THE POPPY WIFE

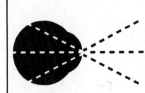

This Large Print Book carries the
Seal of Approval of N.A.V.H.

THE POPPY WIFE

A NOVEL OF THE GREAT WAR

CAROLINE SCOTT

THORNDIKE PRESS
A part of Gale, a Cengage Company

GALE
A Cengage Company

LIBRARY OF CONGRESS CIP DATA ON FILE.
CATALOGUING IN PUBLICATION FOR THIS BOOK
IS AVAILABLE FROM THE LIBRARY OF CONGRESS

ISBN-13: 978-1-4328-7237-3 (hardcover alk. paper)

Published in 2020 by arrangement with William Morrow Paperbacks, an imprint of HarperCollins Publishers

*To Mum and Dad,
with love*

BATTLEFIELD PHOTOGRAPHY
If you desire a PHOTOGRAPH of any
particular GRAVE, CEMETERY,
BUILDING, &c.,
MR. WALTER LEE,
LONDON ROAD, GRANTHAM,
has a Representative visiting the
Battlefield Area, early next month. Write
or call for particurlars.

PART I

PART 1

PROLOGUE:
EDIE

Lancashire, May 1921

Edie doesn't hear the postman. She only notices the envelope, there on the linoleum, as she passes back through from the kitchen to the sitting room. She bends to pick it up, sure it is a thing of no great consequence, just another bill that will have to wait, until she sees the postage stamp. It is the same stamp that used to be on their letters from France.

She turns the manila envelope in her hands. The address is typed, so that it has a vague look of being official. She has written a lot of letters to France and Belgium over the past four years and, in return, receives envelopes full of apologies and repetitions. Her mind flicks through the names of agencies and bureaus, charities and associations, official offices and cemeteries.

At first it is just a white sheet of paper inside the envelope, with nothing written or

11

printed upon it, but when she turns it over, she sees it is a photograph. For a moment she doesn't know the face. Just for a moment it is the face of a stranger with no place or purpose being here, in her hallway, in her hand. It is an item of misdirected post, a mistake, a mystery — but that only just for a moment.

Edie leans her back against the wall and slides down the tiles. She hugs her arms around her knees. There's a flutter in her chest like a caged bird beating its wings against the bars. The photograph has fallen from her hands and is there, at an angle to the checkerboard pattern of the floor, just an arm's stretch away. She rocks her head back against the wall and shuts her eyes.

Edie tells herself that she needs to look at it again. She must look. She ought to look, to bring it up close to her eyes, and to be certain, because while those are surely *his* eyes in the photograph, everything else makes no sense. How can it be? Certainly it is just a resemblance? It can't possibly be him, after so long. Can it? But she doesn't really need to see the photograph a second time to know the truth. It is undoubtedly Francis.

She bites at her knee and makes herself look up. She can see her own footprints on the floor, the habitual patterns that she makes around this house. The linoleum needs mopping again. She should find time to paint the scuffed skirting boards and to beat the doormat. An oak leaf has blown under the hall table, and there next to it is that library card she's been searching for. She notices all of these things, so that she doesn't have to look at his face.

"How?" She asks the question out loud.

The envelope has crumpled in her hand, but she needs to check inside it. There must be more than just that picture. There must be an explanation. A meaning. But there is nothing else there. No letter. Not a sentence. Not one word. She turns the envelope over and sees her address has been typed by a machine with worn keys. The curve of the *u* is broken, the dot on the *i* is missing, but the inky perforation of the full stop is emphatic. She can't read the smudged postmark. There are hyphens in the chain of letters, she makes out, and it is perhaps a Saint-Something-or-Other, but the blur is like a divine mystery. Her hands leave damp fingerprints on the brown paper. She has grown to accept that there must be a full stop after Francis's name, but could she have got that wrong? Could there really be a chance? It is strange to see her own fingers tremble like that.

She rocks onto her side and feels the cold of the floor against her cheek. The photograph is there, just inches from her hand. She hears footsteps going up the pavement outside, the buddleia tapping against the sitting-room window in the breeze, the beat of a waltz on Mrs. Wilson's gramophone next door, but mostly there is the noise of her own breathing. She shouldn't be here, lying on the hall floor on a Tuesday morning, with her face pressed down against linoleum that needs mopping, but how hard it is to make herself move. Why is it so difficult to stretch her hand out toward the photograph? To believe that it really is him?

The sun is slanting through the fanlight now, and the harlequin colors of the glass are elongating across the tiles, jeweling his face in red and green and gold. The face of her husband, who has been missing for the past four years.

CHAPTER ONE:
HARRY

The Folkestone-Boulogne ferry, August 1921
"Edie?"

Harry sees her as he steps out onto the deck. She is wearing a gray silk dress, and though her hair is hidden under a broad-brimmed straw hat, he knows her from the shape of her wrist on the railings and the way that she holds a cigarette.

"It is you?"

But when she turns, it isn't Edie at all.

"Pardon?" The woman takes her sun hat off as she looks up at Harry. Dark hair flickers around a pale face. "Forgive me, do I know you?"

"I'm terribly sorry. I was mistaken. Just for an instant I was certain that you were somebody else." He nods an apology and steps back. How could he have thought it? He wants to walk away quickly now, to turn his face from the woman who is not her. He suddenly feels breathless and unsteady, but

15

he hesitates when he sees the woman's eyes. "Are you quite all right, miss?"

"It's just the blasted sun."

"Here. Please."

"You're very kind."

It is only as she takes his handkerchief that he remembers it is embroidered with his brother's initials. It was a shame not to use them, Edie had said, not sounding entirely convinced. He looks away as the woman wipes the tears from her eyes. The blue water is glitteringly bright.

" 'F.B.,' is it? Frank? Fred? To whom do I address my thanks?"

"Harry, actually." He offers her his hand. "Harry Blythe."

"Rachel West." Her face softens when she smiles. "Bother. It doesn't seem quite nice to soil a stranger's handkerchief and then to hand it back. Even if it perhaps wasn't yours to begin with."

"Do keep it. Think nothing of it." He can feel his breath slowing, his center stilling. To focus on the details of a new face, to see her tears drying, and to exchange steady civilities takes that momentary misplaced rush away.

"I'm indebted to you, Mr. Blythe. I assure you, I don't make a habit of commandeering the linen of men I've never met before."

16

"No secret stockpile of pilfered napkins and inveigled cravats, then?"

"This is the first in my collection."

How could he have mistaken her? Her face isn't like Edie's at all, he sees now: the angles are sharper, her colors all darker. But something in her smile, in the animation of her eyes, reminds Harry of her.

"Did I see you drawing pictures earlier?" she asks.

"Quite possibly. I've found myself press-ganged into being a floating portrait artist. A lady asked me to draw her likeness this morning and now they're forming a queue. I've never had more custom or more gratitude. I'm starting to think that I could make a living on this crossing."

"What a thing!"

"They mean to pin themselves up in enquiry offices and cafés and railway stations. They're looking for missing men."

Rachel West blows smoke at the sea and nods, as if she finds this behavior perfectly normal and natural. Her hand goes to the locket around her neck, her fingers stroking the engraved words *Forget Me Not*. He considers, as he watches her, whether it is sometimes best to try to forget.

"They stick up photographs of their husbands and their own faces. Like so many

17

misplaced shoes that need pairing back together again. I didn't know that there would be so many."

When she looks back at him, she seems surprised. "*So many?* But of course."

She puts a hand to the railings and shuts her eyes to the wind. Harry thinks about ships' figureheads as he watches Rachel West's profile against the water. He pictures her as a wooden woman on a ship's prow, crashing through waves, cutting across wide oceans, all baroque curls and barnacled breast, the darling of the crew. Rachel, very much flesh again, blows her nose on his brother's handkerchief and observes that the sea is so bracing. "It's buffing my edges off," she says as she turns back toward him.

Harry looks at the skyline. He can feel the vibration of the engine. The weight of the breaking waves. A glint of light reflects off a faraway fishing boat but there is, as yet, no sign of the French coast. He tastes salt on his lips and wonders if he will be sick again. Edie had once told him that the trick was to stay out on deck, to take deep breaths, and to stare squarely at the water, as if it were a dog that might bite him if he took his eyes away. He thinks again about the postcard he received from her last week.

Has she stood where Rachel West is standing now within the past month? Could she have leaned on these same railings with her eyes fixed on the waves? Did she feel sick as she crossed to France? And just why was she — is she — in Arras?

"You look green," says Rachel. "I take it that you're not an accustomed mariner, Mr. Blythe?"

He shakes his head. "Not my calling."

The boat pitches down and spumes of white water leap. He hears Rachel's intake of breath. "Doesn't it make you feel *vigorous*?" she asks. "Keenly alive? Effervescent with it?"

"Deeply so." He feels vigorously buffeted by the sharp, salty wind, and nauseous with it. He tightens his grip on the railings. "Like I've got a stomach full of baking soda."

" 'I must go down to the seas again, to the vagrant gypsy life,' " she quotes with a grin. " 'To the gull's way and the whale's way where the wind's like a whetted knife.' " All the sadness in her face goes as she enunciates at the waves. Her eyes widen, like she relishes the taste of the words. But then her gaze connects with Harry's and the grin is gone. "I know you were there, weren't you? I can see it on your face. I probably shouldn't ask you — please forgive me for asking — but what was it like the first time? Would you tell me? The first time that you crossed over to France, I mean."

She makes it sound like the River Styx, he thinks. Harry imagines himself and Francis on a small boat, the water all around writhing with the limbs of the wrathful. He imagines his fingers placing a penny in Francis's mouth.

"We had a false start," he says. It would be wrong to romanticize it for her. "They put us on an Isle of Man ferry — a proper old paddle steamer. It had been requisitioned by the Admiralty, but still had wood paneling and velvet upholstery and the Douglas-to-Fleetwood timetable up on the wall. We sang 'Jerusalem' as we pulled out of Folkestone. I mean, can you imagine? 'Bring me my spear! O, clouds unfold!' " He looks at her. She nods in recognition. "Apologies for the singing voice. Bravado, you know? Only our sword did have to sleep in our hands that day. The destroyer that was accompanying us hit a submerged mine — and boom! It ripped a great gash in its side and all flame and smoke poured out. We'd strayed into an unmarked minefield, you see, and at any moment our poor old paddle steamer might have gone boom too. Anyway, we limped cautiously back to Folkestone and slept that night on the dock."

"With some relief?"

"A concrete floor had never seemed so comfortable. But we had to do it all again the next day." The memory of torn steel and treacherous water looms at him like something spectral and leaves a metallic taste in his mouth. It had been there in the box of old photographs: that image of him and Will and Francis all curled together, three brothers asleep on the dockside. It was one of the pictures that made him pause when Edie had given him the box back in May. He had never seen that one before and it had taken him a moment to recognize his own slumped shoulders. She had laughed at him briefly for that. He can't remember who might have taken the photograph, or the feeling of sleeping entwined with his brothers' limbs.

"And so you did."

"Cross again? Yes." He blinks at Rachel. "That was February 1916. The experience rather put me off messing about in boats."

" 'All I ask is a merry yarn from a laughing fellow-rover,' " she quotes, " 'and quiet sleep and a sweet dream when the long trick's over.' "

"Quite," says Harry.

"We learned that one at school."

Seagulls arc and cry in the background of the canvas that he's mentally composing of Rachel West. The wind in her hair makes her look like a mermaid. With his eyes on the water he can't help but scan for mines. Regardless of what Edie might have advised, it calms him more to focus on this woman who offers poetry, rather than on the waves, and focus also on how he might convey her in paint.

"David went over in January," she says.

"David?"

"My husband. Here. Perhaps you might understand this?"

She takes the paper from the envelope with some care and Harry feels a sense of responsibility as the wind tugs against the letter in his hands. He tries to read it through twice, wanting for her sake to understand, but only the date and Rachel's own name are decipherable. There are the shapes of words, strokes and scrolls, which must have had meaning and importance to their maker, but Harry cannot untangle them. It might as well be in Greek.

"Can you read it?"

"I'm sorry. The writing is very difficult to make out, isn't it?"

"He used to write poems. Would you believe it? Verses full of the landscapes of his childhood, and such clever rhymes."

Harry looks back down at the page, which seems to have neither rhyme nor reason.

"It was his last," she says. "The next thing was a typed note saying that David was missing. When I look at this letter I think that part of him was already missing."

"Yes. I can see that." Harry thinks about flinging this sad letter into the wind, pictures it floating away, a white speck retreating into the water, but he hands it to her instead and watches as she folds the paper.

"It's the third time that I've been back," she says. "It's not enough: 'Missing.' "

"No," Harry replies.

The boat is full of Rachels — women who touch their lockets when they speak, traveling to gravesides and searching. It is a ship full of hope and fear. Hers is the fifth portrait that he will draw on the boat and they are all much obliged. He is curious to see these walls full of the seeking and the missing, all of these faces that require pairing together again. He imagines their photograph faces, Edie and Francis, side by side on a wall, coupled and completed again. He recalls twin portraits, his and hers, painted by his own hand, intended for the walls of their house. He remembers the day that he

23

painted Edie's portrait, how he had watched as she curled her fringe around wetted fingers. He can see it still. The silvering was flaking from the reverse of the mirror, so that sections of her reflected face were cracks and absences.

"There. I'm ready for you now," she had said, her mirror smile focusing in on his own face.

He throws his cigarette away as the port comes into sight and takes Edie's postcard from his pocket. The engines check and he feels the vibration of the boat change. Dunes and ramparts and piers emerge. There are the shapes of chimneys then, the dome of the basilica, and the holiday colors of the quayside cafés. Light cuts through the gathering rain clouds and the flags on the casino pull in the wind. As Boulogne slides into focus now, he wonders whether Edie is still on this side of the Channel and whether she has found Francis dead or alive.

CHAPTER TWO:
HARRY

Boulogne-sur-Mer, August 1921

Francis had been here taking photographs six years ago. Harry had watched from behind as his brother had focused in on the patterns of the rigging and nets and ropes, and all of it reflected back on the wet dock. The disembarking passengers tread through those same reflections today, and Harry hears and knows the sound of the rain in this place, the cries of the seagulls and the stevedores, and the screech of the wheels of the railway cars. He remembers the mass of masts and chains and cables scribbled against the rain-filmed sky, the shapes of cranes, the funnels of sailing barges, and the names of the grand hotels beyond. This dockside is all so familiar, and yet the memory of it feels so far away.

It had been such a momentous thing to see the French coast approaching for the first time, to finally be on this side of the

25

Channel, but then they had stepped onto a workaday quayside, with canning sheds and tea huts and old-fashioned fishing boats with red sails. Now, on that same dock, Harry watches a man piling suitcases into a dinghy. Barrels are being rolled along the cobbles. A horse and cart clatter past, the cart loaded with baskets of herrings. There is a strong smell of diesel and fish. So much is the same, five years on, and so much is different.

Harry shoulders his luggage and walks on into the town, past warehouses, hotels, and shopwindows. He catches glimpses of his own reflection against the displays of butchers and bakers and ironmongers, and half expects to see Will and Francis there at his side. He remembers Will's voice haltingly reading all the shop-front names aloud and laughing; their surprise that here too there must be grocers selling cabbages and corsets and colanders. Their eyes had been all over it that first time, he remembers, expecting foreignness but finding familiarity, as they walked through the streets of an extraordinarily ordinary town. When they had stopped pointing at things, the three of them had linked arms, that wordless action needing no acknowledgment, and seeming like the most natural thing.

"Where's this war, then?" Francis had asked.

"Bothering some bugger else," Will had replied.

He can almost hear their voices, their laughter, their footsteps at his side, but Harry's reflection is alone in the shopwindows today. He has to stop and check that it is so. In the display of a milliner's shop, plaster mannequins tilt their chins under a selection of variously embellished cloche hats and a mirrored sign says QU'EST-CE VOUS CHERCHEZ? WHAT ARE *YOU* LOOKING FOR? Harry finds, as he stands here, that he can't quite put it into words.

He takes a table in a corner café and watches, through the steamed windows, as streetcars slide past. He carves his initials in the condensation. Beyond his dripping letters posters are advertising day excursions and the benefits of taking the water. Painted ladies loll in the shallows around bathing machines, smiling like sirens at the procession of umbrellas. He takes a shot of eau-de-vie with his coffee and turns Edie's postcard in his hands.

Something for your photograph album, her handwriting says on the reverse. *Isn't this a bit back-to-front?*

Harry sees her photograph face ask the

27

question; sees her mouth speak the words; hears the inflection in her voice. His focus pulls out and it is the day before he went back to London, a full three months ago now; Edie is standing by the spillway of the reservoir in his image, framed by his lens, the water rushing down the steps to her right, and her head angled as if she can't decide whether she wants to look at him or not. She had told him about the photograph of Francis just minutes earlier. So much had seemed back-to-front at that moment too.

"I've been looking through Francis's old photographs recently," she had said. "The photographs that he took during the war, I mean. I've been trying to sort them out, put them all in order, only none of them make sense to me. It should be a rule, I think, that no one should be permitted to take photographs unless they mark them with the date and the location. What use are they otherwise? How am I meant to understand what I'm looking at?" She had looked toward Harry. "Of course, you'll know one ruined village from another. Perhaps you'll catalogue them for me?"

"I will, if you wish it." He had rewound in recalled clicks of the camera lens. He had reeled back through in snapshot instants. It left him in Epéhy in August 1917. His older brother was sitting across the table from him cutting photographic paper down into rectangles. Around them a bar full of soldiers roared into song, but Francis was concentrating on the angle of his corners. Two months later he was gone.

"I didn't know that you had his photographs," he had said to Edie.

"I've got a whole box of them. He brought some of them home when he came back on leave, and Captain Rose sent on another parcel at the end. I've always meant to look through them, to sort them all out, but have never quite had the heart."

"Why now, then?"

"Because another one turned up a couple of weeks ago. Or, rather, a photograph *of* Francis. It came in the post."

"In the post?"

"Just that in an envelope. Just a photograph of him and nothing else. I suppose that somebody must have found it, and thought to send it on to me, but it's odd not to put a letter in, isn't it?"

"It is," he'd replied. "And the postmark?"

"French. It was sent from France. Do you think it strange too? I'm glad that it's not just me."

"As you say, someone probably found it."

"Perhaps." Edie had shrugged. "What

happened to Captain Rose?"

"He died at Cambrai. I saw it in the newspaper."

She'd nodded. "It was peculiar to see Francis's face fall out of an envelope. It shocked me. I wasn't ready for it. I'll not lie — I had to pour myself a brandy. It was almost like seeing a ghost."

The eau-de-vie hits the back of Harry's throat now and he coughs. He has seen so many ghosts today. For three months he has put off this task, he too hasn't had the heart, but he has begun working his way through the old photographs today, ordering them chronologically, replaying the memories as he tries to put it all back to the way that it was. They are lined up on the café table in front of him now, in rows and sets, like some peculiar game of Patience.

The first image in the top row is taken in Morecambe, in the January of 1915. They make cakewalk poses outside their billet, aligning themselves by size — Francis, himself, and Will — like a set of end-of-pier minstrels. A newspaperman had taken their photograph, in a more sober stance, just minutes earlier. His mother had posted the cutting from the *Manchester Courier* to them and they had laughed at the caption: *"Brothers in Arms."* They are waxed and buffed new soldiers here. Harry recalls the stiffness, the itch, of that uniform. The smell of it. He can almost taste the Brasso and the boot polish. He is struck now by how very young Will looks.

Harry props Edie's postcard against his glass and starts to place the photographs in the album that he has purchased for her, fitting them into their paper brackets one by one. On the first pages they are doing Swedish drills on the promenade, bayonet exercises on the golf links, and digging trenches at Torrisholme. There are inter-battalion sports days and dances and concerts. They grin, standing on either side of their landlady, Mrs. Faulkner. She twists a white handkerchief in her hands. Crowds (and handkerchiefs) wave as their train pulls away. Harry annotates, as Edie entreated, adding dates and details with the pen that he has bought for the purpose.

There are group photographs at Parkhouse Camp then, Will smiling with the woman who sold oranges from a basket, and views of columns marching over Salisbury Plain. Biplanes curve low over Stonehenge. He sees himself, six years younger, leaning against the stones. His younger self squints into the sun. It is like looking at a different person. He thinks of the photograph of

31

Francis that Edie had shown him three months ago. Where has it been, this image of his brother, for the past four years? Why has it surfaced now? Could it simply have been lost in the system somewhere? But for four years — could that be possible?

He looks out at the street and half expects to see Will and Francis there, linking arms again, walking away. Fat raindrops slide down the glass. He imagines Francis's name on a grave and considers how that could connect with Edie sending him a postcard from Arras. What could have taken her there? Have there been more anonymous envelopes? Could there really be a connection between Edie's postcard and Francis's photograph face?

Francis had sent Edie a postcard on that day they first docked in Boulogne, Harry recalls. A chap with an extravagant mustache was peeping out from behind a bunch of giant pansies and pointing at a sign displaying the motto GROS BISOUS DE BOULOGNE. Francis had covered the reverse with crosses for kisses. No words. No name. Its meaning would be understood, Harry knew that, but there was something mischievous in the lack of signature, he had thought. He had recalled that crosshatching of ink kisses again, and its teasing anonymity, when Edie had shown him the envelope in which the photograph of Francis had arrived.

Harry reaches into his jacket pocket and pulls out the postcard that he has just bought for Edie. Baskets of herring are being landed from sailing boats in a pastel-tinted once-upon-a-time version of the harbor in which he has just landed. The sky above the quayside is tinted an improbable blue.

I am here. I am looking. I am trying, he writes on the reverse — and a P.S.: *But are you here too?*

CHAPTER THREE: HARRY

Boulogne-sur-Mer, February 1916

"I thought you'd stopped drawing," said Will. The wind whipped his hair around his face. He squinted into the low sun. "I haven't seen you painting for ages. I thought you'd given all of that up."

"So did I. I tried." Harry smiled up at his brother. "I haven't done this for months."

It had been odd to open the sketchbook again. For nine months he had told himself to leave it closed. After he'd made the difficult decision not to take up the place at the art college, he'd told himself that he must put all of that behind him; he'd chosen to be here with his brothers instead, and he must now look forward, not back. But today the wind whisked and whistled across the dry sand ahead, planes were scribbling over the sea, and Boulogne-sur-Mer was oyster-gray, umbers, and rose. How could he not test that on paper?

"I'm glad," Will said. "You were miserable when you weren't painting."

"Was I? Did you notice that?"

"You kept looking at the sky moodily and glowering at trees. Francis said that you were pining for your paint box, and we had to cheer you up, or else you might artistically top yourself."

Harry laughed.

The blue-green of the sea pooled on the enamel of his palette, curling into paint approximations of sand and sky. He tilted his paper and breathed steadily as he let the colors run. Harry wasn't sure about glowering at trees, but he did admit that today he felt like himself again. Fully himself. Calm. Whole. He sat back, smiled at Will, and lit a cigarette.

"I was collecting seashells."

Will sat down next to him. His fingers uncurled to show a handful of cockleshells. He spilled them out and then busied himself planting them in a neat line in the sand. A squad was drilling up on the promenade. Harry could hear the rhythm of boots and barked orders.

"Can I?"

"Of course."

Harry watched his brother's sandy fingers turning through his sketchbook. The wind

35

flickered through studies of his own mirror features, his brothers' eyes and smiles, and Edie's face there, over and over. He felt conscious of that suddenly, watching Will's fingers turn the pages.

"They haven't told us where we're going yet." Will skimmed a shell down the beach.

"Do you want to be going anywhere? How about we just stay here?"

Will laughed and then frowned. Harry watched his younger brother consider the question. In the bright beach light he was just a boy.

"No," he replied at length. "You know, I don't think I would mind too much. I like playing football on the sand and going in the cafés for ice creams. Francis has found one that does chips and gravy. It's like someone else's war, isn't it?"

Harry nodded and smiled.

"Frannie says we're missing out, though. It's all happening elsewhere and we're just stuck in another seaside town. It's all rushing forward, all going on farther south, and he's still here, taking photographs of fishermen and beach huts and café terraces, and he's done all of that already."

Harry could hear Francis's inflections in Will's voice. "There are worse things."

"Tell him that."

Harry looked at the shifting liquid land-scape ahead. An old woman was raking for cockles down the beach, doubled in reflec-tion in the water beside her. Clouds scud-ded across. He could make out the move-ment of a cluster of wading birds at the water's edge. He shut his eyes to the glitter of it and lay back on the sand, breathing in the hot smell of seaweed, tasting the salt on his lips. The saline wind sharpened his senses and made him feel intensely alive. He considered that he could quite happily see out the war here, painting busy skies and beachscapes, with the warmth of the winter sun on his face.

"Come on," said Will. "I promised Fran-cis that we'd meet him up on the hill."

They picked their way back up the beach, the wind tugging at the roots of their hair and making sails of their clothes. The clouds were moving fast and shadows shifted on the sand. Flags and music pulled in the wind. The dunes were full of khaki camp-ing, like a Scouts' jamboree. As he turned and looked back toward the sea, Harry felt a sudden reluctance to leave the littoral light, which lent itself to watercolor. It sud-denly mattered that he found the time to paint the sand dunes, the salt marsh, and the maritime pines. He needed to draw the cliffs and the herring boats and the moon-light silvering the shingle. Suddenly he felt that he had lost nine months and the need to put it all down on paper was urgent.

As they climbed up toward the calvary, Francis was there, leaning over the railings, taking angles on the plunging rooftops and the busy port below. Will waved and then Harry could tell that Francis was watching them through his lens. He smiled behind the camera as they approached.

"Is that noise the guns?" Will asked. "It's louder from up here, isn't it? Is it closer today?"

"Fret not, *mon petit frère.* It's just the wind playing tricks."

Francis put his arm around Will's shoulders and Harry pushed his hands down into the pockets of his greatcoat.

"It's colder up here," he said.

"Is it meant to be seen by the sailors coming in to the port?" Will looked up at the crucifix.

"I guess so," Harry replied, "to watch them as they go out to sea and return them safely home again."

" 'Such was the wreck of the *Hesperus,* in the midnight and the snow! Christ save us all from a death like this, on the reef of

Norman's Woe!' " Francis exaggerated his enunciation and made exclamatory arms for Will's benefit.

"Norman who?"

"Never mind."

"Your man up there looks like he's only bothered about sailors, though, doesn't he? I mean, don't you get the impression that he's a bit exclusive?" Francis proposed. "I might take my landlubber prayers elsewhere."

The face on the cross looked steadfastly out to sea, eyes fixed on the horizon and seemingly unmoved by the whispered prayers of the women who were kneeling on the ground below.

Harry nodded. "I don't think he can hear them. He doesn't look like he knows they're there."

Beyond, other men in uniform were sitting on the hillside staring out at the flint-gray sea. It struck Harry how so many of them had made this climb on such a windy day, to just stare back at the way that they had come, in silence. It was as if they were all mesmerized by the sea. Harry committed the oddness of the image to memory.

"But I almost forgot." Francis threw his cigarette away and Harry looked at his brother in profile at his side. A curl of smoke left his lips and then he was turning to Harry and grinning. "I saw it in a shop in the town. It's from both of us."

Francis put his hand to his pocket and handed Harry a parcel wrapped in brown paper. "For me?"

"Well, go on, then. Open it. I saw it, and I thought of you."

There was a small tin box inside the parcel. Harry lifted the lid and saw sticks of bright rich pigment inside.

"They're pastels. I didn't think you had any. Will and I put our money together. We decided that we'd had enough of your gloomy abstinence."

"Was it that bad? Was it that obvious? Thank you. It's really kind of you."

Francis shook his head. "Stand together. Let's have a souvenir."

He stepped back, cradling his camera. Harry put his arm around Will as they leaned against the wall. They both made impolite hand gestures at Francis's lens. "Get a ruddy move on!"

Francis's face was all concentration. "My chuffing fingers are cramped with the cold."

"It's not that cold, you coward. Frannie, how you whine!"

"Hang on," said Will. "Look out." They watched as an officer approached Francis

40

from behind, saw the alarm in his eyes as he turned, and then the relief with which he shook Michael Rose's hand.

"You need to be more discreet on this side," said Second Lieutenant Rose. "You know it's prohibited over here now. I've shown you the order. Be grateful it's only me that saw you. I'd be confiscating it, if it wasn't for the fact that it's my own old Kodak and my fingerprints are all over your misdemeanor."

"I'm sorry, sir," said Francis. "That was silly of me. I'll be careful. I know the rules. I wouldn't get you in a bother."

"Don't look so contrite," said Rose. "Go and stand with your brothers. I'll take this one. You can send it home. Something for your girls."

Francis knocked his cap to a jaunty angle and put his arm around Harry. He could feel the pressure of Francis's fingertips and his pent-up laughter. "Smile for the dickey bird, boys!"

Rose grinned from behind the lens. "Something for posterity."

CHAPTER FOUR:
HARRY

Boulogne-sur-Mer, August 1921

Francis had photographed the railway station too, all exotic Gothic and sandbags back then. He had said that it looked like a church organ, Harry remembers. Taking in the detail of the building again, this time through the viewfinder of his own camera, it seems both oversized and over-grand now; the passage of time has left it looking like it's overstating its claims. There are crenulations, rampant lions, and medieval affectations; corner turrets, stepped spires, and classical statues with swords and crowns of laurel leaves. The sandbags are gone, but as the shutter of his camera clicks, Harry fully expects to turn and see Francis there at his side.

He buys himself a coffee in the cheerless station café and watches as birds lunge through the wires and cables above. Starlings cut curves through the crosshatching.

42

"It's our amphibious portrait artist again, isn't it?"

Her feet stop by his table. He looks up and a drawing of a girl with sad eyes and a *Forget Me Not* locket animates into a crease of smile.

"Mrs. West — I hadn't expected to see you again."

"Likewise, but I'm glad to cross paths with you, Mr. Blythe. My train doesn't leave for another half hour. Would I be making a nuisance of myself if I were to join you for a coffee?"

"Of course not." In truth, he would be glad of a voice other than the ones in his head. He pulls a chair out for her. "I'm sorry, I should have asked you where you were traveling on to." He puts his hand up for the waiter.

"Arras. The eleven-thirty train."

"That makes two of us. I would be happy to have some company for the journey."

He watches as the waiter shuffles cups and saucers on his tray and sorts through the small change.

"I was grateful to you for drawing my picture. We all were. Like I said, I would gladly have paid you."

"Nonsense. I wouldn't dream of it. It was my pleasure."

43

"I hope you don't mind my asking, but I wondered afterward — did you draw when you were here during the war?"

"Yes, all the time." He lights a cigarette and offers her the packet, but she shakes her head. "It was likenesses, mostly. I drew them so they could send themselves back, put their face in an envelope and post it to their mothers and their sweethearts. They paid me for it sometimes. Other times it was a trade for a piece of chocolate or a cigarette. Mostly it was because I wanted to. I like faces — how people's personality and experience show through — and you have to practice."

"You do?"

"Francis said that." He looks at Rachel West and sees the shadows of her eyelashes, the fine lines at the corners of her mouth. There are freckles under her face powder. "And you always have to be looking."

"Francis?"

"My brother. Although his thing was cameras. He wanted to be a photographer, you see, to do it professionally." He knocks back the last of his coffee. "I've somehow ended up doing it for him, though. It's what I do for a living now, it's my everyday bread and butter, but really it was always much more Francis's passion than mine."

44

"Doing it for him? Am I wrong in assuming that he didn't get the chance?"

"A small matter of a war rather got in the way."

"It does that, doesn't it?"

Rachel has placed a guidebook down on the table: an *Illustrated Michelin Guide to the Battlefields*. She has moved it aside to make way for her coffee, but flicks through the pages and shows him a photograph of Arras in ruins. There are tips for motoring tourists, he sees, and day-trip itineraries. "It looks like Pompeii," says Rachel and shuts the page on Arras. "I have to be there tomorrow. I have an appointment to look through lost property."

"Lost property?"

"Lost men's property. Personal effects. Potentially identifying items found on bodies which haven't yet been named. Although it's not officially phrased that directly."

"No, I expect not." Harry picks dirt from under his fingernails. He thinks about what items might have been in Francis's pockets. He considers how that photograph of his brother's face might have been identified and found its way to Edie. "I have some business to do in Arras too. I could ac-

45

company you to your lost property office, if you'd like?"

Rachel plays with her teaspoon. "Would you? You wouldn't mind? Thank you. I'd be grateful for some moral support." Her thin fingers are ringed with hearts and flowers formed in tin and brass and aluminum. Harry has seen similar before, worked from spent cartridges and corned beef cans.

" 'Rings on her fingers and bells on her toes. She shall have music wherever she goes.' Did your husband make them?" He nods at her fingers.

"Yes. David was a silversmith. Always clever with his hands and a pair of pliers in his pocket. He took his pliers away with him, because that's just part of who he was — who he *is*. He made me some napkin rings too, from some sort of shell casing, and a box with pansies engraved onto it. *Pensées* in French, you see. He told me that. It meant that he was thinking of me."

"An artist and a poet and a linguist?"

"Ten," she says. She flexes her fingers. "He sent me one each month. Ten months in France. I look at my fingers and I know where he was each month. I know the location that each parcel arrived from. The one that matters, though — the only one that *really* matters — is the eleventh month, and

46

I know hardly anything about that."

"And the eleventh month was?"

"November 1916." Staring at her fingers, Rachel suddenly looks as if she might cry. "I've been here before, you know. This is my third trip. How many more do I have to make?" She clatters the teaspoon into her cup and the ringed fingers are then in her hair. "I should be an expert at this by now, but — once again — I don't know where to start."

"You've written to your husband's regiment? He could be in England by now. Maybe in one of the hospitals?" There are still twenty thousand men in the special hospitals, Harry has read. Looking for Francis, he has sat in the waiting rooms of many of those hospitals. He has written those letters. Spoken to those doctors and seen them shake their heads. "He could be staring down a ward waiting for you to arrive."

"I told you on the boat, didn't I?" She looks suddenly forceful. "I wrote to his officers, to the men who had written to me at the time, to all the men who he had ever named in his letters. They couldn't tell me anything. So many men are missing. That's what they all say. It's like the word *missing* is a code and I'm meant to get the nod as to what it really means."

"How about the army enquiry office? Or the British Legion?"

"Yes, haven't I already told you? They couldn't help."

"The Red Cross?"

"I even saw a clairvoyant. She told me that David wasn't dead. She was quite certain about it. She couldn't find him on the other side. It was near Arras that he went missing — in *that* place, and it all tumbled down to ruin. I think that David might be lost, or might have lost his mind."

When she looks at Harry he feels like she expects him to know, as if she expects an answer, and, with the intensity of that look, he finds himself examining his trouser leg.

"You don't have to help me," she says.

Her fingers turn the *Forget Me Not* locket. He wonders if it contains her husband's photograph and if she believes that he has forgotten her. Could Edie too believe that Francis has merely forgotten to come home? Two weeks on from writing that postcard, could Edie still be in Arras? Could she have found reason to stay there? "I need to call in Arras this week, anyway," he says.

"Yes, what exactly are you doing here?" It comes out, evidently, a little sharper than she intends, because she adjusts her tone. "I would have thought that this would be the last place that you'd ever want to see again."

"As I said, I work as a photographer and I'm being paid to be here. I'm here on an assignment, as it were. My assignment is a list of graves. My job is taking photographs of graves."

The train is quiet. He leans against the window and watches the suburbs blur. He's aware of Rachel's voice, its tone and rhythm and not-quite-heard words. The fields are green. It still surprises him that they can be. She fusses with an apple and talks about the price of bread. She talks a lot. Harry remembers other railway carriages, stinking of horse and soldier, and sees it slide by.

In February 1916 they had entrained inland in cattle cars, with instructions to keep the noise down. Harry had looked out at France through wooden slats. There seemed to be a lot of empty villages and waterlogged agriculture.

"It feels like sneaking up on the war from behind," Will had said.

But the train had brought them to a town that seemed by-passed by war and time. In between lectures on automatic gun fire and rifle-grenade instruction, they placed bets on turns of playing cards and dominoes and traded tinned rations for silk postcards stitched with sentimental slogans. They paraded in the driving rain, fixed feet at ten-to-two, and dripped. They played mouth organs and tin whistles and tug-of-war.

"Is this it?" Francis had asked.

Harry had started to write it all down that spring, long illustrated letters that lingered over the details, and he crammed all that was new and curious into a diary. He drew kit inspection, bombing practice, and drill. He drew the lime trees, the red-brick farms, and the rippling fields of wheat. He drew Will playing cricket, Francis taking photographs, and their hands passing playing cards across café tables. Harry found comfort in committing it all to paper, felt lightened by the act and the concentration it required. He recorded his brothers' faces in every attitude and expression.

"You don't have much luggage," Rachel observes.

"Luggage?" Harry refocuses on her face, winds back, and finds himself five years later, on a train heading east again. "It's enough to lug around. I don't expect to be invited to many cocktail parties."

"You've renounced dinner jackets? How reckless. How austere. You're not fasting too?" She offers him a bag of sweets and a half smile.

"I'm uncomplicating it," he says and wonders if it's true. "But I do succumb to caramels."

There are potted tulips on the steps of the hotel, a glossy, rich, grotesque red. He looks up to the boarded panes above as Rachel reads the card in the window.

"Deux chambres?" says the woman at the desk.

"Did you see that eyebrow?" Rachel laughs as they climb the stairs. "Is it humanly possible to look more arch? I'm not sure that I've ever felt more scrutinized and doubted."

"Nice to see that propriety is being policed. She's marked you down in the register as doubtful, you know. Better mind your manners, miss."

"Mrs.," she corrects.

"Of course." He is sad to see that the humor in her face has gone. "I'm sorry."

An English voice down the corridor complains over the quality of pillows and the lack of hot water. Harry shuts the door on it, but they're all around: there are voices in the ceiling, under the floor, and in the walls. This hotel is full of voices. They are all talking, all passing a commentary, all pushing their words through the walls. He props Edie's postcard beside the bedside lamp and it is her voice that he hears again then, as clear as if she were here, in this room, speaking into his ear.

"It was almost like seeing a ghost," she had said, as she told him about the photograph of Francis.

"I can understand that."

"It wasn't you who sent it?"

Did she suspect that? Was that why her eyes had searched his face? "No, of course not."

"And not *him*?"

"How could it be?"

Harry had stepped away from her, looking through the lens. For a moment he had been glad to have the barrier of the camera between them, not to have to look her directly in the eye, as he considered his response to her question. In that reeling moment, he had asked himself how she could think that — but then why was it not easier to reply?

He focused in on her features, but her face told him nothing more. Backlit, she glowed at the edges. He watched her eyes lift, following an arrow of geese overhead. Should it not be Francis — her husband, his brother — on this side of the camera? Should it not still be that way around? Did she have any good reason to be asking *that* question?

Harry had leaned against the wall to steady himself. Edie's photograph image offered him the bag of peppermint candies.

"I want you to take a photograph of Francis's grave."

She had rolled a sweet on her tongue, he remembers. Her recalled words smelled of peppermints.

"I will try for you," he had replied.

He'd gone back to London with good intentions. He would talk to all the appropriate agencies and do all that he could to find some evidence. If a grave existed, he would go there and take the photograph for her. But did it? Could it? He had written letters and waited in offices, checked through casualty and prisoner lists, circulated descriptions, and visited hospitals, but all of his inquiries had come to no end. There was nothing. He had tried and failed again, as he had warned her that he probably would. The days went by, the file of correspondence thickening and the possibilities diminishing, and it was only when he received her postcard from Arras last week that he realized another three months had passed.

Isn't this a bit back-to-front? Edie's postcard handwriting insists. *Shouldn't it be you sending this to me?*

There is a picture of the Hôtel de Ville on the card and a July postmark. Could Edie have found something, then? Could she somehow have succeeded where he has failed? Has something of Francis surfaced in Arras?

Harry tries to block out the voices in the walls. He tries to shut out the photograph faces, and the thoughts of ghosts and graves, and just to focus on the pattern of the wallpaper. His hotel room has yellow walls and overlarge pieces of furniture that look like they have come out of a grander house. There is a dead bird on his window ledge. He watches its feathers shift. The sheets smell of stale sweat. The ceiling is water-marked in the shape of Africa. Shadows creep from the corners until he is staring into darkness.

He meets Rachel at six, as arranged, in the next-door restaurant. The room is full of people who look lost. At the tables all around they are telling each other their stories. There is slightly too much gesticulation to be normal. Conversations are conducted in a slightly higher emotional register. Confidences spill out over the soup. It is like everyone in the room is slightly drunk, Harry thinks. They eat steaming boiled potatoes and mutton with gray fat. Photographs of the missing are posted on the greasy floral walls. He finds himself looking for faces that he might recognize, that he might himself once have committed to paper. He finds himself looking for Francis's face.

"He hasn't gone," says Rachel suddenly, after two glasses of wine. "David, I mean. He is a robust man, a strong man, a man full of life."

Harry feels himself being eyed comparably and not coming up to the mark. "There you are, then," he says.

"I haven't shown you, have I?"

She takes a photograph from her handbag and smiles as she pushes it across the table. The young man staring back has tidy features and strikingly pale eyes. Harry thinks that, if he were taking the photograph, he would focus in on the young man's eyes. Whatever Rachel's certainty as to the man in the photograph being full of life, there is something already ghostlike about those eyes.

"A handsome chap."

"Yes." Rachel takes the photograph back. She runs her hands over it as if she is reading it with her fingertips. "I've seen every spiritualist in Sunderland. He's not on the other side."

Harry wonders how many seers have run their fingers over David West's image and what they have felt. He has read about psychics and spiritualist meetings, about widows and mothers communing with the souls of their lost men, connecting again and saying the things that they never had a chance to speak to their faces. But he can feel no sense of Francis as he holds his hand over his photographs. There is nothing there. No presence itching at his palm, no signs, no sense of a soul; only an absence, only a space, a gap, and memories that need to be kept covered up. Francis isn't there to converse through a medium. If he is, Harry can't think what Francis would say. And he's not sure that he would want to hear it.

Chapter Five:
Edie

Arras, August 1921

There is a young couple in the corner of the café, not much more than teenagers, their fingers linked under the table, their heads touching, mouthing words only meant for each other. Edie catches the girl's eye and quickly looks away, a brief, awkward moment of uninvited connection, but then _his_ voice is there.

" 'Fasten your hair with a golden pin,' " Francis's voice whispers. She can almost feel his breath in her ear again and hear the grin shaping his recited words. " 'And bind up every wandering tress.' "

It is eight years ago and she is a girl in the lending library, looking for a story to briefly take her away from her mother's illness — and suddenly he is there, on the other side of the bookshelf, the blond boy with his flamboyant manners, and his rhymes, and that smile. She can see the gloss of his hair

57

again. His smell of soap and cigarettes. His words that tasted of pear drops. Edie thinks of that boy's confidence, and the irresistible vitality that shone so brightly out of him that day, and she can't help but smile at the memory.

" 'You need but lift a pearl-pale hand,' " he says, his soft voice lingering through the words, like the sound of them is delicious to him. " 'And bind up your long hair and sigh; and all men's hearts must burn and beat.' "

It had been a displaced voice at first, whistling through the Poetry section, until she had seen his movement on the other side of the shelves. She had looked through the gap between Dickinson and Donne and then his mouth had been there, making the whispered words.

" 'And the stars climbing the dew-dropping sky, live but to light your passing feet.' "

She had wanted to tell him to shush, that this sort of thing isn't allowed in the public library, to wave her hands and make the embarrassing words go away, but she could see the smile curling at the edges of his seashell-pink lips.

He was just a white-toothed grin, disembodied like the Cheshire Cat, and words with a scent of boiled sweets. But then he was eyes that watched her through the Romantics and the Classics; a flicker of long lashes and clear bright blue-green eyes that creased at the corners, so that she knew he was smiling on the other side. He existed only in fragments and glimpses and elements, and a voice that linked them all. But then he was a flash of profile, and finally a face that had looked directly down into her own as she had stepped out at the end of the row, as if he had always been there waiting for her.

" 'I bade my heart build these poor rhymes,' " he recites. " 'It worked at them, day out, day in, building a sorrowful loveliness.' "

The whisper of his voice was so soft that she had to step closer to hear him. He had put his eyes to the ceiling to recall the last line and then his gaze had connected with hers. He smiled with something that seemed like satisfaction.

"Yeats," he had said. "It's a poem."

"I gathered that much."

"Only, when I saw you through the bookcase, I suddenly knew what it meant. I learned it by heart last week."

"And since then you've been like a coiled spring in the Poetry section, waiting to pounce it on unsuspecting females?"

"Not a bit of it." He had laughed and shaken his head. "It's not like that at all. I would take your hand and introduce myself properly, only . . ."

His arms were full of books. He braced them with his chin to keep them from slipping. She looked at his chest and read the spines of atlases, a history of Roman Britain, walking guides, and a book of birdsongs.

"You'll get in trouble for whispering in the library," she had said. "It's bad manners. There's a notice up. They don't like it."

"I'll only be in bother if you report me. Would you tell on me, miss? Will you get me into trouble?"

There was something mischievous about his mouth. The directness of his eyes made her feel like she ought to look away. She knew that she was blushing under the feel of his eyes, which must follow hers, and the invitation of his grin.

"I wouldn't tell on you," she heard herself say.

He had been sitting on the steps when she left the library. That profile again and his broad shoulders. He had thrown his cigarettes away and turned to her with a book in his hands.

"Here, for you. I took it out for you. That's not a liberty, is it? I thought that, since you were haunting the Poetry section, you might like it."

She had turned the book in her hands. The cover design was a woven net of reeds and the gilding glinted in the sunshine.

"It's like a cage made of leaves, isn't it? Is it meant to be a trap to catch something?"

"I hope so. Only, I'm afraid that you'll have to meet me here again next week, because it's out on my library card."

She had nodded. There was something about his smile, something about his eyes, so intently focused on her, that made it difficult to look up.

"Do I get to know your name, miss?"

"Edie."

"And will you be here again next Saturday, Edie? Around the same time? Can I count on you for that?"

"I wouldn't want you to incur a library fine."

He laughed and looked away then. His eyes, which up to now had been so bold, suddenly seemed shy.

"Since I hold the future of your library privileges in my hands, am I permitted to know *your* name?" she had asked.

"Francis Blythe."

He pushed his fringe off his forehead. His fingernails were all bitten down, she saw, but his hair was golden in the sunlight. He was ivory, coral, and gilt, and glimmering grin, and might well have stepped out of a painting or a poem.

"I am pleased to meet you, Francis Blythe."

He had turned to go, but then somehow his mouth was there by her ear again and his voice is in her head. As it will always be there in her head. As it still is there at this moment. " 'I have spread my dreams under your feet,' " he whispers. So quietly. So very faintly today. " 'Tread softly because you tread on my dreams.' " Edie looks around the café now, eight years on and a country's distance away, and he is so near and yet so terribly far away.

"Please, do you recognize the buildings at all?"

Edie watches the waitress's face, waiting for a flicker of recognition. She watches the steady side-to-side of her eyes, the silent line of her lips, her still fingers at the edges of Francis's photograph, but then the girl is shaking her head.

"I'm sorry, madame. I don't know it."

It is always the same. It has been the same

for the past fortnight. They all shake their heads.

"You don't think it's Arras? I thought it might be the Grand Place?"

"*Non.* No. *Je suis désolée. Ce n'est pas ici.*"

"Thank you, anyway."

"*Peut-être en Belgique?*" says the girl as she hands back the photograph.

"In Belgium? Yes, perhaps."

Edie pushes her soup plate away and tilts the photograph to the light. She turns the image between her fingers. Still the reverse tells her nothing. She tries to read Francis's face in the photograph, but it gives nothing away. For four years she has been certain that he is dead. When they had used those words, "Missing, believed killed," she had believed it. She had felt it. But then, three months ago, this photograph arrived. At first she had asked herself who could have sent it. Now she asks herself why *he* has sent it.

She can tell from his stance that he is taking the photograph of himself. His arms stretch out toward the sides of the print and his eyes are focused just slightly above the top of the paper, so that he is caught perpetually both embracing and evading the gaze of the viewer. She can imagine him looking into the lens of his own camera, seeing the reflection of his own face curving in the glass. She has seen him do it before, when he was young, but always with a smart sideways grin, a raised eyebrow, an expression knowingly composed for film. There is no grin in this image, no larking or posing. There is no hint of humor in his eyes. There is something terribly blank about Francis's face. This black-and-white misplaced man is so far away from that jewel-colored boy in the lending library.

Under her magnifying glass he is pinpricks of silver ink and she cannot piece them together. She can't join the dots and understand the image. She leans back in her chair and rubs her eyes, but it doesn't help. In the picture he is wearing a collarless shirt that doesn't look exactly clean, and a jacket that is fraying at the collar. Edie doesn't know these clothes. These are not clothes that she has laundered or mended or folded. They are poor clothes, she thinks, not the smart cuts and colors that used to be Francis's choices, but still they matter to her. It is important that these are civilian clothes. It matters that he is not in uniform. Surely that confirms that this photograph was taken after 1917? Could she be sitting in the same town as Francis now?

The coffee machine hisses, the woman at

the next table laughs, and Edie looks up. The café doubles in the mirror behind the counter and the men on the barstools watch themselves as they drink. The bottles on the bar shelves contain liquids of strange, exotic colors and they glimmer like rubies and emeralds as the evening sun slants in. A string of Allied flags droops above and looks like a forgotten Christmas decoration. The room smells of garlic and beeswax polish. She wonders if she would still know the scent of her husband's clothes.

The buildings in the background of the photograph do not look like peacetime, but then she has spent fourteen days walking through a town that is still all rubble and ruin. Behind Francis's shoulders there is what looks to be the shape of a wide square, except the buildings around its edges have all been brought down. The square looks as frayed as the collar of Francis's coat. She has stood and stared and turned and compared in every square in Arras this week.

Edie watches the waitress moving around the room, singing along to the gramophone as she weaves between the tables with plates stacked up in her arms. All of the china in this café seems to have different patterns, Edie notices. She imagines that this tumbledown town must be full of smashed-up and mixed-up crockery.

"C'était bon?" The waitress smiles as she takes Edie's soup dish away.

"Yes. *Très bon.* It was very good. Thank you."

Is it wrong that she should still notice the taste of the soup? Is it wrong that she should want someone to share that with? She imagines Francis's face across the table. It doesn't seem right.

Why would Francis be in Arras? How could he be? She remembers that this town was mentioned in his letters at the end of 1916. As she walks through its streets, she thinks that there are lintels and arcades and shop signs that she recognizes from his 1916 photographs. She knows that he has been here, that he has walked these same streets, but that last photograph can't be from 1916. Could he really be here still?

She looks around the café, noticing how the wood paneling on the walls needs repainting, and the tablecloths have been laundered too many times. But the gramophone is quietly playing songs from before the war and the bread is good. There are jugs of white larkspur on each table and the smell takes her back to sitting at Harry's hospital bedside.

She had written to Harry after the photograph of Francis had arrived, because, well, who else was there to ask? He had come up from London the next weekend and she had watched him turn the photograph over in his hand. As Harry had brought the image close to his eyes, she had wanted to ask him so many questions, and to know what questions he was asking himself. He had been the last person to see Francis alive, and couldn't Harry see now, as she did, that this photograph must have been taken after October 1917? But how could that be possible? It didn't make sense. When Harry had shaken his head, she had found herself telling him that she needed to know if there was a grave. If Harry was meant to be in France taking photographs of soldiers' gravestones, why couldn't he show her a picture of Francis's grave?

"But there isn't a grave," he had said. "You know that. Or, if there is one, his name's not on it and there are no records. You've already made all those enquiries and had that reply. You told me yourself, it's always the same response."

"But he can't be *nowhere*," she had said to him. "He hasn't just disappeared, has he? He needs to be *somewhere,* either dead or alive."

"You know he's not alive," he had replied softly.

"Do I?"

Harry had gone back to London and promised her that he would do something. He would make calls and write letters again, revisit all the leads to see if something new had surfaced since she had last tried. But then three months have passed without a word from Harry and it's not enough. Through those weeks all her questions have multiplied, and what does Harry's silence mean? In the end, she had bought a train ticket, and then a boat ticket, and had sent him a postcard from Arras. Only she is not quite sure what she is meant to do now, and she wishes that Harry were here so that she could ask him.

"Madame?"

She looks up to meet the waitress's eyes.

"You can leave a photograph here. *Si vous le souhaitez.* If you wish. People do." She points to the wall at the back of the café.

Edie swivels in her chair. How had she not seen it when she walked in? "May I?"

"Bien sûr."

She walks toward the rear wall and the pattern adjusts itself into a mass of faces, of appeals, of searches. She touches her hand to a chair back to steady herself and then

68

apologizes to the family at the table who all tilt their eyes upward to look at her. The wall is full of photographs of men, and around them the details of the people who are searching for them. So many faces. So many searches. How could so many men be misplaced? Could so many men really just have disappeared?

"*Si vous voulez?*"

She turns, and the waitress is standing at her side. There is a thumbtack in the palm of her outstretched hand.

"My brother is also *disparu,*" she says and gestures toward a tinted image of a boy in a blue uniform.

"*Disparu?*"

The girl hesitates for the word. "Missed? Missing?" There is a purple bow at the collar of her white blouse and she winds the ends of it around her fingers as she stares at the wall. Her hands look like they work hard, her fingers are red and her nails are short. She has a crease between her eyebrows as if she frowns a lot, but she brightens when she turns back to the tables. "There's a chance, isn't there?" she says.

Edie looks again at the photograph of Francis that came through the mail slot in her door three months ago. It is not enough just to pin it to a wall and hope that someone might chance upon it. She needs to do more than that: she needs to stand in that square, to know that he has been there, and to sense if he is still there yet. Simply pinning his face here will not answer these loud questions and, besides, she doesn't want to leave the photograph behind.

In her handbag she carries a miniature portrait of Francis painted by Harry in 1914. As she unfolds it, she is struck again by just how different this face looks from the figure in the photograph. Here he is still the golden youth who whispered poetry to her in the library. This ink-and-watercolor boy could be the son of the man in the photograph. For just a second she checks herself again: Is it really Francis? Is that the man to whom she pledged her future? Is that the man who shared her bed?

She writes his name, together with her own, across the painting and fixes it to the wall. As she does so she is struck with the realization that she will miss this image. She had once meant it to be framed and hung on a wall and she can't now remember why that never happened. It hurts to part with it. She will miss the kindness of Harry's composition perhaps as much as she will miss this handsome once-upon-a-time man to whom she was married.

"Un beau gosse." The waitress nods. *"Un bel homme.* I hope you find him, madame." "Yes," Edie replies.

CHAPTER SIX:
HARRY

North of Béthune, February 1916

Harry watched the flat of Francis's hand moving over the plaster wall. "Have you seen?" Francis asked as he turned.

Harry stood at his brother's shoulder. The wall of the barn was carved with the dates when other regiments had passed through this place. There were initials and insignia and cartoons scratched into the wall. There were ciphers and monograms and shields. The walls of the barn were like the massed voice of the men who had been before them.

"It's like a visitors' book, isn't it?"

"Frannie, could we leave something?"

"We should leave our mark," said Will.

Harry watched as Francis cut away the plaster with his penknife, making the shape of his initials. He stood back and blew the plaster dust away. "Now you."

"Yes." The knife felt strangely heavy in Harry's hand. The plaster yielded easily to

72

its blade, making a sharp, clean angle. He was struck by the seriousness of his brother's face. There was no glimmer of humor in Francis's eyes. It seemed that this was no joke, or light act of mischief. He ran inspecting fingertips over his work before handing the knife on to Will. "Mind your fingers."

They watched as Francis scratched the date in below. There was something oddly ceremonial about the moment, Harry thought. A strange, solemn sense of ritual. He recalled fragments of half-forgotten stories in which brothers mingled their blood. The action seemed to have more than its immediate significance, particularly when Will took both their hands.

"We stick together," said Francis.

They all laughed at their own intensity then. Their eyes met, the moment and the emotion broke, and they mocked themselves with grinned curses. Harry knew, though, that he wouldn't forget the image of their three linked initials.

They were told that they were to march east the next morning.

"This is it," said Will. "This is our turn. What is the point in us being here otherwise?"

Behind the bravado, Harry saw fear flickering over his brother's face. He contemplated what their turn would entail.

"I'd put up with being pointless," he said.

They marched for two days toward the war. On the advice of the old-timers they had packed their pockets with chocolate, cigarettes, and candle stubs. The wax was warm and pliant between Harry's fingers; the cold air caught at the back of his throat. They told them that each one of them, fighting men and fighting fit, was equal to three Germans.

Harry's head filled with songs, worked to the rhythm of their tramping feet, moving as one rhythmic being. As they marched, they left something of themselves behind, cast off a singularity, and became soldiers. It was surprising how easy it was to fall into the tempo. It propelled them with some hypnotic compulsion, turning them into one soldierly unit.

" 'We are Fred Karno's army,' " they sang. " 'We are the ragtime infantry. We cannot fight, we cannot shoot, what bloody use are we?' "

They were billeted on a farm on the outskirts of a blasted village, where all the angles seemed peculiarly askew. The farm buildings formed a square around a courtyard full of spilled tiles and rotting cart wheels. The abandoned plow and rake looked like instruments of medieval warfare. The barns, where they were quartered, still smelled of the breath of patient cattle. They made makeshift mattresses, encasing the sharp straw in groundsheets, and watched the officers drinking café au lait, all domesticity around the farmhouse table.

"We can roll together for the warmth," said Will.

"Hark at the Boy Scout."

There was talk of campaigns in the candlelight that night, of offensives and shifting fronts. Only Mac McCabe marred the collective bravado, with the clink of rosary beads in the afterward blackness.

"I wish the old git would give it a rest," hissed Will in a whisper that seemed meant to be heard. "It puts the wind up."

McCabe had been at Mafeking. He was their old-timer, their grousing warhorse, their yardstick of old soldiering. It didn't seem right that he should be afraid. But it also didn't seem quite right to hear Will dismissing that fear.

Harry looked up through the beams and cobwebs to a roof that was more sky than tile. Stars slid in the spaces.

"As it was in the beginning, is now, and

ever shall be," intoned Francis's voice.
"World without bleeding end."

CHAPTER SEVEN:
HARRY

Arras, August 1921

Location image order: Mrs. Kathleen
Gibson requests a photograph of the
sugar factory at the junction of the Douai
road, Arras. Pte. Michael Gibson (23791,
Durham Light Infantry), the client's
husband, died in England in October
1916, three weeks on from receiving an
injury in this location.

"I suppose that for them the war hasn't
ended, that it won't ever finish until they're
found," Rachel had said, as they walked into
the hospital grounds.

"Found?"

"Amnesiacs," she'd replied. "Men who
don't know who they are. They can't remember their names, their wives, or their
children. They've forgotten where their
homes are. I suppose it's like a sort of

limbo, isn't it? Some of them no longer even remember what nationality they are."

"So there could be Englishmen among them?"

"Yes. That's what I've been told. It's a possibility."

It wasn't a possibility that he had previously considered. Harry had looked at the windows of the asylum ahead. Were they all looking out and waiting? Were eyes even now watching Rachel and wondering, considering, hoping for her recognition? Were eyes at this moment searching for familiarity in his own face?

"Did David make your locket?"

"Yes. He gave it to me on the day that we were married." She had put her hand to her throat and smiled. *"Forget Me Not.* You see? And I won't."

"I don't think he will have forgotten you, then."

A door closes behind her and Harry sits in the corridor. He lifts his feet for the woman with the mop and watches her progress across the floor, the tiles glossed briefly to glistening black and white and then dulling and leaving only the smell of bleach behind. The metal mop bucket scrapes, someone coughs in a room off the corridor, and somewhere in the hospital a piano is playing. Harry pictures an audience of mute men, dulled men, dead-eyed lost men, and imagines his brother's eyes blinking with the sudden recognition of a string of musical notes. Could it yet be? Should he have followed Rachel into the office? He photographs the shadows on the corridor, the doors on the corridor, the handles on the doors.

At length an officer emerges, ushering Rachel. He shakes her gloved hand and nods his head at Harry as he stands. "Nobody in England has any idea of the logistics of this thing. It will be years before it's cleared up." He has weak eyes, Harry notices. He rubs at the red marks on either side of his nose where his reading glasses evidently pinch. The smile that appears, when his hand pulls away from his face, is weary but sympathetic. "It is a dreadful mess," he says.

"Isn't it?" Harry replies.

They walk back toward the village down a straight road. To the left, a farmer is struggling with a plow. Harry has read about the iron harvest, the barbed wire and spent shells that block the plowshare's path — and worse too. He watches the pointed toes of Rachel's boots strike out. Her heels click sharply on the newly metaled road. Her mouth is a tense line.

"So, could they tell you anything useful?"

"Not really. He took all the details. I had to look through cards and pick out the color of David's eyes and hair. I had to point to the nearest match for the shape of his nose and his mouth. It shouldn't have been as difficult as it was." She laughs oddly. "He said there are thousands that they haven't identified, hundreds of men who have completely forgotten who they are. They're photographing them, *cataloguing* them. That was the word he used. Can you imagine it? It made me think about butterflies in a collector's cabinet."

Harry thinks of Francis's face as he painted it once long ago. He sees the color of his eyes and the line of his nose and lips. His brother's eyes are the blue of a butterfly's wing. "I can imagine," he says. Surely Francis couldn't yet be somewhere, nameless and waiting? Surely there was no way back? "So what happens now?"

"They know where I am and, in the meantime, I have an appointment in town this afternoon."

"Your lost property?"

"He talked to me about it in the hospital. Preparing me, I suppose, only there were so many polite euphemisms crammed into his sentence that for a moment I thought I was being invited to view some back room in a railway station. As if my husband might be idling among the forgotten umbrellas and lost gloves, just waiting for me to reclaim him." She stares at her own gloves and flexes her fingers. "He advised me to go home."

They eat thin soup and slices of ham. Rachel sometimes talks with her mouth full, he notices. Harry watches the room, surveying this strange collection of company. There are women who appear to be widows, French officers in uniform, and workmen in shirtsleeves. A couple in Parisian fashions are sharing a table with men who look like they've just come in from the fields. A bottle of wine passes between the hands of those who are plowing and those who are grieving and those who have come to see the sights. This war has been a curious leveler, Harry thinks. The woman at the next table is sitting alone and staring at her soup, her expression suggesting that she is not at all sure how she has found herself in front of this particular bowl. Harry looks down at his own bowl and thinks of Edie. Is she somewhere close by also wondering how she came to be here?

"You're not listening, are you?" Rachel

waves her fork.

"I am. You were talking about the amnesiacs."

She places her cutlery down neatly. "You don't have to stay here, you know, Harry. It's very kind of you to have accompanied me this far, but I really don't need chaperoning. You don't have to help me."

"I want to help you," he replies.

A bus takes them into the town, bumping along the patched roads, looking out at the healing-over land. Among the chaos and the corrugated iron, new buildings are rising. It is being reclaimed in red brick and wire-defined boundaries. Rachel points a finger and passes comment on the architecture. This utility is ugly, she says; there is no sympathy, no softness, no acknowledging nod to the past.

"I might feel inclined to snub the past if I lived here," he replies. "That or make a rude gesture at it."

Much of the square is shored up. Rachel's directions bring them to a building with a columned portico and potted camellias on the steps. Pocks and splinters scar the symmetrical façade and there are still piles of fallen stone all around. This architecture communicates its recent past all too amply,

Harry thinks. How very strange it is to be back here.

They are directed to a large salon that has an ornate plasterwork ceiling. The floor has been boarded over, presumably to protect the parquet, and trestle tables are arranged in a U-shape and loaded with assorted personal effects. It looks like the most ghastly church jumble sale. Each item has an attached luggage label, the number upon which seemingly corresponds to a nameless burial, to a man who is now not even a number. Harry wonders how these things, these ubiquitous things — the standard army-issue pencils; the belts, buttons, and badges; the penknives and combs; the rings and razors; the cigarette cases, compasses, and picture postcards — could identify an individual. These objects could well have been his own. He mentally inventories the items in his old kit bag. Where now are his penknife and cigarette case, his letters and his diary? Could Francis's belongings surface in a place like this? Should he too be looking for clues? And how would Edie feel if Francis's penknife did turn up on a trestle table with a ticket attached? Does she really believe that her husband — his brother — could yet be alive and the past four years have just been errors and lies?

The women sniff as they sift. Rachel examines items diligently, picking them up and turning them over as if she expects them to exude some familiar energy, as if she is willing there to be a crackle of connection. She brings them close to her eyes and to her nose. Harry looks at her fingers working and wonders how many other women have already picked over the same debris. As her hands stroke a leather wallet he imagines Edie making the same gesture. Perhaps she has already been in this same room, has picked over these same tables. He wants to take Rachel away, to tell her not to put herself through this, but she stays until the end, until the officer in charge has watched his watch for long enough. Harry wonders at her tenacity, wonders if it is hope or fear that keeps her eyes searching, and considers which of those two sentiments brought Edie to this town.

They walk back through Arras empty-handed. There are still great chasms in the cobbles. He tries to steer Rachel on a safe path. From many buildings it is only the chimney stacks that have survived. They soar skyward. "Like exclamation marks," she observes.

The arcades are scaffolded and crumbling. On the broken walls above he can see the spaces that fireplaces and kitchen ranges formerly occupied. The remains of an electric chandelier are suspended from a ceiling and there are tatters of curtains at windows. These partially intact houses, with their hints to the lives that once went on inside them, are more moving than those that are completely leveled.

"All wrecked," Rachel says. "All ruin."

"Yes." He turns in the center of the square. "I saw an advert in the *Times* on the way out: six pounds to see the Somme. It's almost laughable, don't you think? People are choosing to holiday here now. I can't fathom why you'd want to come here unless you had to."

"I have to."

"I understand that." Harry shakes his head. A stall is selling trinkets and nougat and shell cases. A woman holds a waffle pan over a burner. The smell of hot fat and sugar is making him feel slightly sick. "I must take a photograph. May I deposit you in a friendly café?"

"I'd rather come with you, if I wouldn't get in the way."

The building is all boarded up. He peers through a shutter and sees a room that is full of mangled metalwork. There are giant boilers at crazy angles and a lot of tumbled-together pipework. He wouldn't know it as a factory, but for the fact that he remembers the junction of the roads. Rachel watches him set up the camera. He focuses in on the nibbled brickwork and wonders which fragment of it finished off Private Michael Gibson.

"Did he die here?" she asks.

"No. Back in England. But he never recovered from the wound that he got here."

"It was a sugar factory, wasn't it? It would certainly put me off taking a lump in my tea. You didn't know him?"

"I never know them. My employer places advertisements in the newspapers and people reply to them. I exchange letters with the families in some cases, in certain instances I meet up with them to discuss what they know and what they want, and sometimes I just deliver the photograph. It rather depends on how good their information is and the particulars of what they want."

"What a thing to do for a living," she observes. "What a burden to be tasked with! You do make it all sound rather business-like."

"It's not businesslike at all, if I'm honest. But I'm very conscious of the responsibility — of the importance of trying to get it right

86

and make the process as smooth and easy for the families as it can possibly be. Not that it's ever really easy."

"In this case it's the man's wife who wants the photograph, isn't it?"

He nods.

"Have you met her?"

"We've exchanged correspondence."

He doesn't tell Rachel how Mrs. Gibson had described her husband's long death. How she had shared the ways in which he had suffered through those weeks, and told Harry of all the anger that still builds up inside her and which she can't yet focus. He would never tell anyone else about all the secret anger and agonies and sorrow that people send him in letters. This isn't his to share, he feels. He only hopes that the evidence that he can provide, and the actions that he can take on their behalf, can go some small way to quietening all those raw and open-ended emotions; that the placing of flowers and the knowledge of the details can bring the families some peace. But all the words and images in those letters stay in Harry's head, compounding his own private agonies and angers, and he knows no peace.

"Do you think that she feels some malice towards these walls?" Rachel asks. "Do you think that she wants it to be all broken down and blasted?"

"Perhaps she wants a photograph of it just so she can tear it up."

"And would you mind if she did?"

"No. Of course not. Not if it makes her feel better." He hopes that it is so.

"I suppose it's a full stop, isn't it?" says Rachel, who has found no full stop again today. "That it's some proof. That it makes it real and final."

"I think that in most cases they just want to be able to picture it and to understand." Is this what Edie wants? Could that be the limit of it? "And I hope it helps them move forwards."

"I'm not sure how I'd feel if I were sent a photograph of this place and told that a fragment of brick had finished David off. I think I might feel cheated. I think I'd feel angry. I mean, it doesn't scream 'right and might,' does it? I'm not seeing 'just and worthy cause.' It doesn't look like something worth dying for."

He shrugs. "No. Perhaps not. But it's different now than it was in 1916. This town was a battlefield. The trenches were cut all through the suburbs, right through the factories and the cellars and the shops."

"You were here yourself?"

"At about the same time," he tells her. So many memories of that autumn in Arras are dark and difficult — the gas scares, Francis's drinking, and the grief hanging over all of it — but he doesn't mean to tell Rachel any of that. "Our sector was just a few streets farther east. It was all shaken apart, but not so much that this wasn't still obviously a place where people had recently lived. It made it feel like the rules were shaken up too, though, and so we had no qualms about picking over it all and scavenging what comforts we could. In some billets we had pianos and armchairs. The luxury of that! Can you imagine?" He looks at Rachel and wonders if she can. "Houses were blown apart and yet, when you looked, there were still slippers on rugs and books waiting for their readers under bedside lamps."

"What a sad image."

"It was lonely, more than anything. If that makes sense? Arras was full of troops, but strangely deserted. I remember hearing a gramophone playing one day on an empty street and thinking that it was the loneliest sound that I'd ever heard."

He also remembers helping to develop photographs in the dark of a cellar on the Douai Road, trays of chemicals and curling reels of film. The recalled smell of the fixer is sharp and immediate. He sees Francis's face in the red light.

Harry's lens clicks on Mrs. Gibson's photograph. The loneliness of Arras strikes him again.

He buys a postcard for Edie before they go. On the newsdealer's rack Arras is photographed in every angle of ruination. He recognizes the blasted basilica, the citadel, and the cemetery gates. *Les fantômes d'Arras,* reads the annotation on an image of the ruined Grand Place. The rickety frontages look like something out of a Gothic horror story, Harry thinks. He selects an image of the Rue de Douai, a fire-blackened façade, leaning girders, and a spill of tiles. *This was once our happy home,* he writes on the reverse of the card. *We lived like troglodytes in caves, pillaged and looted and danced drunken waltzes to gramophone records. We picked blackberries in a forgotten walled garden, I read* Wuthering Heights, *and Francis set up a darkroom in a cellar on this street. But perhaps you have already been here and recognized it from his photographs? Perhaps you have already stood here?*

Back on the bus, he turns the pages of the

90

album and shows Rachel the streets and the cellars where they lived. Francis liked to photograph the strange, fragile, left-behind domestic details that they found in the wrecked houses. There are china shepherd-esses on a mantelpiece, stuffed finches under a glass dome, and plumed hats on stands in the blown-out window of a mil-liner's shop. The details are crisp and eloquent. He admires his brother's sense of composition and the stories that these photographs tell. On the next page they are striking poses wearing the same millinery confections. Francis is grinning under tulle and paper flowers.

"Is that your brother?"

He nods. "Francis."

"You look alike."

"Is it the taste in hats?"

"You're wearing an ostrich feather." She grins and points. "Your face is the same shape. It's the chin and the cheekbones."

"He looks like my father there — by which I'm not alluding to the hat."

"So he photographed your war and you drew it. I wonder if your eyes saw it all the same. Do you ever look back at your draw-ings?"

"I don't have them any longer. I lost everything in 1917." He looks at Rachel. "I lost my sketchbook, I mean."

"That must have felt like a big loss at the time, I imagine."

He watches the landscape rushing past the window. "There was a time when it felt important to me to put it all down on paper. It was just the way that I coped with what was going on around me, and I suppose that was easier than carrying things around in my head. When I lost all my papers, I realized that because I'd been drawing and writing it all down, I hadn't quite committed it all properly to memory, like I hadn't *really* been living in that moment. I realize now that I sometimes remember things wrongly, you see. Like my brain has chosen the wrong bits to keep and some of the important parts are just missing."

"I think that's called self-preservation," says Rachel and pats his hand. She smiles slowly and he sees understanding in her smile.

"Does Francis have your coloring?" she asks then, and her smile curls at the corner. "Your hair is terribly red. Like a fox in winter."

"I apologize for it."

"Like a stoat — or a weasel."

"Couldn't we have stopped at the wintry fox?"

92

It is starting to go dark as they walk back to the village. The evening light sharpens the lines of plowed furrows. The air smells of turned-over soil.

"You do believe he was killed?" she asks.

"I'm sorry?"

"Francis, your brother. You said that he was reported 'Missing, believed killed.' Do you *believe* it?"

"I know he was shot. I was there. I saw it. He had a gunshot wound to his chest. In 1917 I had no doubt, but his body was never recovered. When the dead and wounded were brought in, he wasn't there."

"So there's a chance?"

"For four years I've gone around seizing the sleeves of half-familiar strangers and jumping at shadows. But, no, I've no proper reason to doubt any more now than I did in 1917. Time passes, we search, and still nothing surfaces. But that's not enough for his wife."

"I understand. And I'm sorry," says Rachel.

"Aren't we all?" he replies.

The volume rises in the café that night. A party of French colonial troops, bright soldiers in uniforms of bold red and blue, have pushed the tables together and are now singing something about Paris, beating a ragtime rhythm with their soup spoons. Their songs and their laughter are loud, and soon everyone in the café seems to be shouting. Rachel's fingers tap along with the rhythm. Harry can see how she is drinking to try to forget, and forcing herself to smile at him over the rim of her glass. Only suddenly that effort of will seems to fail.

"What am I doing, Harry? This is foolish, isn't it? He's not coming home. I'm never going to find him. You don't think I will, do you?"

"I honestly don't know." He says it as kindly as he can. "But I do understand why you have to try."

Harry wonders: If he hadn't come home, would Edie have come to look for him? Would she have made the journey to identify his eyes and his belt buckle?

"If he is alive, why doesn't he let me know?"

"Maybe he can't. Maybe he doesn't remember where home is. Maybe he isn't ready yet. I didn't go home until a year after I was demobbed."

"But you did. You eventually *did* go home."

"Briefly. And then left again," he says. "It's difficult. So much has changed. *We* have

94

changed. There's so much complication."

"David isn't complicated."

"Isn't he?"

She turns her glass. "What do I do?"

"I admire you for coming here. I understand your reasons and I think you're brave, but would David really want you to spend the next decade of your life searching? To sacrifice whatever chance of happiness you might now have?"

"I can't mourn him," says Rachel. "I can't wear black. I envy other women having a grave to go to, if I'm honest. I envy their knowing. They are putting it in stone now: *the missing.* It is as if it's over, like the balance sheet has now been totaled up and signed off, as if those that will be found have been found, as if they've decided now that it's done."

"I don't want you to have a graveside. I've got a list of thirteen names in my pocket. I have to send photographs of their graves back to their families. Only I hate doing that, really. When my envelope arrives it will end their hope, won't it? It will snuff it out — and what then? I wouldn't wish a graveside on anyone." He moves cheese rinds around his plate and considers whether this is absolutely true.

"But this limbo! What use is hope to me?

I can't move backwards and I can't move forwards."

"I know. I do understand that."

"I shall end in bitterness and secreted sweet sherry." She turns tragic eyes to him and laughs. The amusement in her face glimmers only momentarily.

"I sincerely hope not."

She stares at him. "Why are you helping me?"

He takes a mouthful of wine and considers. "In part because, if I were David, if I were out there alive and lost, I would want you to find me; in part because you remind me of my sister-in-law; and in part because I'm living in limbo too."

"You're a kind man, Mr. Blythe. I do, however, suspect that you are perhaps a ghost."

"Perhaps I am."

"I also think that you should forgive yourself and move forward too."

He smiles at her and shakes his head, not quite sure how to otherwise reply.

"So when you've crossed off your thirteen names, will you go home again?"

"I don't know. If I'm honest, I'm not sure where home is any longer." He had said the same to Edie eighteen months ago.

"Do you just mean to keep on moving,

then?" she had asked. They had stood side by side in silence in the doorway of the house in which he had always lived.

"I'm not sure. There are just too many memories here."

"Can you force yourself to forget?"

He had replied that he meant to try.

"And do you mean to forget me too?"

He remembers, four years ago, a letter that he had written to Edie and not sent. He had asked her to forget him then. And to forgive him. Eighteen months ago he had asked it again.

"Why was it so complicated?" asks Rachel.

"I felt guilty. Why should I have survived? Why, when others didn't, did I have the right to come back? How did the odds work out in my favor? My brother William had an apprenticeship to come back to. Francis had a wife." He looks from his wineglass to Rachel's face. "It didn't seem fair that I was the one who came through and I don't know what I'm meant to do next."

"Is Francis's wife the woman who you write to?"

"Edie." He nodded.

"Am I wrong in supposing that she's part of the complication?"

"She always has been," he replies.

Chapter Eight: Harry

Arras, August 1921

Harry dreams about the eyes and noses that night, the mouths and chins piecing together into faces, the faces with parts missing, and Francis incomplete. He wakes up sweating in the strange yellow room. Its shadows lurch about him for a second, with the eyes and the mouths, and then the rapping at the door comes again. He rubs the nightmare from his eyes.

"Just a minute."

Rachel is in the corridor. She looks as if she is about to speak but can't remember what she meant to say.

"Are you all right? Did I wake you?"

Has he screamed again? When the nightmares wake wives and babies he normally moves on. He has spent the past twelve months moving on. The nightmares keep him moving.

Still Rachel doesn't speak.

"I had a bad dream. What a fool." He sees the shadows under her eyes. "Are you quite well? You look like you've woken from a nightmare too."

She seems to consider the question. "Can I come in?"

He lights the bedside lamp, wishing it had more power to push back the shadows. Her white nightdress is just a glow around the lines of her body. He sits on the bed and looks at his hands. "I dreamed about the faces," he says, in need of something to say. "The faces that you told me about in the catalogues."

"Don't, Harry." She stands in front of him. "Please don't speak."

She begins to unbutton the nightdress. He sees her collarbone and her angular shoulders and the locket at her throat, its glimmer accentuating the quickening rhythm of her breath. The dress falls to her feet. She stands naked in front of him and bends, then, to put her mouth to his. Rachel's pale lips touch Harry's. Her mouth is soft, hesitant, and then insistent. He sees her closed eyes and closes his own. And it is Edie's mouth then. It is Edie's voice that says his name in his ear. It is her skin, her scent, her touch, as he has imagined it all, and everything else falls away. Her fingers

99

pull him to her, twist and tug in his hair — but suddenly the illusion breaks, and they are Rachel West's fingers once more, her ringed fingers that have stirred lost property, that have touched the buckles and cigarette cases and postcards. He sees Rachel's hands turn the combs and razors and Francis's penknife.

"I can't," he says. He stands, pushes her away. "Rachel, don't." He turns his back to her. "You don't mean this."

"I do."

"You don't." He turns back to her and sees she has covered her eyes with her ringed fingers. "You're just upset and I just happen to be the person in the next room."

"It's not that."

"It is. You're married."

"Am I?" She looks up. "Or am I a widow? Or, worse, abandoned? Who is he with? You must have had that thought yourself." Her dark eyes shimmer. "And now you don't want me."

"It's not that I don't want you." He studies the pattern of the yellow wallpaper as she steps back into the nightdress. "I can't do this because you'll regret it. I know that. If you did this you wouldn't forgive yourself, and I like you enough that I wouldn't want you to feel that way."

"But you think he's dead, don't you?"

"Do you want me to say it?"

She looks down. "I just want to know."

"You could find him tomorrow, and then how would you feel about this?" He nods at her white dress. He finds it hard to look at her. "Your telephone might ring next week. There might be a knock at your door. He might be there on your doorstep when you get home."

"I could also find him dead tomorrow."

He supposes that she may be right. "I can't do this to you. I can't do this to your husband. I can't take that chance."

"Even though you think he's dead?"

He shakes his head.

"You told me to get on with my life."

"I didn't mean this."

"It's all right." She turns to go, her shoulders hunched now. "I'm sorry, Harry. That maybe wasn't fair of me. It's all just such a dreadful mess."

It's the second time today that he has heard the phrase. She stares at him in the doorway. Her dark eyes are solemn. Her hands close around the *Forget Me Not* locket.

"I know," he says.

He thinks of the last time he saw Francis's face. He thinks of his mother framing

101

photographs of her dead sons, draping them in black crepe to confirm that they weren't coming back. He thinks of Edie watching a section of the station, waiting for him to step into that space. Has he walked away again and left another absence? He doesn't know whether he should be here. He doesn't know where he should be. But he knows that he couldn't assume the space that David West has left.

"Don't not tell her," says Rachel. "Don't leave it too late."

CHAPTER NINE:
EDIE

Lancashire, March 1920

She hadn't expected it to be him at the door. Although more than a year had passed, maybe because of that, Edie still wasn't ready for him to be there. And, as she looked at the expression on Harry's face, she could see that he wasn't really ready either. As they stood there in the doorway, wordlessly taking in one another's faces, her mind went back through his last letter, back through all those enveloped words to the winter of 1918. Had their silence really stretched for so long? Why had he chosen to break it now?

"It was an impulse thing," he said, as she stepped back and watched his feet crossing the threshold. "I saw a girl with red hair." He paused. "She was walking down Euston Road, and then went into King's Cross station, and I suddenly realized that I was following her. Of course it wasn't you, but for a moment it might have been. And I thought then, as I stood in the station and looked up at the departures board, that it was time I came back. You don't mind that I'm here, do you?"

She shook her head. "You shouldn't follow strange women. That sort of thing will get you into trouble."

It was a relief when at last he smiled.

"It's very odd to be standing here and looking at you again."

"Isn't it?" she said.

They were lined up on the mantelpiece, Margaret Blythe's soldier sons: three in a row, with potted hyacinths in between them. Edie stood behind Harry and watched his face in the mirror as he looked at the framed photographs of his brothers. Francis's image was still draped in black ribbons. Somehow, although this was Harry's house now, she hadn't quite ever expected him to be standing here and seeing that.

"I remember that day," he said. "We went to a photographic studio in Morecambe. We decided to have it done proper since we were finally in uniform."

"I remember them coming in the post and your mother going out to buy the frames."

All three brothers were making the same

pose, a plaster balustrade to their left and a backdrop that was painted ferns and soft green shadows, like some sort of Victorian fairy glen. Edie lived with these images every day, these three smiling, long-ago khaki boys, but realized, as Harry turned Francis's photograph to the light, that she hadn't actually looked at them closely for a long time.

"I'd forgotten about it. I'd forgotten these photographs existed." He turned toward her. "You know, it feels like a long time since I last looked them in the eye. Were the ribbons my mother's too?"

"Yes."

"It's so decisive. So absolute."

"And shouldn't it be?" She watched him as he touched the black ribbons. "Is it wrong? You're the one best positioned to judge that."

"No. Of course. She wasn't wrong. It just surprises me to see that she was so sure. That she felt he was so definitely dead."

"She ran out of hope. I wish you could have come to her funeral. I wish you could have got leave for that."

"It was too late by the time they told me. You know that. I would have been here if I could."

"It didn't seem fair that none of you were

here. Fair to her, I mean. That there wasn't one of you to see her go into the ground."

He turned Francis's picture in his hands, as if he expected to find something on the reverse, and then placed it back on the mantelpiece. "This is Francis's house now, I suppose," he said.

"Only it's not, is it?" she replied, then paused. "I didn't know whether I was meant to put black ribbons on you too."

"I'm sorry. I should have written, shouldn't I?"

"You've got heather in your buttonhole."

"A woman pressed it on me in town."

She looked at the man Harry had become. She could see Francis's 1914 face in Harry's mirrored features, that man who had packed a bag and told her that he would be back by the next spring. Except six springs had passed and Francis hadn't come back. When she looked at Harry's reflection, she saw glimmers of the golden boy who had whispered lines of poetry at her through library shelves, but Harry's eyes connected with hers then and he was resolutely himself again. When she looked at Harry's face she could still see traces of the young man who had so wanted to go to art college, and who spent his Saturday afternoons drawing her face. Except six springs had left a sadness on Harry's face. Those were still his gentle green eyes, that still his patient smile, but there was also a melancholy there now, casting a different shadow over his features.

"Heather for luck," she said. "Is that why I don't need to bring home a black ribbon for you?"

"I'm not sure that I believe in luck."

She watched as he washed his hands and face at the sink, saw his eyes looking all around his mother's kitchen.

"I am permitted to make a fool of myself because I might die tomorrow," Harry had said to her in August 1917, as they had stood together on the driveway of the hospital. He had put his hand on the sleeve of her green velvet coat. Two months later Francis was gone. She noticed, as Harry turned now, how he stared at her green coat on the back of the chair. Was he remembering that moment too?

"What happened to your hand?" he asked.

"Munitions. I did fuses for a while. Your mother didn't like it at all."

"I can imagine. It must have made her hate the war to see your hands like that. It makes me hate it."

"But I can work a lathe. And I can ride Frannie's bicycle. I rather enjoyed all the greasy camaraderie and I liked feeling independent. We used to sing sometimes. Though, when I think what we were making, I'm not certain that singing wasn't awful."

"Depends on how despicable your songs were."

"Dreadfully so. And we swore like soldiers. We were gleefully vulgar and we laughed at it. But you're not here to hear my new swear words, are you? And what about *your* hand?"

"Munitions." She saw him smile as his words echoed hers. "Shrapnel. It ended it for me. I was in hospital in London for two months."

"I didn't know that. You should have told me that. You should have written to me. I would have come and seen you."

"Would you?"

"You know I would."

"Perhaps that's why I didn't write."

He leaned back on a chair, kicked off his boots, and lit a cigarette. She watched his fingertips moving over the surface of the kitchen table, refinding familiar textures, knowing that he was remembering his mother placing down saucepans here, the flash of her working knife, his mother's hands scrubbing soap into circles of bubbles on this tabletop. He had moved all around this room touching things, and Edie knew that in doing so he was reconnecting, pulling the detail back into focus, putting the memories all back into place.

"I don't remember these teacups. I don't remember the bluebells."

"They were my mother's," she said. "It's all jumbled up now. When I moved back in I brought everything from next door with me and the two houses got all muddled up together. This house used to be so full of voices, but now it's just me and all these cupboards full of other people's china patterns."

"I have never known this house so quiet."

"Isn't it? You're all still here with me, though. I hear your voices every day when I enter rooms, and then I have to check myself. I sound quite mad, don't I? But I still open doors and fully expect you all to be there. It's oddly comforting to have all your possessions around me. All your things are still in your bedroom, by the way, all your paints and pencils."

Harry's room was still as it had been when he went away six years ago. That was how his mother had left it, and it was waiting for him still, as if he might yet come home. Edie didn't often go in there, because she didn't feel that she had the right. Occasionally she asked herself if he hadn't come home because she was here now, in his mother's house.

"Can you still draw?"

"Yes. Though it's taken some time to get the control back. And it's different than it was."

He dabbed his cigarette out. She remembered a boy who had paint down his fingernails. The version of Harry that she had known before the war always seemed to have hands creased in ink or charcoal or paint. She had often wanted to walk him to the sink and put the bar of soap and a nailbrush in his hands, but she was almost sorry to see his clean fingernails now.

"You haven't thought about going back to college?"

"No. It's too late now."

In the summer before the war he had applied to Manchester School of Art. He had told Edie before he had the conversation with his mother or his brothers, had shared all those ambitions with her first, and it had delighted her to see the excitement in Harry's face. How could he then have let all of that go? How much had that sacrifice cost him? She used to think that she could see Harry's soul in the way that he painted, and she remembered how the light used to shine through his colors. Had that light gone out too?

"I'm sorry to hear you say that. Did you start taking photographs because it was difficult to draw?"

"It's a job," he said. "It's money. I needed the money."

"It surprised me when I heard you were working as a photographer — mostly because it was always Francis's thing."

"It's because of Francis that I knew how to do it. I'm only a photographer in a backstreet studio. I take photographs of children on their birthdays, engaged couples, and hopeful spinsters."

She smiled. "You don't have to qualify it. You don't have to explain yourself to me."

"Would he begrudge me the hopeful spinsters?"

"Perhaps he'd be glad for you."

"Perhaps."

She could see, when she looked at Harry, that something wasn't quite right. There were new shadows around his eyes and he looked like he wasn't sleeping. Something trembled just occasionally around his mouth, like he wasn't entirely in control. She saw how the cigarette in his hand shook. She felt such pity and tenderness toward this sad, damaged young man, whom she had known as a bright, ambitious boy, and who suddenly looked so very like Francis. She didn't want Harry to be sad, but she hadn't known what to do when she had seen those same flickers pass over Francis's face, and she hardly knew what she might do now for Harry.

"Are you sleeping?" she asked.

He nodded.

"I'm not sure that I believe you. Are you eating?"

He smiled, pulled his eyes away from hers, and ran his fingers through his hair. "I'm grateful for your concern."

"Of course I'm concerned. You've lost weight. You look like you haven't slept properly for weeks. I'd admit that I can smell whiskey on your breath, only you might tell me where to go."

They had been such a unit, the three of them; they were a team, they were linked, their voices always joining and their wordless looks saying even more. They communicated with their eyes, these three brothers, and she wondered how Harry existed now without the sustenance of all that wordless language. She missed her mother's voice and her understanding, but how much worse must it be for Harry to have had all that closeness taken away? She imagined that it must be something like deafness, or blindness, or losing a limb. As brothers they were such a fundamental and overlapping part of one another. How did he cope with that part of him gone? Perhaps, she thought, as he watched the match flame flutter between his fingers, Harry wasn't coping?

"You have blue irises," he said, nodding at the vase on the windowsill. "Francis used to buy you a bunch of irises every spring, didn't he?"

"He did."

"It's odd when I look around this room: everything is the same, and yet it's all different."

"It is."

"You don't have to keep things as they were, though, you know. This is your home now, and if you want to change anything, you must."

"You mean the crows?"

The crows on the kitchen dresser watched them with beady eyes. She had always thought them too laughable to be menacing, with their cocked heads and glass button eyes, but she had noticed how Harry was repeatedly glancing at them now, and then looking away, as if he didn't quite want

113

to see them.

"I didn't expect them to still be here. I've never pictured you in this room with the crows still in the background."

"I'm strangely accustomed to their company. I have been known to talk to them on occasion."

"God, we've trapped you in a Victorian ghost story! Burn them, or bury them, if you feel inclined. It feels like we've imprisoned you in a mausoleum. I'm developing sensations of guilt."

His eyes connected with hers as he smiled, and it felt like the first time he had really looked at her since he walked back through the door. She remembered how Harry would smile at her when he was a young man. He was so often the dreamer, his eyes in the skies, as Francis put it, but when Harry smiled it was like the sun coming into the room. Only those smiles seemed to be so fleeting and so much more complicated now.

"Are you back in the shop again?" he asked.

"I've been back for over a year now. Of course it's all black now. It's all the color of these crows. I did six months at the station as well. I worked in the soup kitchen there and watched through the hatch as they all filed back." Such a long line of faces. Only none of them had been his. "I looked out for you, but you were never there."

"I'm sorry."

She watched his fingers tapping cigarette ash among the bread crusts, his downcast eyelashes, his mouth looking like it was going to say something, but holding its silence. She didn't want Harry to be sorry, and yet there had been so many times when she had needed him to be here.

"She dyed her clothes black, your mother. Everything. Here in this room. Right down to her underclothes and her nightdress. There was a vat of black dye in here. I can still see her underskirt rising up steaming from that vat. I can't be in this kitchen without seeing that again, without remembering the smell of that black dye. I thought about looking for you, only I didn't know where to start."

"I can't stay, you know. I don't feel like I could live in this house again."

"With all my heart I wish it wasn't like that, but I do understand," she said.

Chapter Ten:
Harry

Richebourg, Pas-de-Calais, February 1916
They were told that they would proceed to the trenches, and so they advanced toward names they knew from 1915's newsprint.

They marched past winter-bare orchards and beet fields and roadside shrines. They passed thatched cottages and waterwheels and weedy canals. The road's straightness reminded Harry of the Roman road over Blackstone Edge, where he and Francis had so often walked together, with a history book or binoculars or a camera, photographing the stones worn smooth by the passage of centuries of packhorse trains and the ghosts of old soldiers. He re-heard the cries of lapwings and his brother's voice singing long-ago ballads, but Francis wasn't singing today. The route ahead was demarked with the debris of passage: an either-side litter of bent metal and trampled paper.

116

"I feel like we're late for the party," said Will.

The road's curiosities sustained them for a while; they marched past a dressing station, antiaircraft guns, and red-brick redoubts. Chickens scattered from their feet in Le Touret and children lined along the roadway to stare. Poplar colonnades stretched away and a blackbird sang as they crossed a farmyard. Francis whistled a reply and made it whimsy. The houses were sandbagged in Richebourg and the church a fascination of rococo ruin. Pausing for a rest, they peered into the splintered tombs and saw the antique black bones.

"This place is full of ghosts," said Francis.

They moved up through the old front line, which was all wattle and hurdle and rotting wood. Harry was struck with how makeshift it all looked, how amateur and improvised and vulnerable. It felt like walking through ancient history, and the sweet-rotten smell of it — medieval and full of warning — gagged in his throat. Split sandbags spilled and other people's rubbish striated the earth walls like archaeology. Harry looked at the mud-streaked fragments of candle wax and glass, the crumbling rust and the folds of burlap, and wondered who these people had been. Something about the old derelict trenches made them whisper.

"Like the bastions of Troy." Michael Rose's voice didn't sound entirely steady.

"What a shithole," Francis replied. "What a shambles."

Honeysuckle tangled its claim where barbed wire had failed, and, farther up, they had to negotiate their way through a sagging tent of telegraph wires that caught in their packs and rifles. ("Mind the wire!" came echoing back, too late.) All of Harry's senses seemed to have pushed to the surface with the goose bumps on his arms and he took in every precise sight and sound and smell of it. He had never placed his feet more carefully. He had never been more aware of all the textures that his fingers touched or the sound of his own breath.

"I feel like I'm walking over somebody's grave," said Will.

They picked across pontoons in the fading light, across silent expanses of water, and into the impenetrable darkness of a communication trench. They heard and felt the height of the water and it flickered liquid reflections in movement. It was late by the time they arrived at the line. It was all black but for the sudden flash of matches and the clustered fairy lights of cigarette ends. They fried up bully beef, breaking open iron ra-

tions for the first time, and talked of Trafalgar and Transvaal. Over the top, the flares
lit entanglements of wire and pickets. The
blackness beyond was Goya and Blake and
Bruegel.

The first crack of rifle fire came at dawn.

"Jesus!" said Will.

"But it's just the way it is," reflected the
Welsh corporal, with singsong unconcern.
"This is a 1915 sector and we like to nod to
the old conventions. We exchange fire at
dawn and dusk. Call and reply, see. We
observe manners. It's just the way it's done."

The Welshman, whom they'd been put in
with, had the vocabulary of veterans and
told them that they should be grateful not
to have arrived a year earlier. This was a
nursery sector, they said, and laughed.
"Fritz's snipers are the very devil, mind."

"Some schooling," observed Francis.

It all solidified with the rising light, but
the sandbag ramparts seemed to diminish
and Harry found himself moving at a
crouch.

The snow came in the afternoon. They
marveled, briefly, at the crisp, innocent
cleanness of it, but the fall began to thaw
where it was trampled and left them with
wet boots and curses.

"I need volunteers for a working party," said Lieutenant O'Kane. "We need to get that gap in the wire fixed tonight. Are you with me, Blythe?"

Harry looked up. He couldn't avoid the lieutenant's eyes.

"Can I count on you?"

It didn't seem like it was optional. "Yes, sir."

"Volunteer?" Francis said with a laugh to O'Kane's retreating back.

They dirtied their faces with grease and wood ash before they went out and Harry's fingers smelled like a bonfire. There was something schoolboyish about this action. It felt like breaking the rules of grown-up behavior, and they joked as they smeared their cheeks and widened their eyes to one another. But there was an edge to the jests, a forcefulness to the humor, an overly heightened excitement, and Harry felt his heart beat faster.

"I think I'm going to be sick," said Bartley as they waited in the sap.

Harry nodded. He tried to steady his breath.

"Keep low. Keep quiet," said O'Kane. "We get it done and we get back."

Harry could hear the bandolier of barbed wire around his chest chattering. All the processes in his body seemed to be running too fast. His nerves didn't feel right. He wiped his sweating palms on his tunic and took a clutch of snow in each hand. It ached coldly but concentrating on that sensation took some of the rest of it away.

"Silently, now."

He held his breath as he climbed over the top. His limbs felt clumsy. As he looked up, he braced for the returning crack of rifle fire, but there was just glittering blue-white and silence beyond. He followed Bartley's boots, sliding out on his belly. He tried to crawl in small, low movements, but the wire bandolier around his chest wanted to snag on everything and his rifle felt like an anvil.

"You see it?" Corporal Gibbs whispered at Harry's side. He could smell whiskey on Gibbs's breath.

"Yes." The snow had settled on the tangle of wire out ahead and made it more material, but there was such a lot of ground to cross to reach it.

He could hear Gibbs's labored breathing and the creak of their bodies over the snow. It seemed to highlight every movement, heighten every sound, and fell away under Harry's hands. A cavity opened up beneath him and for a moment he expected to plunge down.

"Fuck's sake!" said Bartley.

Harry clung on. He put his cheek to the snow and lay still as he got his breath back. The rifle in his hand seemed to be the only solid and sure thing in the world.

That was when he saw the face. A movement. Eyes glinting. Just out beyond the wire. The man's exhales hung around him like a halo, betraying life. They stared at one another and time stretched. Harry saw him bite his lip and somehow he knew that he would run. He would let him run. He would let him go. But then Gibbs shouted and it all changed. Suddenly everyone was screaming and the gun in Bartley's hand was going off. When Harry looked again the glinting eyes were gone.

Harry watched morning roll in through a frame of barbed wire. Mist wreathed the in-between, giving an air of antique times, of ancient campaigning. It might well have rolled back and shown Charlemagne in camp. The wire's gilded brambles dripped caught light. The trenches steamed. Blue smoke began to rise from the enemy line, washing through the white sky like water-color. Harry stretched in the raw, numbing cold, yawned, and beat life back into his limbs. He hugged his aching fingers in his armpits. His throat was raw from how he'd retched.

Francis stood at his shoulder. "Their dugouts have rugs and curtains, I heard, electric light and hot running water." He sniffed. "I can smell the bastards' sausages and sauerkraut. Why didn't you bring me a sausage back last night?"

Harry turned his back. He couldn't blink away the face he'd seen last night. Was he still out there in the cold and the mist?

"Are you feeling any better?" Francis persisted. He was cutting kindling on the firing step. "Will said you threw up. You looked like shit when you got back last night."

"I feel like shit. I haven't slept."

"You'll get over it."

"How would you know?"

"Because you always get over it and I'm here to look out for you." Francis took the cigarette from his lips. "Do you remember when you went under at the reservoir?"

The shock of the icy black water came back to Harry and made him gasp. Even here. Even now. Even after last night. He rewound nine years and was a boy again, following Francis out onto the ice. The reservoir was epic when it was frozen and it drew them; there might well have been woolly mammoths in its black unfathomable depths. To step out onto the water, to take that dare, to test their courage and their weight, was just too tempting. And they had pushed each other. They had catcalled after him, Will and Francis, daring him to follow, and so his feet had trailed theirs. He remembered their three sets of footprints on the frozen reservoir, the creak of the ice beneath his boots, the shift of the bubbles below the surface, and then the sudden certainty that it would go.

"You looked like a waxwork when we got you out," said Francis. He blew smoke at the memory. "Even worse than you look this morning. Your lips were blue."

"I remember going under. I remember the shock of it and panicking, but have absolutely no memory of getting out." He had woken up in their mother's bed, aching and trembling all over. "How did you get me home?"

"We dragged you. Will and I lugged you like a sack of spuds. An almighty sack of spuds. You weighed a bloody ton. We did think you were a goner."

Harry struggled to make a struck match connect with his cigarette. His hands were shaking again. He dropped the match and swore.

Francis retrieved it for him. "It's all right, we're all in this together," he said. "We're all scared. Don't think it's just you. But you'll be okay. I will always be there to pull you out of your grave."

CHAPTER ELEVEN:
EDIE

Arras, August 1921

The morning light is creeping across the rooftops. Once upon a time this skyline would have been spiked with belfries and church steeples, but today the towers have all come down and the roofline is tattered. The white shape of the cathedral is like a ghost of a building. Smoke starts to rise from the chimney opposite Edie's window and a flight of starlings streaks along the street below and then wheels above. She envies the birds the lift of their wings as she turns away.

There are prints of Madonnas and saints all around the walls of this rented room and a black wooden crucifix is suspended above the headboard. It is wound around with a string of rosary beads and crumbling sprigs of heather. When she wakes in the night she can see the beads slowly rotating above. It looks like a bed in which an elderly relative has slowly died. She has spent enough nights lying awake in this awful bed trying to match the photograph silhouette of a broken-down town to the streets through which she has spent the day walking.

She splashes her face at the washstand. In the mirror she is surrounded by lithographs of suffering martyrs, but she barely sees the jewels of blood and gilded agonies. Perhaps she has stared at it for too long, but like a double exposure, that photograph face now seems to be imprinted over everything. Francis is here in this room, there behind her own reflection, and he is all over this town. And yet, she is certain now, he isn't actually in Arras.

She had taken the envelope into the post office the previous day. The staff behind the counter had huddled around it, poring over the blur of ink. They debated, gesticulated, and laughed as if this postmark were a puzzle, a riddle to be solved, a code to be cracked, but then all three had turned to face her and had shaken their heads. It is always the same. With the authorities there have been more headshakes, more rooms full of awful remainders of other men, more ledgers full of names that are not his. She puts the photograph back into its envelope and places it on the top of her suitcase. It is time to move on. He isn't here.

They start work early in the masons' yard. Edie can hear the rhythm of striking chisels and see the blocks of white stone waiting. She places her feet carefully on the treacherous cobbles, but up above workmen whistle songs on scaffolds. They are standing in the empty spaces that once glowed with cathedral glass, sawing out the cracked stones so they can put in the new. It all looks so precarious, this work; she can see more hope and determination than engineering. What has been brought down by machined steel and high explosive is being put back with mortar and sweat and courage and care. It matters, she sees, that all of this is made right. This town is fixing itself. They are putting it all back like it was. She thinks of her husband's photograph face. Could she put all that back too?

A wagon passes in front of her loaded with scaffolding and she walks on. The houses of the Grand Place look ragged, rickety, brittle. They are propping each other up like a staggering row of closing-time drunks. Most of the roof tiles have gone, so that the skyline is a zigzag of rafters. It is like the houses are showing their skeletons and it makes them appear terribly vulnerable. Arras is like a model built from matchsticks, she thinks, and the breath of one more big bad wolf could blow it all down.

The gaps in the façades show the fringes of lampshades and the patterns of bedroom curtains. These rudely exposed fragments of lives once lived — the wallpaper choices and the glimpses of wardrobes — are the most moving. It is these details that make these sad stones into ravaged homes. It fills her with such a sense of pity to stand here. It is all so immediately, forcefully tragic, but looking around here, she is finally certain that this is not the place: however ill-used Arras has been, the town in the background of Francis's photograph has suffered worse.

The square is filling up with voices, and footsteps and journeys weave across it. There are still advertising signs on the pockmarked buildings and beneath the painted lettering (VINS ET SPIRITUEUX — BEURRE ET FROMAGES — VÊTEMENTS FEMME) shutters are opening and wares are being shown to the morning street. There are men in straw boaters and women in white weekend dresses and all the crowd has a sense of direction and purpose. A young girl skips, a boy points, and a family groups together to have their photograph taken by the ruins.

As she stands and looks around the square

his whispering voice is there in her head again, telling her to tread softly. She sees a smile curling at the corners of his mouth, and the glimmer of his long-ago eyes through the bookshelves. She turns around and the arcades and crowds spin. Could Francis be watching her even now? Are his eyes there, just out of sight? But she knows that he's not here. She would feel it. And yet, if he's not here, where is he? Edie turns in the middle of the square, with the crowd surging around, and feels that she doesn't know which way to go or what she is meant to do next.

She stands with her suitcase and looks up at the station frontage. Many of the panes of glass are yet to be replaced, so that when it catches the light it seems to twinkle malevolently. The railway station looks rather Gothic in its glittering raggedness, she thinks, like some sort of monstrous fairy palace.

A man in uniform is chalking up departure times on a board and every destination is a question and a possibility. She tries to pull her mind back through Francis's letters, to remember the significant place-names, all the places that mattered to him and where he might now be. A year ago she had been so certain that he was quietly in his grave, but every town on the map now looks like a maybe.

All the destinations on the departures board are names that she knows from newspaper headlines. They are all memories of battles and fronts and big pushes. Did he want her to follow him to these places? Did he need to show her these things? Did he mean to make her understand? She hears her own intake of breath as she steps up to the ticket desk.

She is certain of one place where he will have been.

CHAPTER TWELVE:
HARRY

Arras, August 1921

"I'm going to take a train south," Harry tells her.

Rachel butters her toast and nods. She has come down to breakfast late. He wasn't sure that he would see her again at all.

"Your graves?"

"Yes."

"Good. It's a good thing that you're doing. A kind thing. You ought to have more confidence in that."

She pours tea and raises an eyebrow at him.

"Yes, please."

"It's horribly weak," she says and dabbles in the pot with a spoon. "The French really don't know what they're doing with tea. I wish I'd packed tea leaves."

"Will you be all right on your own?"

"Quite well. Thank you." She bites toast and he looks away from her mouth. She is wearing a high-necked black blouse today and jet earrings that swing as she chews. She gives the appearance of having dressed very deliberately this morning, as if she doesn't mean for there to be any doubt. "I'm grateful to you for being here with me, Harry, but helping me doesn't move *her* forwards, does it? It doesn't get her any closer to the truth. I mean, it doesn't work by proxy, does it?"

"No," he says, considering what that truth might be and what Edie moving forward might mean. "Only I'm not quite sure how to help her. Will you write to me if you have any news?"

"Would you want to know?"

He watches her tidy fingers briskly cutting the toast into smaller triangles. "I wouldn't say it if I didn't mean it. I want you to find him. You're here for the next fortnight?"

"I have a diary full of hospitals and cemetery records and meetings that will probably go nowhere." She looks up from her teacup. "But where will you be? Where do I contact you?"

He considers and, at length, writes Edie's address on the back of a spare postcard. There is an image of Arras Cathedral in ruins on the front. A Tommy in a tin hat is poking gloomily at the fallen stone with a stick.

"It'll get to me there."

"You should tell her," says Rachel.

"I can't," he replies.

At the station he sees there is a train going to Béthune. The place-name brings back interbattalion cricket matches, sessions of practicing their bowling actions with Mills bombs, and the journey back out of the Richebourg trenches. They had moved back out to the rest area at the end of February 1916, marched, eight miles away from the war, back to where the snow glistened rosy and blue again and their boots once more crunched. Harry turns through the album as he waits for his train and sees himself and Will posing in the snow for Francis's camera.

"Smile for the dickey bird!" Francis's voice comes back across the years and miles.

As they marched west, there were garden gates and overblown cabbages. There were painted shutters and shops that sold postcards and chocolate. The lacquered shoots of the overhead branches, glossy with promise of new life, had a fresh beauty, Harry remembers. To no longer strain to listen, to take it as it came, was liberating, and civilian sounds beguiled Harry's ears: a girl's laughter, a baby's cry, a dog's bark. Domesticity looked bright and kind and he put all of its colors down on paper. Francis had photographed roadside shrines and oxcarts, staring children and the splitting seams of their boots. Will is laughing in a goatskin coat by a sign that says NO LOITERING.

He writes down the place-names and the dates for Edie, wondering as he does so whether she might presently be in any of these places. The snow had turned to rain by March. The villages were dirty and straggling. *Grim weather,* he writes. He pages on, fitting photographs into brackets, and it is June and they are again billeted back near Béthune. There are football matches and boxing tournaments and they swim in the canal. There's a brigade horse show and concert parties and they sleep in the sun under the trees. He can still picture the light moving through the branches above and hear Will's voice at his side.

Harry takes the train south to Albert. He watches it all pass by the window and tries to see the woods where they camped and waited to move east. The countryside is all rather trampled hereabouts; he looks out and sees collapsed masonry, strewn timber, and corrugated iron. Letters in plasterwork

135

threaten SUSPICIOUS PERSONS WILL BE SHOT ON SIGHT, while the wall all around the words has crumbled back to lath. There are telltale hollows and mounds of earth. Tree stumps line a lane. Black thistles grow. The barbed wire is mangled and rusted, and, like the plasterwork words, has lost its menace. It is only ugly now and sad to see.

There are duckboard tracks along the roads through the town and piles of debris on either side. It is all coming down and rising up new. He has seen construction sites on the outskirts. Rows of wooden houses are being built. Their design reminds him of the cowboy towns that he has seen on the cinema screen. One of these new properties has a sign outside announcing itself as the VILLA D'ESPÉRANCE; the name had struck him and then he had wondered if he was right to be surprised by it. How could hope better be exemplified than the effort to make this place a home again?

He had been told about the town's leaning Virgin, how she had gazed down all askew from the top of the tower, threatening to end the war for whichever side made her plummet. He had seen newspaper images of her at ever more precarious inclines. It had seemed as if hope and meaning were invested in those angles. A new church is being built now beside the old. It seems that Albert is trying to right itself, to rise and look forward. The golden Virgin is long gone, though. He looks up at the basilica and it is gnarled and scabbed and sorry-looking. Some ruins have a romance, but this is a gloomy pile of stones.

" 'Before the war as many as eighty thousand people made pilgrimages to this basilica yearly,' " he reads from the guidebook that Rachel has given him, " 'to see the ancient statue of the Virgin, discovered in the neighborhood by a shepherd, in the Middle Ages. Today the immense building is a shapeless heap of stones, bricks and debris of all kinds.' " Looking up, he finds it hard to contend this statement.

He eats bread and cheese in a much-patched and scaffolded estaminet called the Café de la Victoire. There is brick dust on the tabletop.

"Pilgrim or tourist?" asks the waitress as she polishes the bar.

He sees through the window that a day-tripper party is huddled around the ruins now. A man is addressing them through a megaphone. "I'm not sure that I'm either," Harry replies.

"They stand too near." She points toward the basilica. "The weather keeps bringing the bricks down. They ought to put a fence around it but people like to look. I really don't know why people want to look."

"When did the statue fall?"

"The whole tower came down in the spring of the last year. Boom!" She brings the palm of her hand down hard on the bar. The unexpected force of the gesture makes Harry jump. A man looks out from a doorway behind and laughs.

"Which side brought it down? Was it finally us or them?"

"Does it matter?" she asks and shrugs.

He finds a cheap room for the night. The proprietor wants payment up front and Harry understands why when he views the accommodation. The windows are patched with paper and the plaster has fallen from one of the walls, leaving only a wattle lattice that looks medieval. There are scorch marks on the bedsheets, but he supposes that this at least indicates that someone has made an effort to launder them. When he snuffs out the candle, stars push through a crack in the wall. He struggles to get to sleep in his shaken-apart room, to trustingly shut his eyes upon it. He feels as if at any moment the rest of it might fissure and the ceiling come plunging down. Each time he manages to let go and give in to sleep he jolts awake with the recalled slam of the waitress's hand on the bar. He bites his fist to stop the shaking. Brick dust grinds against his teeth.

CHAPTER THIRTEEN: HARRY

Aveluy Wood, north of Albert, Somme, July 1916

The guns were louder now. Will had to raise his voice. With the volume and his newspaper enunciation, it sounded like he was making a speech.

" 'The public had for some days been led to believe that we were on the eve of a great advance,' " Will read aloud, " 'and the fact that the British report was so cheering has caused the greatest joy. British casualties are not heavy. There have been exuberant demonstrations of delight in Manchester.' "

"Forgive me if my exuberance is somewhat subdued this morning," said Harry. "I wish that newspaper contained less cheering and more hot chips."

"This cake is stale," said Francis. "And she knows that I can't abide currants. I mean, have you seen? I could break rocks with that."

"Just dunk it in your tea."

Harry watched as his brother's dirt-ingrained fingers picked at the fruitcake. "Jesus, Frannie. Have you misplaced your cake fork again?"

"Ye gods, spare me brotherly discernment." Will held out his hand and ate discarded dried fruit. "At least we got something. Poor Wilkinson here got a jar of insecticide powder and a religious tract."

"Bugger all," confirmed Wilkinson with a nod.

"Ever wish that you'd been orphaned?" asked Francis.

"Dear God what art in heaven, please spare me from thy creatures all greatly bitey and small." Will put his hands together and raised pious eyes skyward. His hair was plastered to his forehead. The smile glowed white in his grimed face.

Wilkinson shrugged and scratched his crotch. "It's a rum do when you need the *Evening News* to know what's going on," he said. "Incidentally, I'm not averse to currants."

"Here." Will passed both the newspaper and the cake. "It's ten days old, mind."

"The newspaper or the cake?"

"Both."

A shell landed some distance ahead. Mud

rained down. The earth seemed to lurch and Harry found himself gripping hard onto his mug.

"Bloody hell," said Will. "If I'd wanted shit in my tea, I'd have ordered it." He rubbed his face, leaving stripes of mud down his cheeks.

"If Mother could see you now, you'd be sent to bed without cake."

"Think of the color of the sheets."

"Oh! Think of white, dry, hot-water-bottle-warmed sheets!"

"Where are we on this?" asked Wilkinson, leaving greasy fingerprints on the newspaper's map of the new and old front lines.

Francis leaned in to see. "Funny, that, eh? Cartographer's oversight? Godforsaken Shit Hole seems to have been missed off this map."

"Godforsaken Shit Hole just north of Albert," said Harry and pointed.

"Miles behind the line, then?"

"Not bastard far enough."

Francis wiped his fingers on his tunic before he opened his letter. Harry watched. Francis seemed to be taking care not to fingerprint Edie's yellow writing paper. "Lord Derby told the papers that the Manchester battalions have covered themselves with glory."

Will looked down at his mud-splattered uniform. "Glory, eh? Is that what this is?" He sniffed his sleeve. "I'm not sure that I like the smell of it."

The yellow notepaper radiated cleanness in the all-around grime and accentuated the trembling in Francis's fingers. He looked up and met Harry's eye. "Just cold," he said.

"What I'd give for a hot bath."

"Or a vaguely tepid one."

"And a mademoiselle to scrub my back."

"She sent you pencils," said Will, retrieving them from the box.

"God bless Mater and all who sail in her."

Wilkinson yawned widely.

"Heavens," said Francis. "Where have our manners gone? Your veneer of civilization is wearing frightfully thin, old thing."

The expletive with which Wilkinson replied was censored by the boom of the guns behind.

"I can't hear myself think," mouthed Will.

"Go in for much of that sort of thing, do you?"

Second Lieutenant Rose came into the bay with his hands over his ears. "Is this a cozy family reunion?" he shouted. There were shadows under his eyes, Harry saw. He didn't look like he'd had any sleep either.

"We had a parcel," said Will in between the guns.

"She sent me film. Two boxes." Francis smiled.

"Splendid," said the lieutenant. "Not achingly picturesque here, though, is it? Not quite the scenic bosky glade?"

"If we put in a complaint do we get our money back?"

The woods through which the trenches ran were considerably smashed. With, seemingly, the majority of the Allied artillery positioned just behind, there was much coming in and falling short. Guns of every caliber bellowed over their heads. The woods were all mud and broken branches. There was a terrible eloquence to the crude blackened trunks that surrounded them, Harry thought. The trench was cut through tree roots, several inches deep in earthy-smelling water, and something about the torn roots struck Harry as a particularly horrible act of violence.

"The sea view is criminally exaggerated," critiqued Will, "and the catering leaves much to be desired."

"I shan't be leaving a tip," put in Wilkinson.

"I think we already have," said Harry. He watched the surface of his tea pulse with

144

the rumble of the artillery. It tasted more of petrol than of tea, but it at least thawed his fingers. If only he could soak his feet in a vat of it.

Francis took off his waterproof cape. Shaken-off water glittered. "I'm not sure whether this thing is keeping the damp off or in."

"Watch out," said Wilkinson, protesting with the newspaper.

"On the catering front, I'd pace myself, if I were you chaps." Rose waved a stick at the remains of the cake. "Might find that the hospitality arrangements are a little disrupted for the foreseeable."

"Is the buffet off?"

"Exceedingly. Here." Rose produced a tin can from his pocket, looked at the label, and threw it toward them.

Francis caught the can. "Pilchards in tomato sauce? Much obliged, sir."

"More of a tinned-salmon man myself, but my sister seems to have invested in a whole shoal of ruddy sardines. Well-meaning, you know, but still —"

"What is the foreseeable?" asked Will. "Do we know how long we're going to be here?"

"Your guess is frankly as good as mine," said the lieutenant. "Moncrief rode forward this morning. He says that the whole place is an utter shambles. Villages that are on the map have just been deleted. They're just not there. Absolutely razed to the ground. Nothing but dust. There's dead Boche everywhere and prisoners streaming back. It's going to take forever to get them all buried. Moncrief says that the flies are infernal. He smoked two cigarettes at once to keep the filthy brutes off his face. He hasn't stopped coughing since he got back."

"So what's the halftime score, then? Are the odds on our side?"

"I'm not a betting man," said Rose. "And I don't know that we're at halftime yet."

"But we'll get our crack?"

Heavy artillery was heaving overhead. The lieutenant crouched and put his hands to his ears. "Good God, this is perfectly deafening."

Will repeated the question. He shuffled a greasy set of playing cards as he spoke, the cards slipping smoothly through his fingers. Harry looked on and admired the agility of his brother's unfaltering fingers, the steadiness of the rhythm, undisturbed by the churning sky and the shuddering ground. Was it really just twelve months ago that Will was a boy arranging seashells on the sand? Had they all changed so much?

"Without doubt," Rose replied. "We're

just awaiting orders as to when and where."

"Forgive my younger brother's eagerness," said Francis. "He's sparring for a scrap."

"Aren't we all?" said Rose.

Harry wasn't entirely convinced by the lieutenant's scrapping eagerness.

"I think that we know less about what's going on than they do in Manchester," said Wilkinson, looking up from the newspaper.

"I'm ready for my front-page photo," said Will, putting aside the playing cards and straightening his tunic.

" 'Lancashire will indeed be proud of them,' " read Wilkinson.

"Given half a chance," said Will.

Chapter Fourteen:
Edie

North of Albert, August 1921

There are two young men sitting opposite her in the railway carriage, obviously two brothers, and Edie is glad of the laughter in their voices as she looks out at the sad country beyond the window. The whistle screams, the steam clears, and she sees villages that are all wooden huts and leveled churches. Those strange undulations of the earth. The straggling belts of brown barbed wire. The endless thistles. She wants to shut her eyes to it, not to see just how desolate and broken it is, but she tells herself that she must look.

The boys grapple arms, laughing, and smile when their eyes meet hers. She can make no sense of their foreign words, but the sounds are the same, and it pulls her back to Francis's teenage bedroom and all those noises that were always coming through the walls.

When she was nineteen years old she had left the calm of her childhood home for a house full of male voices. It wasn't that she'd grown up in a quiet house; there had always been the homemade wine and the gramophone and the nonsense poems that they'd recited in comic voices. But it was just her and her mother: two twinned female voices, ever harmonious, never raised. They had been contented in one another's company, stirring the jamming pan together, and sharing their sewing patterns and their books. And then her mother's voice had been so suddenly silenced. She was no longer there when Edie looked up from her book; there was no one with whom to share the twist in the plot or a new blouse pattern. All of a sudden their busy kitchen was entirely still.

Francis had been so kind to her through those months of her mother's illness; he had been so understanding, no longer the golden youth with the flashing grin and the ready rhymes, but instead a caring, gentle, steady man. He had let her talk when she needed to, and she had found comfort in the words that he returned. She could see how well he understood her, how he wanted to take away her sadness, and how she now hated the silence of her own newly empty home.

And so she had left it for a house full of boys, with their jokes and their boisterous roughhousing, and the secrets that they always seemed to be sharing. She barely remembered her father's presence, and so how odd it had been to suddenly live among the noise and the movement and the scent of these men.

The train lingers in a station that is all corrugated iron and pine planks, and she watches a young couple swinging their legs on a bench. The boy is turning through a book of maps, seemingly following the line of a route with his finger, but the girl pulls his hand away and smiles as she links his fingers through her own.

She hadn't wanted a great fuss of a wedding because she had no family to invite. Even so, the little church had looked so unbalanced, with all the friends and relations on Francis's side, and so few seats taken on the left. But then, having seen her glance back at the empty pews, his brothers had moved over; they had crossed the aisle, and so when she next looked back, there they were smiling on her side. "We're your family now," Harry had said to her afterward, "whether you want us or not, and we always will be." She can still picture Francis in his bridegroom smartness, the shine of his slicked-back hair and the glow of his face, his sudden nervousness and the twitching smile that he seemed to be having difficulty controlling.

As newly married wife and husband, she and Francis had moved into his teenage bedroom, with his cricket bats and fossil collections and his maps of ancient military campaigns on the walls. They had lived like that for two months — his brothers' voices always there through the walls, and laughing into the pillows to dampen the noise — before the house next door had come up for rent and they had moved one door down. It had seemed the most natural thing that they stay on the same street. She would never have taken him from his brothers, and why would they want to go any farther?

She had always liked to watch the three of them together — Francis, Harry, and Will — their secret sibling jokes and looks, and how their faces mirrored one another. When she sat across the table from them, it was like looking at a progression, or a picture of the passage of time. While Francis's features were the most strongly defined — he was the most conventionally handsome of the three of them — Will's face, beneath a mop of blond fringe, was still forming. When she looked from Will to Francis, she could see

151

the man that he would be in ten years' time. And she had assumed that they would always be there across the table from her, turning from boys into men, becoming the men they were meant to be.

The younger boy on the opposite seat catches her eye and she smiles as he looks away. That shy glance reminds her of Harry. She can see his eighteen-year-old features still, facing her across his mother's dinner service, and how his eyes had sometimes caught hers, just like that. All of the elements that she had loved in Francis's face — the curl of his eyelashes, the angularity of his profile, the bow of his top lip — were there in Harry's face too. When she had seen Harry again this May, that resemblance had been all the more obvious.

Steam billows as the train passes under a bridge; they are into a cutting, and in the darkness of the earth bank she catches a glimmer of her own reflected face. Just as Francis had started with cameras in the summer before the war, forever insisting on taking her photograph, so it had been for Harry with his paints, and she always had to sit for her portrait. She can still put herself back in the sitting room, listening to the whisper of his pencil on paper, the chink of his brush against the glass, and her brother-in-law's steady breathing.

Harry used to *look* at her when he painted her portrait. She can remember the sensation of his gaze on her face and the weight of that look. Sometimes it felt like he was looking right through her bones, and she wondered if he could read her thoughts, but he had to look properly, he said, in order to capture her likeness. He also looked at her when he wasn't painting her, though, and she knew how Francis teased him about that. Just occasionally she felt like she was the prize that Francis had won, and it didn't seem nice that Francis taunted Harry for his blushes and those glimpses under his eyelashes.

Harry didn't help himself, though, she supposed. Sometimes she hardly recognized herself in Harry's paintings and she wondered how he could consider that to be her likeness. He made her noble when he put her down on paper, so that she was no longer a girl who worked in a shop, but a woman who might look out proudly from the walls of an art gallery, surrounded by a heavy gilt frame. There was such generosity in the way that Harry painted her, but he also gave so much of himself away.

The railway line is following the meander of a river — it is there on the left-hand side

153

of the tracks now, and then on the right in the next moment — and the land all around is marshy. The ground is pitted and churned and the waterlogged places bounce back the white sky. A lot of branches have come down, as if there has been an almighty wind, but she can see from the crudely broken shapes of the tree trunks that this has been caused by more than a mere summer storm.

She remembers how, in the August of 1914, the newspapers had been full of the Ardennes and Lorraine, photographs of smashed forests, lines of refugees on the roads, and a burned-down library in a Belgian town. Francis had sat across the dinner table from her and told her that three hundred thousand books had turned to ashes in one night, and she had seen how that angered him. It had frightened her to see that look on Francis's face, because she knew what that look might mean. And she knew that if he went, he would take his brothers with him, that it would be their next shared passion, and how could she stop that? But of course, in the end, they did go. In the middle of July 1916, they'd traveled south, when the newspapers were already full of assaults and attacks and such long casualties lists.

The young men leave the train at Aveluy,

and the boy's brown eyes connect with hers once more as he closes the door of the railway carriage.

"Bonne journée," they say to her, and touch their hats, as they step out into a landscape that's all at the wrong angles. The taller brother puts his arm around the younger and they walk down the platform. As the train slides past, it could well be Will and Francis for a moment. Perhaps she, as an only child, had not fully appreciated how much Francis needed his brothers to be there with him? She thinks about the photograph of Francis alone in the square, and is struck by the terrible loneliness of that image.

Chapter Fifteen:
Harry

Montauban, Somme, August 1921

Location image order: Mrs. Eunice
Maxwell requests a photograph of the
church in Montauban. Her son, Pte. Alan
Maxwell (26519, 17th Manchesters), was
KIA on 1st July 1916, has no known
grave.

It is perfectly quiet. The only sound is the wind through the grass. This spot ought to be full of ghosts, ought to writhe with angry energy. Instead it is the absolute emptiness that strikes Harry.

" 'The struggle for the village was short, but fierce and sanguinary,' " he reads. " 'Today it is utterly impossible to locate the site of a street or house. The only remaining landmarks are the pond and the cemetery — the latter considerably enlarged by the addition of numerous German graves. Everywhere else nothing is to be seen, except heaps of stones and rubbish, beams, scrap-iron and debris of all kinds.' "

He looks up from the guidebook and finds that he can't disagree with its assessment. There are not even really ruins here. Nothing but thistles, nettles, broken glass, and piled stone. A sign indicates that a hump in the earth is where the village church once stood. Iron crosses lean crazily around it.

Harry bends down to get an upward angle on the remains of the church. He wants to somehow make it seem as if there is more to this place than just a bulge of earth. He wants to somehow make it seem more significant. He focuses in on the fancy ironwork of the crosses. As there is no grave for Private Maxwell, so too there is no church to photograph for his mother. Harry feels as if he can't help but fail Mrs. Maxwell.

He walks on. It is five years since Private Maxwell died taking this village, and yet there now doesn't seem to be a single soul trying to reclaim this place. He has read in the newspapers about English villages adopting devastated communes on the Somme, organizing raffles and jumble sales and bingo nights to raise money to gift fruit trees, food parcels, and plows. There doesn't seem to be anyone here to whom fruit trees might be gifted. He wonders if people will ever live here again. Would anyone want to plant an orchard here? What strange fruit would grow from this earth?

The roads have been remade to some degree, but the land on either side has yet to be smoothed and tidied and made right. The ground is hummocky, scrambled over with tangling vegetation, and strange stumps of trees stand like sentinels. For an irrational instant Harry feels like the trees are watching him. There is something accusing about this ill-used landscape.

They had read newspaper reports about the attacks of the first of July as they waited north of Albert. On the eighteenth of that month they had finally received their own orders to move forward. The weather had been wet and they had slipped and skidded on roads that were turning to mud. It was the early hours of the morning before they had arrived, swearing then as they were instructed to make bivouac camp in a boggy field. The men who were coming out told them stories about fighting in the woods, about the splintered branches and the tugging brambles, about all the corpses and the confusion. It was an evil place, they said, a regular charnel house. Harry remembers the faces of the men who told them these stories, the whites of their eyes in the dawn light, the rush of their words, how they had almost seemed to want to outdo one another in shocking those who hadn't been in the woods. Some of them had seemed like they'd left their wits in the woods.

In the distance, to his right, there are what must once have been woods. Black sticks bristle on the skyline. To the left the land slopes away and he can see miles and miles of empty ugly nothingness. Harry feels a great oppressive weight of the nothingness. He feels like the last man left.

By the side of the road is a white stone obelisk. TO THE GLORY OF GOD, reads the inscription on the bronze plaque, AND IN IMPERISHABLE MEMORY. He realizes that the trunks and sticks and scrub behind *are* those woods. He passed through there himself in the last days of July, with the mist and the gas shells and the splintering awfulness all around. He photographs the memorial, focusing in on the bronze words. The broken trunks of trees are like phantoms in the background of his image. Blackened and leafless, they give the impression that it is January, but the horizon shimmers with August's heat.

The road ahead glares white. He remembers these roads as a loudly nudging line of traffic: the trucks, wagons, mules, motorcycles, and the dust from the endless columns of men. His eye scans for familiar landmarks. There is hardly anything here that he recognizes. Just south of where the four roads meet, and just before the ruins of the brickworks, there had been a caved-in barn. The grave had been dug in the field beside. He turns at the junction of the roads, trying to find a feature that he would know.

"You lost, mate? Need a lift?" The driver leans out of the window. Harry hadn't heard the vehicle pull up and the sudden breach of the silence had alarmed him momentarily. There are tarpaulins and stakes and a quantity of mangled barbed wire in the back of the van.

"Do you know if there used to be a brickworks off this road? A red-brick building with a fallen chimney?"

The driver laughs. "Once upon a time. Long ago. You're at the wrong crossroads, pal, but I know just where you mean. Hop in. I'll save you some shoe leather."

He turns the truck and they head back past the black woods.

"Not a place for a picnic, eh?" says the driver.

"Not quite," Harry replies. The barbed

wire in the back of the van rattles. "Is that salvage?"

"A drop in that ocean, aye. They reckon that there's at least a hundred thousand tons of wire alone." He raises an eyebrow at Harry and whistles. "And then there's the ammunition and the bones. It'll go on for years, you know."

Harry can't imagine how it will ever end.

"This is your place."

The van brakes and Harry looks out. He recognizes the slump of red bricks, albeit now much diminished and matted over with brambles. Nature seems to have an urgent desire to cover it all.

"If you're staying in the village, the bar does a passable approximation of beer. You'll find me there and thirsty most nights."

The driver honks his horn as he pulls away.

Harry looks about. Suddenly all is stillness and silence again. He tries to rewind and reorient himself. The barn was on the corner of the side road facing the ruin of the brickworks. There is nothing there now but a pile of timber and tile. The field where they buried them was to the right of the barn. He measures his bearing and tries to re-find the angle, riffling mentally through the fixed images. He recalls a line of crosses and sees none. There is just turned earth. Harry's shoes are clogged with mud and his steps falter, stumbling on pieces of chalk in the soil that look like bones. He turns in the field, the field that should contain the bones of his brother. There are no signs that they were ever here. He thinks about Mrs. Maxwell, wanting a photograph if she could not have a grave. He thinks about Rachel, needing a grave to go to and the horrible hugeness of that word — *missing*. He thinks about Edie's uncertainty. There is no grave for his brother. And, if his brother's grave is missing, where is he? Harry's feet slip from under him and he finds himself kneeling in the mud, staring at the empty earth.

CHAPTER SIXTEEN: HARRY

Bivouac camp, Talus Boisé, Somme, July 1916

"Eaton is back. Rose is rushing around like he's got a wasp up his arse."

"Any news?" Harry asked.

Will shook his head. "Not that they're sharing. They've all gone into a huddle. Roberts is screaming down the telephone. Cropper reckons we're definitely going to get sent up now."

"Jesus."

Harry looked across the field. There was a lot of shouting going on, and a lot of quiet surveying of the men doing the shouting. The bombardment had begun at first light. The sky had trembled with it, the sound of artillery signaling the start of the attack. Francis, with W Company, had gone up in the early hours of the morning. Harry had sat with Will and watched the light pitch in the sky. The enemy guns had started too.

The brothers had hardly spoken, but had smoked their way through a lot of cigarettes. He had felt Will shivering where their shoulders touched.

Greene and Rose were moving around the field now between the improvised shelters, and groups of men were standing up.

"Everyone on your feet. We're on the move."

"Any news of W Company?" Will asked.

"It's chaos up there. A lot of this artillery is falling short. Nobody seems to know whether to move backwards or forwards." Second Lieutenant Rose shook his head. "The French attack looks like it's been a success, though, so we've got to push on."

"No news of casualties, then?"

"If I knew, I'd tell you." Rose batted away the midges with his swagger stick. "I'm just ordered to get everyone moving."

"Buggers are biting," said Will.

The sky flashed and boomed ahead.

"Retaliatory bombardment," Wilkinson said with a nod.

"That's a big word for you."

"Heaney heard Roberts on the phone, reckons that they all ended up falling back. Brigade says it has to happen, though. Roberts was effing and blinding when he put the phone down."

There was a pile of packs by the side of the road. Medical Corps men were crouched over them and turning through their contents. Water bottles and items of clothing were littered about. The wind riffled through the pages of an open book. There were spoons and wallets and shaving razors on the ground. Harry saw a photograph of a small blond girl with a dog and then it was gone on the wind.

"What are they doing?" asked Will. His voice sounded outraged on behalf of the owners of the spoons and the shaving razors. "Whose are they?"

"I'm guessing that their owners are beyond caring."

Will frowned at Wilkinson.

"I'd be glad to give up shaving. There are some advantages to wobbling off this mortal coil."

They walked on in silence for a while. The trees along the side of the road had lost a lot of their branches. They looked twisted, somehow pressingly tragic, and Harry briefly wished that he could pause and sketch their shapes. There was also a lot of debris — coils of wire, pickets and posts, and stacks of corrugated iron sheets. Stragglers sat by the roadside and watched it all pass by.

"It's going to get hot today," said Taylor.

Harry looked up. A plane droned through the overhead blue and plumes of pink smoke rose on the skyline.

"I'm not talking about the weather."

A truck full of Irish went the other way. Their feet dangled from the back of the truck bed. One of them had got a drum and was beating a rhythm. They didn't seem to be in the mood for singing, though. A convoy of ambulances followed them, which put anyone off trying to fit a song to the beat.

"Ruddy long way to Tipperary," said Jones and threw his cigarette away.

They were digging in the field by the brickworks, stripped to shirtsleeves and sweating. The digging men went at their task as if they wished to be finished with it.

"Vegetable patch?" queried Wilkinson. "That'll be a lovely row of cabbages come Christmas."

"Give it a rest," said McCabe.

German prisoners were resting by the crossroads while their guards had paused to smoke and pass water bottles between them. They stared at the traffic on the road. Was this then what the enemy looked like? They looked very small, these men, and very tired. Their ordinariness struck Harry. They looked more exhausted and ragged than monstrous. A pair of brown eyes made direct contact with Harry's own. The boy had shorn-short blond hair and stripes of mud down his face. He had a very young, slightly unfinished-looking face, as if his features hadn't quite set yet. The man next to him nudged his arm and the boy turned away.

"Poor bastards."

The woods to the north were being shelled again. Harry could smell them burning. The blackened tree trunks were stark and sharp and didn't really look like a woods any longer. It reminded him of something from a ghost story, something macabre and Gothic and full of dark meaning.

"We'd know, wouldn't we?" said Will.

Walking wounded were coming back. Their faces were white with the dust from the road, crusted with sweat. Some of the wounded moved like old men, all lurching concentration. Others quivered and jittered. Harry and his companions stared at their faces, looking for features that they recognized. Will's hand was on Harry's arm.

"Yes," he said. "I'm sure of it."

A Red Cross flag fluttered from a tree

trunk. Behind the ambulances there seemed to be a good deal of frenzied activity going on. Weary-looking men were sitting in silence on the banking. Others had found places to sleep. The whiteness of dressings glared against their bloodied faces.

"How's the accommodation?" asked Taylor. "Should I have bought a return ticket?"

"Most convivial," observed Jones.

There was a litter of kit by the side of the road as they went into the trench: helmets and packs and water bottles. Harry saw a leather case that looked like Francis's camera and then he was scrambling over all the kit. Groundsheets and mess tins and webbing fell away as he stretched. His hands trembled as he grasped. It was a pair of binoculars.

"You that keen for a close-up?" asked Yates. "I think I'd rather look away."

Harry shook his head as he looked at the pile of once-upon-a-time possessions. He wondered how long it would take to tidy all of this up in the end.

"Like a ruddy church jumble sale," suggested Wilkinson.

"Only less crochet and chipped cups."

A gunner by the entrance to a dugout was picking a tune on a banjo. He nodded to them as they passed. They tried to whistle along but their lips were too dry and the effort was given up. The gunner's melancholy notes followed them down the sunken road.

The ground seemed to lurch as a shell struck ahead. "Is that ours or theirs?"

Will shrugged. "Does it matter?"

"Of course it bloody does!"

There was a flicker in the sky ahead and Harry felt his heart beat faster. Sweat prickled down his back. Francis hadn't seemed afraid as he'd gone up that morning. He'd got on his business-like face, as Will called it. He had checked his kit carefully and shaken both their hands. He had looked older in the electric light. Will had tried to hug him, but Francis had shrugged him off and told him not to be soft. "I'll be back when I've ended the war," he had said.

"Smartly, now," the shout came back. "Get a shift on."

"Are we late for our date?" asked Taylor.

"I am all abuzz," said Will. "My nerves are all tingling and my belly's full of butterflies."

The earth walls narrowed and the noise ahead increased. It was a great drone, a deep bass noise that seemed to be coming both from above and from the ground under Harry's feet. They were going on in single file now. With an explosion ahead Harry found himself thrown against the trench wall. There was grit in his eyes and in his mouth. Though he knew that he was holding the line up, he had to stop for a moment, rub his eyes, and spit it all out. The earth wall trembled behind him.

"Loads of this is our stuff falling short," Yates shouted behind.

They were moving forward faster now. The bottom of the trench was muddy and Harry found it difficult to keep on his feet. There was a sound like a great rending, an enormous noise, like shipyards and foundries and cathedral bells all pushed together and amplified. The ground quaked with it and he felt it vibrate his bones and drum in his diaphragm. It was like the very earth was being torn apart. Above the bass note there were whistles ahead, almost madly shrill, and a rattle of machine guns. Smoke was rising, white and black, and there was a flashing and an acrid smell. He looked back at Will. Harry saw his brother mouthing words but the noise took them away. His eyes said everything, though.

The line ahead was moving at a pace. "We're going straight over," Taylor yelled back. "It's already started."

They were coming up to the frontline trench now. It was blown out in lots of places. Harry saw newly churned-up earth, dropped rifles, and slumped men. Men were cowering and screaming and crouched over wounds; some were wild-eyed and others were crying. He looked at all the faces, wanting and not wanting to see Francis. The rhythm of the machine guns was loud. He could see the steps where the men ahead were going over. Rose was at the top of the ladder, his arm beckoning on and then diving away. Shells were falling just behind, the earth erupting. Harry was panting now, the rattle and the screaming roaring in his head. He placed his foot on the ladder and realized he was screaming too. He reached backward and gripped his brother's hand. Will's hand was shaking, Harry could feel the pulse in his palm, and then their fingers were pulled apart. His heart was in his throat, his throat clogging, choking with it. He stumbled forward into the smoke.

CHAPTER SEVENTEEN:
HARRY

Guillemont, Somme, August 1921

" 'The village (razed to the ground) was finally captured by the British in September 1916,' " Harry reads. " 'Today no trace whatever remains of the houses, the sites of which are now indistinguishable from the surrounding fields. The whole area was devastated and is now overrun with rank vegetation. After its capture it was strewn with wreckage of all kinds — stones, bricks, beams, agricultural implements and household furniture from the shattered farms and houses. The fine modern church, Gothic in style, which stood in the centre of the village, has entirely disappeared.' "

He begs to differ on one score: two years on from the guidebook's publication there is a village here again, of sorts, and a new church. It is a village built of corrugated iron and wood cladding, the church a Gothic arch of curved metal. It is a fine

172

modern Nissen hut. People are scraping out gardens between their iron houses, there are rows of cabbages, and chickens peck. He notices white lace curtains hung at the windows and the face of a young girl, her nose pressed against the glass. He raises his hand in a hello, but the girl's eyes slide solemnly and offer no acknowledgment. The houses remind him of the huts that they spent time in on Salisbury Plain. It has the air of a prospector settlement, its people brave pioneers scratching a mark in the wilderness. They are plowing out, reclaiming the land around the village. He wonders if they are plowing through bones.

The attack of the twentieth of July was officially deemed a failure. Those who could had retired back; those who couldn't would be brought back that night. *This operation did not work according to plan,* Lieutenant Rose wrote in the official battalion diary. He had told Harry that over a bottle of whiskey a week later, framing the phrase with fingers that were seconds later over his eyes. They lost almost all their senior officers. Rose hadn't looked like he was of a mood to have a glass raised to his promotion.

Noise issues from one of the huts and, stepping closer, Harry sees that it is a bar.

173

The name, AU BON RETOUR, is painted in tidy white lettering above the lintel. Inside, he takes in the corrugated iron walls and the framed photographs of the village before the war. Paper garlands droop from the ceiling and a tricolor is hung from the far wall. The bar itself is a sideboard with bottles and potted geraniums set upon it. He orders a whiskey and recognizes a man down the bar as the driver from earlier. Harry points at a bottle and the driver nods.

"So this is what it was all for, eh?" says Harry as they clink glasses together.

The driver introduces himself as Alfred. He is helping clear the land for the cemeteries and hasn't been back to England since the end of the war.

"The Irish brigades finally took this place that September," Alfred tells him. "Only there was no village left by then. What they found was the tunnels — this great network of subterranean passages and shelters under where the village had been. It was like a fortress, like a maze. Is it any wonder that it took months to take it?"

Harry thinks about the lace curtains and the vegetable gardens and wonders what it must be like to live in a place that is surrounded by so much bone-filled land. He wonders if the tunnels are still there beneath his feet.

"It will be a village again," Alfred goes on. "They mean to remake it."

There is a party of farmworkers at the next table, slapping down playing cards and talking loudly. Their cigarette smoke is thick and sweet, and they gesticulate widely, as if still in the fields. Alfred smiles at their frequent outbreaks of laughter. Harry downs his whiskey and thinks about the plowed earth.

"What did you want by the Briqueterie, then? Did you find what you were looking for?"

"I was looking for a grave," Harry says. "There used to be a row of graves there. One of them was my brother."

"You should have said so," Alfred replies. "They were moved last summer and brought up to the cemetery here. I helped with the exhumation. You were nearly there when I picked you up on the main road."

Harry realizes that he is gripping on to his chair. He stares at Alfred's hand on the glass and imagines it on a shovel. He pictures Alfred's shovel digging down. He wants to shake Alfred's hand.

"Will you draw me a map?"

"I'll do better than that."

CHAPTER EIGHTEEN: HARRY

Guillemont, Somme, August 1921

"Captain Fielding." Alfred makes the introductions.

"Heavens, it's Ralph. Can you forgive my hands?" Captain Ralph Fielding holds up his earth-ingrained palms like a gesture of surrender, and then offers Harry a handshake.

"Harry Blythe, private."

Ralph shakes his head and says, "None of that here."

Looking at the field of graves that surrounds him, Harry can see why rank doesn't matter to Captain Ralph Fielding. The field is level and rather full.

"Captain Fielding was our commanding officer," says Alfred. "We were cleaning up here in 1919 and there seemed too much to do to go home."

Ralph Fielding takes out a white handkerchief and polishes his glasses. He is a large man, big hands, broad shoulders, and a somehow open face, with deep creases at the corners of his eyes as if he smiles a lot. Looking around the field, Harry wonders what he finds to smile about.

"There are ten of us," Alfred goes on. "The old guard. Ten Robinson Crusoes on our odd little island, squatting in a sea of mud."

"Are we stubborn, do you think?" Ralph Fielding asks. "Are we obstinate old relics?"

"Something like that," Alfred replies.

Harry looks around the field. The graves stand in orderly lines, quite straight, and the grass is neatly cut around them. Most are a standard wooden cross, a metal strip stamped with the details of the man they represent. He wonders, looking at the stretching lines, how long it is going to take him to find his brother. He thinks about the furrows of the plowed field.

"I am glad of your stubbornness," he says. "I am grateful for it."

"Barnes was our battalion carpenter, Dobson our quartermaster, Alfred here is a scholar with a shovel, Edwards is a wonder with a lawn mower, and I'm good at making lists and waving my arms around."

"All the scattered graves are being rounded up," says Alfred.

177

"You make it sound like sheep."

"That might be easier. Mr. Blythe here has been floundering around in the fields with an old trench map."

"I can't find anything that I recognize."

Ralph lights a cigarette and offers the packet around. "Turkish," he says. "My one vice. Do you think it terribly unpatriotic?"

They share a match. Harry shakes his head. "Will you help me?"

From the window of Ralph Fielding's office he can see piles of iron shards and barbed wire pressed into bales. There are stacks of wooden stakes, corkscrew pickets, and a great tangle of telegraph wire. It looks like some sort of satanic scrapyard.

"I'm a great one for paperwork," Ralph tells Harry over the ledger. His now-washed finger is working along the lines. "I love a bit of alphabetizing and an index card. It makes me feel efficient, you see. It's just a pity that my handwriting is so god-awful."

There are a great many names in the ledger. Harry can't help but scan the page. "A battalion's worth?" he asks.

"And more. The problem is the ones who we can't name — the unlistable, the non-categorizable, the untidy noncompliers with alphabetical register, those who refuse to stand in *A*-to-*Z* line. There are far, far too many graves to which we can't attach a name strip."

Harry thinks about Rachel. Is her David one of the rebelliously noncompliant? Is he lying in a field somewhere under a nameless cross? He thinks about Francis. Could it really all be as simple as an administrative omission? Is he simply sleeping silently in an anonymous grave?

"Far, far too many," repeats Ralph, his eyes entirely unsmiling. "But mercifully your brother isn't among them." He looks up from the ledger and nods.

Harry walks along the line. Ralph has directed him to the third row of Plot 8, fourth grave from the far right, beside Captain Watts, who is wearing a wreath. Harry is aware that they are watching him, leaning on their shovels and smoking, but then forgets as he starts to look at the names. He sees service numbers close to his own. There are a lot of Manchester men under Edwards's well-mown grass. He counts the crosses along the line and thinks about the line of men ahead of him moving down the trench with the banjo playing behind. On some of the crosses there are flowers and ribbons. Captain Watts's wreath is made from paper roses and oak leaves. Harry feels short of breath as he looks at the cross beside it. His knees give way and he sinks down by Will's grave.

CHAPTER NINETEEN: HARRY

La Briqueterie, Somme, July 1916

"It should have been me," said Francis. He looked up with red-rimmed eyes. It was the first time he had spoken that morning.

"How do you come to that conclusion?"

"We crawled into shell holes when we should have carried on forwards. If we'd carried on, if we'd completed the thing, you wouldn't have been sent up."

"If you'd carried on, I'd possibly be burying two brothers today." Harry flicked his cigarette away. He'd tried to sleep but couldn't. The images convulsed. Somebody else's blood was underneath his fingernails. He had worked it out with a matchstick, until determined working made his own blood run. He wrote it down, as well as he was able. Red fingerprints illustrated his account. The whistling noise was still there in his head. His head ached with it now and

181

he wasn't in the mood for a show of remorse.

"I was meant to look after him," said Francis.

"We were all meant to look after each other."

One minute Will had been at his side, and then he wasn't. In the chaos and the eruption and the adrenaline of the instant, Harry hadn't seen him go. It was only when he fell into a shell hole too that he looked back and Will wasn't there.

At dusk they had all crawled back and the relieving battalion had started to bring the dead in. He had found Francis crouched in a cubbyhole in the communication trench. They had barely exchanged a sentence before Will was being carried back. His lips were white and his teeth were red. In their grief and shock Harry and Francis had kicked and clawed at one another.

"You and I have to watch out for each other now," said Harry.

Francis looked away.

The chaplain had barely mentioned God. There was no "nobility," no "rightness" or "justice" or "sacrifice." He talked about having trained with them, about Morecambe and Masham and Salisbury Plain. He talked about the space that they would leave. His voice faltered through the psalm. " 'I will lift up mine eyes unto the hills,' " he spoke. " 'From whence cometh my help?' "

They had been sewn into their own blankets. Harry had cursed at, and been amazed by, his brother's deadweight. Will's name was pronounced and a mute, crude shape that was, and was not, him slumped into the earth. They had all taken up handfuls of soil and thrown them in, only Francis hadn't seemed able to release his. He gripped the dirt as the chaplain spoke the words of the committal. Harry stared at his brother's tensed hand. "Lord, give him peace," the chaplain spoke. Francis stared at the earth in his fist.

They had taken up their spades and filled it over. Fragments of brick and chalk weighed down the soil. When it was done the burial party scraped the blades of their spades until they gleamed bright again. There was care in that act.

Harry wondered if it was wrong of him to have minded that the symmetry of the crosses was not quite true. Were his priorities misplaced that he even noticed? They leaned on their spades. It didn't seem quite real that he had just buried William. He didn't quite feel as if he were in his own body. It was like looking at the actions of a different man.

He looked across at Francis. "One of us needs to write home. One of us needs to tell her." Rose had given Francis a bottle of whiskey and he was progressing through it rapidly.

"You're better with words than me."

"In the circumstances, I can't say that I'm grateful to you for that."

"Write what you want. However nicely you phrase it, it's the same. He's dead. She's lost a son. How can words make that any better?"

"We shouldn't have to write it," said Harry. "It's not something that should be put in a letter." With the prospect of fathoming a way to put it down on paper, imagining his mother opening that letter, he wished that Francis would pass the whiskey bottle.

"They'll send a telegram anyway."

"It's not how she ought to find out. Can you imagine it?"

Francis shrugged. "If it had been me, would you write to Edie?"

"Of course."

"Darling Edie. Guess what?" Francis laughed sourly. "How inconvenient. How disappointing for you that it's not the case."

"By which you mean?"

"You'd be in there before I was cold."

"Jesus, Frannie. How can you say that? How can you be thinking about that now?" He'd landed a good punch on Francis the day previously. His eye was swollen with it and the cut on his cheekbone would leave a scar. As he watched his brother now, smirking and picking at the label on the bottle, Harry felt an urge to hurt him again.

"Well, tell me it's not true."

"Fuck off."

"Exactly. Don't think I don't see it."

"I don't want to have this conversation."

"And I don't want you to have her. If I die, I'll come back and haunt you." Francis's lips were wet with whiskey and grinning then. "Poor Harry," he said with a laugh.

"You're drunk. I'm not listening to you." He stood to leave.

"What the fuck does it matter anyway? We're all sunk, *mon frère.*" Francis threw the empty bottle away. It smashed as it hit the pile of bricks. "Everything is lost now," he said.

CHAPTER TWENTY: HARRY

Guillemont, Somme, August 1921

"Are you all right, old man?" asks Ralph Fielding. He hands Harry a whiskey.

"Nothing that the services of a laundry and some shoe polish won't put right."

"That's the spirit."

He had stayed there by Will's grave for a long time. He didn't speak any words, silent or otherwise, to his brother. He didn't even particularly feel a sense that Will was there. But there was something very basic and oddly comforting about being so close to his bones. The wood of his cross had weathered to a silver-gray, but it was entirely straight and exactly the same as every other cross on this row. A piece of metal tape embossed with the letters R.I.P. had been nailed above the strip bearing his name and number, his rank and regiment, and the date of his death. Harry had put his fingers to those letters, so small and yet saying so

186

much, felt the texture of them under his fingertips. It was exactly the sort of aluminum tape that is punched out for a penny on slot machines in railway stations.

The sun reflected off the nameplates. Beyond the barbed-wire fence he could see the skeleton trees. It struck him suddenly that he was standing in the no-go flat expanse between the woods and the village. The enemy had sprayed bullets across it from the higher ground near the quarry. They had been ordered to try to sprint across it a week after Will's death. Harry remembered the noise and the fear, the roar of their voices and his own blood banging. Today it had been completely quiet. Camomile, charlock, and poppies nodded silently. It was truly peaceful. The only noise was the crows in the field behind and the sound of his own unsteady breath.

"Did I make a fool of myself?" he asks Ralph. Finally he had come and put a hand on Harry's shoulder.

"You're not even on the scale. People howl, people rave. We've had families pulling up the crosses and trying to dig their boys out. We've had wives and mothers arrive with secreted spades and plans to smuggle them back across the Channel. You'd be staggered at what we see."

"I was here, though. I've stood by his grave before. I wasn't expecting it to hit me like that."

"I have a theory: there's only so much that the human brain and heart can process. We were all emotionally switched on to the minimum ticking-over setting then. We had to be, just to get from day to day. Now, when we don't have to subdue ourselves to all-around ghastliness, when we don't have to be constantly clenched against it, small things can trigger a man and all of that pent-up emotion floods out. I've seen some chaps flood terribly, downpours and tidal waves of tears." He clinks his glass against Harry's. "I'd barely rate you a light shower."

"Ralph told me. I am sorry," says Cassie Fielding, stepping out onto the terrace. Like her husband, Cassie is tall, but she is narrow, with a head full of curls, reminding Harry of a Corinthian column. She squeezes his arm, flops into a wicker chair, and closes her eyes. He notices that, in the interval since she opened the door, Cassie has put on lipstick and a string of glass beads. She winds them through her fingers which are flashed with white paint.

"Cassie is painting window frames," says Ralph.

"We have windows!" Her eyes flick open

and she grins. "I must apologize for our informality. Our house is full of holes and our hospitality somewhat likewise. The glazier has just finished. You've no idea how exciting it is to finally have windows."

There is something of the pioneer about Cassie. It struck Harry immediately. She makes him recall those newspaper stories about women who go off to Egypt to manage archaeological excavations, or who decide that they're going to get a pilot's license and learn to loop the loop.

"This place was just walls when we bought it," says Ralph, looking up at the house. "Alfred said that I was a fool to lumber myself with it: four walls, two chimney stacks, and an awful lot of rubbish in between. The farmer who owned it before is building himself a house of bright red new bricks. Mercifully, it's just on the other side of the hill."

"Ralph put the roof on himself. He gives every spare hour to it. The boys helped him with the timbers, but really everything else is the work of his own hands."

The couple look at one another and smile. "Listen to us prattling on. Can you forgive us, Mr. Blythe?"

"Call me Harry. Please. And there's nothing to forgive."

"Ralph says that you're taking photographs?"

"I'm working as an agent for a photographer. I'm here to take photographs of graves on behalf of bereaved families."

"Oh, dear." Cassie wrinkles her nose. "What a sad task. And you called in to see your brother en route?"

"I can't help but think of them as I photograph other families' graves."

"Them?"

"I lost two brothers. My other brother, Francis, doesn't have a grave. I don't know where he is."

"You poor boy. You must give your brother's details to Ralph. He has contacts. He can pull strings, make things happen, find things out."

"Absolutely," says Ralph, his hand again on Harry's shoulder. "Write it all down for me and I'll do my best. If he's findable, I'll find him. But come on, for this evening at least, let me seize you away from graves and my wife's interrogations. I'll give you the interior tour."

Harry walks around the room. The ceiling, rising to new beams, is high, and the walls are white plaster. It looks like a room in which monks, or knights, ought to be lined up along a table. There is a huge fireplace at the far end of it, broad enough to roast an ox. Logs smolder white in the grate. Either side of the fireplace there are arrangements of teasels in old army-issue rum jars. He has a strange taste in his mouth when he looks at the jars. Their furniture, which is somewhat threadbare and diminished by the proportions of the room, is mostly clustered around the fire. Harry smells woodsmoke and new plaster.

"Is the house very old?"

"Thirteenth century, or thereabouts, as far as we can tell. It appears on some military maps as Brokenback Barn, but according to locals it was once some kind of convent. Poor old house. Imagine standing quietly in a field for seven hundred years just to have the twentieth century hurl explosives at you. It was full of rusted barbed wire and water bottles and horse bones, and you don't want to know what they'd done in the cellar. This is interesting, though." He walks Harry toward an area of the wall that hasn't been skimmed smooth with new plaster. "Names, you see? And dates and regiments. We know who has been here. It's like they all signed the guest register."

Harry puts his hand to the plaster. There

191

are regimental numbers and insignia and monograms and initials. There are place-names and nicknames and crudely carved faces.

"Good God," he says.

"Precisely. It reminds me of being a boy in Durham Cathedral. Do you know it? Have you ever been? There's graffiti all over the columns and the tombs. I was fascinated by it as a child. Cromwell incarcerated Scottish prisoners of war in there and threw away the key. Can you imagine? Three thousand men left to die in a cathedral. So they carved their anger all over it. They left behind their marks." Ralph puts the flat of his hand on the wall. There is something in the gesture, in the gentleness and reverence of it, that reminds Harry of Rachel placing her palm over her husband's photograph. "These walls don't resonate anger, though. I don't think so, anyway. Do you? I see pride and a determination and that rather appeals to me. I don't struggle to sleep within these walls."

Harry recalls the rasp of a penknife on the wall of a barn, the weight of it in his hand. He remembers them carving their three initials together, Francis's finger instructing the design and Will laughing at his side.

"I think you're right," he says.

192

He also remembers taking a knife out of Francis's hands. Francis's fingers are trembling around the handle. He is afraid of Francis having the knife and what he is about to do with it. He uncurls Francis's fingers carefully, slowly, one by one. For a moment the recalled image is as sharp as his own fingers now around the glass, but then Ralph's voice and the present push in.

"Shall I top that up?" he asks.

"Yes. Please. Thank you."

"Do stay for dinner," says Cassie, holding out her glass. "It's not much, we don't eat lavishly, but it's nice to have a new face at the table."

"Are you sure?"

"Utterly certain," says Ralph. "I might make one condition, though. Will you take a photograph of Cass for me?"

"A photograph?" Harry looks at Cassie's expressive eyes, her eloquent hands, the playful smile now stretching on her face. "Wouldn't you prefer a portrait instead?"

Harry lays out his pencils and chalks. There is always something of a ceremony at this stage, like a meditation in the preparation. It is when he feels both most and least in control, when it is all possibility. It is this moment that has always excited him, and also the moment when he always expects to look up and see Edie's face.

"Tilt your chin up slightly, would you?"

It's a strong face, a kind face, an intelligent face, good bones and good skin, but it is not Edie's face.

"Like this?" Cassie strikes a haughty pose, is somewhere between a countess and a greyhound, but then collapses into laughter. "I'm sorry. I'm not used to this."

Harry smiles back at her. "Don't worry. Who is? Just try to relax."

He is glad of her laughter to break the tension and with the first brief lines he has started, he is in, and he relaxes into the curve and the sound of his own pencil strokes.

"You've broken your nose at some point."

"Goodness. I'm not accustomed to such scrutiny." Cassie puts her hands to her face as if newly aware of its shape.

Ralph laughs. "There, you see — revenge! A taste of your own medicine!"

"Yes." She narrows her eyes at her husband. "I was a terrible tomboy. My mother despaired. I had three older brothers and was very keen on following them up trees."

Cassie's eyes are gray and heavily lidded, but with a lively sparkle. Her eyebrows have a high arch, so that she constantly looks

194

either doubtful or amused.

"From Venice. A honeymoon present," she says, pulling at the link of beads around her neck, turning them in her hand.

"Is she fidgeting?" Ralph asks from behind a newspaper.

"Terribly."

"She always fidgets. Anyone would think that she had fleas."

"Is there a Mrs. Blythe?" Cassie asks.

Harry's pencil stops. For a second he falters, thinking that she means Edie. "No. I'm really not much of a prospect."

"Cass, don't pry," says Ralph, emerging from behind a headline about ultimatums being issued to Germany. "Cassie always wants there to be a hidden-away romantic story line. She tries to rootle them out of people — and, if they're not there to be rootled, she'll impose one."

"Not a prospect, indeed!" Cassie's beads twirl around in a circle. "You've got a wonderfully old-fashioned face, like a shepherd boy who might point at a miracle in a painting, or an innocent in a William Blake watercolor. There's something beautifully melancholy about you."

"Steady on. She'll be pairing you up next, have you quaking beside a woman in white before you know it. You will be beautifully melancholy then."

Harry thinks of the white nightdress at Rachel's feet, and then of Edie's face as she described his mother's black nightdress rising from the vat of dye. He's not sure that he's up for being paired off.

"Oh, shush," says Cassie.

Ralph replenishes glasses and peers over Harry's shoulder. "He's being kind to you," he says to his wife.

"And so he should."

They sit quietly for a while. Cassie's eyelids droop farther and Harry wonders if she is going to fall asleep. The only noise is the lazy clink of beads through her fingers, the occasional crack from the fire, and the scratch of his pencil on paper.

"I have a photograph of my brother's grave," Cassie says suddenly. "My mother has a framed copy up on the wall, only I'd rather hide mine in a drawer. I do visit him from time to time, though. Keeping him in the sideboard doesn't mean that I've forgotten him. He's in Tyne Cot. The cemetery, I mean."

"I should go there too," Harry says. "I do intend to. I've been told that, if Francis has been buried anywhere, it's likely that's where he'll be."

"You've already checked the registers, I

take it?" Ralph asks.

"We've done all the conventional paper-work trails, but found nothing. It's all blanks and dead ends and just more questions."

"We?"

"Francis's wife, Edie, and I. We've both been chasing paper trails. She has never wanted to come over here before, but last month she sent me a postcard from Arras. I don't know if she's found something."

He recalls Edie's face through the view-finder, her hand extending toward him with the bag of peppermints. The flight of geese moves across the sky above Edie's head. What has changed since then? What new motivation has pushed her to make this journey now?

"Why Arras, if he's likely to be around Ypres? Is there any significance?"

"Possibly. Maybe. She might just have been on her way to Ypres. She might only have been passing through. I honestly don't know."

"You've no way of getting in contact with her?"

"I've called her at home. I keep trying the telephone, but it just rings out. I can only assume that she's still over here." He tries to imagine Edie in Ypres, among all the plunging masonry and the too-close groan of the guns, but he can't quite pull her into that picture.

"What's your own feeling?" Ralph asks. "Do you believe that he is probably dead?"

"For a long time I assumed that he had to be, but then I see him everywhere. I go through life grabbing strangers' elbows and calling their backs by his name. I don't know if Francis is haunting me, or whether my wiring has gone awry." His eyes connect with Cassie's. She smiles sympathetically and shakes her head. "And now I'm picking over his old photographs looking for clues. As if his experience were something removed from my own. Like it was someone else's war. Only I was there. I was by his side all that time. I honestly start to wonder if I've misremembered it all."

"Would you let me see the photographs?" Cassie asks.

Harry watches her flicking through the album, lowering her face to the pages, pointing occasionally and sharing familiar images with Ralph.

"Were you still here then when they took the village?" Cassie asks him.

"No, we never saw it. We never made it in. Today was the first time that I set foot there. We shifted up to Arras at the start of September."

Cassie turns the page. "Some places are strangely beautiful in their ruination. Some aren't. So you never came back to this area after 1916?"

"We moved south in the spring and took over the French lines." He sees glimpses of flooded trenches as she turns, and then boot prints in snow. "March 1917. The Germans had just withdrawn and we were pushing forward. It was quite surreal suddenly to be walking across the enemy lines."

There are photographs of empty enemy trenches, blown bridges, and just-vacated billets. Harry remembers walking into the room that Cassie is looking at in a photograph. There were letters on the floor and a glass by the side of the bed. He had almost expected the sheets to still be warm.

"I was just a little farther north," says Ralph, looking thoughtful, with a corkscrew in his hand. He pulls the cork from another bottle and pours the wine. He fills Cassie's glass right to the top, so that she has to bend to the table and carefully apply her lips to the rim.

"Bloody man," she says.

Ralph stares into his glass and says, "Péronne. We seem to have been near-neighbors for many months."

Cassie is quickly turning through pages. "The people have all gone."

"It was quite eerie. We expected them to be hiding around every corner — and for there to be booby traps everywhere."

"Not just that. Not just the enemy, I mean. You've all gone too. I haven't seen a face for five pages. It's just objects and landscapes now. He doesn't take photographs of people any longer."

He watches as she turns. She's right. He hasn't seen it before. It suddenly strikes him that he had also never taken Francis's photograph again.

"I'd worry for the photographer," says Cassie. "For his state of mind. I know that it's hindsight, and maybe I'm reading too much into his choice of subjects, but looking at these pages I feel that this story isn't going to have a happy ending." She stops and shrugs her theory off. "Oh, no. I'm corrected. Here we go again. Who's the pretty girl?"

There is a photograph of Edie on the next-to-last page of the album. Francis took it on his final leave. She is standing in the doorframe and looking like she doesn't want to have her photograph taken.

"That's Edie."

"She doesn't look very happy," says Cassie, peering closely at the photograph.

"No, I don't suppose so."

"And the men on the last page?"

"I don't know. I wasn't there. I'm writing in the locations for Edie, but I don't know where that is."

Harry can't annotate these images for Edie, he can't write in a place or a precise date, because there is a gap in the chronology, there is a piece missing — and, as time passes, he can't help but feel that there is something important about this missing piece. After all, it was in the days that followed that everything went wrong.

"Your wars went off in separate directions at that point?" Cassie asks.

"Briefly. Unofficially. My brother went missing for a while. He went home on leave in 1917 and didn't come back."

"He went absent without leave?"

"For ten days."

"Golly. I can't imagine that had a good outcome?" Cassie shifts in her chair. He sees her eyes widen.

"No."

"So did he just stay at home?"

Harry shakes his head. "I don't know where he went. I asked him, of course, but he wouldn't tell me where he'd been or why.

He wasn't really talking much at all by then."

And so, it was simply a blank, and remains so. Harry suspects that these images might fill that blank, that this is what Francis did with those missing days, but he would like to know exactly where they were taken, why Francis needed to be in this place at that time, and what happened there that made things change afterward.

"Did something go wrong while he was at home? Something that would have caused him to go absent?"

"I wish I knew."

He has asked Edie about Francis's period of leave, as delicately as possible, but there didn't seem to be much to tell. Harry can't help but wonder if there are parts of that week that she's chosen to edit out; just as, in turn, he has chosen not to tell her about Francis's subsequent absence and arrest.

Cassie points at a slice of townscape in the background of an image. "If I were a betting woman, I'd say that it's somewhere in Ypres. And there, that's quite a distinctive ceiling with the vaulting. Are those faces carved on the ribs? This looks like they're carousing in a crypt."

Beneath the ceiling vaulting there are other faces. Harry looks again at the last page of photographs. Men around a table stare at the camera. The table is cluttered with bottles and glasses, but the men's faces don't suggest that this is any kind of celebration. *Carousing* isn't quite the word. The light carves hollows in their faces and they all have the same bleak, empty look. Harry has seen that look in another photograph recently.

"Ypres could make sense. We were in a camp at Proven, near Poperinghe, so I suppose it's not impossible that he could have been in Ypres."

"Albie would know where this is."

"Albie?"

"My brother's friend. He's still up there, working on the cemeteries. He knows every cellar and every spilled stone of that town."

"As I recall, there's a lot of spilled stone to know."

"Could I perhaps borrow one of these photographs? I'd like to find out for you."

"Of course. I'd appreciate any help. Thank you."

When Edie had shown him that new photograph of Francis, the one that had come through the post, he'd considered whether it could have been taken at this same time. Do other photographs of this missing period exist, then? Are there more images out there that might yet be sent to Edie?

Cassie shuts the album and pushes it back toward Harry. "Did Francis take William's death badly?"

"He felt responsible, though he wasn't at all. There was absolutely nothing that he could have done. If anything, I was the one who ought to feel responsible; I was the one who was with Will."

"Did it make things difficult between you?"

"Yes. At times."

"Mercy!" says Ralph. "Cass, how you pry! Don't you think that the poor chap might have had enough grilling for one night?"

"Harry might like to talk," she says and looks inquiringly toward him. "I wasn't grilling you, was I?"

He would like to talk to Cassie. He would like to tell it all to her. He is used to carrying it around, but it is a weighty burden. It has become like a sin that he can't confess. He can't even say it to a stranger. "Not in the slightest," Harry replies.

CHAPTER TWENTY-ONE: EDIE

Albert, Somme, August 1921

When she leans out of the window she sees wooden huts with corrugated-iron roofs, lines of washing and lettuces, wire fences and chicken runs, and then all the fallen stone beyond. She had walked past the ruins of the basilica as she had looked for somewhere to stay for the night; with its nibbled stone and empty arches, it looks like a forgotten Greek temple, awesome with age, epic with antiquity, and it might well have stood like that for millennia. It is only the lines of spent shell cases by the roadside, the duckboards, and the brick dust that give the game away. Albert is a sad-looking place, Edie thinks, somehow much bleaker than Arras with its determined resurgence. She turns and shuts the window.

They had spent three days camped in those woods, she knows, waiting for their turn, before they had been marched south and then east, toward those place-names that were being mapped out in the newspapers. She had feared for them as she read all those reports, and guessed how their coordinates were matching up with the newspaper arrows. But she hadn't been ready for the news that Will had gone.

When she thinks of Will he is still a boy with a blond fringe, winking at her across the tabletop, over his mother's baked custards and trifles and steamed puddings, and her voice saying the words of grace. It hardly seems to make sense that Will could have been in this place of leveled woods and flattened churches, and that his brothers could have left him here.

Francis had written to her afterward, and told her how he felt responsible, how he should have been there to look after Will, how Will was only there because of him. Reading those words, she could almost feel his guilt. His frustration. His desolation. How fiercely and desperately angry he was with himself. She had barely known how to reply to that letter. What was she supposed to say in response? She sometimes wonders, if she had found the right words, could she have helped him and changed what came after? But, even now, she hardly knows what the right words might have been.

It's my fault. She can picture his handwriting still. *All of this is down to me. Will would never even have been here, Harry neither, if it wasn't for me.*

Francis's letters had changed after that; his voice changed key, and she knew then that he had resolved to stop telling her things. His letters became more formulaic, lighter, inconsequential, like he'd decided only to show her the parts that he thought she ought to see. She knew that he had stopped sharing, that he was censoring himself. And didn't that imply that she'd already failed him in some way? That he thought she wasn't up to the task? He had let her talk after her mother died, let her pour all that upset out, and how grateful for that she had been; she realizes now that Francis had held all of his grief inside, that he hadn't been able to let it out.

She leans back against the window and looks around this sorry hotel room. None of the pieces of furniture match and the bedspread has been patched. The walls look to have been newly papered, but with the telltale undulations beneath the blowsy roses, she's not altogether sure that the paste and paper aren't just holding the whole thing together.

She thinks about Mrs. Blythe and the

animal howl that she had made in the night when she knew that her youngest son was dead. Edie had heard that noise through the walls again and again in the weeks that followed. Even with that cry coming out in the nights, Margaret Blythe spent the days curled into herself and shaking, as if she must keep it all in during daylight hours. Edie had never told Francis about how his mother had suffered; after all, what could he do? But, she considers now, had she told him more, might he have felt permitted to share his own pain? Was Francis too curling in on himself and trembling at that time? If he had let a cry out, if he had been able to spill it out in his letters, might it have made things different?

She cannot associate the places that she has seen from the train with the blue-eyed boy that Francis had been, and she feels the light on that memory going out. His smiling whisper fading away. What with seeing that landscape, and the background it gives to those difficult months after Will's death, she now understands more of how Francis had become the man that she met again in 1917, and why he had turned his head away from hers on the pillow. But she doesn't yet understand how the man in the photograph fits, and why he has arrived in an anonymous envelope. Is it that Francis means for her to come and see all of this? Does he need to make her understand?

In the weeks after Will's death, Margaret Blythe had cleared out his room, boxing up her son's books, birds' eggs, and football boots. Apart from the crows on the kitchen dresser, everything of Will's had moved up into the attic, where Edie supposes it is still. Then Margaret had done it all again in November 1917; there had been so little of the child Francis left when Edie had moved back into his boyhood bedroom a month later. In those difficult days Edie had been glad to let his mother take that responsibility, not to have to fold away Francis's shirts herself and parcel up his handkerchiefs and hairbrush, but sometimes as she looks around Francis's room now, she misses his atlases and poetry books and cameras. The marks are still there on the wallpaper where his maps and his photographs once were. There are spaces on the shelves where his books ought to be, and empty drawers in the dresser, and sometimes that room feels to be so full of Francis's absence. And, yet, could she still have got it wrong? Could she have misunderstood? Is the absence that she senses not quite what she has assumed it to be?

Chapter Twenty-Two:
Harry

Guillemont, Somme, August 1921

The mist is lifting. Harry watches it peel back and half expects to see tents and horses and howitzers, but all that it reveals is wet green grass and silence. It is this silence, this stillness, that is strangest. It is not peaceful, this absence of noise. He ought to breathe it in slowly, but instead he finds himself holding his breath. It is like it has stalled — the film reel has jammed and any second shells will roar their return. A dog howls somewhere in the distance. A pheasant flutters from a hedge. A gramophone starts up somewhere in the house behind. Harry throws his cigarette away.

"Do you want some tea?" asks Cassie from the door. "It's English tea. The proper stuff. Product of Yorkshire's finest tea plantations."

"You're making a garden," he says. He nods at the borders.

"Ralph talks to his seedlings. And knows all their names in Latin. I could get quite jealous." She smiles. "It's in the pot. Come in when you're ready."

He steps into the kitchen. She is leaning against the stove, looking thoughtful, with a slice of toast in her hand. "His mother still sends him food parcels," she says, waving the toast. "Marmalade, gingerbread, tea leaves, the *Times* crossword. I half suspect that no one has told her that the war's over. She used to send him boxes of Craster kippers, only the postal service isn't what it once was."

"My mother used to send us fruitcakes. She worked in a bakery, so we got a lot of just slightly stale cake. What with there being three of us and all, our parcels were the envy of the battalion."

Cassie licks marmalade from her fingers and stirs the teapot. "I talked too much last night. Ralph told me off for it this morning. I'd probably had too much to drink as well. I apologize if I said anything that I shouldn't."

"Not at all." He nods for her to pour the tea. "I enjoyed your company."

Her fingers tap on the table in time with the music that's coming from the floor above. "Thomas Tallis," she says. "He likes a bit of English Renaissance while he shaves. Did I see you with a cigarette? I'm not meant to, but while the cat's away."

Harry lights Cassie's cigarette and she gives him a wink. They drink tea together, listening to the secondhand chorals. Her portrait is propped against the kitchen dresser. She looks toward it from time to time. "You're wasted as a photographer," she says.

"My boss might agree with you."

"How many do you have to take?"

"Twelve, for the present. I have a piece of paper with twelve names on it. I have to cross them off."

"Thirteen," corrects Cassie.

He looks up at her.

"Thirteen including your Francis, I presume?"

"Yes. Of course."

"He's the reason that you're here, isn't he? It's really about him and her, isn't it?"

"Only I fear he's the one name on my list that I'm not going to be able to place. That I'll never be able to place."

"Ralph will help you. Let us help you."

"Thank you."

"And when it's done, when it's all crossed off, you'll go home?"

Harry wonders where home is. He looks

around this kitchen, which seems very much like a home. A tabby cat is circling the table legs. Cassie puts down milk in a saucer and the cat arches its back to her hand. He thinks of a kitchen full of crows and Edie in it. Could that ever be home again? Would they ever again sit either side of that table? Should there be another chair at that table? He wonders where she is now. He replays iterations of possibility in his mind, arranges Edie and graves and ghosts, but can't see what exists beyond. "I'm not sure. It rather depends on how things go over here."

"Number thirteen," Cassie reflects. "Unlucky for some? I'd wish you good luck, although in this case I'm not sure what that happy outcome is."

"Neither am I," he replies.

The van rattles along the newly made-up roads and Harry looks out at the strange hillocky land. The fact that the grass is growing over it makes this terrain seem all the stranger. It is like someone has taken a penknife to a Bruegel landscape. Will it ever be stitched together again and the scars smoothed over? Will time level and soften it? Here and there are piles of rusting debris and groups of crosses. He realizes, as he sees the metal roofs of the village ahead, that they have just driven over the rise that they were meant to have taken on the twentieth of July 1916.

"How do you live here?" he asks Ralph. "I'm not sure I could."

"I couldn't cope with being back in England. The awkward conversations. The comfortable upholstery. The ticking of the clock. My mother's cooking!"

"No?" He looks across at Ralph, profiled against the afterward landscape and tries to picture him in English domesticity.

"But, more than that, the knowledge that all of this was still here." Ralph pats the steering wheel with the flat of his hand. Harry hears him take a breath. "I mean, the job wasn't finished, was it?"

He halts at the junction and they turn into the village. Harry looks out at the huts and the vegetable gardens. He sees a flutter of yellow wings within a wire birdcage. A woman is pegging out a line of white washing. A child chases a dog and stops to stare at the van.

"No, I don't suppose so."

"I'd just been made up to captain in July 1916. I had four platoons under me, one hundred and thirty-odd men. It was my job to take care of them and to bring them home again, but by the start of September twenty of those men were dead, nearly seventy had been wounded, and six of them were missing. I owe it to them, and to their families, to make sure that the missing are accounted for and the dead properly buried. There are going to be cemeteries with white grave markers — gardens of sleep — real English gardens. There will be wallflowers and forget-me-nots and pansies and Bible words cut in stone. They'll be places that their families can visit and hopefully find some comfort. I was meant to bring their boys home; this is the best alternative that I'm able to offer."

Harry watches Ralph's hands on the steering wheel. He can see the veins on the back of his hands. He thinks that this is possibly the most sincere, and the saddest, speech that he has ever heard anyone make. "I am grateful to you," he says.

Ralph turns onto the main road and Harry looks back for a last glimpse of the village. He can see the remains of the woods ahead and the bristling lines of the field full of crosses.

"Do you want to stop for a moment?"

"It's all right. It's enough now to know he's here." He watches the rows of crosses slide, align momentarily, and then stretch apart. A man with a mower raises an arm to

Ralph's van. Harry is not sure whether it is a wave or a salute. The man looks like a last sentry guarding the field and its quiet prisoners. A woman is standing by the roadside. A flock of starlings lifts from the black woods.

"I can hardly believe that there could be birdsong in that place."

Ralph smiles. "Believe it. There were cuckoos in the spring. We kept hearing them and laughing. They were calling and replying. I think they were nesting in there."

Harry pictures a flight of wings through that place of splinters and shrieking and sudden conflagrations. "Good God."

"But that's just how it is, isn't it? Nature takes things back. The circle goes round and goes on."

They drive back through the deleted village, past the hump of earth that once upon a time was a church, over the railway lines, over the old front line, and back to the town where virgins plummet and barmaids say, "Boom."

"I'll make enquiries for you," says Ralph. "Leave it with me. There are unofficial channels. I know men on the ground. Just give me a week or two. Say, give me a telephone call in a month's time? If there's anything to find, I'll find it for you. If a grave exists anywhere, I'll pull all the strings that I can to track it down."

Harry thinks, if Francis has a grave, does it lean like the iron crosses in Montauban? Stand straight, tidily aligned with a thousand others, like a battalion on parade? Or does he have a white marker and Bible words and flowers?

Or could Francis yet not be in a grave?

CHAPTER TWENTY-THREE: HARRY

Albert, Somme, August 1921

Harry telephones Mr. Lee, as arranged, from the railway station.

"Have you got a pen and paper?" a faraway voice issues from the Bakelite.

"Do I need it? Have you had many enquiries?"

"Yes, and if you can summon ghosts and solve whodunits, we'll prosper in this business. A Mrs. Cathcart, a clairvoyant, placed her ad in the paper just below ours. If we could team up, we might do quite well."

"Ah. Like that, is it?"

"Thus far it's ten enquiries from families seeking missing, three requests for photographs of graves, and two killed-in-action locales."

"Could you make that sound any more clinical?"

The station is full of excursionists and pilgrims. There are lots of pale young wives

218

with black trimmings on their hats and French officers with older women on their arms. Harry finds himself pressing the earpiece to his head in case anything unduly indelicate should leak from it.

"A Mrs. Bainbridge asked if you would go to Gallipoli," says Mr. Lee. "I've only agreed to Picardy and Flanders. I take it I did right?"

Harry thinks of how many graves there must be between Amiens and Ypres. He wonders what on earth he has agreed to.

"I've only said yes to commissions for grave photographs where they can furnish the details of the cemetery. I've asked for plot, row, and grave number where possible."

"Good." How terribly efficient this all sounds, he thinks. How horribly sensible it all is.

"Can I order you south, then?"

There is a woman with red hair walking down the platform toward the southbound train. "If you must," says Harry, as he puts down the receiver and his pen.

She is wearing a floral print dress and green shoes. Her hair, grown longer again, is pinned up in a tortoiseshell comb. She puts a hand up to shield her eyes to the sun and then is standing on the tiptoes of her green shoes and waving at someone down the platform.

"Edie?"

He knocks the telephone receiver from its cradle as he steps away, fails to catch it, and leaves it swinging. A man turns and swears at him as he catches his elbow. Anger curls at the corner of the man's mouth, but Harry doesn't linger on it.

She weaves through the crowd ahead, her footsteps getting faster now. She swings a woven straw bag in her hand as she walks. There is something in the way she swings the bag, in the width of the swing, that is carefree and unselfconscious, that tells him that she is smiling.

"Edie!"

A porter is handing suitcases down from the train and stacking them on the platform. Harry stumbles to avoid a trunk that's being lifted down, only just manages to stay on his feet, and when he looks up again she has gone.

"*Attention!*" shouts the porter after him. "*Regardez où vous allez, hein?*"

He runs now down the platform, looking through the train windows in case she has boarded. He scans the waiting room, along the empty benches, and, turning, catches the panic in the eyes of his own reflection in the windows. He pushes through a cluster of children and apologizes his way around a pair of arm-linked nuns.

And then she is there again. A strand of hair has escaped from her barrette. It catches in the breeze and strokes her white neck. Harry's hand is about to reach toward it as she turns and smiles. His mouth is about to make the shape of her name but he stops himself.

"Frank!" she says with laughter in her voice. A man puts his hand on the back of her neck, curls his finger through the strand of loose hair, and pulls her in for a kiss.

CHAPTER TWENTY-FOUR:
HARRY

Cimetière des Pommiers, Somme,
   August 1921

Image order: Mrs. Cora Evans would like a photograph of the grave of her son Pte. George Evans (32049), Lancashire Fusiliers (age 32, KIA 25/02/1917, grave number 186). Flowers requested.

It is an extension to the village cemetery. Harry walks between the civilian graves, some of which have odd wooden constructions above them, like sentry boxes, and others grander creations in glass and iron. These grave housings remind him of greenhouses and he half expects there to be tomatoes climbing inside. He sees fancy ironwork crosses, timber palisades, and ceramic roses. There is something rather showy and competitive about these graves. Something slightly histrionic. He imagines their inhabitants sticking out their chests. The graves are stuck with rosettes, woven metalwork wreaths, and votive arrangements of enamel flowers. In some places the ironwork is terribly twisted, the mangled forms communicating great violence. Much of the stonework is chipped. None of the crosses are at quite the same angle. Whatever the original pretensions of this cemetery's inhabitants, the overall impression is now one of disorder, representative of this village's suffering.

He had watched them, the man called Frank and the woman who was not Edie. Frank had handed her a bunch of pink roses in blue tissue paper and kissed her on the mouth. For a moment it *had* been her face and then they had turned, both of them, and stared Harry right in the eye. She had a kind, gentle face, a face full of laughter, but she was not Edie. They had looked back at him again as they walked away. He had stepped onto the train, leaned his head back against the seat, and, as the platform pulled away, wondered what this sensation was.

A crude arch of bound applewood has been made at the entrance to the area of military graves, and Harry must pass underneath it. The branches have been roughly severed and no effort seems to have been

made to soften that; as if the primitive raggedness of this arch is meant to be unset-
tling. The first rows of crosses have rectangles of brick around them, seemingly
salvaged from the fallen buildings behind.
These are all French burials, mostly from
August 1914, he sees. He walks the path
between the French dead looking for a
Lancashire fusilier. Camomile and corn-
flowers grow in between the crosses. He
hates the fact that the graves have to be
numbered; he is also grateful for it. All that
he has received from Mrs. Cora Evans are
the coordinates of her son's grave and a
request for flowers.

George Evans is to the right-hand side.
His is one of just three English graves —
and the only named one of the three. The
crosses on either side of George's are
marked UNKNOWN BRITISH SOLDIER. Who
do these men belong to? Who has known
and who misses them? Who at home is wishing that they could have a photograph of
this man's grave? Are there women nearby
searching through buttons and belt buckles
for these soldiers?

Harry looks down at the bunch of roses in
his hands. Unable to find anywhere that
would sell him cut flowers, he had had to
beg them from a garden in the village and

pay over the odds. Perhaps Mrs. Evans would wish for something grander, but the roses smell of summer borders and their redness glows in the drab of the cemetery. He places them carefully on George's grave, feeling awkward in knowing so little about the man whose grave he is arranging roses upon. Did George Evans care for roses? Was he a man who would stop and comment on their scent? He wishes that he knew how this Lancashire man came to be in this French cemetery, that he had had the chance to meet Mrs. Evans to find out more about her son.

Harry steps back and takes out the camera. It is a pity that the grass around hasn't been cut more recently. He focuses in on the name on the tape, hoping Mrs. Evans will be able to make out the lettering. Behind, the French crosses taper away and the apple trees are ragged silhouettes against the sky. The either-side unknown soldiers nudge into the shot. Harry imagines three lads together pausing to have their photograph taken in an apple orchard. The trigger clicks.

He considers what Mrs. Evans will do with the photograph of this place. He pictures a grave with his brother's name on it, frames the image in a photograph, and wonders what Edie would do with it. Does she need it in order to move on? And, if so, what would moving on mean to Edie?

Harry takes his hat off and bows his head to the English boys. He steps forward and takes two roses from George's grave and places one on each of his neighbors'. He hopes that Mrs. Evans would not mind. He decides that he will write to her when he has developed the photograph and tell her about this place. He feels that he needs to give her more than the photograph and, in turn, needs something more from her. If these visits are just a matter of connecting coordinates and the delivery of flowers, too many questions remain and he has to carry all the maybes of who these men were around with him.

When he looks up he sees that there is another man at the end of the row. The presence of another pair of eyes in the cemetery makes him conscious of the camera. He feels conspicuous with it. It doesn't feel quite right, quite polite. He imagines a stranger taking a photograph of Will's grave. He thinks that he would want to put a hand in front of the lens.

He nods goodbye to George Evans and tells him that he will visit his mother for him. The figure along the line is placing a wreath on a grave. He looks up and Harry touches his hat. He wishes that he knew the right words to say to strangers in cemeteries.

CHAPTER TWENTY-FIVE:
EDIE

Guillemont, Somme, August 1921

The sky is blue, broken only by high streamers of cirrus cloud, and the wind comes sweetly across the newly mowed slopes. A skylark is singing and the sun is warm on the back of her neck, but this is not a happy place. Edie had seen cemeteries from the train, but it was quite another thing to stand here and to know that one of these crosses is William Blythe.

Harry had written to her from a place called Happy Valley, she remembers. He had told her that Francis had taken it badly. He didn't seem to be himself, Harry said, like something had snapped in his head. She had heard the distress in Harry's letters, his sense of panic, how he was appealing to her. He wanted her to write to her husband. He wanted her help to make Francis right. She wished now that Harry was here helping

228

her. Had he not heard the panic in her voice?

There are two thousand men in this cemetery, the gardener has told her. So many. The crosses are neat, standing tidily in line, the flower beds around them well tended. These men are cared for. They are not forgotten. They have columbines, campanulas, and pansies. As the gardener tells her about their work here, she hears both pride and apology in his voice. It is the sheer number of crosses that makes her shake her head.

She had thought about looking for Francis in the first weeks and months of peace and possibility, but it was always a grave that she pictured herself searching for, it was always a place like this. She hadn't really ever lingered on the alternative possibility. So many of the men in this cemetery have no names; their crosses bear the words A SOLDIER OF THE GREAT WAR or KNOWN UNTO GOD. Francis could have been any one of these men until that photograph arrived. Was that known unto God all along too?

It is all kind and colorful in this square of English garden, but beyond the boundaries the colors change and the trees tell a different story. The woods on the skyline are tattered, tree trunks torn and blackened, and ragged boughs stretch like beseeching arms. In here it smells of grass clippings and tea roses; out there she knows that it will smell of smoke.

She follows the gardener along the line. It is impossible not to look at the words on the crosses, but the names of the men make her cry. There are so many Manchester men in this flower garden, young men full of ambitions and plans and hope, she imagines, like Will and Harry and Francis. Tokens have been left on some of the crosses to show that they are remembered. There are wreaths of greenery and rings of brass laurel and oak leaves.

"It's funny that you should be here to see this lad," the gardener says, turning back toward her. "He's had two visitors in one week now. There was a chap looking for him just a couple of days ago."

"A man?"

"His brother."

"Francis?"

For a minute it all spins around her, the crosses and the flower beds and the angry trees. For a minute the angles all go askew and the scent of the roses is suffocating, but then the man called Alfred is shaking his head and saying, "Harry."

She laughs, but doesn't know exactly why. Is it relief that she feels? "Harry was here?"

"Yes, miss. Just earlier this week."

She has seen the barbed wire by the side of the roads, and the corrugated iron crumbling into brown dust, and has thought of Harry in a hospital bed, his chest all torn apart by that wire. She remembers the shock of seeing his pale face that day and the weight of his hand on her arm. The thought of it makes her hate the wire and want to link her arm through his again.

"I'm glad that he's been here," she says.

"There you are." The gardener's feet still and he stands square in front of a cross. He takes his hat off and touches Edie's shoulder. "I'll leave you with him. My condolences."

She recalls the blue of a robin's egg cupped in a boy's palms. His fingers rubbing away the dirt to show her the pattern on a shard of pottery. She remembers Will's hands stretching out toward her and showing her flints and flowers, the skull of a mouse, a pine cone, a bronze buckle caked in earth. His pockets were full of treasures and always something that he wanted to share. She remembers his endless boy's curiosity. How did that end? How did that boy end up in this place? On his grave Wil-

231

liam Blythe is nineteen years old. Edie thinks that his grave is the saddest thing she has ever seen.

She kneels and puts her hand to the wood of Will's cross, touching the tape that bears his name. She has an odd urge to hug his cross. She feels both overwhelming affection toward it and intense anger. How could this be that boy? There are blood-red petunias growing at the base of his grave, orange zinnias, and a black feather. That at least seems right. She would like to bring him fossils and seashells, marbles and caramels and cigarette cards, but all she can offer him today are her tears. She thinks about Harry sitting by his brother's grave and can't help but cry for him too.

Knowing that Harry is on this journey with her makes it feel better. She is not so alone. She is not such a fool. And yet, she can't help but think about why Harry has taken so long to start it. Why has he been so reluctant to come here? But she checks herself: she looks around and knows exactly why. Suddenly she realizes that it perhaps wasn't fair of her to ask him to come back.

She knows that Francis would have come here, if he could. He would visit Will. She is certain of that. She remembers Francis's arm around his younger brother's shoulders,

Francis's fingers ruffling Will's hair, their gripped fingers as they arm-wrestled across the kitchen table. Francis letting Will win and feigning pain. Will always following Francis. He had followed him to this place. Surely Francis wouldn't just leave him here? She pictures Francis's photograph features in this place. The color of the columbines looks like overcompensation against Francis's black-and-white afterward face.

"Did Harry leave him the feather?"

The gardener is spaying the roses at the end of the row. He smiles at her as he looks up. "The feather?"

She twirls it between her fingers. It is a feather from a crow's wing, she thinks. It is glossy and bounces back the blue of the sky. "It was there." She points. "Pushed into the soil at the base of William's grave. He must have left it."

"What a thing," says the gardener and shakes his head at the feather. "It wasn't there this morning, miss, I swear it. I weeded along that row and I'd have noticed it."

"No?" She wonders.

"Perhaps it blew there?" he suggests.

"Yes, perhaps."

She places it back at the base of the grave and stares at it there. It was so deliberately planted in the soil. She can't imagine how the wind might have done that.

"Is he still here?"

"I'm sorry?"

"Harry."

"No. Ralph took him to the station. The day before yesterday, if I recall rightly. He was going south, I think, and then on to Ypres."

"Ypres?"

"It was something to do with his brother there. His other brother. Something about a photograph of him turning up."

CHAPTER TWENTY-SIX:
HARRY

Rosières, Somme, August 1921
" '*Apres la guerre fini, soldats anglais parti,*' "
sings Élodie as she moves between the
tables with soup tureens. Everyone in the
café knows her name and the words to the
song. The room hums along.

From his table Harry can see the spire. It
seems so improbable, this soaring height of
brickwork. He had not expected it still to
be intact. Much of the tile has slid from the
roof of the church, and the building to the
near side reminds him of a house of cards
that has slumped, but the spire is much the
same as it had been in a drawing he made
four years earlier. They had sought its shape
on the skyline as they had marched back to
brigade reserve. He had remarked that it
was like a lighthouse then, steering them
into safe harbor. Today it looks like a miracle.

"Monsieur, would it disturb you?" Élodie

is standing by his table, her eyebrows raised in inquiry. She gestures from the empty chair facing Harry to a figure waiting by the bar. "I am sorry, but we are very full today."

A family is occupying the greater part of the restaurant with loud bonhomie. They are raising glasses and making toasts to a white-haired woman at the head of the table.

"No, I don't mind at all. Please." He stands and beckons his arm toward the stranger. As the man approaches Harry's table, he recognizes a face. He puts out his hand. "I think we may have passed earlier today?"

The stranger shakes Harry's hand. "In the cemetery, yes? My name is Gabriel Bousquet and this is very kind." He takes the opposite chair.

"Harry Blythe."

"If you wish to be quiet, I will not disturb your thoughts."

"No, not at all. I am pleased to make your acquaintance."

"Excellent. I am happy to practice my English. I like to collect English words — like *butterflies.*" His eyes slide upward as he searches for the word. "But, like butterflies, they flap away from me." He makes his fingers into a busy flutter of wings. They float back down to the tablecloth and he looks up and laughs.

For a second Harry thinks of the catalogue in Arras, the collections of eyes and noses and mouths awaiting identification. His mind flicks through iterations before they still into the features across the table. Gabriel Bousquet's eyes are green, set widely apart, and amused. His face is all triangles, so that he looks somehow catlike. Harry finds himself mentally calculating the angles of Gabriel's face, thinking how he would put it down onto paper. He grins at the girl as she delivers bread and wine to the table. She blushes in the white glare of Gabriel's smile.

"I hope that I didn't disturb you in the cemetery," Harry says.

"No. Not at all." Gabriel rolls up his shirtsleeves before he pours the wine. "I saw you taking photographs. Is it the grave of a member of your family?"

"No. I was taking a photograph for the man's mother. She cannot travel here."

"Ah, so she will be able to see where her son is?"

"That is the idea."

Gabriel sighs and blows his fringe in the air. "What a thing!"

"Quite."

Harry feels embarrassed to explain it. He

realizes, as he describes the arrangement to Gabriel, that it is not so much the principle that he has any moral difficulty with, or the taking of the photograph itself, but the fact that he is receiving a salary for undertaking the task. Though he knows that Mrs. Evans may find some comfort in finally knowing her son is properly buried, he does not like being paid for delivering this sadness.

"And so you are normally a photographer in England?"

"I work in a portrait studio. I take photographs of brides and holidaying spinsters and babies. I sometimes find the babies frustrating — they cry and they blur and they leave wet patches — but when I go back to the studio, I shall be very glad to see them."

Gabriel touches his glass against Harry's. "I am sure."

The girl brings the soup. Gabriel serves, as if he is accustomed to playing this role.

"And you?" Harry asks. "Is it a friend or a relation that is in the cemetery?"

"It is my brother."

The soup is thin and tastes of nothing much. Gabriel stirs in copious pepper and sneezes into a handkerchief that is embroidered with another man's initials.

"I am sorry."

Gabriel shrugs at his soup. "We were both here, in the Bois de Chaulnes, in the winter of 1916. It was terrible in the woods. The woods were full of graves. We moved north in February and I had to leave my brother in the woods. It is a long time ago, isn't it?"

"Yes. We moved south, to here, that same month. I was here with my brother too." He nods to the window. "I was just remembering drawing that church spire."

Harry also remembers the French graves that they had passed along the road. They heard that the roads all around were full of wire entanglements and machine gun posts and French dead. Mostly he remembers the mud on those roads.

"It is bizarre to be back, isn't it? It is the first time that I have visited my brother's grave. I thought that I should come and see it before I go home. My mother has never seen it." Gabriel gulps at the wine as if he wishes to be rid of it and then refills his glass. "Would you perhaps take a photograph for me? I would pay you."

"Of course," says Harry. "But only on condition that you do not give me any money for it."

"Perhaps I can buy you a bottle of whiskey instead?"

"I am more amenable to such suggestions."

Gabriel raises his glass toward Harry and smiles.

"So you are going home?" asks Harry.

"Yes. *Enfin.* At last. I am traveling south now. I have been working on building sites in Clichy for the past two years. I am a stonemason."

Harry nods and takes a mouthful of the wine. "There is plenty of work?"

"Enough. But I must return home. Like a fish on a wire, I am reeled in." He makes an action like he is casting a line to catch a salmon and grins unconvincingly.

The café behind Gabriel, in the background of his portrait, is loud. A party of workmen, their faces white with plaster dust, all glance at the clock as they drink. They josh with Élodie and roar at her lightly delivered put-downs.

"Unwillingly reeled in?" Harry asks.

"Duty," says Gabriel, his eyes widening. He looks like he doesn't have much fondness for the word.

"To your mother?"

"She writes letters telling me to return. We have a farm — sheep and tobacco." His gestures suggest expansiveness. "I was the second son, but Marcellin is dead five years and my father is ill. He has not turned the soil this last year. I go back for my mother, for duty to my mother, who now sleeps in the *bergerie* and worries for bread. I should have returned home two years ago. I am two years too late."

Élodie clears the soup bowls and presents slices of meat, of undisclosed variety, in a mahogany-colored sauce. Gabriel replenishes the glasses.

"I should perhaps have gone back, but I didn't," says Harry. "I know that it's not easy."

"My mother wants me to take Marcellin's place in the fields and in his widow's bed. But I do not return home with any enthusiasm. It is complicated."

Harry watches Gabriel attack the meat with his knife. "It is always complicated," he says.

There are farmers from the market at the tables, traders, shopworkers, clerks, and the butcher in whites. The chef stands at the kitchen door and surveys the reception of the meat.

"She writes to me each week, piles of letters, begging me. I do not have a choice." Gabriel steers the meat about his plate. There are old scars on his arms. "This meat is not good," he says.

Harry thinks about the scars that the war has left on Edie's hands. Would she have accepted him if he'd come home and said that he meant to take Francis's place? Was that ever a choice? Could it ever be?

"So you are a stonemason no longer?"

"Not a poor mason, but I am to be a monument sculptor." Gabriel brightens and then flags. "I am to make the monument — the *monument aux morts.* I have been asked by the commune. I have to make a statue of a soldier and a plinth where their names can be carved. I have to make something which expresses the village's loss, something that sums up all the men that I left the village with." He turns his wineglass. "The statue has to summarize eleven dead men — three brothers, including my own, among them. They are already preparing the ground."

"That must be an honor," says Harry, not sure of what else to say.

"Apparently. Though today it feels like a big weight on my back. I do not sleep because when I dream of it the statue always has Marcellin's face. It can't have his face."

Harry imagines a statue with Francis's face. He does not envy Gabriel this task.

"They began collecting for it — the sub-scription — in 1916." Gabriel wipes bread

242

around his plate. "It was, at first, to be Monsieur Abanes's tomb to make. Then it passed to Eloi Alazard, to whom I was apprenticed in 1914. But then Eloi is dead and so it passes to me. It is a thirdhand honor and not an inheritance that I would have wished for."

"No, I suppose not."

"I make drawings: heroic soldiers, crying soldiers, writhing soldiers." Gabriel assumes demonstrative poses. "My head is full of dead soldiers in stone. Perhaps our burden is not so different."

Despite the scars, there is something elegant about Gabriel's hands. When he talks about drawing, his hands curl and scroll and carve arabesques in the air between them. He has the wrists of an Indian dancer. The girl scrapes together the fat and gristle and stacks the plates. Gabriel attempts eye contact and is rejected. He rolls his eyes at Harry.

"But I am ignorant. I talk of myself. I have no manners. You are here just for work?"

"Duty too. I'm trying to find some clues as to my brother's whereabouts. I suspect that he is dead, but don't know that he isn't alive. My sister-in-law needs to know either way. Only I'm not sure that I'll ever be able to deliver that certainty to her."

Gabriel nods. "Even if you find a grave, can you be sure that the right man is in it?" He peels the skin from a pear with his knife in one deft, smooth, circular movement. "When I stood by Marcellin's grave I wasn't entirely certain that he was there. I didn't feel like I was standing next to my brother. I read that the burial records are often incorrect, because the earth has been turned over so many times, because it has all been shaken up. Who can really be sure? But it is very difficult to explain that to someone who wasn't here, isn't it?"

"It is," Harry replies.

CHAPTER TWENTY-SEVEN: HARRY

French communications trenches west of Chaulnes, Somme, February 1917

They went on in silence for a while, with just the noise of the hurdles dripping. The earth had been frozen hard since the start of the month. They had woken with stiff limbs and with ice-rimed beards. It made their eyes ache, their throats raw, and it gnawed at their finger ends. They had cursed the cold and prayed for the thaw. It had now set in and the sky looked full of rain. Harry could hear water running under the duckboards.

"Single file," said Lieutenant Rose from farther up the line. "Quietly as possible, now."

Harry listened to the noise of their boots on the wet boards. He put his head down and his hands in the pockets of his greatcoat. They had been told that the line ahead had been hairy up until a couple of months back, as the French tried to take the woods. The landscape testified to it. The roads behind were churned and cratered. The village was all ruins. There was no noise of guns ahead now, though. The only sound was the dripping of water and the wet tramp of their boots.

"Thus we nobly slithered into battle," said Pembridge under his breath.

The sky above was wide and gray. They had left behind the last signs of the village and there was nothing to navigate by now; no hills or trees or roof timbers broke into the peripheries of their vision. There was just the high earth walls, a funnel of sky, and Wilkinson's pack in front with its swinging mess tin.

"Mind, now." Bartley's voice came from up ahead.

Part of the trench wall had collapsed, a small landslide spilling across their path. They clambered over it, complaining as their feet sank into the waterlogged earth. Harry felt the cold seep into his boots.

"They're falling in with the thaw," said Jones.

Earth was sliding from either side. In front, the bottom of the trench was a line of winter sky and feet splashing through it.

"The whole thing is crumbling," said

Wilkinson. "It's all going to fall apart."

It came over their boots, to their ankles, creeping up their calves. The water was sharply cold. Harry watched the first raindrops spatter in Wilkinson's mess tin. His own movements, reflected in the metal, were the color of mud. They discussed the efficaciousness of various patent embrocations, to pass the time, and speculated as to whether they would all have pneumonia by the morning.

"Goose grease is the only thing."

"I'd rather have the roast goose."

"Right now I'd gladly sell my wife if I could buy a hot bath with the proceeds."

"I've seen your wife. They might let you have the hot water free out of sympathy."

The line was moving slowly now. It was like walking up a stream at first, but now the stream had thickened and was rising. It had turned to a heavy sludge. They took difficult, careful, deliberate footsteps. It sucked and pulled, as if the landscape itself were now against them, wanting to drag them down. The enemy was forgotten. They stumbled and swore and the struggle now was to stay upright. Harry's hands pushed into the earth walls on either side. The walls oozed water and fell away. Each step was an effort.

"What's going on?"

Ahead, the men had stopped.

"It's a bog," said Pembridge. "It's like a trap."

"Is there a way around?" asked Bartley. "Like climb over the top?"

"Or build a boat?"

The wickerwork revetments were collapsing. Wires sagged and the walls slumped. Everything was falling down into the mud ahead.

Bartley nudged into Harry's back. The line behind pressed.

"Go on," said Fearnley's voice.

"We can't go back," said Jones.

It was up beyond Harry's knees now and moving against the glutinous thickness of it was so tiring. His greatcoat felt like an enormous weight.

"My legs are screaming," said Pembridge.

Harry took large, exaggerated, slow steps. Each movement required concentration. Getting across it was the only thing that he thought about now, but there didn't seem to be a far side. The mud-colored figures ahead were staggering like old men. He wished that he could shrug off his kit and his greatcoat. He watched the rain pitting the surface of the mud.

"I feel about a hundred years old," said

Bartley. Harry could hear the effort of his breath.

"I feel like I could fall down and sleep for a hundred years." Pembridge leaned against a post with his eyes closed. "I am clinging to the mast," he said. His eyes opened and rolled skyward. In the gathering dusk and the all-around mud the whites of his eyes glinted.

"This ship is well sunk," he said.

From the thighs down Harry was all clay; he was a statue struggling into life. He felt the coldness of it circling around his thighs. It was soft, but sharp. It chilled and burned. Someone up ahead was yelling. The cries sounded hysterical.

"I'm not sure that I can go on," said Bartley. "I'm not sure that I want to go on."

The rain streamed down Harry's face. He tasted the salt of his skin and it stung in his eyes. He thought about just giving in to it, just spreading his arms and sinking in. He imagined the mud pushing into his mouth and his nose, claiming his throat and his lungs. He stumbled in his panic.

"Go on," said Francis's voice behind. Harry looked back. The line of men were just shadows now, the mist of breath and the shimmer of rain on tin hats and capes.

Harry's foot sank as he turned and he felt

it lurch. The cold rushed up. His hands grasped but there was nothing to grab on to, nothing to stop him from falling. He tried to move his feet, to find purchase, but the weight and thickness of the mud was too great. It crept beyond his waist. His hands flailed but there was nothing to cling on to. He felt it rising up his chest. The figure of Pembridge was pulling away. He tried to turn, to reach to the man behind.

Francis was there, then. His face flared into light as he put a match to a cigarette. The match arced away and Francis's hands were gripping Harry's. He felt his brother's pulse and pulled against his hands, kicking, fighting, heaving, frantic. Then the red glare of the cigarette was gone and Harry was falling again. He felt the cold pushing up and panic surging through his body.

"Francis!"

Other hands were at his armpits then, pulling his pack and his greatcoat away. He felt hot breath against his cheek and caught glints of half-familiar faces. He screamed as they pulled. He felt like the sockets of his arms were going to spring loose and his bones were going to tear apart. The mud let him go. He clung to Bartley, found himself blinking into his up-close eyes. He wanted to say thank you but couldn't seem to quite make words. The line ahead went on and they were pulled with it. He looked back to see his greatcoat sinking into the mud.

"Leave it," Bartley said.

Harry remembered how he had once spent an afternoon watching a butterfly slowly shrug off its cocoon, struggling free of its constriction to stretch its wings. Moving on through the darkness and the thigh-high mire, he wished for a set of wings. He thought of Francis's hands pulling away from his own. Had he imagined it? He could hear his own teeth chattering.

"The guide is a spy," Fearnley's voice was proposing behind. "He's one of theirs. He's led us into a bog to finish us off."

"Bastard is just lost," said Pembridge. "He's got no more clue than we have."

Harry looked back. All that he could make out now was occasional glimmers of reflection and a swaying line of cigarettes. Was one of those red lights Francis? Was he still behind?

"We're all lost," said Bartley.

They went on with just the noise of their legs in the mud and the patter of the rain. The moonlight seemed to heighten the texture of everything. The flooded ditch ahead shivered.

"What's that?"

There were voices ahead, notes of hilarity and fast foreign words. He looked up to see the silhouettes of men standing up on the top of the parapet. Pembridge stopped. He turned back toward Harry. He could see Pembridge's breath and the question in his eye.

"Boche?"

"French."

The poilus were standing up on top of the trenches that they were meant to be holding. Harry could see the shapes of them. They were walking about apparently without any concern for the facing enemy and offering their hands then to the men who had come to relieve them. He could see the men in front clambering up.

"Are they mad?"

"Perhaps we are."

The figures on the tops of the parapets were patting each other on their backs. Someone was singing. Cigarettes were being passed and lit. It looked as if the war were quite forgotten. It looked like the war was over.

"Allons! Venez! Ne restez pas dans la merde."

Hands were beckoning, stretching down to them, pulling them up.

"Is it safe?"

The men on the parapet were laughing. Harry took offered hands, kicked and clambered. He rolled onto the top.

"Bien. C'est mieux, hein?"

Hands were patting him, then. He lay on his back and looked up at the faces. They grinned and joshed in the gloom. Were they madmen or satyrs or ghosts? He took a proffered cigarette and a hand that helped him to his feet.

"Allez, regardez là!"

An arm pointed away. Harry looked out across no-man's-land, across the dark shadows of the churned and cratered land, flooded shell holes glowing like milky pools, and the sharp twists of torn trees. On the far side was a bobbing line of yellow lights. Harry looked at the cigarette in his own hand and realized what it was.

"They're on the tops too?"

"They climbed out this evening, and so we did the same. Their trenches are flooded too," said a voice without a face in heavily accented English. Harry could discern what might have been the shape of a church spire beyond the enemy lines. "It is as bad for them as it is for us. And why should we stay in the mud just because politicians say it ought to be so? The village behind is Chaulnes. We have been fighting for it for seven months."

The noise of laughter carried across the darkness.

"*C'est complétement fou. Tout est foutu.* It is all madness," said the voice in the blackness.

Chapter Twenty-Eight:
Harry

Chaulnes, Somme, August 1921

"Give me your hand," says Gabriel. *"Allez!"*

They clamber through the grassed ditches that once were trenches and climb to stand on the parapet. The ground ahead, though now scrambled over with green, still looks churned and dangerous. As they pick through the old wire Harry remembers walking along the top of the parapet searching for Francis. He had finally found him smoking with Harrison. Francis had offered Harry the packet of cigarettes and said, "It makes you wonder what the point is, doesn't it?" Harry hadn't been able to quite make his hand still as Francis held the struck match out toward him. With that memory seeming so close by at this moment, Harry has to cross his arms over his chest again.

"We came here in September 1916," says Gabriel, shading his eyes to the sun. "By then the line had circled half around the town. We were fighting in the woods to the north, trying to complete the circle, but it was like a fortress."

Beyond, to the north, the skyline bristles with tree stumps. It looks horribly sharp and unfriendly, like a wicked woods in a children's fable.

"Marcellin died here in the woods?"

"Yes."

He had taken a photograph of Marcellin Bousquet's grave that morning, and a second of his brother standing at its side, Gabriel's hand stretching out to touch the cross. There was a simple tenderness to the gesture. Behind the lens, Harry had pictured Gabriel's hand on his brother's shoulder. He can't imagine himself posing for his portrait at the side of Francis's grave.

"I am sorry." Brambles and barbed wire pluck at Harry's trouser legs. He kicks them away. "We walked into the town, or what was left of it, in March 1917. It was completely deserted."

He remembers following Francis into a burnt-out house, its smell of blistered woodwork. Harry's fingers had brushed against a cast-iron stove and he had been shocked by the heat that still issued from it.

"I read that they are going to plant pine woods from here south, great stretches of them. They think that pine trees may grow in this earth if nothing else will."

Harry looks up at Gabriel. "Shall we walk to the town together?"

"Yes. I would like that."

They take cautious steps between the tangles of old wire, over the dips and rises of the ground. He sees a hand grenade flaking into rust, and a bolt of machine gun cartridges. They look like something left by an ancient civilization. An ironwork gate is bent into a frightful shape, there is the mangled frame of a daybed, and Harry realizes how hard he has tried to put all of this out of his mind. He treads carefully, not wanting to see it all, yet needing to see. There are moldered sandbags, scraps of rag, and brown lengths that might be branches or bones. His boot touches the spine of a book. He nudges it and it falls stiffly open. The white pages inside are pristine, the print crisp and uncompromised.

"A Bible?"

"I think so."

Just for an instant it might have been his own lost notebook, the book of sketches and thoughts that had been so important to him, into which he could put all his sorrows and fears, confine the images that he meant to forget, and preserve the memories that he chose to keep. Putting it down on the page had seemed to keep it all in balance, it had worked for him for a long time, but then his book had no longer been there. Harry wonders if anyone has ever curiously kicked at that cover as they've walked through the ruins and, if so, which page the book split open on.

"We were at school together, Marcellin, Madeleine, and I," Gabriel goes on. Harry watches as he pokes a stick at a helmet and turns it. Mercifully it is empty. Gabriel throws the stick away and shrugs. "She had a brown face and yellow plaits. She took the sheep out and knew birdcalls. She had quick hands. She could catch lizards and could dance. She danced with us both."

Harry sees gavottes spin around Gabriel and his brother's grave and a girl's white-toothed smile. He sees the spin of a long-ago garden, a woman's lips forming the words to a song being played on a gramophone. But the woman is his brother's wife and he should not recall those words on her lips. He blinks the rest away.

"They were married before the war?"

"Yes. Him in uniform. But when we were sixteen I thought that it was me who Madeleine would choose. It was my eyes that she smiled into. But Marcellin had the confidence. He was the one who had all the talk, who knew the right words to say to girls, and he would have the farm one day. Marcellin had a future. Now he has no future." Gabriel picks up a piece of brown metal and turns it over in his hands. "Shrapnel?" he says. "I do miss my brother, you understand."

"I understand," says Harry.

They rejoin the road, which looks as if it has recently been relaid. The new surface makes the roadside trees, splintered and severed, look all the more tragic. Today the sun is high and these trees can offer no shade. Harry takes off his jacket and passes a water bottle to Gabriel. This must once have been a handsome avenue, he considers. The well-spaced slumps of brick to either side must have been smart houses. There are fragments of dressed stone still, and roses scramble over fallen walls to which they were perhaps once trellised. The grandeur of the gateposts looks almost mocking.

" 'Following the Enemy withdrawal to the Hindenburg Line, British troops entered Chaulnes, almost without striking a blow, on March eighteenth, 1917. But the town would be recaptured by the Germans in March 1918,' " he reads aloud from his

259

guidebook. " 'It was only finally taken by the Allies on August twenty-eighth, after being surrounded. It was razed to the ground. The low brick-and-rubble houses which lined the wide straight streets sheltered a population of about twelve hundred fifty inhabitants. Very few of them escaped total destruction.' "

Gabriel passes the water bottle back and they walk on. A couple in black are staring at a pile of stones. The woman turns rheumy eyes to Harry. He takes off his hat.

"I saw a proposal written in a newspaper that the trenches should be left, should be kept an open wound for all to see. I thought that it was right; but now I see that it's wrong. This is someone's home. I feel as if I ought to apologize," he says to Gabriel. When he looks back the woman is staring after them.

"But still people do want to see. There is talk of building an Office National du Tourisme, with barracks to house the sightseers and fleets of motor buses to take them over the battlefields. They say that it will be a new invasion." A girl with blond hair passes them, cradling a loaf of bread to her chest. Gabriel says, *"Bonjour,"* but the girl doesn't take her eyes from the road ahead. "I don't know that it will be welcomed," he says.

Curtains twitch at the windows of wooden huts. The houses here look like gardener's sheds, Harry thinks. Another town is being remade in pine and corrugated iron. An old man carries pails of water from a pump. Children stand and stare on the junction.

"These places make me think about photographs that I've seen of prospector towns. Is this what it was like in the Klondike and California?"

"I don't know that the prize was quite so high."

Their feet stop by a Nissen hut. There is the noise of a piano playing and voices joining within, shaping into the tune of a hymn that Harry recognizes. Pieces of colored paper have been glued onto the windows to give the impression of stained glass. There is a large wooden cross nailed to the apex of the corrugated iron roof. It looks like it has been salvaged from an older place. It looks somehow declamatory. Harry wonders how these people can cling on to faith and hope.

"Communion," says Gabriel.

"Perhaps that is what matters: the coming together?"

Chickens scatter ahead of them. A dog stretches lazily and watches them pass. There is a burnt-out house at the end of the road, the pink brick scorched and blackened roof beams slumped. Harry imagines how it must have roared when the roof gave way. They sit on the remains of a garden wall and pass a packet of cigarettes between them. A child hits at the dirt with a twig.

"I get letters," Gabriel says. "They all know what they want the memorial to be and what they don't want it to be. The trouble is that they don't agree. One person writes that the figure has to be realistic, *un fils de la terre,* while a second wants a heroic *homme de guerre.* Another says that it should not be a soldier at all, but a mother, a Vierge Marie, a mother of Christ stripped of her son. Others tell me that it must not be triumphal; it must be a proletarian, socialist expression of loss — an old man struggling with the plow. Others want a symbol of Peace, a figure of Justice, a winged Victory, and I have no idea what is right!" He throws his hands in the air and looks at Harry. "Is this peace? Is this victory? Is this justice? How am I supposed to make that decision? How can I sum all of this up?"

"You were a soldier. You saw it. I guess that, as far as they're concerned, you're more able to sum it up than someone who wasn't here."

"Do you think? I wish I had your confidence."

"I have confidence in you. Will you send me a sketch when you get there?"

"Of course. I must give you my address for the photograph," he says, then pauses. "Or you can bring it — you can deliver it by hand. If the weather holds, I'll get a second cut of hay by the end of the month. Come with me. Another pair of hands would be very welcome. It is heavy work, but lighter than all of this."

"I am tempted. Believe me, I'd love to leave this place behind, but I have sixteen names in my pocket and I've promised to deliver these photographs."

"Well then, cross off your sixteenth name as soon as you are able and get on a train."

Harry thinks about the possibility of crossing the last name — Francis's name — off his list, and what the likelihood of being able to decisively do so would entail. It would require a grave, or to stand face-to-face with Francis again. Both scenarios seem remote at this moment, and their consequences beyond contemplation, but he watches Gabriel writing out the address on the back of a used train ticket, the foreign name forming in his copperplate letters.

"Calvaire du Quercy? As in Calvary? The place of the cross?"

"The place of my childhood is all crosses and saints' bones and shrines." Gabriel shrugs. "We hope fiercely and are probably fools."

Apples are ripening in the field at the side of the road. These young trees look to have been newly planted and the stumps of the old trees in between are almost indistinguishable now. Harry remembers how buds had broken on the old trees' severed limbs in March 1917. Though they had been cut clean across at the trunk, green leaves had sprouted from the boughs. They had stared at this inexplicable show of new life. That too had once looked like hope.

"Rebirth. It all goes round. It all carries on." Gabriel points at the name painted above the door of a roadside shack. It is called the Buvette de la Renaissance. A man is smoking as he leans in the doorway. He raises a glass to them. "When I have completed my memorial I intend to stop remembering. I will work hard at forgetting all of this. I will work until my bones are tired each day, and not dream. I will breathe in each new morning and be glad of it and I will not look back."

"You're probably right."

"And you should too." Gabriel offers him his hand. "We will meet again, my friend. I know it."

"I hope so," Harry replies.

CHAPTER TWENTY-NINE: HARRY

East of Chaulnes, Somme, March 1917
"Why did they have to cut down the orchards?" asked Bartley. They were standing in a field of newly felled trees. Bartley was a corporation gardener at home and this destruction seemed to strike him as profoundly as if he had found himself surrounded by a field full of felled men.

"Why are the bridges blown? Why are there craters at every crossroads? It's the same reason: they didn't want to leave behind anything of any use."

It had seemed like a strange dream to be climbing up out of the trenches, out of the line that they thought they might have to hold forevermore. Then they had marched down roads that, just hours earlier, had been behind the enemy lines. They had stared at the belts of wire, the enemy dugouts, and the green grass beyond. They had laughed, linked arms, felt almost giddy with it. It had seemed like the first day of a holiday. It had sobered them, though, when they had seen the cans of petroleum and the cottages that were still smoking. It was the small inconsequential things that had touched Harry most: the smashed greenhouse, the goldfish floating in a pond, and now this field full of felled apple trees.

"But trees? There are new buds," said Bartley, holding up a severed branch. "At home I prune at the start of March."

"These have been well pruned," said Pembridge.

"It's barbaric."

Harry sketched them as they lolled in the leveled orchard, Bartley holding branches to his chest, Pembridge dozing among the rotting apples, Fearnley and Robertson crouched over hands of cards. The bright spring light gave the fallen trees sharp shadows. He could smell the sweetness of the new-cut wood. A collared dove took off from among the grass. He was startled at the sudden flash of wings.

"Jumpy?" Fearnley said with a laugh.

"Too bloody right!" He put the sketchbook away and stretched. "Where's Frannie?"

"In the house, I think, with his camera."

The near side of the farmhouse was still

standing, though the windows had gone and floral curtains billowed out from the upper floor. Harry trod through broken glass and fallen tiles. The door was swinging on a hinge. He stepped inside. The furniture looked like someone had taken an ax to it. A kitchen dresser had been pulled over, spilling an avalanche of plates and bowls and a porcelain coffee service. The floor was all splinters and smashed willow-pattern china. It was silent now but for the noise of the wind. There were moony woodland glades in the design of the wallpaper. What orgy of destruction had roared through these walls? What loud violence had filled this room just hours earlier?

Their portraits were still above the fireplace, facing photographs of him and her, their side-by-side faces angled so that their eyes seemed to triangulate upon Harry as he approached. She had braided hair, pale eyelashes, and a hydrangea flower in her hands. He had last-century side-whiskers and was holding out an open book. Harry thought them rather mannered images; they were slightly forced and awkward, like they were trying to be Pre-Raphaelite portraits. Were these unsmiling faces those of the couple who had chosen the willow-pattern china and the moony wallpaper? Was this their home? Harry heard his brother's tread on the floor above and remembered twinned portraits of him and Edie that he had once painted long ago.

On the landing there were chunks of plaster that had come down from the ceiling, and a baby carriage. He pushed a door and saw a room with papers all over the floor, like an explosion in a library. He stared at the pages around his feet, most of which seemed to have been torn from travel books. He stepped over maps of Abyssinia and images of Arctic expeditions and wondered why it was so important that these pages be wrenched from their spines. What crime had this litter of words committed? The next room was full of feathers and clothes and his brother taking photographs.

"Has someone had a pillow fight in here?"

The white feathers were everywhere. They trembled as he stepped into the room. He could smell the spilled powders and perfumes. Francis laughed behind the lens. "Happen that's how we'll finish it."

All of the drawers had been pulled out of the dressing table, as if someone had been searching. Francis was photographing the scent bottles and hairbrushes that had been left by the mirror, things of quiet femininity, and the room's angry reflection. Harry stood in the doorway and watched his brother trying to find the right angle.

"You're in my shot," he said.

He took a step back onto the landing and lit a cigarette. Had the soldiers laughed as they tore this house apart? he wondered. Or had they felt anger and hatred for these people and their possessions? Had they looked the downstairs portraits in the eye? He heard the click of the camera shutter.

"Done?"

Francis was sitting at the dressing table. There was a vase of violets doubled in the mirror, the freshness in the petals indicating that they hadn't been picked many hours earlier. Harry had seen violets growing under the hedge and was struck with how fast time moves; was it really only hours since the man with the earnest mouth had picked these stems and presented them to the woman with the pale eyelashes? The intactness of so fragile a thing seemed surprising among the wreckage. There was something suddenly terribly poignant and important about this small vase of flowers.

"Most of this stuff is rubbish," said Francis.

Harry refocused. He could see his brother's fingers in the mirror going through a box of buttons and trinkets. He pulled out a brooch and held it to his own chest.

"It's only paste," Francis said, his mirror eyes meeting Harry's. "Only a cheap thing, but still . . ."

"We shouldn't be in here."

" 'I will make you brooches and toys for your delight. Of birdsong at morning and star-shine at night.' "

There was something disturbing about Francis's singsong voice and his eyes in the mirror. Did he mean to provoke? Did he want to start a fight? Harry watched as Francis slipped the brooch into his pocket.

"You shouldn't be touching that stuff."

"Don't look like that. It's for Edie," he said. "I'm going to give it to Edie when I go home on leave."

"You can't."

"It'll look pretty on her, won't it?" Francis's eyes in the mirror challenged Harry.

"You can't take it."

"Who has seen? Who will know? It's only you and me. And you wouldn't tell on me, would you? Edie will wear it and think about me."

"You can't just take things."

He didn't see Francis's hands move. He didn't see him throw the box, but suddenly it was all in the air. Buttons and beads and trinkets leapt. Harry put his hands over his face and crouched as cuff links and buckles and bobbins of cotton struck him. Thimbles, bracelets, and embroidery scissors hit his arms. The vase exploded as it connected with the wall behind him. When it all finally stilled, there were violets around his feet and he could hear Francis laughing.

CHAPTER THIRTY: HARRY

Epéhy, Somme, August 1921

Image order: Miss Winifred Uttley requests a photograph of the grave of her fiancé, Pte. William Horace Stubbs (27891, East Yorkshire Regiment), KIA 22nd March 1918.

George Bartley is just feet away from Private Stubbs. Harry stares at the name on the cross. When he shuts his eyes, and recalls Bartley's face, he's still sitting in an orchard in 1917. Harry had drawn him that day, quickly, surreptitiously, struck by Bartley's depth of feeling for the fallen trees and the way that it had shown on his face. He recalls the symmetry — and the not-quite sym-metry — of the orchard, and looks at the lines of graves that now multiply behind George Bartley. He leans in to see the date on the cross; it is five months on from that day when Bartley had cried for the felled trees and Francis had stolen the brooch from the room that smelled of violets.

Remembering the apple in his pocket, Harry takes out his penknife. Bartley had told him about the five-pointed star at the center of an apple, how it represents atonement and immortality. "A symbol of both sin and of eternal life," he had explained to Harry that day in the orchard, the former notion at that moment seeming more convincing than the latter. Harry carefully cuts the apple and pulls out the pips. He pushes them into the earth around Bartley's grave. He likes to imagine that one day Bartley might be under an apple tree, its own fruit falling and forever beginning again. He wishes that he could offer something more to William Stubbs other than to tell him that Miss Winifred Uttley is thinking about him.

There is nobody else in the cemetery. It is not the same here as it is in the headline villages of the Somme; the pilgrimages and parties of excursionists don't come this far east. He stands and looks along the row. They are mostly men from September 1918 here, their graves closely packed together. When Harry had known this area it was green with copses and hedges. The summer of 1917 had been all fights for posts, over hills and farms and woodlands. Was it still green in September 1918? With the numbers of dead in this cemetery, he can't imagine how it could have been.

"I didn't know that you were here," he says to Bartley's cross. He does recognize the date on the grave, though; the day that Bartley died is the same day that Harry had been wounded. His memories of that day are of the panic on the wire, the wire being everywhere, and it all shrieking and bursting over his head. Many of the graves in the cemetery are decorated with woven wire wreaths. The tangling trap of the barbed wire, and the journey back in an ambulance train, had taken Harry to a garden in Cheshire. Just for an instant the recalled sound of a blackbird and the smell of new-cut grass push into the here and now. She is saying his name, the gramophone is playing, and Edie is shutting her eyes as it all spins around her. But this isn't a place that he's permitted to go back to and he blinks the memory away.

Bartley liked to pass around a photograph of a girl called Jane whom he one day meant to marry. Harry recalls the girl's photograph face. Has she ever visited him here? Does she have a photograph of his grave? Will she ever marry anyone else? He puts his hand to Bartley's cross. He will write to his family later and let them know that he has been here. He will ask them for the address of the girl called Jane, so that he may tell her about the day in the felled apple orchard and how, even through the worst of it, he would catch Bartley smiling at her photograph.

There is a man selling wire wreaths by the cemetery gates — the same wreaths, Harry recognizes, that are on so many of the graves here. He thinks about buying one for Bartley, but on reflection decides that he would be happy enough with his ring of apple pips. He watches the wreath maker's hands work, admiring his dexterity. There is speed and sureness in this man's fingers as he weaves the metal wire. The meshed wire makes Harry think about the trap of barbed wire, but there is skill and art in the geometric forms that this man is conjuring with a pair of pliers. He is in control of the wire.

"Je peux prendre votre photographie?"

"I'm not much of a one for posing for photographs," the man replies in unexpected English. He has a soft, courteous voice and strikingly pale eyes when he looks up. "But if you must."

"I promise not to steal your soul." He offers the man his hand. "Harry Blythe."

"East. Daniel East."

He frames Daniel East among his wreaths. His fingers never stop working. He wears an old blue French army overcoat and a pink chrysanthemum flower in his buttonhole. Harry wishes that he could capture the colors — the coat and the flower and the barely blue of the man's eyes. On film his irises will look like an absence.

"I'll send you a copy if you want."

"No fixed abode," replies Daniel East and shrugs. He wishes Harry *"Bonne route."*

He walks from the cemetery toward the village. It's now another township of huts, rising up in corrugated iron and prefabricated panels between the ruins. He can hear the noise of a saw. Old foundations are being flattened. Children are chasing a dog through the new-made streets, laughing and banging a can.

There is a statue among the tumbled masonry, bright and crisp in clean new-cast concrete. Harry leans on the railings, which are threaded with red, white, and blue ribbons, and reads the words *Monument aux Morts.* Dedicated to the dead of the village, *Nos Enfants,* the figure of a woman embodies the sense of loss. Her eyes are cast down upon a poilu's helmet. She touches it with the flat of her right hand, while with her left

277

hand she holds a palm leaf to her breast. The way she is holding the palm, the tenderness of the gesture, reminds Harry of Bartley with the apple branch. Whose face was the artist resisting thinking of, he wonders, when he put this statue's classically Greek features down onto paper? Wreaths and garlands and simple bunches of flowers have been placed at the base of the memorial. Harry counts the carved names: there are fifty-eight of them. It seems a heavy cost from this small village. The children and the dog chase around the railings.

He sits outside a street-corner bar and shuts his eyes into the sun. A gramophone inside is playing something with a jazz beat. Harry thinks about the apple pips around Bartley's grave wriggling into life and reprimands himself for his melancholy. He reminds himself that he is lucky. He orders a beer from the barman and asks him if there is somewhere in the village where he can buy a postcard.

"Vous voulez un souvenir de ce coin?" The barman looks at him with surprise and laughs. But he places two picture postcards on Harry's table with an apologetic shrug.

"C'est tout que je peux vous offrir. C'est avant. Before the war."

Harry offers the man a palmful of coins,

but he shakes his head. It is as if what came before now bears no relevance, is obsolete, and can be of little value to a traveler requiring a memento.

"Merci bien," says Harry.

The first card is emblazoned with the caption *"Souvenir de Notre Village."* Swallows swoop, each of them bearing a pastel-tinted image in their beaks — a chateau, a schoolhouse, the columned frontage of a church — all now gone. It is like an offering of memories. The second postcard is a photograph of three men standing in a field, paused with a plow. In the background a valley slopes down toward the canal. Harry knows the slope.

At the sound of laughter he looks up. A woman with a jazz voice is arm in arm with a man in a white apron, and they're dancing their way out of the bar and circling between the café furniture. " 'Now I got the crazy blues,' " sing Mamie Smith and the dancing woman. She has dark plaits twisted around her head and silver bangles that clatter up her arms. Harry thinks of Rachel's ringed fingers, of the wreath maker's weaving fingers, and it is only at that moment that it strikes him.

CHAPTER THIRTY-ONE:
EDIE

Poperinghe, August 1921

Edie remembers Francis's photograph of this place: all the men crowded onto the platform of Poperinghe station brandishing their leave papers for his camera. The men in the photograph squint into the sun and grin. They fill every inch of that image with the flourish of their papers and the flash of their smiles. But today she is the only person on the station platform and at this moment she can no longer recall what her husband's smile looks like.

Harry had told her that he had seen his brother on that day back in September 1917. Their paths had crossed on this railway platform; as Harry was going back to the battalion, so Francis had been on his way home on leave. It was the last time he would come home, the last time she would see him, but she wasn't sure she knew the man who had sat and stared at the fire for hours and curled in the sheets of her bed.

Swallows streak down the railway lines and she remembers how Francis had given her a brooch on the day he came back. As he had stooped to kiss her in the doorway, he had placed it in her palm, folding his hand around hers. She can feel the brief sharpness of that grip as she thinks about it now, and that was what had caused her to withdraw from that awkward embrace. Their lips hadn't met. And so it was.

"For you," he had said. "Do you like it?"

When she had opened her fingers there was a silver swallow in her hand, set with paste stones and a ruby eye. Somebody else's fingerprints were tarnished into the metal, and there was something about that glittering red eye that she didn't like. She had nodded and thanked him, but she can't recall that she has ever worn the brooch. Was that a mistake? Did he see that she didn't like it? Was that where it all went wrong?

She remembers that last week with Francis strangely, almost as if it is not her own life that she is recalling, but a story that she once read, or a play that she's seen. It feels secondhand, as if during those days she hadn't been living at the surface. The images that she brings to mind now aren't quite in focus and she can't remember all of the words. What she recalls most clearly about that week is the tension, and when she forces her mind back there, she can feel it again.

It wasn't that she had expected it to be easy. After all, it had been more than two years, and she already knew from the voice in his letters, or rather the lack of voice, that something wasn't right. She wasn't fool enough to have imagined things would be like they had been before, that they would instantly fall back into laughter and easy intimacy, but she had at least expected that they would be close together. And, as she had prepared for his visit, she had wanted to be close to him; to wash his skin and ease his aches, to soothe him and care for him, to show him that he was loved, and that he had all of this to come back to. She had also wanted him to talk to her. To tell her what was troubling him. To share. To unburden himself. Did it all go wrong because she didn't ask the right questions? Or was it that first awkward touch on the doorstep that spoiled everything that came after?

The platform clock ticks. Its gilt hands move around the Roman numerals too fast. It was not Francis's fault that there was dirt down his fingernails, she told herself, and that he hadn't washed his hair all week, but she had found herself not wanting to be close to him. Every room in the house smelled of him, a sweet-sour smell that his skin had never had before, and she had to lean out of the windows to breathe. She was glad that he didn't try to touch her after that first difficult moment. She can't recall that she touched him. When she lay at this stranger's side, she couldn't sleep and the hands on the bedroom clock had moved so terribly slowly.

The railway tracks in Poperinghe stretch east and west. She is seven miles — one train stop — from Ypres, where he now might be. If she steps onto the next train, will she have to lie at his side again? Will she have to listen to his breath and launder his shirts and put her hands through his hair? There was a time, before all this began, when she had liked to put her face to Francis's neck and just breathe him in, when she couldn't keep her fingers away from his strong white shoulders and the glossed curl of his hair. There was a time when she couldn't lie close enough to him. The man who had left her house in 1914 knew the names of all the birds and the trees, and she loved him for that. He read books about ancient civilizations and African countries. He whispered poems in her ear and plaited her hair. But that was not the man who had come back in September 1917. Could all those fundamental parts of him really have permanently disappeared? What had happened to all that they had shared? How had they moved so far apart?

When he had walked back in, Francis had brought strangeness into the house and she had found herself moving around him. She could no longer predict the reactions of the man whom she'd lived with since she was seventeen. There was something wild and unknowable about this version of Francis. The look that he gave her when she asked him if he wanted to talk about Will. The way his lip curled when she laid a blanket over him. It wasn't that he had raised a hand to her, or even raised his voice, but she saw the flinch on his face. The trigger. She no longer knew how he would react to anything she said, and so fewer and fewer words had passed between them. What might he need to say to her now, then? She looks at her watch.

She has never told anyone how difficult it was, that last week with Francis, because it makes her sound like a terrible woman. A terrible wife. How could she admit to anyone how difficult she had found it to be

284

with him? That she didn't know how to speak to him? That she felt some relief when the week ended and he went back? How can she tell anyone how she opened all of the windows after he went, and scrubbed the floors, and boiled the bedsheets? How could she admit to anyone that she had been frightened of that man and how she felt about him?

If there is a chance that she might see him again, that it might be true, which version of himself is he now? Could that strong young man with the carefree grin and the whispered poems ever really come back? But she has seen the cemeteries and the smashed villages now, what the war has done to this country, and finally realizes that Francis was like that because of all of this. And how can that ever be reversed? How could they ever go back to what they were?

When she had first opened that envelope and seen the photograph, she had dropped it. The image sent a shock through her fingers and she had slid to the floor. She has had four years of getting used to his death, was quite certain that was what it was. It was silent. It was settled. She hadn't doubted it. What did it mean now, though? He had pushed his way back in through the mail slot. What did he want to happen next?

A guard steps out onto the platform and touches his cap to her. The church bells have stopped ringing.

Six weeks prior to the day that Francis had boarded his leave train at this station, she had danced on the lawn of the hospital with Harry. She remembers Harry's breath on her cheek, the creases at the corners of his mouth when he smiled, the shadows of his eyelashes, the nape of his neck, and how she hadn't wanted him to have to come back here. She had felt so fiercely protective of Harry at that instant. So close to him. She had watched him walk back up the drive and wished that she didn't have to walk away. Would she be feeling different now if she had Harry's hand to hold?

She hears the tracks begin to vibrate with the approach of the eastbound train. The lines hum and rattle and she feels it through the soles of her feet and in her chest. The Ypres train comes into sight and she sees Francis's face there waiting at the other end.

It is her duty to stand in that square, to hold the photograph to the skyline, and to know that she has matched it up. It would be the right thing to do, the proper thing to do, and surely what Francis meant when he put that photograph in an envelope. But how can the right thing feel so wrong?

She puts herself back in a room where he is curled in a tangle of damp bedsheets. The animal sound of his breath and the smell of his sweat fill the room. She can taste it. She is standing on the platform of Poperinghe station, but she can hear the awful liquid rattle of Francis's breathing and feel the hot dampness of those sheets on her own clothes. The guard blows his whistle and panic surges through her body.

287

CHAPTER THIRTY-TWO: HARRY

Vimy Ridge, August 1921

Location image order: Miss Esme Stewart requests general photographs of Vimy Ridge. Her brother, Captain Albert Stewart (13th Brigade), was reported missing, believed killed, on 10th April 1917. Remains yet to be identified.

"I wasn't certain whether you'd still be here. When I phoned your hotel, I fully expected them to tell me that you'd gone."

"I honestly start to think that I'll still be here in a hundred years' time," says Rachel.

Harry hadn't known whether, or how, to say it down the telephone. Now that he's here, standing at her side, he's even more unsure of where, or indeed if, to start.

"I leave David's details with everyone I meet."

"That's good of you," she says.

They're walking together up the ridge. The grass is thin and the white chalk below shows through. He remembers reading how it had snowed on the ninth of April 1917, as the Allied attack had been launched. Though the gradient does not seem aggressive, he has to take a break and catch his breath. Rachel puffs her cheeks out and puts a hand on his arm.

"I'm so glad you stopped. I didn't want to be the one to wave the white flag first."

"It's deceptive, isn't it? That or I'm very out of practice."

He looks at Rachel West's ringed fingers on his arm and thinks about Daniel East's hands twisting the wire. His image is inside Harry's camera. Is it enough, though, this coincidence of pliers and eyes and compass points, to raise her hopes? She smiles at him. If he were to say it, would he take the smile from her face? Would it just be giving her false hope, sending her in the wrong direction?

"Have you been here before?"

She nods. "Just last week."

She pulls her windblown hair from her eyes and he recalls the pull of those same fingers through his hair. He wasn't sure that she would turn up, but she shows no apparent embarrassment. She doesn't avoid his eyes or his questions. Her straight gaze makes him start to question the scene that he recalls. Did it really happen? Might it just have been a dream?

"You should have said. I wouldn't have dragged you back had I known."

She shrugs. "I'm glad to revisit with someone to talk to. It makes a change from talking to myself."

It was not inconvenient to come here. Meeting her fit in with the other tasks he had to do. When he had spoken to her on the telephone he had felt sure that it was meant and right that he tell her, but now he is no longer quite so certain of what he saw, or what he ought to say.

"The family asked me to take general photographs of the ridge," he explains. "That was the brief. Only it seems excessively brief. *General* just seems a bit too general, don't you think? I don't know where to start."

When they turn and look back, the road is long and straight, tapering out in the haze on the skyline. There are other groups advancing up the hill, tourists in sneakers and pilgrims in black. The slope is pitted with shell holes and crumbling earthworks. The village below looks like a feature that someone has tried to scratch off a canvas.

"I can see for miles," says Rachel. "You can see why they had to take it."

The plain below is flat. There is the smudge of an industrial town in the distance and a stretching scar (not a neat cut — but like something troublesomely healed) that might perhaps once have been the front line. He takes the view looking back down toward the village.

"It's the man's sister who has asked for the photographs?"

"Yes. I haven't met or corresponded with her. My employer just passed this request on. All I know is that her brother was reported missing here in April 1917."

He wishes that Mr. Lee's instructions weren't so scant and unspecific. The landscape framed in his viewfinder might have no relation to the whereabouts of Captain Albert Stewart. He has no idea where precisely the line was on the tenth of April 1917. He doesn't want to palm Miss Esme Stewart off with a meaningless image. It is too important for that.

"Perhaps she just wants a sense of the place?" Rachel suggests.

"I suppose. But what direction am I meant to point the camera in? I might be completely off the mark. Would you want a photograph of it if you couldn't get here?"

"Yes. I might," she replies. "Just to know the lay of the land, so that I could imagine it correctly."

He wonders what Miss Esme Stewart imagines. He looks down at the scabbed slope and considers whether he ought to show it to her at its worst, or whether to try to select kinder angles. Would it be kindness to show Rachel the image on his camera? Could he not be completely off the mark there too?

"You've been working farther east?" she asks.

"Northeast of here. I was in Epéhy yesterday. Four years ago I thought that I might never leave there. I was injured there," he clarifies as he looks up at Rachel. "It was quite sobering to go back."

"And who would be visiting your grave?"

"I don't know." He considers: Would Edie make that journey? Would she have come to look for him? Would it have mattered to her to know the lay of that land? "But instead I ended up on an ambulance train back to England."

"Come on," says Rachel, leading him toward the top of the ridge.

A family is having a picnic at the top. They have laid out a blanket and are passing sandwiches and a thermos flask. A man in pin-striped trousers is pointing. The children look bored. There are circles of sweat under the father's pointing arms.

"There's going to be a Canadian memorial up here," she says. "I've read about it. They've launched a competition to design a monument."

Harry thinks about Gabriel, once again struck by the enormity of the task of designing a memorial, of capturing and commemorating an experience in stone, to be seen for miles and forevermore. It seems so much more epic than framing it in a camera lens.

"That's quite a responsibility," he says.

They walk along the top of the ridge. The children behind them are now tumbling and giggling over a game of leapfrog. The father is still pointing. Harry circles, taking photographs until the film comes to an end.

"This heat," she says.

They sit down and take in the view. Harry leans back, into the sharp grass, and shuts his eyes to the glare. The camera is heavy on his chest and the white light throbs through his closed eyes. He is very aware of the image of the wreath maker inside his camera. How can a chemical reaction between light and silver salts be such a weighty thing?

"You'll get sunburnt," says Rachel's voice. "I can see you sizzling. I can almost *hear* you sizzling. You'll be like a lobster by this evening."

A headache is beginning to throb. He feels slightly too large for his own skin. "Is a lobster better than a weasel?"

He sits up and she hands him a bottle of lemonade, apologizing for the fact that it's not cold. It hits the back of his parched throat, sweet and sharp. Rachel wipes the top of the bottle before she puts it to her own lips. Did his lips really once touch hers? Did he really dream the scene in his hotel room? He's not quite sure that his memory hasn't perhaps started to play tricks. A horse-drawn cart struggles to the top of the slope and sets up selling ice-cream wafers.

"The things you can buy on a battlefield these days."

He shelters the camera under his jacket while he changes over the film. As he puts the used roll in his pocket he is very conscious of the face of the man imprinted on it.

"You look furtive," observes Rachel.

"Just keeping it out of the sun. If the light gets in it will all just disappear."

"It seems almost callous that the sun should shine, doesn't it?" Rachel asks.

"Almost cruel. It's not weather for loss or regret. If only the light could make it all disappear."

"Will you show me your photograph of David again?"

He's unsure about the wisdom of his words as soon as they're out of his mouth. Rachel looks at him, as if measuring the question.

"Yes." She reaches into her bag. "Why?" She holds the card out toward him. He knows that her fingers won't release until he has given her an answer.

"I'm traveling a lot. I'm seeing a lot of faces."

Her fingers let go. She nods as if his answer makes sufficient sense. "Of course."

It is a much younger man in the photograph. He would like to compare this image side by side with the one of Daniel East. There is some similarity around the eyes. He is not sure that it is enough, though. He looks up at Rachel. It's not enough.

"Thank you." He hands her the photograph back and watches as she smiles at the young man's face. Her left hand abstractedly plucks at daisies.

"I'm the one who should be saying thank you."

They walk on and he photographs the

country below. Where within that stretching plain is Captain Albert Stewart? Will he ever surface and point out landmarks for his sister? Will his features ever turn up on a stranger's photographic film? A couple are picnicking in the shade of one of the shell holes. At first he is careful to keep them out of his shot, but then he finds his lens focusing in on them. The girl is laughing as the man gently places a daisy chain around her neck.

"I would rather see him in a shell hole with another woman than not ever see him again at all."

He turns to Rachel. She is shielding the sun from her eyes with her hand. Are there tears in the shadow of her hand?

"Sometimes when I wake up he's breathing at my side. Just for a moment. I hear his footsteps on the floor above. I smell his cigarette when I walk into a room. I just can't believe that I'll never see him again."

Harry shakes his head. "I'm sorry."

"I used to smell his shirt collars, you know. That's stupid, isn't it? I've never admitted that to anyone before. I could breathe him in, though — bring him close. But now he's fading. Now he's barely there."

Harry thinks about a pair of pale eyes caught on his camera film and imagines them fading. He wants to give that news to her, wants to bring David close, but he's not certain that he can hand her that fragile hope.

"Oh, I nearly forgot — your handkerchief. I had it laundered."

He looks down at Francis's embroidered initials.

"Your journey hasn't crossed with your sister-in-law's?"

"No."

"You should try to contact her."

"It's been four weeks since I received her postcard. I don't know where she is. She might be at home again by now."

"Write to her there, then. Telephone her."

"To say . . . ?"

"You told me about going back to the place you were injured. How you thought for a moment that might be your end. Did you think of her on that day?"

"Yes," he eventually replies.

"Tell her that."

CHAPTER THIRTY-THREE: HARRY

Canal Wood, east of Epéhy, Somme, August 1917

It hit just to the rear. Earth leapt up and showered over them. Harry leant against the wall of the jumping-off trench and listened to it all falling down.

"Two minutes," said Captain Wear. He peered at the luminous face of his wrist-watch.

It was all that Harry could see, the glow of the watch hands and then flashing in the sky. They hadn't expected the incoming shelling. There had been no preliminary wire-cutting, Captain Wear had been telling them ten minutes earlier, as they didn't want to give any indication of a planned raid. Did this bombardment signify that they knew anyway?

"Official report is that the wire is thin. The barrage is going to roll forward and we just follow it through. All right? The wire

298

isn't going to be an issue."

"I do have a bit of a personal issue with getting strafed," said Pembridge under his breath.

"At least there's no moon."

"This war has made me hate the moon," said Jones, "its dozy great silvery beams. Big silvery-beamed bastard."

Harry felt the earth jolt. "How long?"

"Thirty seconds."

". . . Loving Jesus, gentle lamb, in thy gracious hands I am . . ." Nicholson's voice quavered as he worked through the rhymes of a childhood prayer.

"Jesus, I wish you wouldn't do that."

Another explosion hit just behind. Harry pushed his fingers into the earth. He could hear the rapid whistle of Nicholson's breath to his left.

"You know the routine, right?" said Corporal Wright. "In and out. Get an identity if you can, but really this is just a diversion. Is that understood?"

"Have these, Blythe," said Lieutenant Redmond. Harry felt a pair of wire cutters — the weight and the cold of the metal — placed in his hand. They had blackened their faces and he could just see the here-and-there glimmer of the whites of the lieutenant's eyes.

"But I thought —"

"Just take them."

With another lurch of the earth, Harry felt Redmond's hand momentarily grip his shoulder. He tasted blood in his mouth and realized that he had bitten his lip.

"All right, lads. Keep low. Keep quiet."

He saw Captain Wear's profile as he clambered over. Harry heard his own heart racing.

The land sloped down toward the canal, which was a ribbon of light. Between here and the canal was just clotted darkness, dense and entirely quiet now.

They slid out on their bellies. He could smell the wet grass. There was dampness and roots under his hands. He pushed his fingers into the soft cold.

"Straight forwards," hissed Redmond's whisper.

Harry felt a stone push against his rib cage. His fingers pulled back from the shock of something sharp.

"Where's that barrage?" asked Pembridge.

It started before the end of his question. Suddenly the valley below was all alight. Harry felt the earth beneath him quake as the light leapt. Like white paint thrown at a black canvas, it splattered and stretched. Smoke billowed into the sky and the valley below was full of a flickering phosphorescence that looked almost supernatural. It was completely contrary to instinct, it was an anathema, it was absurd, to crawl toward this rending light, but, to left and to right, they were scuttling, creeping, running forward. His fast breath and startled eyes told him that this was madness, but Harry's feet were on the slope of the hill and now dashing down.

The barrage boomed across again, beyond their wire now. The sky seemed to churn with it. The star shells stretched, white trajectories sliding back into the black. It looked like it was burning beyond. The canal was now lost in smoke. He could see the posts and the wire silhouetted against the white.

The ordered silence was forgotten now as they stumbled down the slope. Harry couldn't see the men around him, but he could hear their ragged breath, their oaths and prayers. There was a roar rising from their feet and from their mouths. He staggered in the soft, unseen earth, but they were pushing on as one and plunging toward the enemy wire.

The barrage came down again. Louder now. Throwing him off his feet. The earth kicked up under him and white light ripped across. It looked like the sky was tearing ahead. Fragments screeched through the air. He could feel the heat of it, the searing wind on his face, the smell of hot metal. Particles of earth flew up, seeming to fluoresce as they fell.

"It's gone forward too fast," said a voice that was almost a yelp in the black. When Harry looked back, all that he could see was an echo of the shape of a starburst, like the bright light had burnt itself onto his retina. His eyes ached.

It looked like a fairy thing ahead, the glitter and intricacy of it, like some web spun from mischief to catch mortals. It looked like that only for an instant. They were plunging toward the wire. It slid into focus now, the pickets and the web in between, all too real and thick and intact. The sky lit again and Harry looked forward into the belts of wire. He heard the blood pump through his head with a roaring beat. He felt his body accelerate, his rhythms run awry, as if his body were betraying him. He was suddenly vulnerable within himself and he gasped, full of fear as he fell.

"Keep down!" a warning voice bellowed as rifle bullets zipped toward them; they left behind lines of hanging light that cut through the wire. Lots of them were cutting through the wire now.

"How are we supposed to . . . ?"

"For fuck's sake!"

Harry heard teeth chattering, a fragment of prayer, and a metallic clatter that came to him through his fingers as much as his ears. Their hands were on the wire, pulling, clambering, clawing at it. Cutters were working, rifles trying to push it down. To his left a figure leapt forward, running at it, plunging and then convulsing.

A shell hit just behind. Theirs now. It sent them all rearing up and thrown onto the tangled trap. Harry's clippers were working. The wire tore at him as he cut. Its barbs were yanking at his sleeves and scratching at his wrists. He could see that his hands were sticky. He pulled the wire apart, inched forward, and began again.

"In and out, eh?" a humorless voice to his side asked with a laugh.

Shells were landing behind again and he found himself facedown in the wire. It was stuck in his puttees and his tunic and his sleeves now. He felt like a fly in a spider's web. It pulled and cut against him when he tried to move. The white arcs of bullets fizzed through the darkness. In the shell light he stared at the clippers in his hand. How could he ever cut his way out of this?

The last thing he saw, as the earth plunged up, was Pembridge's face at his side. There were tears on his cheeks. Then it was all convulsing up underneath him, like the wire had an energy of its own, the brambles and the pickets lashing and writhing. He heard the wire whip and felt it rush all around him. His legs were wet and the whistling light rushed to white.

CHAPTER THIRTY-FOUR: HARRY

Péronne, Somme, August 1921

Harry isn't accustomed to lingering on his own reflection, but today something has changed. Today he walked back down the field toward the canal. Four years ago the doctor had told him that he would always have fragments of shrapnel inside him; was it just a fancy this afternoon that, returning to the place where it had entered his body, he had felt all those metal fragments tingle? Was it some strange magnetism, or just the memory that had made him tremble? His knees had buckled on the slope, it had all rushed back, and he had crouched down in the place where the belts of barbed wire once were, and rocked with his arms around his knees; but then he had got up and walked on. He looks at his arms in the mirror. The scars are white now where the wire lashed around him. The skin is still puckered on his stomach where they stitched him back together. The hotel mirror has a long crack across it; it is in as sorry a state as he is, Harry considers. But, like him, it is still here.

He can hear the couple talking in the room above. All of the plaster has fallen from the ceiling, leaving only floorboards overhead. The male voice says that the sanitary arrangements are like "Japan in the old days"; she says that she is going to write a letter to the paper when they get back to Basingstoke. They agree: the standard of accommodation isn't at all like Bournemouth. Harry smiles. Small showers of plaster follow their footsteps. He watches, over his mirrored shoulder, as they progress across the room. Billows sigh from the ceiling and dust skitters across the pages of the photograph album.

It is still open on the bed. He turned through its pages when he got back here, but he cannot annotate the images after August 1917 for Edie, and he will never know if he has put them in exactly the correct chronological order. Francis had photographed trophies from the trench raid while Harry was in the casualty clearing station. He wonders whether his brother had known, as he was taking those photographs, that he'd been injured. On the next pages of the album there are pictures of the vegetable gardens that they had cultivated through September in the deserted village behind, a bunch of flowers in a dugout, and a length of dusty road. At the end of September the battalion had come to this town. Harry, though, has never been here before, has never seen these things. He can't write dates and locations underneath these photographs because he wasn't there. He buttons his shirt and steps out into the evening.

A breeze has got up and he pulls his jacket around him. When the wind blows, everything seems to rattle; the scaffolds shake, the tin roofs hum, and the tarpaulins lash. His guidebook tells him that, in the Middle Ages, this was a proud fortified city, with important ramparts and moats. In Francis's photographs it is all fallen down. It had all been dynamited. Nissen huts have now been constructed around what was the central square, and everything is patched and impermanent, but he sees signs that that long-ago pride has not been entirely crushed. Today the town seems to be almost entirely inhabited by workmen. The rubble is being cleared away and new bricks are rising. There is a lot of energy and determination and noise. Péronne clearly means to come back.

He orders a beer in a bar and remembers the piece of wire in his pocket. A three-inch-or-so fragment, twisted and rusted and looking like a relic from the Middle Ages, it was all that he could find. The field had been plowed and green lines of wheat were showing. He had walked between those green rows looking for an indication that he was in the right place, but this scrap was all that remained of the old barbed wire. There were just the clean new shoots and the canal peacefully glimmering below. Perhaps it was walking back down that slope, completing that journey, or seeing Bartley's grave, or the fact that the wire had gone, but he feels a strangely powerful sense of being alive tonight. It seems to fizz in his veins. He feels more than the sum of his broken parts, and for the first time he feels that he might truly be lucky. Like Péronne, he feels determined. He leaves coins — and the wire — on the table.

"Are you in Spain yet?" Edie's voice on the telephone sounds very distant.

"Spain?"

"Only your postcards seem to be getting farther away. I looked on a map. You're going south."

"Just following orders. I'm heading back

north again this week."

"And talking of postcards, your mail is building up here. People keep sending you cards at this address. I'm not your secretary, you know."

He laughs. "I apologize. I'll give you a tip at Christmas. Anyway, you're at home! I was fully expecting that the telephone would ring out again. I've kept calling and just thought I'd take another chance."

"I only got back here yesterday."

"Did you find anything? How far did you make it?"

The line goes silent for a moment, then crackles, and he thinks he's lost her, but then her voice is back again.

"Not far enough. Not as far as I intended. Listen, Harry, can I ask you something?"

"Yes?"

"It's a big something."

He hears her hesitation. "Go on."

"Is there any possibility that you could be in Ypres on Friday?"

"This Friday? Yes, I suppose so. Why?"

"Because, as I said, I didn't get as far as I intended."

"I'm sorry?"

"If you'll be in Ypres, then I will be."

He sits on the curb and lights a cigarette.

Men are playing billiards in one of the bars and their ease and laughter spill out of the windows. A waiter weaves between the café tables, a tray stacked with glasses carried high and confident in his hand. A girl in a white dress turns and smiles as he places her drink down. With the thought of seeing Edie again, it's all pushing through Harry's veins too fast, like all his chemicals have gone slightly off-kilter; he doesn't feel to be quite in control of his own body. He breathes in the smoke and the laughter and the warm breeze. He counts his breaths. But when he opens his eyes again he sees that the cigarette in his hand is shaking.

"I found an old photograph of Denham Hall recently. A postcard. You sent it to me. I want to see you," she had said on the telephone.

He throws the cigarette away and walks back through the early evening streets. The shape of a tank looms in a corner of the square. A plaque has been attached to it informing the onlooker (in three languages) that it is a gift from an English town and a war memorial. A gang of children are chasing around it. He stops to take a photograph and the children grin and wave at the camera. The tank might as well be a lump of stone.

"I want to see you. And there is a place that I need to visit," she had said.

He wants to see her too, he craves seeing her, but the thought of why she needs to meet him in Ypres, and what that implies, leaves him with so many difficult questions. Did she really see something significant in that photograph of Francis? Could there really be some clue that he has missed?

"Where?" he had asked.

"I'll tell you when I get there."

Her voice had gone. The line was dead. But he had stood there still with the telephone receiver pressed against his ear. Just for a moment he had allowed himself to remember her dancing in a garden four years ago. The smell of a summer evening. Reflections in a lake. The grip of her hand on his arm. But then her voice was asking him to meet her in Ypres. Needing to visit Ypres.

His own mirror face startles him as he steps back into the hotel room. For a second the reflection in the glass is his brother's. Francis's eyes. The shape of his mouth.

"I'll come back and haunt you," says Francis's faraway and all-too-close voice.

CHAPTER THIRTY-FIVE:
HARRY

*Denham Hall Military Hospital, Cheshire,
   August 1917*

Harry wanted to tell her to sit still. He wanted to draw her just as she was in this instant, but his hands were bandaged up and she was walking down the ward saying, "Good afternoon," to each bedstead that she passed. It struck him that she was completely unaware of how they stared after her. He wanted to tell her that it wasn't the way to behave. It wasn't the way it was done. But still he couldn't help but smile as she walked toward him.

"You look ghastly," Edie said.

"Thank you."

Harry tried to remember how long it was since he had last seen her. Almost two years? Her skin was very white and her hair dark red. She was not soft and sensuous, like a redhead in a Rossetti painting, he considered, but she was handsome. She was wearing a knitted green beret over her red hair. There were blue shadows under her eyes.

"Does it hurt?"

"I'm full of medication. Can't you hear me rattle when I move?"

"The doctor says you're full of metal." She took the beret off. Her fingers played with the comb in her hair.

"But only small pieces. I shan't go around trailing magnets or get rusty if I go out in the rain."

"That's a mercy," she said. "May I?"

"Please."

She took the chair next to his bed and curled her long limbs around. Did she realize, Harry wondered, that every man in the room was watching her?

"I cut you flowers from the garden. Larkspur. Do you remember?" She held the bunch out for him to smell. "I thought that it might be horrid in here, that it might need cheering up, but it's like a palace."

"Isn't it? Almost worth having a few stitches for, eh?"

She put the flowers on the bedside table. The stems were wrapped in a newspaper headline that pronounced stormy weather in France and Flanders. She picked up the novel at his bedside.

"Tess of the d'Urbervilles?"

313

"I like a tragic heroine," he said.

"Dear me. I bought you this as well." She reached into her bag and handed him a tissue-wrapped parcel.

"A book?"

"Open it, then."

The marbled-paper cover was the softest blues and browns and hints of pink and looked like the paint had been stirred with a feather. He ran his fingers over the leather spine. "It's beautiful."

"It doesn't contain any tragic heroines, I'm afraid. It's a sketchbook. A proper one. Francis says that you're always scrounging around for scraps of paper. Well, there's plenty to go at there. Full of pristine white paper for you to spoil."

"Thank you. It must have cost you a lot of money. That's tremendously kind."

"Hand it back to me one day full of pictures."

"I shall. I will put your picture on the first page."

"If I'd known you'd do that I might not have given it to you." She stared at his hand on the book. "You'll be all right, though? You haven't hurt your hands badly?"

"Only cuts."

She nodded, smiled briefly, and looked away.

He watched her as she looked around the room, seeing the now-familiar walls anew through Edie's eyes. The rows of plain beds were rather at odds with the grandeur of the plasterwork ceiling. Ferguson, in the next bed, picked at his blanket and stared at Edie from behind. His hands looked clawlike, Harry thought, as if the tendons had shrunk. Sometimes Ferguson's clawlike hands beckoned at him when he wanted to talk. His voice was a thin thing and sounded as if it came from very far within him. His lips seemed to want to stick together, seemed, with a glistening whiteness, to want to glue in his words. Harry had to lean in close to hear, but Ferguson's too-close words smelled sour. He was starting to dread the beckon of Ferguson's fingers. He watched him watch Edie now and then suddenly Ferguson's eyes flicked and connected with his own. Did he wink? Did he really just see Ferguson wink? Harry felt a rush of affronted protectiveness. He wanted to get out of the bed and hit Ferguson, whether his lungs were rotten or not.

"I'm not sure that the flowery bedspreads are entirely soldierly," Edie said.

He refocused on her face. "The firmness of this mattress is appropriately military."

"It is very nice to see you, even pale and

315

bedraggled and bandaged." Edie looked at her hands in her lap.

"We should do this more often."

She looked up. "Please, not in these circumstances."

The sunlight made bright rectangles on the parquet. Johnson in the bed across was snoring. The smell of the larkspur was making Harry slightly nauseous. He felt Edie's blue-green gaze on his face. It prickled on his skin.

"It's terribly quiet in here," she said. "They're all listening, aren't they? It makes me feel noisy and clumsy and indiscreet — like everything that I'm saying is a pronouncement on a stage."

"Isn't it? I can't stand the quiet. I am glad of your noisy indiscretions."

In truth, when it was quiet he could still hear the roar of the incoming shell. Its echo seemed to have got stuck in his head, as if it were ricocheting in his skull. In his dreams the wire was still writhing around him.

"You're jittery," she observed.

"What makes you say that?"

She nodded to the matchbox that he was turning between his bandaged fingers. "Fidget."

"Sorry. My springs are all wound up tight and it takes a while to remember how to relax, but I'll get there." He rattled the matchbox and put it down. Ferguson was still staring.

"Forgiven."

"Do you think that we might go for a walk? I've been glowering at the same ceiling for a fortnight. They'll trust me not to topple over if you're here to mind me."

"Lord, do you topple? Are you well enough to walk?"

"I'm actually A1," he said in a stage whisper. "I just secretly like hospital food and nurses' uniforms."

Harry passed commentary on the walls as they walked along the picture-lined corridor. They walked through earnest Victoriana, grand tours, and seascapes. His identifying finger pointed out Dutch landscapes, mild-faced Madonnas, and the Battle of Balaclava. The door of the red room was open at the far end. He was conscious of not wanting to lean on her too heavily. The effort of it left him slightly breathless.

"You're doing very well," she said.

He stared down at his arm through hers. It struck him that this was the most physically intimate moment that they had ever shared, or were possibly ever likely to. He wished the corridor longer.

"Had I known that you were invalided in an art gallery, I wouldn't have felt sorry for you."

"What luck, eh? It's all downhill from now, isn't it? This might just be the best day of my life."

She squeezed his arm and looked away.

Three years earlier he had talked about the future with Edie. He had told her that he had applied to the college, about the bright and bold marks that he meant to make on canvas. He told her things that he had never dared to say to anyone else before and she had encouraged his ambitions. She had let him talk and it had all seemed possible.

"I might lean against the door for a minute. Would you mind?"

He watched her walk ahead of him into the red room. They were all new paintings in here, a collection of canvases that the family had bought in the south of France just before the war, all hot southern intensity. There were yellow mountains and blue trees, houses that thrust crystalline, precipitating from the sea, and bacchic dancers curling arabesques. He watched Edie's fingertips extend, testing texture, looking back at him to check that she wasn't doing the wrong thing. He took in all the details

318

so that he might draw her later. There was a vase of white roses on the fireplace. The smell of the white roses filled the red room.

"Is this what France is like?"

"Not the parts that I've seen yet."

"Very bright, isn't it? Violently bright. It makes my eyes hurt. I think that I might have a permanent headache if I had to live with these pictures, or in this place."

"They make my eyes hungry," he said.

"You must think that you've bounced out of the down-below place and ricocheted up into Paradise." She looked back at him over her shoulder.

He put his arm out toward her. "If I cling on to you, will you help me not to bounce back down?"

There was a crowd out on the back steps in hospital blues and dressing gowns, with newspapers and novels and the ears of the family's dog requiring attention. They smiled into the sun and passed cigarettes. It was only the lean of crutches and the white of bandages that compromised the idyll. The men moved apart as Edie linked him down the steps.

"When you've perambulated Blythe, will you do me, miss?"

"How did he manage that?"

"Would you like to polish my medals, miss? I've a Victoria Cross in my trouser pocket."

Edie laughed as they walked toward the lake. "Good God. Is that the plucky Tommy's saucy badinage?"

"You don't know the half of it."

They sat on a bench and looked out over the water. Edie plucked a daisy and pulled its petals away. The reflection of the house shivered in the lake. He skimmed a stone toward it.

"Loves me or loves me not?"

"I didn't count." Her chin tilted as she smiled. "You do look a bit peaky in the daylight. Am I not meant to put a blanket over you, or some such?"

"Never ever think of training as a nurse."

She wrinkled her nose as she passed him a bag of sweets. "Licorice rock. See, I'm good for something. They told me that you're doing well — that you're making excellent progress."

"I am. It's not nearly as bad as it looks."

"Trust you to make an almighty fuss over a bit of a cut. Do you think you'll be here for long?"

"No. Not at all. The major told me this morning that they'll have me back in France before September is out. I honestly think that he expected me to give a cheer."

She pointed at the fleeting glimmer of a
dragonfly. Sitting here, with just the noise
of the ducks and the pleasant chatter behind, it was difficult to believe that France
existed.

"Maybe you should stop making such
excellent progress?" she suggested.

He looked at her. Backlit by the sun, she
had a bright silhouette.

"What?"

"You're all fiery around the edges. You
look like a star shell."

"You do talk nonsense, Harry."

Coleman had brought the gramophone
out onto the steps again and Italian arias
were crackling across the garden. Caruso
was singing something about dying despair-
ingly. Pickering was miming along with the
music, making exaggerated arm gestures.
"Oh, dear me," said Edie.

"Have you heard from Francis?" he asked.
Not speaking his brother's name extended
the spell, but eventually he had to say it. "I
sent him a postcard but I've had no reply."

"Yes. They've made him a lance corporal.
Would you believe it? Apparently he covered
himself in glory in this little show of yours."

"A lance corporal? Frannie? Good God."

"I'm sure that he'll love giving you orders

when you get back. He's got leave, as well. This is what you get for being a good boy, you see. You should try it. He thinks that he might get home for a few days in September."

"You don't look particularly pleased."

"Of course I'm pleased."

Pickering was now conducting the choir as the men on the steps sang the chorus. Edie looked back and laughed, but when she turned toward Harry all the light had gone out in her face.

"How is he?"

"Francis?"

She nodded.

"Muddling along — as much as anyone else is. You know what he's like: it's never easy to know what Francis is thinking. Or, at least, when I try to read him I always seem to get it wrong. You'd think that we'd speak the same language, wouldn't you? He writes to you, doesn't he?"

"I get pages full of words but they don't really say anything. It's almost the same letter every time, like it's a formula that he feels he has to send me. The same phrases. The same sentiments. The same not-quite-convincing cheeriness. Oh, I know that I shouldn't complain. He's kind, he's caring, he never criticizes, but it's like the model letter that a soldier ought to send his wife, and I can't hear Francis's voice in it. Like he's disappearing. Slipping away. The voice in his letters isn't that of the man who I lived with. It could be from anyone and I worry about that. You write to me more often than he does and I open your letters with more relish. That's awful, isn't it?"

"Yes. You're a terrible woman. I shall endeavor to send you duller letters. In fact, as you're such a perfidious floozy, I might stop writing to you altogether."

"Please don't," she said. "But he is all right?"

"He is. Don't worry. He's just ready for a break. He needs a rest. Coming home on leave will do him good."

"I do hope you're right."

Phrases of music seemed to hang over the water, as the mist clung to the lake in the mornings. The sun was warm on the back of his neck. A breath of air shifted a strand of hair across Edie's cheek.

"Ever wish that you could just hold your breath and make it all stop — make it all stand still?"

"Yes. Right at this instant," she replied.

The reflection of the house, bright in the early evening light, had the heightened color of an illustration from a child's book. It looked like something that might disappear at any moment.

"Is it always like this?" She turned toward him. "I expected to be visiting some grimly sober institution. I was braced for gray wards and the smell of antiseptic. I expected to feel sorry for you, but I can't remotely."

"Not even slightly? Not even for having to suffer sentimental tenors? Do you know how much light operatic we must endure?"

"Poor Harry!"

"It's agony. Can't you possibly summon up enough pity to dance with me?"

She smiled slowly as she stood and offered him her hand. "I'm only doing this for the war effort."

They danced just there on the lawn. Turning slowly. Feet faltering to the uncertain notes. The men on the steps whistled and shouted as they spun, but Harry didn't hear them at all. He held on to her and the rest of it spun away. Edie shut her eyes and leaned her head back as she laughed. The flat of her hand was between his shoulder blades. Her laughing mouth was just inches from his own.

"What?" she said, as she opened her eyes and looked back at him.

He leaned the side of his head against hers and could feel her breathing. He breathed in her smell of soap and licorice, and the swoop of the orchestra strings, and wanted to tell her that he had never felt more exquisitely happy or more sad.

Harry walked her back along the driveway. He ought to talk to her, he felt, ought to keep it light and bright and her entertained, but he struggled even to find airy words now that she was leaving. The roses, along the path, had passed their best. The petals of the poppies had blown. He named lilies and foxgloves and delphiniums because of the need to keep on speaking, to keep on sharing, to have her eyes lift and meet his. He pointed out seed heads and leaf shapes and gave her the Latin names, all of these details already like a memory. He told her about the palm house and the fern garden and the espaliered apricot trees. Harry filled the space between them with all of these things, so that he didn't have to tell her about the other places. So that her eyes were only full of the images that he had selected to show her. So that he didn't have to speak Francis's name again.

"I keep thinking about Will," she said suddenly. "I remember you having handstand races down Rochdale Road and then having to pick glass out of your palms. I remember the three of you getting slung out of the Black Horse for horseplay and Will always saying that Francis had started it. I remember Francis coming home and saying that he'd signed up and then knowing with absolute certainty that you and Will would too. Because it always *was* Francis who started it. I can't imagine the two of you out there without Will. Everything must be out of balance. I fear for the two of you now."

He remembered Francis by Will's grave. He had held up his hands, like a gesture of capitulation, and Harry had noticed that the creases of his palms were picked out in brick dust. He had looked at Harry and then looked away. Something had changed in that instant.

"We'll watch each other's backs now," Harry assured her.

"Will you?"

"As much as we can."

"Why doesn't that fill me with confidence?"

What was it that he had seen in Edie's eyes at that moment? As she stopped and turned toward him, she looked as if she were about to say more, but then had changed her mind.

"What?"

She shook her head. "Just be careful, eh?"

They carried on up the driveway. He watched their side-by-side feet on the gravel and felt a great weight of unsayable words.

"Here," she said, her footsteps stopping abruptly. "I want you to have this." She pulled a ribbon over her head and handed it to him.

"What it is?"

"It's a Saint Christopher. It was my grandmother's. She believed it was lucky."

"I wondered what the ribbon was. I haven't seen you wearing it before."

"I didn't. I haven't. It's been quite a year, though, hasn't it? I'm not sure that I believe in luck, but I figured that it was worth a chance."

"You can't give me this."

"Yes, I can. It's mine to do with as I choose, and I choose to give it to you. I can't vouch for its luck-delivering properties, but it can't do any harm, can it?"

"No." He looked at the gray metallic medal in his palm. The ribbon was still warm. He closed his fingers around it. "I want to say something to you. If I don't say it now, I might never say it."

She looked down as she shook her head. "Harry —"

"I am permitted to make a fool of myself

327

because I might die tomorrow."

"Tomorrow? In Altrincham?"

"I'm not being literal."

"You are being dramatic." Edie pushed her hair behind her ears and put the beret back on. She smiled at him and widened her eyes. "You might not die tomorrow, and then what a fool would you feel?"

"Edie, please, let me be serious."

"No, because you will say something that you regret. And then I will say things that I regret."

"Will you?"

"I have to get my bus," she said. "Saint Christopher protects travelers. Now you'll always be able to find your way back to me, won't you?"

"I will. You know I always will."

"Don't really stop writing to me, will you?"

"How could I? I promise: I won't ever stop."

CHAPTER THIRTY-SIX: HARRY

Talbot House, Poperinghe, September 1921

Location image order: Mr. & Mrs. Reeth
would like photographs of the garden of
Talbot House, Poperinghe. Sgt. Claude
Reeth (23765) was decl. missing
28/11/17. He had last written to his
parents from this location.

What did Sergeant Reeth see here? What did he put in a letter to his parents? Did he send them the shrub roses and potted geraniums and the monkey-puzzle tree? Did he send them the sound of the wood pigeons, the bumblebees, and the church bells? Harry rewinds and corrects himself; he remembers that there weren't church bells, then; there was eastward grumble of the guns. He considers what Mr. and Mrs. Reeth would like to see. He considers whether Sergeant Reeth's last letter — like

Harry's lens — composed well-meaning lies. Did he tell them about the smell of the larkspur?

The garden is full of birdsong on this afternoon four years on. Calla lilies are flowering in pots and there are salad greens coming on under cold frames. Chickens scratch on the gravel footpath and a woman is singing as she scrubs the tiles in the summerhouse. The scent of the lilac is heady. He sits down on a bench and watches the trees' dappled light shift on the lawn. The monkey-puzzle makes sharp-toothed shadows.

"If it had been me, would you write to Edie?" Francis had asked. And, of course, he had. Harry tries to remember what he had said, what kind and polite form of words he had framed that news in. She had sent him back letters that were full of questions, demanding details that he couldn't supply. She had wanted him to go back over the ground. She had wanted to come out to Belgium herself. Did she not understand what it was like? There were lots of letters in those weeks, and then fewer. In the winter of 1918, their exchange of envelopes had just ended. Not a word had passed between them — not a word for over a year — until he had seen a girl that looked like her on another station and found himself boarding a train heading north. In all that silent time had she been going over those same questions? And, if so, why hadn't she spoken out and asked him to help her before? What had prompted the need for a photograph of a grave? What had made her need for the truth suddenly urgent? Was it the anonymity of the envelope containing Francis's photograph? Did she really picture Francis posting it to her?

A blackbird hops across the lawn. It tilts its head to one side, listening for worms. Very carefully, with slow controlled movements, he reaches for the camera. Wings flap away with the click of the shutter. His image will be a blur of feathers.

They had passed through the station here on the same day, he and Francis. He was coming back as Francis was going home. "Like a couple on a weather house," he had said. It had been raining in Poperinghe that day. Was Sergeant Reeth here at the same time? Was his last letter full of dripping trees? He has spoken to Mrs. Reeth on the telephone, and heard the sadness in her voice as she told him how happy her son had sounded in his last letter. Harry wishes now that he had asked her more about the details in that letter, so that he may match his photographs up with Claude Reeth's words, so that he may give his mother some proof of the sincerity of that happiness, and in turn perhaps take away some of her sadness.

The sun makes shifting patterns through the branches onto an empty bench. White roses glow in the shadows behind and light glints on wet paving stones. He commits it to film, thinking as he does so of the alchemy of chemistry and light and its capacity to capture an instant, a chemical reaction making the scene in front of him forevermore. The face of Daniel East is still in his pocket. What reaction will that caught instant set off? Will it trigger happiness or sadness? He means to develop the film when he gets the chance. Then, when he sees the wreath weaver's face again, when he has had the chance to test it against his memory of David West's photo, he will make a decision whether to write to Rachel. His shutter clicks on the shadows of the beech trees, on the bark of the silver birch, and on the two men at the bottom of the garden playing cards across a table. He means to give Mr. and Mrs. Reeth a peaceful forevermore image that might perhaps echo something in their son's last letter, that might perhaps bring them some peace.

Harry is struck by both the permanence and the fragility of the scene in front of him.

Standing next to Francis on the station platform, he had been very conscious of the red ribbon around his neck. Did he really have cause to feel guilty? It was hardly a betrayal of his brother. He can still remember the texture of it, the feel of her placing it in his hand. He can still see Edie pulling it over her own head, smiling through her hair. "For luck," she said. Would it have changed Francis's luck if he had passed it to his brother that day? Harry isn't sure that he believes in luck either. He wonders where the ribbon is now. Has it too survived somewhere?

A man is raking the gravel paths. He touches his hat to Harry as he passes. A gramophone is playing inside the white house. The windows are open and a curtain billows out. The carillon bells are ringing. He wishes that he could send it all to Mr. and Mrs. Reeth.

CHAPTER THIRTY-SEVEN:
HARRY

Poperinghe station, September 1917
"Frannie!"

Harry saw his brother from across the station. He had clambered up on top of a wagon and was angling his lens down at the men on the platform. There was a great crowd of them, all flourishing their leave papers at Francis's camera. He put his thumb up and the crowd erupted into a cheer.

"He wants to be careful with that. He's going to find himself in a bother." Pembridge was leaning against a railing. His grin spread as Harry turned toward him.

"Jack! Bloody hell, it's good to see you." He took Pembridge's extended arm and grabbed him into a hug.

"You look well, Harry. They stitched you tidily back together?"

"A few souvenir scars but otherwise as good as new. You got leave too?"

334

Pembridge held up his white paper.

"Lucky sod."

"He needs it." Pembridge nodded toward Francis. He was just clambering down from the wagon. Harry waved toward him.

"When did you move up here?"

"Only a couple of days ago. We were west of Arras for a fortnight, being prepared for 'conditions prevailing in the Passchendaele sector.' " He made quotation marks with his fingers and an officerly voice.

"And in English?"

"Mud. We've had a lot of lectures about looking after our feet."

It was just coming on to rain again. The crowd of men was quickly dispersing. Harry stepped back under the shelter. A transport column was grinding its way up the road behind. Rain glistened off the roofs. "Where's the camp?"

"Up to the northwest. It's pretty lively. Supply depots and munitions dumps all around. They've started shelling it. The roads are something to see. It's like Piccadilly Circus."

"Have you ever been to Piccadilly Circus, Pembridge?"

Harry turned around as he heard his brother's voice. Rain was coursing off his cap.

"Francis." They shook hands. "It's good to see you."

"It was nose to nose on the road as we came in. Rather be heading in our direction than yours."

Harry was struck by how much older Francis looked. There were new hollows in his cheeks, and his eyes seemed to have shrunken back. When Francis put a cigarette to his lips Harry noticed how ingrained the dirt had become in Francis's fingers. For an instant he thought of those fingers on Edie's white throat.

"New camera?"

"It was Rose's."

"He doesn't give me photographic equipment," complained Pembridge. "He gave me latrine duty last week."

Harry laughed. "You've got ten days?"

"Aye," Francis replied. "I might not get out of bed."

He imagined Francis, a few hours on, sitting across the table from Edie. He imagined Francis's hands in her hair. He imagined them in the same bed. "Give Edie my regards," he said.

"I will." Francis's eyes met his own for the first time. "Did you see her?"

Harry was suddenly very aware of Edie's ribbon around his own throat. Had Francis seen it? "Edie?"

Francis nodded.

He felt the weight of his brother's assessing eye. "She came to see me once at the hospital. She brought me in a bunch of flowers and a bag of licorice rock, but she ate them herself — the sweets, not the flowers, that is."

Pembridge laughed. Francis looked at the railway lines.

"Get a feed in town before you go back," said Pembridge. "You can buy anything here."

"Send us a postcard," said Francis.

" 'Wish you were here'?"

"Hardly."

"We'd better go and get our train."

"You do that. I'm glad that I saw you," Harry said.

"Keep your head down." Francis shook his hand. It struck Harry that there was something strangely final about the way he said it. It was as if Francis didn't expect to come back.

"Au revoir," said Harry.

"Not if I can bloody help it."

Francis looked back as they walked across the railway lines. Harry had nothing to feel guilty for. Why, then, did that look make him feel like he had betrayed his brother?

CHAPTER THIRTY-EIGHT:
EDIE

Ypres, September 1921

She sees him from the window of the slowing train. His profile. His face turning. There, on the platform. She hears her own intake of breath, pushes herself back against her seat, and turns her face away from the window. Because, for this moment, it *is* him. It is Francis. But then, when she looks again, the man has stepped forward and it's Harry, shifting from foot to foot, looking up and down the length of the train, his face all concern and nervousness, and brightening now as he sees her.

"Let me take your suitcase."

"Dear God, I'm glad to see you!"

Is it relief that makes her hug him so tightly? She clings on to Harry as the train pulls away and the crowds shift and thin around them. With her face against Harry's chest, the clean smell of his shirt, and his arms closed around her back, she is eighteen

338

again, and safe and certain, and none of this has happened. She really doesn't want to pull away and step back into this afterward life.

"I think I just heard one of my ribs crack."

She feels his laughter. She hears the smile in his voice. And she is so glad of him.

"I'm sorry. I just worried that you might not be here. I'm so relieved to see you."

She leans back. It is glorious to see the smile that he can't quite seem to straighten out, and she has an urge to put her fingertips to Harry's twitching lips, but she smooths her hair instead, pats his hand, and nods her head.

"Come on," he says.

She watches him as they walk along the platform. It has been four months since she last saw him. Four months through which she has needed him and doubted him and worried about him. She is not sure what it is that makes the ground seem to shift beneath her feet just now — whether it is finally walking down the platform in Ypres station, or looking at Harry's face again.

"You're not eating enough. I could feel your ribs. Is it any wonder if I broke a couple?"

He looks tired too, looks like he hasn't been sleeping again, but he glances toward her and grins. "It's delightful to have you telling me off again. Utterly ruddy joyous. Don't feel that you can't wag a finger at me. Don't feel you have to stop."

But his grin fades as they step out onto the station steps, and then she must turn and look at it too.

"My God. I knew it was bad, but not this bad. We had no idea at home," she says. "Absolutely no idea. How you must have hated us."

She looks to him, wishing that he would say something, wishing that he had some explanation for the wreck of a town in front of them, but Harry just shakes his head.

"It's not what I expected," she says, because there has to be something to say. "Though I'm not sure what I expected." She needs to put a hand to his shoulder as they walk down the steps. "Do you mind? I feel like my knees might go at any minute."

"Don't worry. It's only a short walk and I've managed to find a hotel with walls — and even some roof."

"Is it the first time that you've been back?" she asks.

"Yes, it's almost three years. It actually looks more knocked about now than it did then. I think it's the fact that people are living among it, that there are shops again and schoolchildren and curtains at windows. It highlights what a wilderness it is."

Many of the buildings on the street from the station have lost their top floors. They are just fragments of frontage. An arm-in-arm couple stroll ahead of them with a black dog, its tail ticktocking. They have to keep stepping off the pavement to avoid the piles of bricks.

"It's like something fantastical," she says. "It's not quite of this earth and our time. I'm horrified and fascinated all at once. I want to babble and yet I'm utterly lost for words. Is that the wrong reaction?"

He shrugs. "I don't know that there is a right reaction."

"I feel like I've arrived in Africa."

She watches his boots at her side. She feels steadier looking at Harry's sensible, serviceable boots making a straight line, but the ground still feels like it's trembling beneath her feet.

"I made it as far as Poperinghe," she says. She's not sure where to start, so she just says it, although it feels like admitting a weakness. "I meant to come here. I planned to, I even bought my ticket for the train. I stood on the station platform in Poperinghe and watched the train for Ypres leave. It was something like panic. Can you understand that? I couldn't quite find the courage to come here on my own and then I bolted for home. That's terribly cowardly, isn't it?"

"No. I don't think that of you at all." He glances at her and glances away. "I am sorry that you're here," he says. "I feel like I've let you down. I'm sorry that I couldn't have done this for you. That I can't give you more answers."

"I'm no longer certain what the question is. Or exactly what answer I want."

"You said on the telephone that there's somewhere you want to see?"

She isn't quite ready for the question, but she sees that he needs to ask it. "Yes. I'd like you to take me back to that place."

"*That* place?"

"Where he last was. Where you last saw him."

"Because?"

She considers. "Just because."

"If that's what you wish," he replies.

"It is."

There are areas of recent demolition on either side of the road, she sees. A strange sort of a scrub seems to be growing over much of it now. There are nettles and thistles. Cats slink between the rubble.

"That photograph of Francis . . ." he begins, and as she looks at him she sees that he isn't entirely sure where to go next. "Have you seen something in it? Is there something there that has made you come here?"

What can she say to him? "I think it might have been taken here."

"Here? Ypres?"

"I thought it was Arras at first. I thought I recognized the buildings in the background. He's standing in a ruined square, you see, but no: all arrows now seem to point to Ypres."

"And you've received nothing else since? No other photographs? No letters?"

"No, and that's the most frustrating part of the whole thing. Why the anonymity? Why be so cryptic? It could be from anyone, couldn't it?"

"It could."

"Is that the Cloth Hall?"

The tower is under scaffolding. She has seen photographs of the Cloth Hall in the newspapers, but that doesn't prepare her for how emphatically broken-down it all is now. How very little of it there is. A lot of what remains of Ypres is being shored up. So much of it is just façades, and it reminds her of a stage set. Some of it looks as if a strong gust of wind might bring it down.

"It was."

"Like Roman ruins," she says. "Like some antique site. I almost expect to see grand tourists quoting poetry among the fallen stones."

" 'Look on my works, ye mighty, and despair'?"

"And how!"

There are piles of broken old stone, and dressed new stone, stacks of timbers, iron beams, and roof tiles. It is all waiting by the roadsides. There is so very much of it to be put back.

"Have you been here long?" she asks.

"I only got in this morning."

"I'm not distracting you from your work?"

"Terribly. Entirely. And I'm glad of it."

"It's heavy going, then?" She sees it on his face.

"I just wish that I could do more for the families. When I've met them, when I've spoken to them, the size of the gaps in their lives is so apparent. How can just a few photographs fill that? I wish that I could give them more of my time. That I could give them whys and wherefores and more comfort. But I can't."

She looks at him and sees what a burden on him this responsibility is. She wishes he didn't have to carry that. Has she been fair to Harry in expecting him to answer her question too? "You underestimate what you're doing. I'm sure that having those photographs does give them some comfort."

"To know that their sons and husbands and brothers are definitely dead?"

"Don't undervalue the significance of that. It will be a comfort to them to know that the facts they have are correct and that their loved ones are properly buried."

"Properly? As in respectfully buried, or definitely buried?"

"Both, I suppose."

They walk on. Her footsteps still for a moment by the window of a patisserie shop. There are towers of stacked sweetmeats behind the glass, tidily boxed chocolates, and a gingerbread model of the Cloth Hall as it must have been before. The wall above the shopwindow has been blown entirely out, exposing a first-floor interior that looks so terribly violated, with its sprigged wallpaper there for all to see, and its curtains bleached and tattered by the weather and catching in the breeze now.

"In May you told me that you couldn't come here," he says, "that you couldn't bring yourself to make this journey."

"Female prerogative."

"Am I allowed to ask what changed your mind?"

"I started to wonder if you'd ever get round to it."

"Of course I would."

"I do know that. I'm only teasing." She smiles at him and is glad to see his profile eventually return it. "There was a letter waiting for me when I got home. It was from an acquaintance of yours, I assume. A woman called Rachel? She told me that I ought to find out about Francis, one way or another, and then move on with my life. I was rather affronted when I first read it. I mean, *that* from an absolute stranger! It is a bit presumptuous, isn't it? I screwed it up and very nearly threw it in the fire. It was a rather bossy letter."

She doesn't know who this Rachel is, but it is obvious that she means something to Harry. Was it wrong that Edie had also felt something like jealousy as this stranger's handwriting told her how she ought to have more respect for Harry's finer feelings?

He laughs. "That sounds about right. Rachel is looking for her husband. She's already been out here three times. She can't accept that he's dead, she's not convinced that's right, but every time she comes back she feels like she's getting farther away from finding him. It's like she's on this endless, impossible quest."

346

"You make it sound like some trial from Greek mythology."

"I just think that she's tired of it, really. And lonely. She'd just like to have a grave that she could put flowers on and to be able to move forwards herself."

Something passes over Harry's face as he talks about this woman called Rachel and her loneliness, and Edie can't quite place what it is. Is he saying that Edie ought to see herself in this other woman's quest for finality?

"I wondered if it might be that photograph of Francis," Harry says.

"The one that came in the post?" His eyes move over her face. For some reason she has a sense that he's testing her response. "What do you mean?"

"I thought receiving that photograph might have prompted you to come here."

She feels his eyes on her, and has to look down at her feet before she can meet his gaze again. "You mean the suspicion that Francis himself might have sent it?"

"Yes."

It both relieves and disturbs her that he has voiced that thought too. "And do you think he might? Could Francis have sent it?"

"You know it's impossible."

"Do I?"

They walk on through the tumbledown streets. A troop of schoolgirls moves along the pavement ahead of them in white blouses and green hats. Edie watches the brims of the hats circling as the girls look about. She looks at the schoolgirls walking ahead, watching their reactions to this broken-down town, because she doesn't want to look at it herself. On the corner a man is turning the handle of a barrel organ. He raises his hat to the schoolgirls, but might as well be invisible.

"This is us," says Harry.

There are flags flying outside the hotel. They look absurdly victorious. "Ever catch your mirror image and wonder how you got here?"

When she looks ahead they are reflected side by side in a shopwindow, he and she, framed in Gothic architrave. It looks like a portrait of two alarmed people. They stare at their mirrored selves.

"Frequently," he replies.

CHAPTER THIRTY-NINE: HARRY

Ypres, September 1921

Harry lies on the bed in his hotel room. The woman at the desk downstairs had bragged of hot water and electric light, but the walls of his room are patched over with brown paper. It reminds him of a nursery rhyme — Jack and Jill tumbling down the hill and vinegar to draw the bruises out. He can hear Edie unpacking in the next room, her footsteps moving back and forth from suitcase to wardrobe. Light comes through a join in the paper walls, which her movement now and then blocks.

"We can talk through the walls," he says.

"Yes," says Edie's voice.

"I used to hear the sound of snoring through Francis's bedroom walls at home. It wasn't you, was it?"

"You'll find out tonight."

He works to slow his breathing, still a bit in disbelief she is there, in the next room.

349

He hadn't expected her to put her arms around him at the station. He wasn't prepared for that, or for just how difficult it would be to pull away. He has to keep it light and bright now, to joke and tease, and make them brother and sister once again, because it could all too easily, too quickly, become something else. He can't let himself look through the gap in the paper walls.

The stairwell is all shadows. He follows the light down and then sees her from the turn of the stairs. As arranged, she's waiting by the door. He watches her for a moment before she realizes he's there. She is silhouetted in profile against the window and staring down at her hand on a chair back. The pose reminds him of the woman that he'd seen topping a war memorial four days earlier. Edie's circling ankle is the only thing that gives away that she isn't an allegory cast from concrete. Like the memorial figure, her eyes aren't focused; her face gives the impression that her thoughts aren't in this room. But then a moth starts to flicker at the window, the insistent throb of wings seemingly bringing her back into the here and now. She puts her fingers to the glass.

" 'And when white moths were on the wing, and moth-like stars were flickering out, I dropped the berry in a stream and caught a little silver trout.' "

"Harry! It's you. I didn't see you," she says as she turns. "Yeats?" Her whole face changes when she smiles.

"The trout became 'a glimmering girl with apple blossom in her hair who called me by my name and ran and faded through the brightening air.' "

They step out into the evening. Swallows are plunging through the overhead blue. They swoop, as one wing, between the tattered rooftops.

The hotel is just off the square. It is a wide square and must once have been prosperous, only now it is all brought down. It surprises him again, when they walk into it, how little remains. There's much less of it than he remembers there being in 1917. The leveling of the buildings, the flattening of it all, makes the sky seem very wide and rather heavy.

"It's like a half-excavated Roman town," Edie remarks. "Don't you think? Where's the bathhouse? Which way to the barracks? Where's the ditch to keep the barbarians out? Doesn't it strike you how quickly we can roll back to that?"

"Yes," he answers.

"It's like something left by an ancient

civilization," she says, "like all the clues that remain at the end of a civilization. I know that I'm staring, and yet I feel as if I ought not to look, as if it's impolite to let my eyes linger on it. Irreverent, almost. I don't know whether to whisper. Should I whisper?"

He shakes his head. "Is this the square in that photograph, do you think?"

"It is."

Wreaths have been placed against the ruins of the cathedral, as if it were a grave or a tomb. It is circled in barbed wire. They stand to look at the notice that has been placed there. " 'This is holy ground,' " he reads aloud. " 'No stone of this fabric may be taken away. It is a heritage for all civilized peoples.' "

Edie raises an eyebrow. "Would anyone really want to? Would someone seriously want to pocket a chunk of it as a souvenir? It looks entirely unholy to me. *Civilized* is a bit of a stretch too."

"Perhaps."

"You'd already been posted here when Francis came back on leave, hadn't you?"

"Not far away. We were in a camp up to the northwest."

"I wish that I could have understood it then, that I could have had some notion of what this place was like."

"When Francis came back?"

"I didn't seem to be able to connect with him. It was like part of him had already gone. Maybe that part of him was here? If I'd seen this, perhaps I could have understood him better. Perhaps I might have known how to start a conversation."

"But you couldn't have made it better. How could you?"

"I don't know."

The lights are just starting to come on in the cafés, which seem to be making a great effort to be cheerful. The bars and hotels brag their resilience in confident names — they are the Grand, the Victoire, the Splendid, and the Excelsior. It seems to Harry like they're overstating their claims. They take a table outside and order glasses of beer. She smiles at him between sips. Harry gets the impression that Edie too is making a great effort to be cheerful, though her hand shakes, he sees, when she lifts her glass.

"Don't you draw any longer?"

"Occasionally. I live my life surrounded by cameras now. They make me feel rather inadequate as a copyist."

"You were ambitious once. You were more than a copyist."

"Would you write that down for me?" He

raps his knuckles on the table and can't help but grin. Edie shakes her head, and her smile is gone when she looks back. "That photograph," he says. "Can I see it again?"

"I understand." She retrieves a brown envelope from her bag and passes it across the table to Harry. "I still keep looking in the envelope expecting to find a letter that I've missed, but there's nothing."

"It is a French postmark. Saint-Christophe de Something? It's blurred. I can't read the remainder of it."

"Do you know how many villages in France are called Saint-Christophe? I took it into the post office in Arras. It could take you ten years to travel round them all."

The photograph slides out of the envelope. It is peculiar to see Francis's face again in this place, with Edie sitting across the table from him. It is a version of Francis's face that he has tried to forget, a version he never wanted Edie to see. "He's taking it of himself."

"He was here, wasn't he?"

Harry stands up with the photograph and circles until the background slots into place. "Yes." He hears her intake of breath.

"He looks older, don't you think? Much older?"

He remembers the rain falling down

354

Francis's cheeks. He remembers the whites of his brother's eyes turning toward him as they lay in a shell hole. He remembers the noise of the barrage, how it throbbed through his own body, and how Francis's lips had trembled. "He does."

"But I saw him in September 1917, Harry. He was reported missing at the end of October. Yes, he didn't exactly look his best when he came home in September, I was shocked when I first saw him, but the face in that photograph isn't one month older than the man who sat in my house that week. This man is years older."

He looks at her. How can he tell her? "It must have been taken towards the end."

"I can hardly believe that," she says. The liquid in her glass shakes as she puts it to her mouth. "I'm grateful to whoever sent it. I can't say that I like it, that it didn't shock me, I'm not exactly going to put it in a photograph frame, but I'd rather have it than not. I just wish I knew who it was that sent it and why now." She takes the envelope back and returns it to her bag. "Don't you? Don't you wonder what it means?"

"Things just surface." He considers what is making her hands shake, what has surfaced for her with this photograph, why she is looking at him like that. "I saw it with

Rachel. There are rooms full of personal effects. You could fill cathedrals with all of this stuff. It'll be decades before it all shakes down and makes its way back to its rightful owners."

"Your Rachel woman sent me a postcard of a cathedral."

"I told her that you like a nice topographical feature."

"Only it was all toppled down. You've had some odd post. The postman probably wonders what's going on. A man somewhere in France is sending you postcards of war memorials."

"That would be Gabriel."

"And then another woman sent you a saucy postcard. There was a poem written on the back in French. I looked some of the words up. It was quite vulgar."

Harry laughs. He is glad to finally see a smile twitch across her face. "It's all right. Cassie was a nurse."

"That makes it all right? And this?" says Edie. She rummages in her bag again and passes a card across the table. "What cryptic mischief is this?"

It is a postcard of a William Blake watercolor, a shepherd and his sheep, an image from *Songs of Innocence and of Experience*, he thinks. He smiles as he turns it. The reverse reads: *Didn't I tell you that I'd be useful to you? Your mystery ceiling is in Ypres. Ask for the Blue Angel.*

"Does it make sense to you?"

"Not in the slightest. Cassie's husband works for the war graves people. He's making some enquiries for me. I have to call him at the end of the month."

Edie nods, but looks unconvinced. "That's very kind."

They eat steak and fried potatoes. She prods at the meat with her fork and accuses it of being horse. The waiter brings them an unlabeled bottle of white wine, serving *madame* and then *monsieur* with no compromising of ceremony, and they drink it even though it tastes strangely sour. When she shivers he gives her his jacket. The café has a corrugated-iron awning and looks very temporary. It calls itself the Grand Hôtel and it is evident that it has grand plans — or a sense of humor. The shape of the cathedral looms ghostly behind Edie. Jackdaws croak from the tops of the ruins.

"I never expected that he'd come back," she says quite suddenly with her fork in her hand. "I didn't have doubts. It never nagged at me. But it all changed when that envelope came. Now, whenever there's a knock at the door, I start. Whenever the telephone rings,

357

I'm waiting to hear his voice. When the train came into the station here, I expected to see his face on the platform. Well, don't you? Didn't you? I can no longer quite believe that he isn't here, that everything that Francis was can just have been snuffed out. Nullified. Neutralized. Nil. I mean, it can't, can it?"

"I'm sorry."

"He isn't here? He won't come back?"

Harry shakes his head. "I can't see how."

"I want to go to the place where he was wounded and to Tyne Cot Cemetery. Fingers keep pointing there. People keep telling me that if he's buried anywhere, that's likely to be the place."

"I've been told that too. And I've gone through all the burial registers already. He isn't there. His name isn't on the list."

"But you said that there are so many nameless burials. If I go there, I might know if he is one of those. I might *feel* it."

"You honestly think so?"

"Don't look at me like I'm foolish."

"I'm not. I'm truly not."

From inside the restaurant comes the noise of scraped chairs and china. The waitress collects bread crusts from the next table and pours salt where the wine had run red through the tablecloth. Her mouth

358

recites a silent ceremony. In truth, being back here, he sees Francis everywhere. He's there in shadows and at shuttered windows, in movements, in memories, in his own reflection. Francis's name is in the shape that the waitress's mouth makes. But he can't tell Edie that.

"You were right in what you said: I do think that he might have sent that photograph himself. You don't think he did?"

"No."

"But are you certain? Can you be absolutely sure?"

"Edie, I was there."

A moth flickers at the candle flame. She licks her fingers and snuffs the flame out. "Of course. You know, I think I might be losing my marbles."

They walk back slowly through the dim streets. Waiters are taking the chairs and tables in and emptying ice buckets on the potted plants. At night, with so few lights at windows, it's all the more a city of backless façades and ghosts. Bats are streaking between the ruins, arrowing across the night-blue sky. They listen to the sound of the town: a motor engine starts up, a shutter closes, the wind seems to hum as it moves through the ruins. They are the only people on the street.

"Twenty thousand people used to live in this town," he tells her.

"Don't you find it all terribly lonely?"

"Yes."

She says that she's glad she's not here on her own now. She tells him that she needs him to be here. She thanks him by her bedroom door.

Harry stares at the ceiling. A vehicle passes with a sudden roar and its headlights strobe across the walls. For a second he tenses. When it is gone it leaves behind a thin sliver of light through the paper wall. He can hear her crying in the next room. It takes all his willpower not to walk to the wall.

CHAPTER FORTY:
EDIE

Ypres, September 1921

"Did you sleep?" Harry asks.

"Not terribly well. My brain was all in a fizz. I kept imagining that I could hear crunching shells and marching feet. Are there armies of ghost soldiers out there?"

"Only armies of builders."

She listens to him talk about masons and carpenters, and a six a.m. percussion of chisels and saws that had drilled into his dreams, but he looks like he hasn't slept at all either.

"We need tea. Shall I serve?"

He smells of peppermint and shaving soap as he leans toward her, and just for a moment it is the long-ago scent of his brother's skin. Just for a moment she wants to close her eyes and put her face to Harry's neck, just to breathe him in and forget the rest.

"What?" he says.

She shakes her head and watches as he

361

folds away his newspaper.

"You're folding bread crumbs into the paper. Can you understand much of it, then?"

"Some of it. A little. I stumble through. My French is survival-grade, really. I'm better equipped for restaurant menus than international politics."

"How like you to feel the need to try." The tea is scaldingly hot and tastes of nothing much. "Are tea leaves still rationed here?"

"Quite. It makes you quickly develop a taste for coffee."

The rattle of his teaspoon seems to clatter in her head. She wonders if she had too much to drink last night. The barrel-organ man has started up again. The piped waltz is slightly too fast and somehow insistent.

"Strauss? Is Strauss still allowed?"

The waitress sings along as she clears crockery from the next table. Edie thinks about sitting in a café in Arras and how convinced she had been then that Francis might be there. Is he any more likely to be here? Across the table Harry's fingers are breaking bread into pieces. She notices that he doesn't eat any of it.

His eyes meet hers. "Penny for them?" he says to her.

She shrugs and looks down at her hands. "You're not eating. You should eat. I worry that you're not looking after yourself."

"I am. You mustn't worry about me." He pushes the plate of broken bread away. "Do you want to go to Tyne Cot today?"

The too-hot tea scalds her mouth. "They're in time with each other." She points to the street beyond the window. A woman is sweeping the pavement in front of her shop, the broom working to the rhythm of the waltz. "It will never be real unless I see a grave. I won't ever quite believe it. Your friend Rachel was right about that part."

"Do you want it to be real?"

"Can it be real tomorrow? Can we go for a walk today instead?"

They clamber up onto the ramparts and take in the panorama. Weeds are growing through the stones, softening the jaggedness of it. There is clover in the crumbling mortar. Yellow grass and slender saplings are reclaiming the ramparts. It strikes her how determined nature seems to be to take it all back. The town — or what remains of it — is laid out before them.

" 'Few names awaken more memories than that of Ypres,' " Harry reads aloud

from his guidebook, " 'a city of incompara-
ble splendor in the Middle Ages, and of
which nothing now remains but a heap of
ruins. History furnishes few examples of
such grandeur followed by destruction so
swift and so complete. Ypres is now but a
memory.' "

She turns and looks at him. "What memories you must all have. It makes me feel
rather inadequate. I don't know how to
begin to comprehend it."

What memories does he see as he gazes
out across the moat? What version of Francis does he see in those memories? She can't
help but feel there are some memories that
Harry has chosen not to share with her.
They stand side by side and swallows' bellies glimmer blue over the water. A man is
sculling, concentric circles stretching out
from his quiet blades. Harry skims a stone.
It skips three times.

"Ducks and drakes," she says.

Beyond the ramparts there is an area of
new housing. It is a township of huts, yellow wood walls and pitch roofs. These
streets look like something made of matchsticks, she thinks, like something that a
strong wind might easily level.

"It's called the Plaine d'Amour," he tells

her. "The Plain of Love! It's not very lovely, is it?"

"I remember reading that it was all going to be preserved," she says. She has followed all of the stories about Ypres in the newspapers, knowing that this is the area where Francis was. "That it was going to just be left as untouched ruins, that the town was to be made into a symbol and a souvenir and war memorial."

"This was home to people, though. They wanted that back more than they wanted a monument for the British to visit. I read in the paper yesterday that five thousand men are presently employed in construction in Ypres."

"What great days these are for joiners and carpenters." Her foot strikes against a piece of metal then. "What is it?"

"An air shaft."

Edie crouches and peers down. There is only blackness and a smell of stale air below.

"The ramparts were full of dugouts," Harry says. "We sheltered here one night in 1917. I remember an earth-floored cellar, furnished with a salvaged velvet armchair, a long-case clock, and needlework alphabets on the walls." He widens his eyes and smiles. "It was a long night. I was down there with an Australian, a second lieutenant from Melbourne, who swore each time the clock struck the quarter hour and kept standing up to straighten the pictures. We finished a bottle of Benedictine together, and talked about spin bowlers and parrots and wildflowers, but the shells were splintering the walls outside."

"*We?* Was Francis there? He was with you?"

"No. This was after."

"After," she repeats. She is no longer sure what *after* means. A church clock somewhere repeats the hour.

"Will you tell me again? About that last day, I mean."

"Edie, please —"

"It's all I have."

"I've told you a hundred times."

"But there might have been something that we've missed. Some possibility that you've overlooked which, in the one-hundred-and-first telling, might jump out at me."

"Edie, he was dying. He had gunshot wounds to the chest. We were ordered forward. There was no one to help him. And it was too late. At the time I had absolutely no doubt about that. I wouldn't have left him, if I had any doubt. It *was* too late."

"I'd like to get rather drunk," she says.

"Can I draw your picture?"

"It's a very long time since you last asked me that."

"Isn't it? Too long. For old times' sake, then?"

"I'm not a girl of eighteen any longer."

"And I'm not a boy of seventeen, who only dares to look you in the eye when he's given permission to draw your portrait." He looks at her then. "But don't make me remember that. Please. I'm not sure that it's manly to blush."

She smiles, and nods, and he draws her there in the café. She watches Harry's eyes and his moving hands, as she has done so many times before.

"It's the sketchbook that I gave you, isn't it? I thought you'd lost all of that."

"It's the only thing I didn't lose. It was in my pocket at the time, when everything else went." He looks up and closes the book. "What was it that you said to me — hand it back to me one day full of pictures?"

"I did! And will you? May I?"

He gives her the book and she turns to the first page and sees her own likeness. "Denham Hall?" It's her, standing in the doorframe of the red gallery. "Four years ago? It seems longer, doesn't it?"

"It does."

"Goodness, you always flattered."

"I never did. Not one bit."

" 'If I cling on to you, will you help me not to bounce back down?' " She smiles as she recalls his voice. "That's right, isn't it? That was your line?"

He stares at her. "You remembered that?"

"I did. Of course I did."

She pages through the book and her own face flickers at her. Again and again. It's there so many times. She looks up and catches his eye, and there's suddenly something difficult in that connection. Why does she feel like she's overheard him whispering a secret? Like she's listening in to him making a confession?

"There were no other women to draw," he says. "I like female faces, and I'd drawn yours so many times before that I could do it from memory."

"I understand." She looks at Harry's face, his obvious embarrassment, and feels like she needs to be cautious about what she says next.

"We were a bloody ugly lot. A real rough bunch. You've never seen so many unlovely faces."

He swirls his drink in his glass, will look at everything but her face now, and she feels so desperately sorry for him at this moment. "I wish there'd been more pretty nurses for you, or barmaids, or farmers' daughters, or conveniently proximate winsome nuns."

"Nuns?"

It's a mercy when at last he looks up and smiles, but as she puts the book down on the table, the breeze catches the pages and then Francis's face is there. "I didn't tell him that I'd been to see you in hospital," she says. "I don't know why. It was an omission, though, not a lie — and we didn't do anything that we need to feel guilty about, did we?" She tilts his brother's likeness toward Harry.

"No."

"When did you draw this?"

"Just after I'd got back from England. Our journeys crossed. I saw him on the station as he was coming home on leave. It's the last time I drew him."

"What would that be, then — September?"

"Yes. Towards the end of the month."

She looks closely at Harry's drawing and can't help but think that this isn't the man in that photograph. Francis would be declared missing within a month of Harry

369

drawing this picture, but the man in that photograph isn't just one month older. She leans across and unwinds Harry's fingers from around his cigarette. "You do miss him, don't you?"

"Of course I do."

"It's just that you didn't seem shocked by that photograph."

"The one that was sent to you?"

"Yes. You didn't seem surprised by Francis's appearance in that photograph."

There was just something about the way that Harry had looked at it. When she handed the photograph to him back in May, she had watched as he turned it to the light. Why hadn't he seemed more disturbed by it, as she had been? Why didn't he see that the face of the man in the photograph was much older? Why did Harry look like he'd seen that face before?

He shakes his head, as if he's not sure what to reply. "We saw each other at our worst."

She doesn't feel like she can press him and nods. But it doesn't silence her questions.

He comes back from the bar with a piece of paper in his hand. He passes it to her across the table as he puts down the drinks.

"What is it?"

"The Blue Angel. My mystery. Apparently it's some sort of drinking dive."

"This is the place that you don't recognize in Francis's photographs? You think he might have been there — that he was there sometime in that October?"

"It was a cellar full of gloomy drinkers then, and seemingly it still is now."

"Sounds like just my sort of place," she says.

He finds the street in his tourist guide and reads the description aloud. " 'The fine double-gabled houses markedly illustrated the transition from fifteenth to sixteenth century architectural fashions — irregular arches to the lower floors, full semicircles framing the regular window bays above. Today little but rubble remains,' " he reads.

"How terribly twentieth century of it."

Evidently the carpenters and masons have been busy in the two years since Harry's guidebook was published, and wooden buildings now stand in many of the gaps that were seemingly formerly admirable stone. Where old walls remain, they are shored up, the protected plasterwork terribly nibbled and pitted.

There is no sign to indicate that it is a

drinking establishment (of dubious repute or otherwise), but there are flecks of blue paint around the carved wings above the door.

"Is it a secret club, do you think?" she asks. "Will we be expected to whisper a password and to give a special handshake?"

"Nothing so fun."

They are momentarily light-blind. From the brightness of the street they flounder into black.

"I can't see a thing," he says.

In the dark, just for a second, it is Francis's voice at her side, his voice that had once whispered unseen through library shelves, but then he strikes a match, light bounces off a low curved ceiling and a stone staircase descending, and Harry's face is there again.

"I'm glad you're here with me," she says.

Harry goes ahead. She feels the temperature drop as they go down.

The staircase bends around and opens onto what seems to essentially be a cellar. Light flickers off a vaulted roof and damp fluoresces on the red-brick walls. It might as well be midnight outside. The air is thick with cigarette smoke and there is a sour-sweet smell of old dirt. A dozen or so men sit at tables, candlelit and crouched over glasses. Nobody is talking. A gramophone plays a jazz track that seems entirely inappropriate with its forcible jollity. Edie knows which photographs Harry was thinking of, and she recognizes the curve of the ceiling and the bottle-cluttered tables. She imagines the flash of Francis's camera and needs to reach for Harry's arm to steady herself. Has Harry pored over those photographs too, then, not able to date and place them? Has he too sought meaning and explanation in those images?

A man looks up from beside the gramophone. He seems to be the only person who has registered their presence. It is as if everybody else in the room is in a trance. Have they realized that the war is over, that it is 1921 and summer outside? She feels that she has walked into Francis's photographs. The faces might well be the same. But why had Francis been in this place? What was he doing? What was he feeling here? And why does this seem to matter so much to Harry?

"I can't decide whether this was a chapel or a beer cellar," he says.

She nods. There are columns of swirling stone, incised at the top with grapes and grains, and saints and angels on the bosses. "Why was he here?" she asks.

"I don't know."

"I do know that he shouldn't have been here."

The gramophone man places a bottle and glasses on their table and returns to study his records. The blues are blaring out now. A brassy lament. It sounds like a New Orleans funeral. Edie clinks her glass against Harry's. She imagines the candlelight dipping and dust dropping from the ceiling as artillery roars in, pulverizing the street above; she imagines the floor lurching and the bottles clinking; she pictures Francis stumbling. When she looks up at Harry, she can see how the surface of the wine in his glass quivers.

"Is that really a funeral march?"

"I think so."

Harry is staring at the scarred tabletop, as if he expects to find some meaning in it. There are names gouged into the wood, branded monograms and scorch marks, and his fingers trace these shapes. Is he expecting to find Francis's initials? What meaning is Harry looking for here?

"Good God." She downs her glass. She clenches and unclenches her hands. "This is probably the most depressing place I have ever been. Have you seen enough?"

"For a lifetime."

Harry returns the bottle to the gramophone man and says the name as he places coins in his palm.

"Blythe?" The man doesn't look up from his newspaper.

"Francis."

"Ask Dillon. If he was here, then Dillon would know."

"Dillon?"

"The Wunderkammer — it's a shop — Mr. Dillon's cabinet of curiosities." The man looks back down at the paper and laughs.

They blink as they step back into the light. It seems too bright. She hears Harry take a deep breath and sees him shut his eyes. What does he see behind his eyes?

"Why was Francis here? Why does it matter that he was here? Was he in trouble? Is he still in trouble?"

The shake of Harry's head is not the answer that she needs.

Chapter Forty-One:
Harry

Ypres, September 1921

Edie wipes her sleeve on the shopwindow. They are building above it, new plaster and lath rising up, and all the dust of old Ypres falling down.

"Is it open?"

"There's a light on in the back."

Through the window Harry can see a curious accumulation of items for sale: tourist guides, maps, books about the region before, chunks of architecture, items of uniform, shell cases, helmets of all nationalities, and fragments of colored glass. A handwritten sign proclaims: SOUVENIRS OF YPRES. AUTHENTICITY GUARANTEED. ALL CURRENCIES ACCEPTED. SOMETHING TO SUIT EVERY PURSE AND EVERY PALATE! It looks like the haul of the most almighty trench raid. He is momentarily startled by the ring of the bell as Edie pushes the door.

Inside it is arranged into classes of curio.

On the first table there are stone heads, fragments of carving, and shards of letter-cut marble that look like sections of a blown-apart tomb. Edie holds up a piece of stained glass to the light. It is a lively gem-blue, the lead around it horribly bent and buckled.

"Beautiful blue," she says. "Ecclesiastical blue? A fragment of sky, do you think, or the Virgin Mary's cloak?"

A triangle of refracted blue light trembles on Edie's throat. It takes all of his willpower not to extend a finger and touch it. "Supernatural blue. The windows of the cathedral, I guess?"

She raises an eyebrow.

The next table is all variations of shell cases. They are worked into napkin rings, ashtrays, money boxes, vases, tobacco jars, milk jugs, inkwells, dinner gongs, and crucifixes. They are engraved, embossed, beaten into patterns, and emblazoned with slogans. The metalworkers of Ypres cannot be faulted for any want of variety or inventiveness, it seems. Stacks of copper driving bands and aluminum nose caps (on sale at two francs apiece) look almost abstract.

"I am odd that I think it all rather grim?" she asks.

"Not in the slightest."

There are smaller items laid out for more

modest budgets. As he watches Edie's hand glide over the brooches, bracelets, and rings, he recalls the touch of Rachel's ringed fingers.

"Who would want such things now?" Edie grimaces as she holds earrings either side of her face. "They are worked from bullet cartridges and engraved with the words *Vive la France!*"

He dips his hand into a bowl of brass buttons (BON MARCHÉ says the sign, at fifty centimes) and pulls out one that bears the insignia of a Yorkshire regiment. A trestle table at the back is lined with helmets, an arrangement of rusty-bladed bayonets, and a collection of variously twisted pieces of metal. Edie shakes her head and turns away.

"You mean you don't want a souvenir pickelhaube? I can't tempt you with a lump of shrapnel?"

She moves ahead of him, her steps slowing as she peers into the display cases down the right-hand side of the room. She is standing on her tiptoes. She leans closer, and he can see her reflection and her breath misting the glass. The cases are full of salvaged personal belongings. He sees pipes and tobacco tins, cigarette cases, shaving sets, and mechanical pencils. There are penknives, rosaries, and a row of spectacles, looking poignantly fragile. There is something terrible, he thinks, about these spectacles, the light blinking off their blind ownerless eyes. Edie's reflection moves over tie pins, framed photographs, and wedding rings. She turns around to Harry and wrinkles her nose. He thinks about Rachel moving around the room of identifying objects. What price would her rings fetch? Are these things too the property of missing men? He both looks for — and doesn't want to see — items that might have been his own.

"Can I help you young folks?" says the man at the back of the room.

Edie gasps and then laughs.

He steps forward out of the shadows and smiles. He is wearing an army greatcoat over a smoking jacket that has seen better days. Licking the palm of his fingerless gloves, he smooths his yellow hair and then offers the hand to Harry. Damp wool presses against his palm.

"Michael Dillon at your service, sir. A pair of redheads, eh? There's trouble ahead!" He whistles through his teeth and touches a joshing fist to Harry's chest. "Is it a souvenir for your lovely girl that you're after?"

"Not quite," says Harry.

"Anything that you want, we can get it for

you. A trinket? A jewel? A keepsake? Or perhaps it's something more personal? No request too exotic or too awkward. The world begins again here and we can make it what we want it to be." Michael Dillon's eyes narrow as he grins.

"We were told that you might be able to give us some information," Harry says.

Edie steps forward. Harry is aware of the pressure of her fingertips on his shoulder.

"Information, is it? And what would that be, then?"

"You might know someone," says Edie. "Or might *have known* someone."

Dillon tilts his chin. "Well, I might! Did the particular someone have a name, or is it a guessing game?"

"Does the name Francis Blythe mean anything to you?"

"Blythe?" Dillon speaks the name slowly. Harry watches his mouth shape the word. His eyes slide to the ceiling. His mouth looks like it's about to make an answer, but he shakes his head instead.

"We think that he might have been here in October 1917 — in the place called the Blue Angel."

"I'm sorry," says Dillon. "So many names. So many faces. Blythe? October 1917? It was hardly blithe times. I can't put a face to

380

the name. Why is it that you want to know?"

"Only to fit together a piece in a puzzle."

"Fair enough," Dillon says and smiles.

Harry feels Edie's fingers release. She turns away behind him.

"Could I maybe leave you the address of our hotel, just in case anything comes to mind?"

"I doubt that it will, but it can't hurt, can it?"

Dillon has long yellow fingernails, Harry sees, as he hands the piece of paper over. Dillon folds the paper and winks as he stows it in his smoking jacket pocket.

"Harry?"

When he turns, Edie is pointing at the display cabinet.

"Harry, this is mine."

Her finger is pressed against the glass. Beyond it is a lozenge of gray metal suspended from a tattered brown ribbon.

"It can't be," he says.

"Would you like to see the item, miss?"

Dillon unlocks the cabinet with a key and then dangles the object from his finger. Edie watches it as if it is some kind of power-issuing amulet.

"It's mine, Harry. It's my Saint Christopher."

Dillon twists the ribbon around in his

fingers. It spins in the light, and the relief shows on the metal. Harry feels inexplicably repulsed by the thing.

"Patron saint of travelers — happen it's traveled back to you, miss? Would you like me to find you the price?"

"It could be anyone's." Harry looks beyond the turning medal. Edie seems to be mesmerized by it. "It's not yours," he says.

"You think he knows something, don't you?" The bell rings behind Edie as they step out onto the street.

"Yes."

"Why is it that you want to know about this?" Edie repeats the question that Dillon asked of Harry. "Why does this Blue Angel business matter? What exactly is it that you want to know?"

"There were some days, toward the end, when we weren't together, when I don't know where Francis was. I'd just like to know where he went. Who did he talk to? How was he feeling? If he came into Ypres, what for? It would just satisfy my curiosity to have the pieces complete."

"Your puzzle might have just got more complicated. That was my Saint Christopher, and you know it."

CHAPTER FORTY-TWO:
HARRY

Ypres, September 1921

"When did you last have it?"

Harry turns his glass. The table is gritty beneath it. Edie puts her hand to the other side of the glass, jamming his movement, forcing him to look up. The tower, behind her, is gnarled into a shape that looks feudal, like a relic of the twelfth century. It all seems so long ago.

"October 1917."

He remembers the feel of the ribbon around his neck, the sensation of that moment as she put it over his head. Seconds earlier it had been against her skin and it had held her warmth, he recalls. Could it be the same? He had felt himself blush on the station in Poperinghe, under his brother's appraising gaze, a hot rush rising up from the red ribbon. As he had walked away from the railway tracks, he had taken it off and buttoned it into his pack.

"It can't be yours," he says again.

"How can you be so sure?"

He's not certain that he is.

She shields her eyes with her hand, cuts out the glare. He follows the direction of her gaze. A fairground has been set up in the square over the course of the day. There are tourist buses in from Ostend and a determined show of gaiety and animation. Children are riding on a merry-go-round. Green horses with flaming red nostrils are gently ebbing and rising to a plucked-metal rendition of an old song about love and roses and Colinette with the sea-blue eyes. Men are taking their chances on the shooting gallery. The crack of the rifles makes Harry jump.

"Steady," Edie says and smiles at him across the table. She stretches, points her toes, and extends fingertips to receive a sky that is uncomplicatedly blue, as pure and unblemished as a robin's egg. "Have you got a cigarette? I'll permit you to appease me with a cigarette."

"Do you never buy your own packet?"

"No."

"Did you see his fingernails? He reminded me of a rat. I bet he goes out picking over the ground. I can just see his busy fingers — *scrit, scrat* — scratching in the ground."

"You didn't like him much, did you?"

"All of that stuff belongs to other people. I could almost feel him digging in my own grave."

"Only you're not in your grave, are you?"

A Neapolitan tune is jangling out from the merry-go-round. He remembers Caruso's gramophone voice crackling over the lake. Edie's fingers tap the beat on her glass.

"Don't worry, I wouldn't dream of making you dance," says Edie.

She turns her glass and the prisms spin. A stall is selling waffles and its smell of burnt fat and sugar makes him feel slightly sick.

"It's a bit like a carnival in a graveyard, isn't it?"

"Just be grateful that there isn't a chorus line and clowns."

He hears American accents above the jangling music. White grins cluster together in front of a camera lens. He can't imagine wanting to take Edie's photograph in this place. A wasp is drowning noisily in the bottom of his glass. He tips it out, rinses the glass with water, and refills it with wine.

"You're drinking a lot now," she says.

"And so are you." He touches his glass to hers.

"More now, though." She raises her glass to him. "What will we do, Harry?"

She exhales. He watches the smoke curl from her lips. "I don't know."

They leave their coins on the table and walk back toward the hotel. They pass a bag of fried potatoes between them and Edie links his arm. Her eyelids are drooping slightly and he wonders if she is perhaps slightly drunk. Ahead of them a woman pushes a man in a wheelchair.

"It is a good and noble and proper thing for a widow-woman to take on a damaged man," she says, "to come to a mutually beneficial arrangement, to betroth him a lifetime of care, as it were."

"And where did you read that?"

"In a newspaper. Do you think they resent each other?"

"Sometimes. They probably also need each other."

"I did love him, you know," she says. "I never stopped loving him. But he'd changed when he came back on leave. It was difficult. We didn't know how to talk to each other. When I read that word *damaged* in the newspaper recently, I thought of how he'd been that week. I mean, it's not just walking sticks and wheelchairs, is it? I'm not wrong, am I?"

"No. I understand. I know how he was,

386

and I worried for you when he was coming home. I guessed that it might have been like that for you."

"That doesn't mean that I want it to be this way, though." She waves a chip in emphasis. "We would have found a way through it. I would have looked after him. If I could have him walk down this street towards me now, I would."

She says it a little too forcefully to be convincing. Harry stares down the street. The houses ahead have all been shorn up with scaffolding to make them safe. "Of course."

"I cried in a department store after the letter came, when they told me that he wasn't coming back. There was a vase of irises on the counter, and suddenly it struck me that he would never again be there with a bunch of flowers in his hands. The smell of them! The poor shop assistant didn't know where to look."

He thinks of the blue irises in her kitchen. How long after the letter had she made the decision to start buying flowers for herself? He looks at Edie and considers what conclusions that decision process must have contained. "Francis wouldn't want you to cry," he says and wonders if that is quite true.

"Sometimes I look up at you and it's him.

387

It takes me aback. I forget sometimes just how very alike you are."

Her words catch him out and he looks down. When he shaves he is aware of his bones, how they are more visible now, how they more obviously determine the shape of his face. He sees Francis in the shape of his bones, in the angle of his cheeks and the line of his jaw. He considers what Francis would look like now, four years on. It more troubles than reassures him that he sees Francis in his own face.

"Just occasionally," she goes on, "in a certain light, it's like you're him."

"I'm sorry, Edie."

It surprises him that she laughs. "Sorry again, eh? Why *sorry*?"

"That I'm not him."

"And that's just it. The bones and the muscles are all the same, but your expressions are completely different — what's going on below the surface is completely different — and the worst of it is that I'm not sure whether I'm glad of that or not." She looks up at him as if she expects his judgment. He looks down at the bag of chips. "Oh dear. I've had too much to drink, haven't I?"

"It's this place," says Harry.

He's noticed that she looks at him a lot.

He catches her sometimes, sees her reflected eyes following him in mirrors and window-panes. He does the same to her. He is frightened sometimes that if he takes his eyes off her she won't be there when he looks again.

"We should just go home," she says, "and pretend all of this never happened. Not look back. Refuse to remember. Make ourselves deaf to the doubts. Just start completely new lives." When she turns to him her eyelashes are full of tears. She blinks and they fall.

"You need to sleep."

She leans her forehead against his shoulder as they stand at the bottom of the stairs. He can feel the rhythm of her breath and wants to both break away and stay like this forever. He remembers her laughing mouth spinning in a long-ago garden and the confusion of feelings that had whirled around him in that instant. There is no laughter in her face now, though, as she looks at him. He watches Edie's up-close eyes scan across his face. Is she searching to find Francis there?

"I have to phone Mr. Lee tonight," he says.

Edie nods slowly. "You must do what you have to."

He leans against the wall as soon as he is out of the hotel door and lights a cigarette.

The match shakes in his hand. He kicks at the wall.

Mr. Lee's faraway voice spells out names and regimental numbers and issues directions to cemeteries. Harry draws merry-go-round horses and angels around the names and numbers. He draws question marks around Francis's name.

After he returns to his room, the sound of her breathing is slowing, he can hear it through the paper wall, that fine line between his dreams and hers, and so Harry makes tentative steps around the unfamiliar floorboards, not wanting to disturb her sleep. Careful movements. Shallow breaths. When he closes his eyes he sees the cabinets full of framed photographs and shaving sets and penknives. He sees Francis's photographs and razor and knife — and the lucky charm that perhaps ought to have been his.

Chapter Forty-Three:
Harry

Ypres, September 1921
Harry whittles a pencil to a point and goes to retrieve the sketchbook from his bunk. He treads carefully on the stairs. It is dark in the dugout and his fingertips stretch to find the walls. He curses as he kicks at a fallen-over stool, kicks it into Alfred Mc-Cabe's suspended shins.

He staggers back. Hanging from the beam, his belt about his throat, Alfred McCabe creaks. His tongue protrudes horribly. There is a crust of blood in his beard. His eyes bulge, but there is no brightness of life behind them. Only the red ribbon, wound through McCabe's dead fingers, stirs. A silver-plated Saint Christopher spins.

Harry vomits. McCabe is their old contemptible, their regular, their warhorse; he is all swagger and soldiering lingo, is all talk of Boers and cavalry and Mafeking medals on his chest. It doesn't seem right that

McCabe should be dead. Harry straightens and wipes his mouth on his sleeve. Now they are all as good as dead. "Old soldiers never die," he whispers. "Young ones wish they would."

The electric bulb dips and buzzes and suddenly Harry sees that McCabe's face is not his, but his brother's. Francis Blythe, wrongly and rightly, is hanging dead in a dugout south of Cambrai. Harry stares. He gulps for breath, his chest shudders, blood bangs in his ears, but his brain and his eyes cannot align. Gravity jolts. He is transfixed by the face of his four-months-maybe-dead brother. He scans the dugout. All is as it was: he touches the ironclad walls, the wooden props, the pressed-earth floor, the mirror and the pinups and posted poems, and McCabe's boots, suspended still six inches off the earth. He hears water drip and smells damp clay and tastes blood where he has bitten his lip.

He takes a step closer, his legs unsteady. Francis's lips are cracked and all the color has gone out of them. But his lips are parted, as if he does yet have something to say. Harry doesn't want to hear what his brother's dead mouth might have to say. He doesn't want to look at his dead face up close like this, but fear fixes him to the spot.

Francis's hair sticks to his forehead in damp curls. Dirt accentuates the contours of his cheeks. Fatigue hollows his eyes. But then Francis's eyes flash open, pupils dilated. His wide, dark-lashed, blue eyes address Harry's own.

Harry screams. Terror tears out of him and then there is the shock of black silence. The black is the dilation of a pupil just an inch from his own. When he gasps, his breath mists the mirror. His eyes refocus and the mirror is breaking. He watches the fissures spread. It is a sigh and then a crackle and only the shattering rush of noise right then at the end. His own reflected face falls in fragments.

"Harry!" It is her voice through the paper wall. "Harry, what's happening?"

He slides down to the floor and sits among the splinters. There is glass everywhere now. The half-lit lines of the room are alien for a second. He puts his head between his knees and tries to remember how to breathe. He hears her door open and close and then she is banging at his. He watches the handle turning. She keeps banging. He reels back, re-tracks.

"Harry! Please let me in."

He cuts his hand on the glass as he stands.

There is blood on his shirt and now hand-printed on the door. Edie looks pale under the electric light. There are other voices and faces in the corridor. She pushes him back into the room and shuts the door behind them.

"Harry, what's happened?"

She holds his hands between hers and steers him toward the washbasin. Harry watches as she pours from the jug. His blood swirls pink in the white basin. The water is cold. His hands are trembling. He can hear Edie breathing.

"Harry?"

"I'm sorry," he says.

She takes his hands from the water and dries them on a towel. She turns his hands over, runs her fingertips over them, and pulls a piece of glass from his palm. Her fingers tremble, he sees, and she gasps at the same moment that he does, as if that sharp flinch of pain is her own. There is a smear of red on the shard of glass. He recalls her, earlier that day, holding a piece of blue glass up to the light, the quivering triangle of blue light on her throat.

"You're shivering. Talk to me," she says.

"I broke the mirror."

"But why?"

"I didn't mean to."

394

He thinks about Francis's face in the mirror of the ransacked house, their eyes meeting in the mirror and then the trinkets and violets raining down on his head. The memory makes him want to put his hands over his head. *"Don't look like that,"* he hears Francis's voice again. *"It's for Edie."*

"I had a dream," Harry says. "A nightmare. I must have sleepwalked."

"Have you cut your feet?" She pulls her shawl around her shoulders. It is embroidered with Indian flowers, he sees. The fringe of the shawl brushes softly against his hand. Harry imagines that he can smell the musky silk roses.

"I don't think so."

He sits on the edge of the bed while she washes his feet. His eyes keep closing. He's not sure that he isn't still asleep. She sweeps the glass shards together and folds them into a newspaper. His hand aches where she pulled the glass from it. Her hands lift up his feet and pull over the sheets. She puts a finger to her lips and then there is nothing but the black.

"It will be all right," says Edie's voice.

He shuts his eyes and briefly believes her.

CHAPTER FORTY-FOUR:
HARRY

Proven military camp, west of Ypres, October 1917

"You've heard nothing from him?" asked Captain Rose.

"Not a word. I last saw him on the station in Poperinghe — that was on his way out."

Rose was writing in a book. Harry could see that he'd drawn a pair of eyes and a dog in the margins. The dog had forlorn hound eyes and its tail between its legs. "That would be the twenty-fourth of September, then?"

"Yes, sir. I suppose so. Nearly three weeks ago now."

"So tell me: How come Corporal Butterworth reported seeing him in the vicinity of the camp ten days ago?" Rose checked the notes in his book. "Butterworth swears that he saw him here on the fourth of October — the day that he was due back from home leave. He says that your brother came back

396

into the camp, but then left again."

It was the first that Harry had heard of this. "I don't know anything about that, sir. Could Butterworth have been mistaken?"

"He's made a sworn statement. He says that he saw Francis going out through the gates."

Harry shook his head.

"Why would he come back into camp, but then leave again?" Rose asked.

"I can't imagine why he'd do that. It doesn't sound right. Like I say, I've heard nothing from him."

Rose looked up. "All right, Harry. I believe you. But this isn't good for him, you know. We can't have men just wandering off. It isn't tolerated."

"I understand that," said Harry, wondering quite what that nontoleration meant.

"Did you have any concerns about his peace of mind when he left? Was Lance Corporal Blythe quite himself?"

He had forgotten about the change of rank. For a moment he wasn't sure who Lance Corporal Blythe was. "I hadn't noticed any recent change," he replied, wondering if that was true. He thought about his brother's face at the station. How much older he had suddenly looked. How his eyes didn't quite seem to be there. How he had worried about that man going back to be with Edie. Should he be concerned now for Edie?

Rose twisted the cap onto his fountain pen. There was ink on his fingers and parts of a camera on his desk. He'd had a new Autographic sent out from England, Harry knew, and had recently given his old Kodak to Francis. Wouldn't Rose himself know if there was something significantly wrong with Francis's mind, if something had broken in his brother's head? Rose pushed his notebook away and looked up at Harry. "If you were a betting man, where would you say he is?"

"At home. With his wife. It makes no sense that he'd come back here only to leave again."

"I can sit on Captain Frean for three more days. You do understand the seriousness of this, don't you?"

"I do, sir, yes."

"Very well. Let's hope that Lance Corporal Blythe's train has just been delayed. By ten days."

Harry walked back across the field. A band was playing behind the huts, men standing in groups and looking on. " 'She is watching by the poplars,' " they sang along,

" 'Colinette with the sea-blue eyes. She is watching and longing and waiting, where the long white roadway lies.' " Two men in kilts were laughing as their feet picked out dainty steps. The sky behind, which the previous night had rained long-range shells, was now pink and perfectly serene. At another time he might have stopped and drawn the scene.

"What did Rose say?" asked Pembridge. He was sitting on the steps of the hut scraping mud out of the tread of his boots with a stick.

"That Francis is for it."

"Do you think he's still in England?"

He wondered if he should write to Edie. Could Francis still be there with her? If Francis wasn't right in his mind, what would that mean for Edie? Could he find a way to get a message through to her to check that nothing had happened? But what if Francis was there and just meant not to be found? "Part of me hopes that he's bribed his way onto a boat and is halfway to Argentina."

Pembridge didn't look convinced by this hypothesis. He handed Harry a cigarette and shrugged.

Armstrong, leaning in the doorway, whistled. "Is he that keen on corned beef?"

"He'll lose his stripe at least," said Pembridge.

Harry sat on his bed. Rose had disclosed that they were likely to be shifting north next week, up beyond Langemarck, where it was all marsh and gas. Perhaps Francis was right to have got away, then? Perhaps that's all it was, and how could Harry blame him if he'd made that decision?

Beyond the windows of the hut they were encoring the chorus of the song. There was no noise of guns, and stars were just starting to show in the pink-tinted sky. He wanted to sit on the steps and draw it, to smoke Pembridge's cigarettes, and to not think about anything more than whether his line was true and his composition balanced. He touched the drawing book in his pocket. The book that she had given him. But, if Francis was there with her now, and not in his right mind, shouldn't Harry be doing something? Shouldn't he at least check that nothing bad had happened? He had to write to Edie. His fingers stretched under the bed toward his haversack. It must have been kicked farther under. He knelt down on the boards and peered beneath the metal frame. His stretching fingers found only an old blanket. He lit a match but it illuminated

400

just a spider's web and a forgotten spoon.

Pembridge, out on the steps still, was singing about shining roses and the hush of the silvery dew.

"Jack, my bag has gone."

"Don't be daft," said the older man.

They searched the cupboards, the latrines, and behind the iron stove. Harry thought about his sketchbooks, his pencils, his letters, his diary, and Edie's red ribbon wound around it. They searched the recreation hut, the cookhouse, and the laundry.

"It's gone," said Harry. "Some bastard has offed it."

"When did you last have it?"

"I don't know. A week ago? A week and a half? I haven't looked for it. I haven't needed it."

"Don't worry, son. We'll club together and sort you out."

Harry thought about his drawings and his private words and the luck token that she had handed him. How could they club together and bring that back? How could that be sorted out?

"You should go and tell Rose," said Pembridge. "It's probably been taken by accident, or some sticky-fingered sod will just have pilfered your cash and your smokes and dumped the rest somewhere."

Harry looked around the dim field. The band had finished playing now and groups of men — faces he knew and didn't know — were milling about. He looked at the milling faces with a sudden new suspicion.

Pembridge put a hand on Harry's shoulder as they walked back toward their hut. "Happen we head into the village and I shout you a chin-up beer?"

Harry turned to reply, but then a cry was coming from the hut. He recognized Armstrong's accent. "No sign of Blythe's kit," came his voice in the dark, "but his brother has just turned up."

"Lose sixpence and find a shilling, eh?" said Pembridge, patting Harry's back. Harry couldn't put into words the sensation that made the lights of the camp suddenly spin around him.

CHAPTER FORTY-FIVE:
HARRY

Ypres, September 1921

Image order: Mrs. Alice Gray would like a photograph of the grave of her husband, Pte. Percy Gray (46389, 15th Sherwood Foresters, died of wounds 30th October 1917). Grave number 153.

"I bought it," Edie says. The medal is there on the breakfast table. He thinks it looks slightly unsanitary and moves his coffee cup away.

"How?"

"*How?* I didn't have to slay lions or walk across bridges of fire. I just went over to the shop before breakfast and handed over money in exchange for it."

"I shan't ask how much money he made you hand over."

"Don't look like that. I'll clean it up. You didn't mind taking it off me once."

"But it's not yours, Edie. It can't be. Don't you see? It doesn't make any sense."

"There's so much that doesn't make sense," she says. She takes a bite of her toast and turns away from him.

"Edie?"

"Do you always have to be right?"

"Hardly," he says. "I lost mine fifteen miles west of here and four years ago. It's probably been buried under mud since then, all rusted and flaked away." He stares at the dull and grimed object on the white tablecloth.

"Probably, probably," says Edie.

"What are the odds?"

The waitress hovers with a coffeepot and they silently watch as she fills their cups. Edie pockets the medal and apologizes.

"No, I'm sorry," he says.

She shakes her head. "How's your hand now?" Her cool fingers stretch across the table and take his, turning over his palm. "Does it hurt?"

"It's nothing." He might have believed that he had dreamed it but for the red handprint on the door and the disappearance of his reflection. "I cut myself more trying to shave without a mirror this morning."

"I'll ask if they can find you a replacement. I did notice that there was shaving soap in your ear." She laughs at him and then stops. "Does it happen often?"

"Shaving misadventures?"

"That you have nightmares."

"No."

"*No?* I'm not sure that I believe you." She narrows her eyes like she's not convinced. "Seven years' bad luck for breaking a mirror."

It's not the first broken mirror, but in his nightmares he's usually in the woods. The images come back with the night, with the dark, flickering like newsreel. His dreaming eyes open in the black-green light, under the canopy, among the broken and the twisted things, with the living, the dead, and the in-between. The dead walk abroad again in the woods of his dreams, unwhole and unwholesome in rags and black blood. He stumbles with them and away from them over tree roots and brambles. He doesn't need Edie to know how often he has that nightmare, how he walks in the night, or how often he's screaming when he lurches awake.

"You scared me last night," says Edie. "I was frightened for you."

"It's just being back in this place."

"Of course. I understand that." She turns

405

her coffee cup and then looks back up at him. "You dreamed about Francis last night, didn't you?"

"What makes you say that?"

"I could almost see it printed on your eyes — that, and I dreamed about him too."

He looks at Edie. What image of Francis did her dreaming eyes see? What did she see of Francis in his eyes? The only image in Edie's eyes now is his own reflection. "Do you want to go to Tyne Cot today?"

She shakes her head.

"You do still mean to?"

"I do, but not today."

"You know that you don't have to," he says. "Like you said last night, we could just go home and try to forget."

"Could we? Could you? What kind of life could we have if we never know? What sort of decisions could we build on that doubt?"

"We might never know."

"I have to try," she replies.

He puts the flowers on Percy Gray's grave, as requested by his wife. Edie watches as he takes the photograph.

"Poor lad," she says. "How old was he?"

"Twenty-six, the same age as I am now. I talked with his wife. He had two children."

"How terrible for them. I wonder if one

day, when they're grown up, they'll make this journey."

There were burlap sacks laid out by the roadside just outside the cemetery. Harry had seen bits of leather that might have been boots, a second lieutenant's epaulets, some unidentifiably mangled pieces of metalwork, and what looked horribly like a jawbone. He had steered Edie aside. He hopes that, if this is what they might see, his photograph will steer Percy Gray's children away from ever making this journey. He hopes that it will be enough to silence all of the questions that he had heard in Percy's wife's voice. He also rather hopes that seeing this cemetery might deter Edie from wanting to visit Tyne Cot.

He has read about the white stone cemeteries — "God's Acres," as the newspaper article called them — but this is the first one that he has seen. He is struck by the cleanness of the new-cut stone, the tidiness of it all. They are smart, these men, fixed forevermore in parade-ground order, well turned out, and playing by the rules. He thinks about standing at Edie's side by the lych-gate four months ago and looking into the overgrown churchyard by the reservoir. The tombs in the old graveyard were carved with sleeping angels and acanthus leaves and ivy for fidelity. Lichen bloomed across the messages of IN MEMORIAM and LOVING MEMORY. Harry could see it all as sharp as a photograph still, and smell the peppermints in her mouth and the verbena soap on her skin. He looks at her now as she walks along the white line and wonders what it is that she really wants back.

They walk through the rows together. There are English garden flowers planted around the graves — pansies, harebells, and columbines. They look strange here, these cottage garden plants and clipped lawns, oddly foreign, assertively English, but also somehow not quite right. It is perhaps the straight-lined planting and the clean soil in between. There are rosebushes at the end of the rows, their scent strong. He wonders: Does Francis too now have a clean white stone and a smell of roses? There is something about this place that strikes him as a white lie.

"Five hundred thousand headstones have been ordered," he tells her. "They all have to be shipped over from England. They sink a concrete beam into the ground and the graves all slot neatly into it, so that they'll never fall over. Straight and true for all eternity. I suppose that they could all go down like a set of dominoes, otherwise."

"I'm not sure that I wanted to know that."

"There's something slightly too tidy and practical and decent about it. Don't you think?"

"*Decent?* You mean that it shouldn't be?"

" 'The stones will endure for all time and excite the wonder and the reverence of remote generations' — I read that phrase. It rather struck me."

There are lines of young, flimsy-looking trees planted around the edges of the cemetery. Beyond them are other trees, bent and blasted, with metal splinters embedded in some of their trunks. They are both ugly and beautiful, these stubborn trees; they are both candid witnesses and resurgent life. New growth breaks from scarred trunks, which are older than his brothers might ever be.

At the front of the cemetery is a cross. They pause for a while and look up. Edie links her arm through his. The stone is inscribed with the words THEIR NAMES LIVETH FOREVERMORE. He remembers Francis on the post, his arms and ankles tied, the shape of his bound body reminding Harry of a painting of the crucifixion that he had once seen. He remembers Francis then with his arms spread and his face at that last moment. That is the image of Francis that will endure in his mind forevermore. It's an image that he means Edie's eyes to never know.

"Come away," he says to her.

CHAPTER FORTY-SIX: HARRY

Proven military camp, west of Ypres, October 1917

There had been a painting of the crucifixion in Denham Hall. Harry had stood in front of it for some time. It was a gilded panel that, one of the staff had told him, was a section from a fifteenth century altarpiece; it had been brought back by a member of the family two centuries earlier, a grand tour souvenir from Siena. Harry had stared at the painting's blue receding hills, the curve of the valleys, and the flooded low places. There was great serenity and antiquity in that smoky retreating landscape. It was a smooth and still backdrop that he would like to have walked into with a day's leisure and a thermos flask. In the foreground figures in robes of vermilion and ultramarine were making busy gesticulations. In the center Christ was a small, thin mortal man on a cross too diminutive to inspire awe.

411

His face, eyes cast down, was just weary.

Harry hadn't seen anything divine in this painting, it hadn't filled him with righteousness or courage; he had just felt pity for the poor pained arms and the quiet sadness that showed in the shadows around Christ's eyes. Looking now, beyond the window of Rose's hut, and seeing his brother slumped on the cross, he felt pity again, but also an anger that he hadn't found in the painting.

"They've taken his stripe off him," said Rose.

"*They?* None of this is your doing, then?"

"I spoke up for him, Harry. I told them that he'd been under strain and that this was completely out of character."

"It's barbaric."

"It's two hours per day. It's not like he's being flogged."

"Only because it's been outlawed. It's two hours a day for *thirty-five* days! It's humiliating. Have you seen his face? His disgrace is written all over it."

"Regrettably, it's meant to be. It's a show — a demonstration. He's being made an example of."

"He won't speak to me."

"I am sorry, Harry, but there have to be rules. He was absent without leave for ten days. If Francis isn't punished for that,

412

what's to stop everyone from taking a fortnight's holiday? What's to stop us all from just going home?"

"But he came back, didn't he?"

"That's not the point," said Rose, "as you well know."

"Did he tell you why he didn't come back on time? Did he tell you where he went?"

"He hardly spoke when they questioned him. They might have been more lenient if he'd been more forthcoming. It wound Frean up, his silence. He took it for insolence."

Harry looked down at Rose's desk. Among the paperwork he could see a tin of sprats and a jar of Gentleman's Relish. Rose's fingers worked discarded toffee papers into twists. "It's only a couple of months ago that Frean was putting him up for promotion. You instigated that."

"And with no regret. He deserved it. I regard Francis as a friend. I respect him. I think he's a good soldier. You can hardly imagine that I'm happy about this, can you, Harry?"

"We volunteered for this. He came back *voluntarily.*"

"I do know that." Rose pushed away papers and stood up. Harry thought he could smell whiskey on his breath. "If you want to know the truth, we're expecting to move out of here within days. I shouldn't tell you this, and it must stay within these walls, but we're going up towards the front next week. He won't really have to do thirty-five days. This will just get forgotten."

"But he won't forget it. I won't forget it."

"We all must make an effort," said the captain.

They had tied him to the post, his hands bound behind his back and his legs tethered by the ankles. The camp was thronging with people, but it was as if Francis were issuing some unfriendly energy, creating a circle of green space around him. Harry stepped into the space.

Francis had shouted at first. Harry had heard him. They had stood and watched from the windows of the hut as Francis was brought out. All of the anger had gone out of him now, though. His head hung down. His eyes were almost closed. He looked as penitent, as humiliated, as disgraced as a man could be.

Harry felt Francis flinch as he put a hand to his shoulder. He kept his face turned away.

"It's for another twenty minutes," Harry said and looked at his wristwatch. "Rose reckons that it'll stop next week anyway because we're on the move."

Francis barely seemed to register his presence. There were dark shadows under his eyes. He looked like he hadn't slept or washed for days.

"It will all get forgotten, Frannie, so long as you don't take it to heart."

Francis laughed mirthlessly and angled his face away.

"Francis, where were you? Why did you do it?"

He shut his eyes and leaned his head back against the post.

"Frannie, I'm sorry. I wish you'd just talk to me. I wish that there's something that I could do."

"Sorry?" said Francis.

His eyes flashed open then. Harry could see the red veins in the whites of Francis's eyes.

"You're *sorry*?"

In truth, beyond his pity, Harry wasn't quite sure what he was sorry for. He wasn't certain what act he was meant to repent. But the look that Francis gave him made him feel as if he had betrayed him utterly. Francis stared at him. His gaze was impossible to hold. Harry turned and walked away.

415

CHAPTER FORTY-SEVEN: EDIE

Ypres, September 1921

Edie watches the man hovering in the street down below, retracing his steps backward and forward along the frontage of the hotel. When he looks up, his hat tilting, his eyes obviously scanning the floors above, she knows who it is and why he is here, and she steps back from her window.

She had known that there was something more. Something had flashed across Michael Dillon's face when Harry said Francis's name. When she had gone back to buy the Saint Christopher, she had half expected him to tell her. It was part of the reason she had gone back. But then she had asked Dillon how the ribbon came into his possession, and he had just smiled wistfully and told her that things fell into his hands. She knows now, though, that there is more to all of this. That he knows more.

Edie steps to the curtains and glances

down again. He is still there, pushing open the door of the hotel now. She sits down on the bed and readies herself for the noise of his feet on the stairs, and then his knock on her door, but why does that cause her heart to race?

She makes herself walk to the washbasin and turn her hands in the cold water. The pale woman in the mirror looks her in the eye, straightens her dress, and smooths her hair. Edie tells herself that she is ready for this, that she will cope with whatever comes next. She can do this.

His hand is at the door quicker than she anticipates. She has hardly had time to compose herself before he is standing in the doorway, inviting himself in, his eyes all around her room. She is not sure whether she feels more affronted or frightened, and half wishes that she had turned the key in the lock, so that she might be able to hold her breath, so that she might have been given a choice about what comes next.

"Mr. Dillon?"

"Mrs. Blythe — dear lovely Mrs. Blythe! Please excuse the incursion, only the young lady at the reception desk was kind enough to let me have your room number."

"She did?"

"It's not a liberty, is it? Can you forgive

me the liberty?"

His smile fixes on her face. She's not sure why Michael Dillon's smile makes her tremble. "Do you have something to tell me, Mr. Dillon? There is something more, isn't there?"

"Oh, well," he says. He shrugs. He takes his hat off and turns it in his hands. "It might be nothing, now."

It is only at that moment that she notices the bag over his shoulder. It is a canvas khaki haversack, of the sort that Francis came home with all that time ago. She can still picture Francis's bag waiting in the hallway. He had shrugged it off there when he came through the door, and she had hardly dared to touch it in the days that followed. Could this be the same bag? If Dillon has this, then surely it's true that he met Francis. Does Dillon now know where Francis is?

"It's his?" she asks.

She watches as Dillon swings the pack off and holds it out toward her. Once again, she finds herself afraid to touch it.

"I don't know about that, miss."

"The man who gave you that bag — do you know where he is?" She watches it swing, suspended between them. Eventually he puts it down on the floor.

"The young chap who you're with is the spit of him, isn't he? For a moment I thought it was the same man walking back into the shop."

"Then you have met Francis." She stares at the bag on the floor. "He's here? You've seen him recently?"

"No, Mrs. Blythe. Don't misunderstand me. I was running a store of sorts, back in the day — razor blades, pencils, writing paper, bars of soap, bars of chocolate — all the requisites that your fighting man might need, you see? Well, we all did what we could. I bought and sold and did a bit of barter. I seem to recall that your man exchanged it for a bottle of beer, but it was a rum deal. It was no bargain. It's only papers inside, see? Apart from your old Saint Chris, there was nothing worth having. The trinket was yours, miss, wasn't it? Has the old feller found his way back to you? Call me a tender heart, but I do like a happy ending."

"When was Francis here? When did you see him?"

Dillon runs his hands through his hair and then shakes his head.

"Please?"

"Back end of '17? Early '18? In the black days, certainly. I was moving from cellar to

419

cellar. Now, those were rum times." He looks at her. "It's been in my storeroom for a long time, but it's where your Saint Christopher came from, and so I figured it might have some significance to you. That it might have some emotional *value,* I mean."

She looks at Dillon and realizes that he means her to give him money for it. She looks at the bag on the floor, at Francis's bag, and is not certain that she wants to possess it.

"Nineteen-*eighteen*? Are you sure of that?"

"There or thereabouts. It gives me satisfaction to return a treasure to its owner," he says.

"Did you see him again? The man who gave you the pack, I mean. Have you seen him since?"

"Not that I can recall, but a lot of faces have passed through."

"Do you know where he went after?"

"Where did any of them go?"

She knows that he won't tell her more, and she wants Dillon to be gone, then. She hears Harry's recalled voice saying *scrit-scrat* and knows this man is a rat. "Please. Do have this. For your trouble." She takes a note from her purse and puts it in his outstretched palm.

"No trouble at all, dear lady. It's my pleasure to reunite you with it. I do like to see a lost thing found."

He grins as he bends into a bow, and then winks at her as he straightens.

For a moment the winking eye is Francis's black-and-white eye in that photograph, and then a blue eye that had once watched her through a library bookcase. Has Francis been watching her all along? Is he still out there watching her now? She looks at his bag on the floor and suddenly it all seems so much more plausible.

With the close of the door, she stands alone again in her hotel room, and stares at the bag on the worn-down rug. She wants both to tear into its contents, to know what those papers say, and to never have to touch the thing; she is at the same time compelled and repelled by it. She slides down onto the floor and covers her face with her hands until the walls stop moving around her.

Chapter Forty-Eight: Harry

Ypres, September 1921

Harry looks out across the water. The old city gate is nothing now, just a grass-grown slouch of stones. He has read that it is to be rebuilt as a great archway spanning over the road, with the names of all the missing recorded on the vault. He imagines his brother's name arching over that space, along with David West and all the others. The plan to list them in stone as THE MISSING implies that they will now never be found, he supposes. Chiseling them onto a memorial implies a finality. It draws a line. But what a difficult line to negotiate. How do they move beyond that?

Bullfrogs croak unseen in the water below. He sees mangled metalwork in the water, fallen stones, and limbs of trees. He thinks about the water on either side of the duck-board tracks. There had been bloated bodies in the water too. There had been so many bodies. He wonders how the names of all the missing might fit within the width of the street behind him. And how many damaged lives multiply out of that? How many derailed expectations? How many unanswered questions? How many years of waiting?

He has seen a sign for Boesinghe on the road. Does anything exist there now? Two days after Francis had been put on the post, they were back in railway carriages and heading for that destination. There had been nothing left of the village but ruins. All around it was just churned mud and broken stones. The devastated landscape had no mystery and they had exchanged few words as they moved north along the tracks.

Francis had been ahead of him. Harry had seen the marks on his wrists, the red welts where they had been bound. He wanted Captain Rose to see them, to see the shame marked on Francis's skin, to share his anger. He also wanted to see Francis's anger. But instead he just seemed to be absent. Francis's eyes wouldn't connect with his. It wasn't that they avoided him. He was just elsewhere.

A man passes on a bicycle, raising a hand in acknowledgment. The roads are still full of potholes. Harry watches the bicycle's weaving progress, stones skittering under its tires. An advertising panel by the side of the road offers English breakfasts and motor tours of the Salient.

Only the signpost at the side of the road — THIS WAS LANGEMARCK — had told them that they had arrived at their destination. Otherwise it had been completely obliterated. There were no clues to prove that a town had ever stood there; there wasn't a building or a tree, just a great stretching desolation. Harry considers what there is now for the motoring tourist to see.

They had been shelled as they moved forward to relieve the frontline trenches. They had crouched and ducked and shouted in their confusion. He had seen Francis up in front moving stiffly, unfalteringly onward. He didn't flinch as earth was flung up, metal shrieked, and the air rushed with shock. It had been at that point that it struck Harry that his brother no longer cared. With that realization he was overwhelmed with the need to protect Francis.

He stands now outside the hotel and looks up at Edie's window. There is no light within but he thinks that he sees a face step back from the glass. In this instant he feels an overwhelming need to protect her.

"We could just go home and try to forget," he had repeated her own words back to her that morning.

He had never told her about the marks on Francis's wrists and didn't suppose that anyone had ever seen fit to inform her. Should he really try to forget that? Could they really forget and move forward, as Rose had suggested?

He stands outside her door. No light leaks from around the edges of it, but he can hear her footsteps on the other side. The door moves ajar when he knocks and so he pushes it open to find her silhouette against the window.

"Edie?"

She doesn't answer him, just stands there, mysterious in the dim light. He can't determine the expression on her face in the darkness. His finger moves to the light switch.

The room flicks into light and he sees it. It comes at him brightly. There are papers everywhere, over the floorboards and the dressing table and the bed. For a moment he is back in the looted house stepping through torn-out accounts of Arctic expeditions and maps of Abyssinia. But that's not what these pages contain and Francis isn't next door in a room full of feathers. These pages are crammed with writing, recorded images of long-ago instants and pencil portraits. The picture of the girl with the

red hair is everywhere. Francis is everywhere. It's a long time since he has seen
these images, but Harry knows the work of
his own hand.

"How?" he says simply.

"It's not *his,* it's *yours,*" she replies.

CHAPTER FORTY-NINE: HARRY

Ypres, September 1921

"But how?" Harry says it again.

"How indeed!" Edie laughs, but there is no humor in her face. There are red lines down her cheeks as if she has clawed at her own face. He wants to take a gentle hand to the red marks. He wants to pull her own hands away, but her laughter pushes him back.

"Dillon had it?"

It all looks to be there, the contents of his haversack, everything that he had lost: his drawings, his notes, her letters, his diary. Harry sees his own life splayed before him, illustrated in a progression of caught instants — in ink, graphite, watercolor, and words. There is Will, at eighteen, in sepia pencil, and Edie with cerulean-blue eyes. There are sketches of smashed woods and broken towns, dugouts, cellars, billets, groups of once-familiar faces, and her face

427

everywhere. He had found comfort in the repetition of her faraway features, like verse rote-learned. It all looks long ago and terribly near.

"Do you remember what you wrote?" asks Edie. She stands up and walks toward him with his diary in her hands. "Do you remember what you put down on paper?"

He tries — and fears — to recall. Her face is fierce. He has never drawn her like that. He watches as she riffles through pages of his words.

"How did Dillon have my bag?"

"Don't you know?" Her fingers still. Her eyes lift from the page.

The truth is suddenly all too obvious. "Francis," he says.

"Did you never guess that it was him that took it? Was it not obvious? He gave the bag to Dillon," she replies with a matter-of-fact tone. "Francis must have gone back into the camp and taken it from you, then he came back here with it, learned what he wanted to know, and told Dillon to do what he would with the rest."

"He told you that?"

She nods but doesn't look up from the notebook. He thinks of Francis reading the words that she's now riffling through. Of course, he had suspected that it might be

428

Francis who had taken his bag, but he didn't want to believe that could be true. Did this, then, account for those missing days at the start of October? Was this what he did in the Blue Angel? Had Francis seen the ribbon around Harry's neck on Poperinghe station and known that it was hers? There's a pencil portrait of him on the bed — Francis in gallant profile, put down by Harry's hand so that he might post himself back to Edie. The thought of Francis going through all his papers, of him knowing everything, makes Harry want to crouch in a corner.

" 'How I wish that it were otherwise,' " Edie reads. She clears her throat and arches her eyebrows. For a moment she's an actress reciting lines. " 'For a few minutes this afternoon I thought how things might be if he didn't make it back. Am I a wretch that I even for a moment consider that?' " She looks up from the diary and her eyes scan across his face. She's the dispassionate actress no longer.

He remembers recording the thought on paper. It was the day they had danced at Denham Hall. Had Francis then read these words two months on? Had he seen that whole scene?

"I'm sorry."

"You're *sorry*? How can you have been so stupid, Harry? How can you have been so careless?"

"I was careful. I didn't think that he'd ever read it."

"But he *did* read it! And then by the end of that month he was gone." She turns her back to him. He stretches his hand toward her. She flinches with his touch.

"You've no reason to feel guilty. You never did anything wrong. We never did anything wrong."

"But I didn't tell him the truth, and once he'd read this, he knew that, didn't he? I hadn't told him that I'd seen you in the hospital. If he knew I'd chosen to keep that from him, what else might I have been lying about?"

She turns and thrusts the opened page toward him. He sees his own writing. *I fear that I love the one woman that I absolutely shouldn't,* he had written.

"No wonder he couldn't look at you," she says. "I'm not sure that I can look at you. Francis suspected me of something that I hadn't done. You made me a guilty party."

"I'm the only one that's guilty — and only guilty of thoughts, never deeds. There's nothing written there that implies that you returned my feelings. Is there?"

"But I did," she says. "That's the worst of it."

He stares at her with the ruins of his war all around her. Might it really have been different? Could it still be?

"Edie —"

She pushes his hand back. "Please, just leave me alone, Harry," she says.

What is she feeling, he considers, as she reads his hidden words? Does she feel like she's prying? Does she realize that all of his words are addressed to her? Does it strike her that he wrote to her every day?

He watches her through the gap in the wall as she reads the words that he couldn't — and still can't — say to her face. She is sitting on the bed. Quite still. The only movement is the occasional flick of the page.

When she has read it all, will she forgive him? Can she understand how he felt? Could she still return it? He is only grateful that the diary ends before Francis came back, before he was put on the cross and fell. She still doesn't need to know that part.

Several times her head rises from the page, as if she is considering the words that she has just read. She looks toward the window, and he glimpses her profile, but she turns away from him. Occasionally she puts her finger to the page and he wonders what word it is that her finger touches.

She stands and pours herself a glass of water. Her shadowed face shifts in the mirror as she looks at her own reflection, pulling her hands through her hair. He leans his cheek against the paper wall and watches her in the mirror. He hears his own heart beating; the silent room throbs with the pulse of his heart. He is shaking.

He thinks about Francis in the Blue Angel. Did he sit in that cellar turning pages while the glasses rattled and plaster fell from the ceiling? Was this the act that caused him to be tied to a post? Was it Harry's own words that were responsible for his brother's humiliation? Or was it her action in putting the ribbon around his neck? His mind replays the action. Everything that comes after is an unbearable blur.

His crouched limbs ache. He watches her until she puts out the light.

CHAPTER FIFTY: HARRY

Ypres, September 1921

Harry moves fingertips, touches the floorboards, then his wrist. He turns his head to the cool wood. His limbs feel wasted, like after a route march, and his head feels as fragile as glass. He feels all hollowed out. The curtains billow, bright with sunlight, and there is the noise of crockery being set out somewhere downstairs. He rights himself cautiously. When he puts his eye to the wall, there is nothing in her room but tidy order and absence.

He splashes water onto his face and looks himself in the eye in the replaced mirror. What should he say to her today? Must he now speak the words that she has already read? Or, her having read them, should he forget that he had ever felt that way? He buttons a clean shirt, dampens his hair, and tries to make it lie flat. Will she cry? Will she scream at him? Or will it be a day of terrible silence?

When he opens the door it is all there in the corridor — the papers stacked neatly and buttoned back into his haversack. The ribbon, once again, is circling the diary. Edie, though, isn't there.

The bus rattles along the road. He looks out the window and tries to find features that he recognizes. Only there are very few features. There is only agriculture interspersed here and there with new red roofs. The wind makes waves across a field of wheat. There are lines of sugar beets. Cows graze in fields where pillboxes crumble.

The woman at the reception desk had looked at him coolly as he had asked her the question. She told him that Edie had paid for her room and left early that morning with her suitcase. He had run through the streets to the station. The train had gone two hours earlier. It had then occurred to him that, instead of going straight for the train, she might have first come here. Might he yet find her at Tyne Cot?

He knows that it is the most likely place. That is what they have told him — and what, in turn, he has told Edie. Those casualties that were hurriedly buried behind the railway lines had all been transferred to this cemetery. He looks down at the directions to this place formed in her handwriting, and thinks about how she had suspected that Francis himself could have sent that photograph. Did she really have a doubt? Is that really why she made this journey? Surely she would need to silence that doubt before she went home?

There are vans parked by the side of the road and parties of men digging in the fields beyond. He thinks of Ralph and is aware that their spades have no agricultural purpose. He leaves the bus at Zonnebeke and guides himself with an atlas of the fighting line that he had bought for two shillings back in Tidworth in 1916. The line on the front cover looks like ancient history; it might as well be a map of Carthage. He remembers Francis looking in this map book in 1916, all trepidation and excitement, as they had traveled east in cattle trucks. He thinks of Francis, just eighteen months after that, turning the pages of his diary.

Along the sides of the road there are the usual sentinel trees. They show its line ahead. He recalls reading about the taking of this village when he was waiting for his return train in London in 1917. It is now nothing but ruins — a stack of roof tiles by the side of the road, a pile of anonymous masonry parts, some curiosities of old carving, and yellow grass in between. The name of the cemetery doesn't exist on his map and so he is glad now of Edie's directions. It is terribly desolate all around, as if an effort has been made to erase every feature from the map. The only landmarks are clues to things that no longer exist.

Harry walks through the cemetery gate. The crosses are straight and orderly and stretch a long way. He starts to count rows but gives up. There are thousands here. Maybe tens of thousands. The scale of it, even after having already seen so many dead men and so many graves, shocks him. There is a gun emplacement among the graves, the concrete crumbling away. He has read that it is the only German pillbox that is going to be allowed to remain on Flemish soil, serving as an instruction and a reminder. He thinks that no more reminder is needed than the crosses that fill his vision all around.

Most of the burials here have no names, he sees. These men have all been swallowed up by the earth, their identities gone along with their futures. They have lost their bones, their blood, and the name that bound it all together and made them into that particular man. These men are now nothing but gaps and question marks. It matters then that someone is asking the question, that someone is searching for these nameless men, but what a big and terrible question it is. He thinks of Rachel's search and how impossibly vast it has been. It seems, in this instant, like a definition of hope. Looking at the stretching crosses, at this place full of terrible questions (with only tidiness and order for an answer), he rather hopes that Edie hasn't come here.

Other figures move between the graves. He stares at the women, bending with flowers and private words and tears, but none of them are her. The shadows of the crosses swing around as he walks along the path. He thinks of Francis's spread arms, the awful shadow swinging around the cross to which he was tied, and is glad, regardless of what happens next, that she will never see that.

He remembers looking into Francis's eyes at the end, that last moment, his eyes full of half-formed suspicions and Harry's own stolen words. Could his brother be here? Could he be one of the nameless burials? To find him, among so many men, so many other names and absences, seems like an impossible quest. All the paper trails that he has pursued have ended. It feels like the end of the line.

Has she walked through this cemetery earlier today? Has she stood where he is now standing and spoken her guilt and innocence to the nameless graves? Could she really feel Francis's presence if he was here? All that Harry can feel is an awful sense of emptiness.

When he looks at it through his viewfinder, the rectangle is full of crosses, like a postcard that his brother sent once long ago. The crosses crowd into the frame and stretch away beyond it. Harry supposes that he is the lucky one, but at this instant he can't muster much positive feeling. The shutter clicks. He cries.

CHAPTER FIFTY-ONE: HARRY

Houthulst Forest, north of Ypres, October 1917

The first light was in the sky now and Harry could more clearly see the tape line stretching out across the mud. There was something almost laughable about the precision of this white line. It looked feeble and false; such a small, silly thing amid the rule-breaking bigness of the landscape that it demarcated. It didn't look like something that trust ought to be invested in. They had obediently followed the tapes forward, though, past the dead mules and the dead men, all churning together as the heavy shells fell and the columns of black water roared into the air.

Lines of other men had been moving the other way, following the tape lines back. Harry couldn't see their faces in the gloom — they were anonymous, invisible men, only there in the jostle and the noise of their boots and breath. They could well have been a ghost army retreating. The duckboard tracks, the heaving howitzers, and the tapes were the only things that had kept the scene from being some vision from the Old Testament. Armstrong had said that it was like going through Dante's seven circles. Summerfield said that this Dante clearly had a nasty imagination. The night air billowed hot and cold and smelled of sulfur. Harry had been reminded of a William Blake illustration for the *Divine Comedy* — a writhing whirlwind of doomed lovers — and had kept his eye on Francis's back moving on in front of him, following the tape into the flood and fire and darkness.

This tape line had been laid out by the engineers in advance of the front line. The men had been crouched on it since two a.m. It gave a strange illusion, Harry thought, like this was the start of a race — as if there would be an engraved cup and a congratulations cream tea for the first man across the finish line. Summerfield tapped the face of the wristwatch that his mother had just sent him. Tate tested his rifle, kissed it, and spat. His rifle had kept jamming with the damp and so he now played with it like a nervous tic. Flares glimmered occasionally ahead. The finishing tape, such as it was, was the line of the forest, just beyond the road junction that rose some thousand or so yards ahead. At 5:35 a.m. they were due to start advancing toward it. They were waiting for the rolling barrage to start. He could see Francis just a few yards away to his left. He still hadn't spoken.

Harry had been trying not to stare at his brother. When their eyes met he saw that his attention was not welcome, but it was difficult now not to watch Francis. He didn't trust him to look after himself. When Harry went forward it was not just his own skin that he must steer out of trouble.

"Bleeding rain again," said Armstrong.

The flooded shell craters ahead shimmered as the rain moved over them in waves. They waited for the waves of artillery to come.

"How long now?" asked Tate.

"Anytime."

It seemed like only a fraction of a second between them hearing it roaring up behind and then the shells actually hitting. The earth thundered up ahead, just yards away. Great convulsions of mud and wood and water leapt and then heaved down. Harry realized that he had dived back. His hands clawed into the earth, which was cold and liquid. There didn't seem to be anything solid to hold on to. He watched the line of artillery boom down again. Summerfield next to him was screaming. His mouth stretched into silent words. Harry couldn't hear a thing. There was just the eruption of the barrage. The sky sounded like it was rending ahead.

Lieutenant O'Kane blew his whistle, only much of the artillery seemed to be falling short. They were told to advance and, within seconds, told to get back.

"Flaming hokey cokey," shouted Armstrong in Harry's ear. Harry laughed, though he didn't know why. Above the bellow of the bombardment he could hear his own heart pounding in his ears. His whole head felt like it was throbbing. His throat was dry and his eyes smarted. He looked across at Francis, who looked back to Harry. Was that fear finally in Francis's eyes?

"Go on!" screamed Sergeant Foy.

Harry stepped forward, the ground giving beneath his feet, pulling him down into panic. They edged on, crouching, stumbling, cursing the artillery, which too often was falling short. It seemed to be all around them rather than ahead. Earth pitched and splinters zipped. It was all churning and sharp and black smoke billowing. Instinct told him to run away from it, but which way to run?

"Two hundred and fifty yards," yelled O'Kane.

"Are you pacing it?"

"Thirty minutes gone." Summerfield tapped his wristwatch.

They had worked out the mathematics as they had waited on the tapes. Based on the advance rate of the barrage, Harry had calculated that it would take them eighty minutes to reach the enemy line. Looking forward, through the barrage, there was just leaping mud and a sharp line of trees beyond the rise in the distance. Could this really go on for another fifty minutes? At this moment, it seemed impossible.

"Your watch must have stopped," he shouted back.

Francis was on the other side of Pembridge. He was struggling forward with the rest of them, his feet moving, his eyes on the rise ahead. The aircraft seemed to come in from nowhere. It swooped low overhead, spraying bullets along the line. Harry toppled forward, his cheek in the cold mud. A shell hit just ahead of him, hurling it all up and leaving behind a smoking crater. He felt the earth jolt and got to his feet. He saw that Summerfield hadn't. His hand was outstretched and the glass of his wristwatch was smashed. Francis was standing perfectly still, just watching the sky.

It all came in as they crested the rise. It slammed in. Machine gun fire was coming from the front and behind the railway lines over to the right. Harry was on the ground again, Pembridge flattening himself at his side.

"Jesus wept," said the older man. "Are we meant to go on into that? *How* are we meant to go into that?"

When Harry looked across at him his lips were trembling. Beyond Pembridge he could see that Francis was still standing. He wanted to leap over Pembridge and grab Francis, but then Corporal Allan was dragging them both to their feet. "On, not back," he said unsteadily. To the left Harry could see Captain Rose on all fours, teeth and blood spilling out of his mouth.

They ran forward at a crouch, but suddenly Pembridge was pitching back. Harry looked over his shoulder and saw his empty, broken face.

Lieutenant O'Kane was shouting to the right. "Our right flank is completely up in the air," he protested, but then he was falling, holding red hands to his chest.

Harry stumbled into a shell hole and let

his legs slide down. Rifle fire was coming from the left now as well. It seemed to be all around them — and so few of them suddenly seemed to be moving on. Water splashed behind and he turned to see Francis. He staggered forward and lay down at Harry's side. Above the noise of the artillery and the machine gun fire he could hear Francis panting. For a moment he remembered them having races by the reservoir and then Francis there next to him on the grass, chest heaving and grinning. Francis's grin seemed like a long time ago. He touched his brother's shoulder and he turned his head toward Harry. There was mud on his face. He pulled back his lips and showed his teeth, but it was more of a grimace than a grin. His lips were cracked and trembling. His eyelids fluttered. His breath was hot and sour and whistled through his lips.

Something heavy hit the earth just behind and dirt skittered across the surface of the water in the shell hole. He heard a catch in Francis's breath. It was only then, as Harry looked up, that he saw it. The blade in Francis's hand glimmered as light rolled in the sky above. The rhythm of his breathing quickened. The white blade moved. Francis's grimed fingers held the knife out toward Harry. For just a moment he felt its cool steel touch on his throat, at the very spot where Edie's red ribbon had burned. He heard himself gasp. Whatever menace there was in the gesture, though, it wasn't there in Francis's eyes.

"I know. I've always known. Do you love her?" he said.

Harry put his hand out to the knife. He curled his hand around his brother's and pulled Francis's fingers away. "Yes," he said. There was no firmness, no resolution, in Francis's grip. The penknife fell from his fingers. Harry folded it shut. He almost wished that there had been more certainty, more strength, in Francis's grip. He looked at the knife. It was the same penknife with which they had carved their initials onto the wall of a barn; three sets of joined letters, side by side and so long ago. "Yes," he said again, "I always have." Was it grief or relief or just fatigue that showed in Francis's eyes then? He nodded and his eyes closed. Rifle fire spat earth from the lip of the shell hole. Francis's eyelids didn't flinch. Would their plaster initials still be there after they had all gone? Would she outlive them all? Did it matter then if they both loved her?

Francis rolled onto his front and lay with his cheek against the earth. Harry wondered if they could just stay here, could just crawl backward or forward later when this thing had resolved itself in either direction. It stank worse than a latrine in this shell hole and the cold was creeping up his legs, but he didn't want to leave. He watched his brother's sleeping face. Harry wanted to sleep too, deep undreaming sleep. He wanted to curl into his brother's back and to sleep it all away. But then Corporal Brady was bellowing and there was a bayonet between his shoulder blades.

"Up, scum." Spittle hit Francis's back as Corporal Brady screamed down at him.

Harry took his brother's arm and they clambered up and over together. He felt the air move against his face as machine gun fire zipped across. Francis was sagging, but Harry kept hold of his arm. They flailed and staggered on as it erupted and tore all around them. Francis's footing seemed to go again and suddenly he was ahead of Harry and facing him. Harry stared at his brother's face inches from his own. He put his hands to Francis's shoulder, wanting to push him away, to pull him back and put himself between him and danger, but Francis had dropped his rifle and was now spreading out his arms. Harry watched his brother's pupils dilate. He felt him sigh

against his cheek. He also felt the bullets'
thrust. It surprised him, the volume of the
violence in that jolt. Francis convulsed and
slumped. Harry fell to the ground with the
weight of his brother in his arms.

PART II

CHAPTER FIFTY-TWO: HARRY

Amiens, September 1921

"You don't look well," says Cassie. "Not at all."

"I'm all right." Harry pulls out the chair for her and puts his hand up for the waiter.

"Are you sure? You didn't sound it on the telephone."

He had called, as arranged, on the fifteenth. He had meant to talk to Ralph about Francis, but had ended up telling Cassie about Edie. Facing her questions and her concern, he had crumbled and spoken it all into the telephone receiver. The voice that had replied was calm and kind, but now she is sitting across the table from him. There are Japanese pagodas in the print of Cassie's blouse and ostrich feathers in her hat and she is staring at him from under its brim.

"So she's gone?"

"Disappeared. Might never have been

here. I might as well have imagined her."

"Oh, dear," Cassie says and looks disappointedly down at the hat, which is now in her lap. She absentmindedly strokes the feathers as if they are a cat. "I am sorry to hear that, Harry. *Really* sorry. And I have to pass on Ralph's apologies too: he apologizes for not being here and for having drawn a blank."

"Nothing?"

"Nothing at all beyond what you already know. He made a lot of telephone calls, wrote several letters, pulled on all his strings of contacts, but he found nothing beyond what you've already been told. There's no grave with your brother's name on it, but neither does he seem to have surfaced anywhere alive."

"I can't say that I'm too surprised. I'm coming to the conclusion that we'll never get beyond this point, that this is it: this is as much information as we are ever going to have."

"I'm sorry that I haven't brought you any answers. You must despair of what direction to go in next."

"You could say that." He pulls the ribbon out of his pocket and holds it out toward Cassie.

"Hers?"

"Yes."

"Saint Christopher, who looks after travelers? What's the line from the story? 'The whole world couldn't have been as heavy on my shoulders as you were'? He doesn't seem to have done you many favors, does he?"

He winds the ribbon through his fingers and rewinds time. "It can't do any harm, can it?" Edie had said as she handed it to him on the driveway of the hospital. If she hadn't given it to him, could things have been different? Would Francis ever have been in the Blue Angel? Would she have given it to Francis instead, and where then would they all be now? Would Francis have come home at the end of the war and been a husband again, even a father? Did all of that harm happen as a consequence of that action? Harry shakes his head. "I can't load much blame onto a trinket and a ribbon."

"Aren't you a bit furious at him, though?"

"At Francis, you mean?" He looks down at his glass. "How could I be? Why should I be? He wasn't well. I see that now. He wasn't thinking rationally. Everything had just got out of proportion. I understand now just how unwell he was, and with his mind in that state, an ungrounded suspicion became an obsession, and then tore him apart. Perhaps I should have taken better care of him. Perhaps there's more that I could have done. If anything, it's me that's the guilty party, only I'm not sure that I'm guilty of any sin beyond the occasional thought."

"Occasional?" She raises an eyebrow.

"But I didn't do anything about it. I wouldn't have done. I never said anything to her. Not really. I wouldn't have betrayed him, or encouraged Edie to do anything that she shouldn't. That just wouldn't have happened."

"You do seem to have been a bit hard-done-by."

Beyond the window of the brasserie a woman is pushing a man in a wheelchair through the square. She is pointing up at the architecture; he is staring at the blanket over his knees. "No," Harry replies. "Not in the grand scheme of things. I'm the one that made it through, aren't I? I'm vaguely whole and healthy. I don't think I have a right to feel wronged."

"Don't be so ruddy reasonable," says Cassie.

He laughs. She rolls her eyes and reaches across for his packet of cigarettes.

"What will you do now, then?"

"I've got a list of twenty-odd graves that I've still got to photograph." That list, in his pocket, presently seems like a heavy thing to have to carry around. It is so much more than just a piece of paper — so many people's hopes and fears and needs. He feels the magnitude and rawness of that more than ever now.

"Oh, Harry. Do you really *have* to do it?"

"It's different for Ralph, isn't it?"

"Ralph does it because he's driven to do it. It's more of a calling than work. He has absolutely no doubts that he's doing the right thing. I sometimes wonder if it's some sort of penance too — him working himself back to a moral even keel — but I wouldn't say that to him and, however he reasons it, he wouldn't have it otherwise." She takes a sip of her drink and looks at Harry over the rim of her glass. "It hasn't settled at all yet, has it? It's like all the debris is all still falling down. We're just finding our feet and picking our way through the ruins."

"And that's just it: I don't know the way. I don't know which direction I'm meant to be going in now." He pushes the ribbon away. "I want to do the right thing, but I don't know what that is any longer."

"You sound like a man in need of a compass." Cassie dabs her cigarette out and looks up at him through her fringe. "You should go after her."

"What can I say?"

"Be straight. Tell her how you feel."

"She already knows that and she chose to go. I think that's my answer."

The woman with the disabled man is struggling to push his chair through the door of the brasserie. The man's hand is caught between the chair and the doorframe and Harry sees his face flinch with pain. When his head leans back there is such profound weariness in his face. A waiter rushes forward to help the woman. She smiles thanks to the young man but the exhaustion is marked all around her eyes too. Perhaps, Harry considers, it is best for Edie's sake that she has gone.

"You said that she left the photograph behind."

"I'm sorry?"

"The photograph of Francis? The one that someone sent her?"

"Yes. Here. I'll show you."

The envelope had been there beneath the diary. It had saddened him to see Edie had left that too. Did she feel let down by them both? He recalls her fingers touching the edge of Francis's photograph.

"Hell," says Cassie. She turns over the photograph. "Poor man. His poor face. It's like a cry for help, isn't it? No wonder it spooked her."

"I think she's convinced herself that it was taken after 1917, that it might be more recent. I couldn't quite bring myself to tell her that was how he looked at the end."

"You mean she thinks it was taken after he was declared missing?"

"And that Francis himself might have sent it to her."

"Jesus. She thinks he might still be alive and sending her a calling card?" Cassie's eyes widen.

"She looked scared when I met her at the station. I didn't expect that. She kept looking around in Ypres, as if she thought he might be there watching us."

"Are you absolutely certain that she's wrong?"

"Yes. I think so. Surely?"

"You don't sound one hundred percent convinced." Cassie blows up her fringe. Her fingers push away the photograph. "Your poor Edie. What an awful thing. It's sad that she didn't want to keep it, but I can absolutely understand why." She turns the envelope over and squints at the postmark. "Saint-Christophe du Quercy?"

"Is it? I couldn't make it out. How can you tell?"

"Three years as a doctor's secretary. Does

it ring any bells for you?"

He shakes his head. "But . . ." It then strikes him. "I met someone from a place called Calvaire du Quercy." Gabriel's address is still in his pocket. "A few weeks ago. Just a stranger who I met in a cemetery."

"Could that stranger have known your brother?"

"No, I can't see how."

"Same region, though. I'd guess that it's down in the southwest, with a name like that. You should go and find out."

He thinks about the photograph that he took of Gabriel. Could there be any link between that and the image of Francis that Cassie is turning in her hands? "Yes. I should, shouldn't I?"

"Listen, I don't mean to pile another rock onto your shoulders, but I've something for you from Ralph." She fishes in her handbag and pushes a cream envelope across the table.

"What is it?"

She wrinkles her nose and frowns. "You gave him the name of another missing soldier. He had more of a result there. That's what he found out."

"You mean David West?"

"Yes, that's the name."

Harry picks the envelope up and weighs it

in his hands. He thinks about Rachel and how much depends on the contents of this envelope. He thinks about the wreath maker whose undeveloped image is still on the film in his bag. "I really hope that this contains an address?"

Cassie looks down at the ostrich feathers in her lap. "I'm sorry. I think it's the address of a cemetery."

Chapter Fifty-Three:
Edie

Amiens, September 1921

Edie had watched Harry leave the cemetery. She had seen him turning among the crosses, where she had been standing herself just minutes earlier, and knew that he too was trying to feel whether Francis was there. She saw Harry's eyes searching, his mouth moving. Were those words for Francis? Did he speak with anger or regret? Did he ask for pardon, or offer his apology? Edie had wished that she could hear what words Harry was saying, could more clearly see what expression his face wore.

Rain spatters against the glass suddenly and she looks out, beyond her own reflected face, and sees apple orchards and fields of cattle, sugar beets, potatoes, and barley. It is all pastoral again here now: fertile, productive Picardy. The fields are green and full of wet life and Edie is struck by the contrast between this place and that. There, north of

Ypres, it had all been churned earth and new earthworks, like a whole county had been bulldozed, brought down, and was being started again. There was no sense of rejuvenation, though; it wasn't as optimistic as that; it was more reclaiming and sanitizing. Had it once been as bright and bountiful as the landscape that is now accelerating past?

As she had boarded the bus back to Ypres the man ahead of her had shown her a piece of twisted metal. "Lead," he had said. "From the church roof."

Edie watched the man's hands turning the object, his fingers examining where the melting lead had run. It conveyed so much heat and violence, and Edie was reminded of all the scrap metal, all that salvaged ugliness and sadness, in Dillon's shop. "Are you taking it home?"

"Yes, it's quite all right: I did ask permission. It's a souvenir," the man had said.

Sitting beside her on the bus, he had told her that this was his holiday, his fortnight away from the accountancy office. He had been at Passchendaele in 1917 and had now come back to see the sights. Edie wondered how anyone might want to come back. How might one choose this as a holiday? A fortnight among accountancy ledgers seemed infinitely preferable. As she looked out at the sour and scabbed land, the bus rattling along the newly laid road, she had felt like she was watching a film reel: what flickered past the glass was unreal, surreal, black-and-white cinematography that might snap at any moment. Once again, she realizes it had perhaps been unfair of her to expect Harry to come back.

"S'il vous plaît?"

She shows her ticket to the guard as the train slows through suburbs. Sidings and terraces and a canal blur past. Workshops and warehouses and allotments pull away. She sees church spires, factory chimneys, and intact streets that look medieval. How lucky this town is, with its solid bridges and sound architecture. What fortune to be back behind that line.

There are twelve thousand men buried in Tyne Cot, eight thousand of them without a name. Edie had read that fact, had known that number for a long time. And, whatever the odds, she had told herself that if Francis was there, she would know it. Maybe she wouldn't be able to walk directly to his cross, but she would feel that he was nearby. Standing among so very many crosses, though, she had only felt a sense of shock, of horror, of confusion. With the size of the cemetery, the scale of the thing, it was almost too much to comprehend. They could all be Francis, or he might be none of them. She didn't feel a prickle of connection to any particular cross. Just a terrible sadness and anger for all of them.

The train pulls into a station and Edie sees the sign for Amiens. She watches the exchange of passengers, the sightseers, pilgrims, and widows alighting, guidebooks and suitcases in hand, and the onward travelers joining the train. Beyond the gantries the stonework of the station has been cleaved and shored up. Nothing is quite intact, is quite as it was. Nowhere has entirely escaped.

The movement of the crowd returns her thoughts to the stillness of a field of crosses and his photograph face. Harry had said that that last photograph of Francis must have been taken in October 1917. He had sworn it couldn't be later. But how could he be telling the truth? Francis had slept in her bed in September. How could four weeks do that to a man's face? But then what had Francis learned in those four weeks? And what had he done to himself as a consequence of that learning? She thinks about Francis when he had come home on leave, how he had curled himself away from her and just sat for hours staring at the fire. She had watched him and wondered what terrible thoughts were passing behind his eyes. Now she realizes that, at least in part, it was jealousy and suspicion that were twisting Francis up. At what point had he first suspected? How long had he been storing all of that up? Was it seeing the Saint Christopher that had triggered it? Was it because she wrote letters to Harry too? But had he not read her letters and seen that they were innocent?

She had stood among the unidentified dead and told them that, whatever Francis might have supposed about Harry and her, it wasn't true — that nothing had happened — that whatever conclusion he might have drawn, it was the wrong one. She wouldn't have betrayed him, she tells herself. Not then. Whatever feelings she might have had for Harry, she wouldn't have acted upon them, and however difficult a future might have been with Francis, she would have made it work. She would have done the right thing, however wrong it might have felt. She would have tried. Edie tells herself that. She had also told it to the field of crosses.

" 'I have spread my dreams under your feet,' " his long-ago voice whispers. " 'Tread softly because you tread on my dreams.' "

Was it natural that she had felt some sense of anger toward the graves that might be Francis as well? Was that a proper reaction? Was it so wrong to feel that she had been treated unfairly? That she'd been judged and damned and had not had the right to defend herself? She had unbuttoned the swallow brooch from her coat, remembering his words. "It's only paste," he had said. "Only a cheap thing, but it'll look pretty on her, won't it?" She had seen the scene through Harry's eyes a few hours earlier, visited that looted house through his diary. She knew about the trinket box, the violets, and his sudden violence, and she had remembered the moment when Francis had placed the brooch in her palm and tightened his fingers around her hand. She had thought, after that happened, that perhaps her response had spoiled things. But maybe the Saint Christopher was more to blame? Or perhaps it is just her that is to blame? Edie had looked at the closest cross, at the words KNOWN UNTO GOD, and pushed the brooch into the soil.

With the guard's whistle, and the call for Calais Maritime, she looks out on slate rooftops slipping by, red chimney pots, and the distant towers of Amiens Cathedral. She is leaving it all behind, all the skeleton churches and leveled cathedrals, all the ruins and the boneyards. She imagines Harry waking in Ypres this morning and wishes, for his sake, that he too could leave it behind. All this cemetery searching can't be healthy. It's all too like endlessly digging over the same ground.

She recalls the night when he broke the mirror. His eyes had fluttered when she had first walked into his room and didn't seem to be able to focus, like he wasn't really there, like he was seeing something else, but then his pupils had dilated and stilled as they connected with her own. He had looked like his own death mask then, as his head had rolled back on the pillow. His cheek, against her own, was as cold as a tomb and wet with her tears. She had put her unsteady fingers to his white lips and there had been no thoughts in that moment, no questions or doubts, only the need to care for him. She had watched his chest rise, and falter, and would have given him her own breath. As she switched off the light she had looked back and, lying there with his hands crossed over his chest, he was a marble soldier on a cenotaph. She had returned to her own room and, staring into the darkness, had so very nearly gone back and lain down on the bed next to Harry. How much more complicated it might all be now. Surely it is better not to have that complication?

Edie thinks of him, but tells herself that she mustn't. She has made a decision not to be in contact with him again, knowing what those words in his diary did, knowing how close she has come to being the woman that Francis suspected she was. She can't be with Harry and not feel like she is still proving those suspicions right. And yet she is traveling home to his mother's house. To Harry's house. Can she carry on living there now, surrounded by another woman's china patterns and handed-down cake forks and family photographs? How can she live with the three of them there on the mantelpiece, knowing now what they knew? It can't be as it was. Looking out across the rooftops of Amiens, she realizes it is already all too complicated.

Market gardens and waterways pull past. It turns again to open landscape and a young man apologizes as he takes the seat opposite. Too young to have been in poilu blue, he unrolls a magazine full of American film stars. While his thoughts might be with Rudolph Valentino and Mary Pickford, he has the hands of a farm boy, Edie decides.

He places his finger to the line on the page as he glances out at the passing barns and haystacks and cattle in the shelter of the hawthorns.

She had touched the words on that cross in the graveyard. A SOLDIER OF THE GREAT WAR KNOWN UNTO GOD. She recalls the action. Touched the soil that covered that soldier. Pushed her fingers down through the soil toward his bones. Could it have been Francis there just feet and inches below? Was he really beneath the earth? She had doubted it for the past month and didn't feel any sense of him as she pushed her hands into that soil. Edie leans her head against the cool glass of the window and looks out at farmhouses and wheat fields and hedgerows. She thinks of eight thousand unanswered questions. She feels the distance pull. It is only now that she cries.

"Tout va bien, madame?" The boy with the magazine leans toward her.

"Not remotely," she replies.

Chapter Fifty-Four: Harry

Amiens, September 1921

Harry unpacks his haversack and lays the items out on the bed. They are odd, suddenly, these objects that were once so familiar and so vital. His fingers move over his old mess tin remembering the pattern of the tarnish. There is a set of cutlery, his cutthroat razor, a tin of boot polish, a penknife (still sharp), a fob watch (stopped), and a cigarette lighter (out of flint). He feels both very close to and very far removed from these items. Some of them were once other men's belongings, things that he had found and salvaged, souvenirs of other lives, maybe more even than secondhand. It is not so very different from looking in Dillon's glass cabinets or watching Rachel's hands move over the lost property of the lost men.

In between his items of kit are his papers. There is an envelope full of letters from

469

Edie and the sketchbook that he had bought in Morecambe into which he had recorded everything that came after. The pages have come out of this book, the stitching of its spine long since gone, and so the order of the images is now all awry. Among the wrongly ordered landscapes and seascapes and once-upon-a-time townscapes, there are a lot of images of Edie. It surprises him — shocks him — how many of these there are. And then there is his diary, kept secretly, meant for no eyes but his own, which Edie has just read. Once again, as before, her ribbon is wound around it. He ought to return the Saint Christopher to her, he thinks. Three days ago she had needed to possess it. If he posted it to her now, though, would it repulse her?

There are a handful of pencils, variously sharpened. Some of them are barely more than an inch long. He remembers how he had scrounged for pencils, how important the act of committing to paper once was, and how she has just told him that he was a fool to have done that. "How can you have been so stupid, Harry? How can you have been so careless?" But how was he meant to have got from day to day otherwise? He tests the leads of the pencils, sorts those that are worth salvaging, and carves a point with his penknife, thinking of an identical knife that his brother once held to his throat.

He sits at the dressing table, his writing hand reflected in the cheval glass. When he glances up between sentences he is obliged to look himself in the eye. He remembers Francis's face reflected in the mirror of the looted house, how their eyes had met in that moment, just before the trinkets and violets had all exploded around him. He has revisited that scene in his own diary today, concerned that she has now seen it too, but how glad he is that there are other parts that his diary couldn't show her. He knows that there are sections of time that he needs to account for, though, and questions that she will have, and so he puts pencil on paper now and gives her a version of what happened in the days either side of Francis's death. He folds the ribbon into the letter. As an afterthought he adds a photograph of Will and Francis, laughing in Boulogne, right back at the start.

He seals one envelope and opens another. He reads again the note that Ralph has sent. In parentheses of apologies there is the address of a cemetery. It is unequivocally that. There is, Ralph says, no doubt. The face on his film, then, is a mistake. Harry looks up at his own face as he thinks how to begin a letter to Rachel. She had told him that she would be relieved just to know, but he can't really imagine that could be true. In communicating these facts he will end her awful searching and her hope. Is this an act of cruelty or kindness? He wishes that he could say it to her rather than write it, but then it would be so very difficult to say it to her. He hesitates over words, thinks hard how best to frame the phrases, imagines himself saying those same phrases to Rachel's face. Though he knows her eyes will rush through his politenesses, he tries to put it in kind terms. He thinks of Daniel East's eyes and crumples the letter in his hand. When he looks up he sees the reflection of his camera in the mirror. He recalls the insistent eye of Francis's camera in the mirror of the broken house. He has had to call Mr. Lee this afternoon, which has resulted in another five names being added to the list of graves that he must photograph. He wonders if he will ever be able to escape the graves.

He stands up from the dressing table and takes the camera in his hands. It hits the wall with a convincing thud, leaving another gouge in the already scarred plasterwork. There is broken glass on the floorboards again. He thinks about Edie pulling a fragment of glass from his hand and turns away.

CHAPTER FIFTY-FIVE:
EDIE

Plage de Calais, September 1921

Edie startles at the noise of breaking glass. The wind has taken over a café table, dashing glasses to the ground. A waiter fusses in with a dustpan and brush as the drinkers gesticulate over their lost aperitifs.

"Quelle catastrophe!" says a woman in black silk crêpe and laughs.

"Quite," Edie replies.

"Of course, you're English." The woman in black is leaning on the railings. "I did have suspicions about the color of your hair."

The café table is righted, glasses are replenished, and the waiter is applauded. Beyond, the promenade is busy with day trippers, admiring the sea and the seafront properties. The houses at the top of the beach have a maritime cottage style, half timbered and balconied, with turreted rooflines. There are white-painted railings and

palm trees and potted lemons. The prom-
enaders point at the dahlias and bougainvil-
leas and the smartly varnished shutters, as
if this decorative appraising is the thing to
do. Edie looks down the sand and wonders
how she has come to be watching the stroll-
ers and having her coloring critiqued in
Calais.

"I'm sorry. Where are my manners? I'm
Clara Lawrence." The woman in black offers Edie her hand.

"I'm pleased to meet you. Edie Blythe."

The woman is eating a cornet of cockles
and Edie can smell the vinegar. "Will you?"

Edie shakes her head. "No, thank you."
She can smell waffles and hot toffee too. It
takes her back to Ypres and makes her feel
slightly nauseous. She realizes that she
hasn't eaten since the previous day.

"Are you here on holiday?" asks Clara,
who seems determined to have a conversation.

"No. I wish it were the case. I have been
to Ypres. I thought my husband might be
buried there." It seems almost impolite to
say it, like she's thrusting too much unsa-
vory unsolicited information at a stranger.

"Oh, dear. How sad. Do I presume correctly that you didn't find him, then?"

"Yes." Edie shields her eyes to the bright

light. She wonders if Clara Lawrence, in her well-cut mourning, is a veteran of these matters. "I mean, I didn't. And you?"

"A holiday. A break. I've been taking the waters in Le Touquet. I feel more liquid than solid at present. If the sun gets too strong I might start to steam."

Edie walks down the beach with the woman in black silk crêpe. There are tents to hire for the day, striped in bright barley-sugar pinks and greens and yellows, and wooden chalets with fretted eaves and spiked parapets that remind Edie of the bourgeois mausoleums that she has seen in French cemeteries. The families who have rented the chalets sit on the steps, drape their towels proprietorially, and take tea from china cups. Siblings are burying one another in the sand. They laugh and fight and conspire. Fathers loosen their collars while the children run feral. Awnings strain in the wind, ropes rattle, and always the sound of the sea.

"It must be difficult for you not to have a grave." Clara squints into the sun before she turns her eyes back to Edie.

"It seems to get more so," she replies. "With time you'd think it might recede, but the questions seem to be getting louder. The telegram said, *Missing, believed killed,* and

475

that word, *believed,* seems to be looking all the more flimsy." Is it right to say it out loud? Is it bad form to share these sentiments with a stranger? She can't seem to stop the words from falling out of her mouth. "I have never felt more unsettled. In the past four years I have never felt more certain that he isn't in his grave."

"Have you any good reason to think that? Have you any evidence that it might not be the case?"

"No. Not really. It's just an instinct."

Women walk with parasols along the shore, dressed in black or white. There seems such a definiteness to that. No in-between. As if the women, like the men, have all been sorted now and allotted their status. Edie feels, watching the women, that she's not certain to which camp she belongs.

"It's the uncertainty that's so difficult to live with, isn't it?" says Clara. "It's all the questions that you ask yourself. The constant needling of the doubt. The being unable to focus on anything else. It's just so exhausting, isn't it? I understand that. My father was reported missing in the spring of 1918 and we heard nothing for ten months. There was just no news, a complete absence of information, but then he turned up in a prisoner-of-war camp. And now I have to say that I'm not sure which was worse, really: the not knowing, or having him back so changed. That sounds awful, doesn't it? It must sound terrible to you. But he's in a neurasthenic hospital now. He came back to us, but the father that I knew is still missing."

Edie shakes her head. "I'm so sorry." She looks at the woman in black at her side and realizes that this is a sort of mourning.

"He doesn't know me any longer. He doesn't remember his own name. The doctors say that he'll probably never come out of the hospital."

Clara stares at the sea, then turns to Edie and shrugs.

"I can't tell you how sorry I am."

"Daddy's war probably won't ever end, and there's so little I can do about that." There is a conclusiveness in Clara's voice, as if she's spent a long time coming to this decision. "We shouldn't linger in these places unless we have to. Don't let doubt eat you up. I know it's not easy, but try to think about other things. Occupy yourself. Look for the positives and look forward. This war has taken enough already, hasn't it?"

Children dip in the shallows with fishing nets. A group having a swimming lesson splash and laugh. A yacht with orange sails comes to the shore and men heave it up onto the beach. Donkeys repeat the same path up and down the length of the sand. It is only the children on their backs that change. They tread endlessly through their own hoof marks. Edie considers whether Clara is perhaps right.

"Are you leaving today?" Clara asks.

They watch a steamer pulling out from the jetty. Smoke billows behind. Edie looks down at her damp feet and considers whether to make the crossing. The wind whips her hair at her face and she tastes salt on her lips. Gulls hang and cry above. Does moving on mean heading north or south? In which direction is she meant to look forward? Can she leave Harry on this side of the Channel, condemned to never move on, always lingering in these memories? But, after everything that has happened, after all the mess and hurt that they've caused, she knows that their paths have to part here.

"Yes. My boat is at five."

Clara squeezes Edie's arm. "Don't look back," she says.

CHAPTER FIFTY-SIX:
HARRY

Amiens, September 1921

The dawn is full of birdsong. It feels like something newly made, something that hope might be invested in. Except Harry is feeling short on hope. He tosses a coin at the station and, with his decision thus determined, he trades it for a postcard. He tells Edie that he is going south and copies out the address that Gabriel gave him. Beyond that he is unsure of what more to say. Harry doesn't know what exists in Saint-Christophe du Quercy, but he has a hunch that it might not be a happy discovery. Ralph's note had concluded by giving him the same advice again: that if Francis was killed, he's likely to be one of the nameless burials at Tyne Cot. And if he is not? If Francis is in Saint-Christophe du Quercy, if that really is a possibility, why has he chosen to let Edie believe that he is dead all this time? And why is he reminding her of his existence now? Will she return home to further envelopes?

The train is packed. At length he manages to find a seat, but is crushed between an overweight widow and an amputee. While he is packed in such close proximity, Harry's eyes cannot help but be drawn to the hemmed edge of the steel-blue trousers to his right. He stares down at his own hand, the scar white across his palm. Edie had once, years earlier, shown him which crease was supposedly his life line. He had been reminded of that on the day he was discharged from the hospital, the ward sister jokingly advising him to henceforth steer clear of gypsy fortune-tellers. He can still hear the woman's singsong Dublin accent and see the wink of a dark eye. His life line is cut straight across. Is this, then, the start of the second part? He thinks of Edie's fingers tracing the line. Those same fingers touching Francis's photograph. He is not sure that he has much enthusiasm for the second act if she is not a player in it.

The carriage is airless and all alien chatter. A fly lurches at the glass. Beyond there is a gang of men with spades. They pause from their work and stare at the train. Behind them a field of temporary crosses is being replaced with lines of permanent white graves. He wonders, as the train pulls away, how far the cemeteries stretch. He thinks of the stretch of tape lines and train lines and of how little of this country he really knows. Is Edie now on a train in England? As he pulls south, is she pulling north? He smells the earthy riverbanks, the glasswork fumes, and, at nine, as they linger at the station of a provincial town, the day's new bread. The morning light makes a lantern of the chestnut trees.

In his atlas of the Western Front he looks for the station names that he passes, but he has already moved far beyond its pages. He is off the map and into the unknown. He remembers being on a troop train, Francis at his side, and the sense of momentum as they moved south. He feels that momentum again; only it is not his destination that he fears now, it is a sense of alarm that he feels at the thought of the accelerating distance between him and Edie. He feels a sense that there is no going back now. It is done. He puts the atlas on the vacated seat at his side and knows that he will never need it again.

The amputee disembarks into an anonymous station, leaving Harry with his newspaper. Only the pictures are intelligible to him, but they say enough. There are photographs of groups of men around new war memorials, women by panels of stone-cut names, and design blueprints presented for the reading public's approval. He is suddenly aware that it is not just in the north. It is happening all the way down this country, in hamlets and villages, in towns and cities — the marking of it, the celebration in stone and metal, as if it is a landmark, a thing to have a line drawn under. All down the country men like Gabriel must now chisel out a history, must find an appropriate expression. He imagines it like a shock wave stretching out from the cemetery with the gun emplacement at its center. It ripples out from that place, beyond the pages of his atlas, expressing itself in monoliths and mausoleums and menhirs, in arches and obelisks, in catafalques and cruciforms — and, in their multiplication, these things mean nothing and everything. He folds the paper away.

In the afternoon the landscape changes. The railway line follows a river, which churns muscular beneath its glassy width. Willows dip and shiver and a figure fishes off a sandbank, the line glistening crystal as it arcs. Time runs awry. It races and dawdles, its rhythm lost to the train's crazy beat. A father and daughter, sitting opposite, whisper and sleep, sleep and whisper. Harry envies their cocoon, the completeness of their circle. South, south, into the evening, with the weight of the world dragging in their slipstream. The sky is the softest watercolors.

He spends the night in a station hotel where the pillowcase smells of soap and the walls are solid. He pushes back the shutters and lets in the evening light. There is no one with whom to share the color of the hot roof tiles, the silhouette of the belfry, or the way that swallows swoop across, and so, once again, he finds himself putting it onto paper. The view that his window frames is all the colors of a Matisse painting, but still he wishes for brown paper walls and the rhythm of her breathing in the next room. He puts the terra-cotta tiles and the belfry and the swallows into a letter. He knows that she will possibly never read it, that his descriptions and drawings are probably mute and blank, but he still has to try to share them with her. Without that, they too might as well not exist.

He sits on the edge of the bed and stares beyond his feet. The floorboards have parted with age. They have warped in places, with water or heat. There are scratches — arcs and curves — their repetition looking like frenzy, like struggle, like panic. But, he tells himself, it is only where furnishings have been rearranged. These boards tell a story, but it is a quiet story with no crescendos or exclamation marks. They have never been shaken by explosives. They have never lurched and shuddered the plaster from the walls. The shock waves do not stretch that far. The bell tower sounds. Shadows creep from the corners of the room. Harry cries into the soap-smelling pillow.

CHAPTER FIFTY-SEVEN:
EDIE

Lancashire, October 1921

The church bells strike twelve notes and Edie looks up from the grave. She leans on the spade and contemplates her efforts. She has had to dig much deeper than she expected, as they wouldn't lie right and she couldn't bear to break the wings. A childhood rhyme comes back to her with the bells. " 'All the birds of the air fell a-sighing and a-sobbing,' " she recites to the crows' grave. Should she say some solemn words? Some formula to wish them a fortunate onward flight? As she looks down at the small wooden cross that she has fashioned, she isn't sure whether to laugh or cry.

They had been much lighter than she expected, much less solid than their presence suggested, and terribly, horribly brittle. That brittleness set her teeth on edge somehow; it had both an awful fragility and a sense of pent-up potential. Despite their very obvious desiccating deadness, she almost expected the wings to flinch under her hand.

Edie had felt a great sense of Will's presence as she took the crows down from the dresser. They were so obviously the work of his hand. In removing them, in erasing their presence, did she push him out too? She had found herself talking aloud to Will's memory, carrying on a conversation with a recalled image of a cross in France. She also found herself asking him about Francis. Was there something more that Will knew? Is Francis with him on the other side?

Condemned to a cardboard box, the crows had less menace. There, at unnatural angles, they looked less like they might beat into life. And yet there was still something threatening about them. Still some suspicion that they weren't yet finished and entirely devoid of the potential to flap their protest. Edie told herself that it was just her imagination. Is imagination getting the better of her with regard to Francis too?

It wouldn't have been right just to put them out for the rag-and-bone, and to burn them would have been too close to sorcery, so she had taken a spade down the garden and dug a grave. Standing here now, she is struck with her own folly, her own ridiculousness. "If you could see me!" she says to a memory of Harry's face, and then tells herself that it is for the best that he can't.

On a whim, taken with a fancy, she cuts a bunch of sweet Williams and places them in the crows' grave with an apology to her brother-in-law. A blackbird is fluting its liquid notes from the lilac. It is a more elegant elegy than Edie can summon. She takes up the spade again and lets the first clods of earth cover them over gently. She works with reverence, carefully at first, but then it becomes an effort to just hide the last of the feathers. The tip of a wing protrudes through the soil. She cannot bear to put a boot to it.

Her hands sting when it is done, and there is dirt in the creases of her palms. She thinks of a graveside gesture of Francis's caught in Harry's diary. She thinks of them covering Will over. She thinks of the cut on Harry's palm. She remembers a black feather on Will's grave that Harry had not put there. Her fingers find the ribbon in her pocket.

Edie surveys the garden and listens to the low sultry hum of the bees. It is overgrown now; poppies have seeded and bindweed twines through the buddleias. In 1917 Mrs. Blythe had helped her dig up the lawn and they had put in lines of potatoes and cabbages and carrots. How has it run rank around her? How has she not noticed the weeds taking it back? She tells herself that she should make the effort again and reverse this neglect. She silently recites notions of efficiency and self-sufficiency; she will make a bonfire and dig the earth over. She will cut back the buddleia and take pruning shears to the overgrown roses. She must plan ahead for next spring. Order seeds. Draw up a scheme. Bring back the lupines and the broad beans and the Canterbury bells. It is healthy to make practical plans, she tells herself. And yet, as she schemes potato trenches and lines of spring greens, she is struck by a sudden sense of alienation. This garden now belongs to Harry. This is *his* house. Can it still be her home? How can she still plan a future here?

There is a pair of men's boots in the border, she notices. The leather is lichened green and moss has claimed the soles. She vaguely recalls them being there, but is no longer sure which brother they belong to. The larkspur has seeded itself around the boots, is still there in the same border where it always grew. Mrs. Blythe had told her that larkspur signified fickleness in the language of flowers. The smell of it takes Edie back to a hospital ward and a café in Arras where

Francis's face is waiting on a wall of missing men. Had these all been acts of fickleness?

She washes her hands at the kitchen sink. The earth swills and circles away and she remembers washing Harry's hands in the Ypres hotel room. The glass might well have been in her own hand, for all the pain it gave her. She had felt such tenderness toward his cut skin in that instant. She leans against the draining board and looks at his letters on the kitchen table.

They had been waiting for her behind the door when she got back. She had put the suitcase down in the hall, turned the card in her hands, and taken his envelopes through to the kitchen. The postcard was a picture of Amiens Cathedral surrounded by sandbags. She had passed it on the train just hours earlier. He wrote from the station as he waited for a train to take him south. Had they passed so close again, then?

She had opened the letter with the Amiens postmark first and heard Harry's voice making apologies and appeals. It had made her cry to see the photograph of Will and Francis laughing, and once again to have the Saint Christopher in her hand. Harry's second letter was from farther south and was full of azure skies, red rooftops, and regret. He seems to be a long way away now and getting farther. She wasn't certain whether she felt relief or regret that there wasn't a letter from Francis behind the door.

Edie makes tea and sits back at the table. The kitchen is different without the crows. It has lightened. She no longer feels watched. And, yet, there is less of them — of Will and Francis and Harry — in here now, and she is sorry for that. She props the photograph of Will and Francis against the milk bottle. *He was dying in my arms,* Harry had written, but she couldn't quite believe his words any longer. The version of Francis in Harry's diary was so far away from the golden-haired young man she had loved, and she now isn't sure that she really knew the story's narrator any longer either. *We were ordered forward,* Harry wrote next. *I couldn't stay with him. It wasn't a choice. Leaving Francis there was the hardest thing I have ever done in my life. But, believe me, Edie, he wasn't going to get up again. It was over. I know you hope that it might not be so, that you want to believe there's a chance that he might still be out there, but it just can't be right. For your own sake, Edie, you need to believe me.*

She looks again at the letter to Harry that

she had begun. *So who was my husband really?* she wrote. *And where is he now?* Edie does not mean to send the letter, it will never be posted, but she somehow can't not reply to Harry's pen. She needs to have her right to reply, and so she tells him about burying the crows, how much more difficult it was than she had expected, how different the room is now, about her plans for the garden, and about what it feels like to hold the Saint Christopher in her hand again. Though he is the one taking trains, Edie has the sensation that she is still traveling, and to grip the medal in her hand gives her some sense of steadiness. But then, didn't the Saint Christopher trigger all of this? Her pen confesses that she wishes Harry was here, not getting farther away, but that she can't be the woman Francis assumed she was, that she feels shame, that she feels guilty — and that she can't believe Harry when he says that Francis is so definitely dead.

491

CHAPTER FIFTY-EIGHT:
HARRY

Quercy, October 1921

The village has a Romanesque church, its gargoyles made more grotesque by time, along with marigolds in terra-cotta pots and rabbits in cages. In noon's heat he circles through streets that are shuttered to the sun. He looks at the map the man in the station ticket office had drawn for him; each village is illuminated with details of its architecture and the shape of its trees, but this plan gives no clues as to the gradients between the gargoyles and the poplars. Harry's route map is like a cluster of holy men, each village going by the name of a saint, and he wonders if Edie has opened his envelope yet and seen her returned Saint Christopher. He can imagine the medal in her hands, but can't picture what expression her face might make. He thinks about a village called Saint-Christophe where someone had kept his brother's photograph

492

face. What links Francis to this alien place?

From the south side of Saint-Jean he surveys his progress. The valley is a bowl before him. The hills recede in declining blue, like the background of a Sienese crucifixion. The land falls away sharply immediately below and Harry realizes that he is standing at the top of a cliff. He wonders what it would be like to step off, to dive into that landscape. He feels himself swoon toward it, sees himself in a gasp of bright terminal light, the ground thrusting up and beckoning blackness. He looks out and feels himself pulled forward, but then a woman is singing on the terraces below and there is laughter in the fields beyond. He takes a breath and leans against a wall for a moment, realizing he is shaking.

From the village he descends through a forest of chestnut and pine. Harry's feet find a rhythm and for a moment it is a route march again and Will and Francis are at his side. He startles a deer in the shadows and it stops him in his tracks. The present presses in again and there is no voice on the road to call him back. To question. To challenge the stretching distance. He listens, but it isn't there. There is nothing but birdsong and shifting light on the road ahead. Beyond, the forest gives way to walnut orchards and bald glades. The light, after the forest, is startlingly sharp.

The road from Saint-Laurent follows the valley, which, in turn, follows the stream. Poplars, tall as church spires, punctuate, indicating the stream's forward meander. He looks up at a height of shimmering leaves and is dizzied by it. Blinking the glare from his eyes, he recalls the tree stumps along the roads in the north where he had walked by Gabriel's side. Is this how it once was? Is this what the war took away? In the fields around they are haymaking, the sickles glinting a rhythm. The people in the fields still and straighten, turning to him as he passes. Do they look out for other men returning along this road? He wonders how many times his gait and his coloring have disappointed.

The valley leads him to Saint-Pierre, where, true to the stationmaster's map, there is a tower framed in yew trees. Washing is suspended in lines across the street and canaries sleep in cages. An old woman, sitting on a doorstep, plucks at sewing and acknowledges him in a language that he doesn't understand. Otherwise the streets are empty. He sees only old women in these villages.

He follows the road straight through

Saint-Pierre to the end of the village, before taking the right fork, where he re-finds the river. Calvaire, Gabriel's village, is red rooftops and the honey colors of old stone. Its church is a patchwork of ages and architectural theft. Mary, smiling benignly in plasterwork, is preserved behind chicken wire. There are offerings of flowers and pebbles and military buttons around her feet.

He had written a hasty letter to Gabriel from Amiens and told him that he would be here by this afternoon. As Harry looks at the square where the memorial will stand, he wonders if Gabriel has yet received his words. The preparations have already started and a workman is skimming out a rectangle of concrete for what must be the monument's base. Gabriel has told him that there is to be a platform, lifted on a wall of faced stone and dressed with a wrought-iron fencing, to discourage unseemly shows and livestock. On the square base the names will be carved: NOS MORTS. They are pushing to have it unveiled on the eleventh of November, Gabriel has told him, when there will be trumpets and silence and those returned, and those not to return, will be honored. Three years on from the end of it, it will be solemnized. In six weeks' time, the memorial will give the square a new perspective. Harry is suddenly aware of the enormity and urgency of Gabriel's task.

He watches the workman mixing the concrete. It seems expertly done. Harry in turn commits it to paper: the wet slap of the worked mixture, the warmth of the afternoon sun on the backs of his hands, the flits of sparrows in the violet sky. He draws it all into a letter to Edie that she might never open. "Don't really stop writing to me, will you?" she had said once. How could she ever imagine that he might stop? He stares at the page of writing in front of him, the paper too brightly white. His skin feels tight with the sun.

The waiter from the bar takes a beer across for the workman. He stands, straightens, arches his back, and raises the glass across the road. Harry watches as men come and go; all seem to feel duty-bound to ask questions, to approve the design, and to distract the workman from his labor and from keeping the concrete from drying out. The workman wipes foam from his mustache and gestures thanks in the café's general direction. Men pat his back as he carries his empty glass across. He shakes the hand of a young man in a black waistcoat. The young man walks on to Harry's table. He recognizes Gabriel's eyes under the brim of his hat.

"It's all happening. Already."

Gabriel nods. "I am glad to see you," he says.

The road climbs out of the village and then descends, through scrub oaks, to the farm. Gabriel takes off his hat and wipes sweat from his face. Harry sees that his green eyes are ringed with red.

"How was it?" he asks.

"Coming back?"

"Yes."

"My mother cried, my father does not know me, my brother is — and is not — everywhere, and Madeleine is making hay. How was Ypres?"

"Too full of memories. My brother is — and is not — everywhere. We didn't find anything."

"And Edie?"

"She's gone."

"Gone?"

"She left. She's gone back to England, I think. I don't know if I'll see her again."

"But why? What happened? You can't let that happen."

"I don't know that I have a choice."

"But you always have a choice."

"I think she genuinely believes that my

brother might still be alive." They stand at a fork in the road and Gabriel shakes his head. "Do you know of a village called Saint-Christophe du Quercy?" Harry asks.

"Yes. Of course. It is south of here. An hour's journey away."

"Will you take me there?"

"If you wish it. But why do you want to go there?"

"Because I need to know if my brother is alive."

Gabriel's finger points out the house that he once called home. It is a square farmhouse and below it, in the valley, there are tobacco fields. Harry watches Gabriel's feet at his side and wonders if he has re-found a connection with the fields. Does the house that they are walking toward again feel like home? The expression that he reads on Gabriel's face indicates that it is not so.

"Et voilà," says Gabriel at the gate. "I must present you to my mother."

White light splinters through the shutters, but the room is dark. It takes Harry's eyes a moment to accustom. Embers indicate the shape of a fireplace. A woman spins around from it as if startled, as if she expects someone else. She says few words in acknowledgment and the little she does say

Harry cannot comprehend. Slowly the details show themselves; he discerns a large table, an assortment of chairs, and little other comfort. It is stiflingly hot in this room. He looks at his feet on the doorstep and wonders what he is doing here. What is he doing among these strangers, these people whose language he does not even understand? Why has he traveled south and not north? But then, how can he travel north before he knows if Edie is right?

"She says that you look lost," Gabriel says with a laugh.

"Is it that obvious?"

He hands Harry a roll of blankets and leads him across the yard to the barn, advising that the mice will trouble him less in the loft.

Harry acquaints himself with his accommodation and makes a mattress of the straw. The scent of it brings back billeted discomforts. He aligns his possessions, such as they are, on the lintel — makes an altar of it with his offering of cigarettes, pencils, and Edie's portrait. He remembers nights in other barns, the rhythm of his brothers' breathing, and the shape of their joined initials scratched into a plaster wall.

At dusk Gabriel returns with a candle, bread, and broth. "My mother tells me off like a child," he complains. Harry suspects that Gabriel envies him his apartness and the shadows of the hayloft. "We used to play in this barn," he remembers aloud, watching Harry eat. "Have you written to her?"

"Every day."

Harry watches the light retreat. It is warm in the barn and the old straw is sweet. He finds sleep easily, with the day's journey weighing on his bones, but wakes with the stars. In the roof-space is a white shape that is either an owl or the ghost of an owl. It stretches, screams at the night, and is gone. For a moment he is back in the nightmare woods.

Gabriel shakes him at dawn. He flops beside him on the straw and sighs at the roof beams. "Madeleine has made a start. They are already in the fields. She says that they do not need us. Women do not need men any longer. It is the same everywhere, she says. We are obsolete, my friend. Extinct. We are as good as dinosaurs." He lights a cigarette and laughs as if he doesn't mean it.

Harry considers how Edie must feel the same. Is she waking in his mother's house today and making plans in which he is not a consideration?

He puts his head under the pump, washing away sleep's warmth and thoughts of Edie waking. Behind the barn they descend along the white road, through the scrub oaks, to the valley. The plum trees are heavy with overripe fruit. The branches are crusted with lichen, making them falsely look like something long dead. They are organizing collections for the fruit trees destroyed in the war zone, Gabriel informs him conversationally. Harry thinks about George Bartley cradling the branches of apple trees and a circle of apple pips around his grave.

As they walk, Gabriel shares the night's sketches. He has drawn an image of a soldier slumped against a wall. There is a great weightiness in the dangle of the man's arms, in the slouch of his shoulders and the droop of his head.

"It is too deathly," says Harry. "You will have the village in tears every time they walk past. They will start avoiding the square. You will do nothing for the takings of the bar."

Gabriel's sketchbook is full of his brother, Marcellin: limp-armed and phantomlike, gesticulating, writhing, Christ-like and dying.

"When must you submit your design?"

"I'm already late. It has to be agreed by

the end of the week."

In the field, Madeleine, her sister Thérèse, and Madame Bousquet advance as a line, swinging scythes and sweeping down the glinting grass. It is a timeless picture — except the workers are all women. Madeleine is dark-skinned and pale-eyed. She leans on the scythe as they approach, looking like she might use it against Gabriel.

Harry watches as Gabriel plays the gallant sergeant in the hayfield, but it is obvious that Madeleine does not want it. He sharpens a scythe for Harry, working it with a whetstone and showing him the action. So much of this is for Madeleine's benefit, Harry realizes. Gabriel laughs at his inexpert efforts, says he hopes he will make up in sweat what he lacks in skill, but still Madeleine does not smile. Gabriel tries to coax her, gives her the comedy and Harry's incompetence to share, but her pale eyes are not here. Harry is struck by how much Gabriel needs Madeleine's gaze to be on him. She shuts her eyes against the brightness and his grin.

They find a rhythm and work until the clock in Calvaire strikes noon. They drop the tools then, where they stand, and retire to the dark cave that is the farmhouse. Harry sits hesitantly; they have brought out an odd three-legged stool for him, even though there is an empty chair at the table. Is that, then, Marcellin's seat? Is no one else permitted to sit there? They eat soup thickened with bread and wedges of sheep's cheese, all of which is consumed in businesslike silence. Gabriel is the only one who tries to make conversation, but there is seemingly little enthusiasm for the words that he wants to share. Gabriel lets the dogs lick his fingers and smiles at their attentions. Only the dogs seem to be glad to have him home.

Harry thinks of his black-framed brothers and imagines an alternate reality in which they have all returned and are now placed around his mother's kitchen table. He cannot picture what their expressions might be and what conversations would pass between them. There is only their photograph faces and an absence of words and Edie alone at that family table now surrounded by empty chairs. Is that where she is sitting at this moment, with blue irises and black crows as her background?

They return grudgingly to the fields. The sweat stings in Harry's eyes. His throat burns and his hands are a weeping mess of blisters.

Gabriel picks a leaf from a walnut tree.

"Here, to mark your book, so you will remember me when you go." Gabriel's hands, which are already all scars, do not blister.

"When I go?"

"You have to go on. You're not there yet."

"Could I ask you to take me to Saint-Christophe du Quercy next week?"

"Of course. If you wish it. I would have taken you yesterday if you wanted."

"I wasn't ready, but now I am."

Chapter Fifty-Nine:
Edie

Lancashire, October 1921

She is standing in exactly the same spot. She is sure of it. Five months ago she had stood here and had finally found the courage to ask Harry.

"I want you to take a photograph of Francis's grave."

Standing here again, Edie wants both to take her words back and to ask them again with more urgency. More imperative. More uncertainty. As she had asked it, she hadn't been sure that she wasn't setting Harry an impossible quest. Five months on, Francis being in a grave feels all the more implausible. But what is the alternative?

"I want you to take a photograph of Francis."

When she says it out loud she is not sure that it sounds any more convincing. She imagines Francis's face, four years older,

505

tracked down and finally caught by Harry's camera.

"And then what happens next?" she asks herself.

Edie looks out across the reservoir. They had often walked up here together, watching the water side by side, Francis's voice telling her about giants and witches and Roman roads. He had pulled flints and fragments of pottery out of his pockets and had talked about the village under the water, she remembers, the cottages and the public house and the Methodist chapel, all submerged when the valley was flooded to make the reservoir. Edie had thought about how the families must have felt as they had watched the waters rising, seeing those well-known walls and floorboards and fireplaces lost to the liquid underworld. She had imagined their sense of dislocation. She feels something similar now when she contemplates the walls of Harry's house. Today those walls had felt like they were closing in on her and she had to get out.

There had been another letter from him that morning. He writes to her about war memorials, haymaking, and the Frenchman who is in love with his brother's widow. She is not sure what he expects her to feel about the latter. What emotions does he wish this information to incite? His letters radiate heat and sunshine but also sadness. Her replies are full of shortages in the shops, the price of coal, and questions. She keeps her letters with his, filing her replies in between, as if this were a conversation. But she will never send him her letters. She will never actually put them in the post. This will never be more that a one-sided conversation.

There are couples doing the circuit of the water today, smiling at the sun on its surface and the silent landscape beyond. A group of children in Sunday best are leading a horse. Two girls twirl parasols, and shadows roll across the moor. She shuts her eyes to it all and listens to the lapwings.

"Edie, isn't it?"

It startles her. For a moment it is Francis's voice. For a moment it is always Francis's voice, but when she opens her eyes a ferry-man is standing at her side. He flicks his cigarette away and offers her his hand.

"Mrs. Blythe? I'm rotten with faces, but you are Francis Blythe's wife, aren't you?"

"Yes." She turns toward him. She is still Francis's wife. She will always be Francis's wife. She just wishes that she could be certain what that now means.

"I thought so. It's the hair." He nods. "I often think about him. Often used to see him up here with his camera."

"You're right." Edie recalls photographs of the pump house machinery, of cotton grass, and the grooved stones of the old packhorse track. Francis was a man who liked history and technology and to understand the landscape around him. He needed to know the names of plants, the geology of the hills, and the reason why stones were worn thus. He wasn't a careless or a clumsy man. Not a man to idly or accidentally let go. There was so much more that he wanted to learn and to try.

"I was in the same battalion. I was sorry when I heard about him."

"Heard about him?" She looks at the man. He is so much older than Francis. Much older even than that photograph. "What did you hear *exactly*? Would you tell me? Were you there in October 1917?"

"And a bloody awful balls-up it was." He wrinkles his nose when he looks back at her. "Forgive me, love. Excuse my language."

"Did you see his body?" She watches the man turn his eyes away and take a step back. "I'm sorry. I shouldn't ask, should I? But there are so many questions in my head. You didn't see Francis, did you? Did you see him dead? Did you hear that he was definitely dead?"

The ferryman shakes his head and looks like he doesn't know what to reply. He looks like he doesn't want to reply. "I saw a lot of things that day that I'd rather forget. I only heard that he was on the casualty list."

"The casualty list?"

"I'm sorry, Mrs. Blythe. That's all I can tell you. But you know that already, don't you?"

There are shadows around the man's eyes. His eyes now don't want to meet hers. There is a tremble in his hands as he puts a match to his cigarette. She remembers that Harry's hands do that. He blows smoke away and apologizes.

A lapwing cries as she watches the ferryman walk away, and she considers: How does Francis being on a casualty list equate with him being missing, believed killed? How does that add up? Surely, being a *casualty* requires a body, be it one injured or dead? A missing man can't be a casualty, or can he? Could the ferryman be mistaken? Could he have misremembered the events? Confused Francis for someone else?

The reservoir is a mirror full of blue sky, but the railings are cold to her hands. She looks down on the water and just for a second, in the movement of the surface, Francis is there by her side. Fleetingly.

Certainly. Possibly. Her pulse races. She is dizzy and nauseous. But she grips onto the railings, makes herself look again, and there is nothing in the water but her own reflected face. Is it elation or fear that she feels? Grief or relief? Wishfulness or madness? She concentrates on her breathing, counts her breaths, shakes away the notion, and tells herself that it is just the tricks of memory, of conscience, of light on the water. Isn't it?

The wind blows across the water and she pulls her coat around her shoulders. Harry had been in this water too, she remembers. She is not sure why she recalls it just now, but she can hear both their voices telling the story, their voices weaving, Francis's lips whispering it into her ear again, and Harry's there too. In the winter of 1907 they had walked out onto the ice together. Three brothers, still boys then. They had dared each other. Pushed each other on. Harry had told her how he had heard the creak of the ice beneath his boots, seen the shift of the bubbles just below the surface and then the sudden cracks. Francis had told her how suddenly Harry had no longer been there, how Harry had screamed Francis's name and then Francis's arm had kept searching in the water until he had finally found Harry's hand. She imagines the panic and racing fear and the moment when their hands connected. Harry gripping on to life and his brother. The gasping as he surfaced. The emotions exchanged between their eyes in that instant. And what if Francis hadn't run to him? What if Francis hadn't got him out? She pictures Harry kicking slowly against the curling weed, the light pulling away from his clamoring hands. She sees him fixed in the glacier cold, like a fly in amber, or a photograph smile. Surely Harry remembers that too? Surely Harry wouldn't have just let Francis go?

"Mrs. Blythe?" The ferryman is there again.

"There is something else, isn't there? You said the casualty list. Not the list of the missing."

"I don't know what I can tell you," he says and looks down at his hands. "There isn't much that I can give you, but perhaps you have a right to know the bit that I have."

"Yes?" She watches him shift his feet and feels both an urgent need and a sense of shame for putting him in this situation.

"All I know is that your husband was taken away to the dressing station. Rose took him there himself. He carried him, they said. That's the only thing that I can tell you. I don't know anything more. That's the only thing that I heard."

"Rose?"

"Captain Rose. Michael Rose. They'd been friends, you see, him and Francis, back before it all began."

"But Captain Rose wrote to me. He sent me a letter at the end and he told me that Francis was missing. How could he be missing if Rose had taken him to get help? He didn't mention a dressing station at all. Why wouldn't he put that in his letter?"

"I don't know." The ferryman looks away. He now looks like he wished he hadn't followed her. "I've no idea. Only don't misunderstand me — the dressing station was just a group of pillboxes, and it was conspicuous, so they shelled it. They kept on shelling it. The fact that Rose got him back there doesn't mean that he wasn't missing in the end. It's not easy to explain to you what it was like."

"Captain Rose died, didn't he?"

He shakes his head. "I'd heard that he was living in Cheshire after the war. If you get in touch with the regiment, they'll be able to tell you."

"Yes, of course. Thank you for helping me."

"I'm not sure that I've helped at all."

She completes the circuit and is back at

the spillway. A rainbow glistens in the spray of the water, but the rushing sound of it down the steps makes her shiver. Five months earlier Harry had taken her photograph, standing on exactly this spot. He had nodded when she had talked about Francis's grave, but then there would be three months with not a word from him. What did that silence mean? Is there really something that he couldn't bring himself to tell her? So many words pour out of Harry's letters now, but she knows that he hasn't told her everything. It was there in Ypres, that hesitation. When she had asked him to find Francis she believed that it would silence the doubts and the questions, but how loud they are now.

CHAPTER SIXTY:
HARRY

Quercy, October 1921

Harry takes a smoke in the cool evening air. The red cliff beyond the goose field glows, and Gabriel, in the foreground, is a silhouette in the twilight. He stares across the green. Harry takes a place at his side, leaning on the gate, and offers him a smoke.

"It is the house of Madeleine. And of Marcellin, of my brother." Gabriel gestures to the house opposite. A lamp defines a yellow square of window. "It is the *lanterne des morts.*"

"Lantern of the dead? To guide Marcellin home or to show her loss?"

Gabriel shrugs. The match betrays the shaking of his hands as he lights a cigarette, Harry notices. "Both? Madeleine resents my heart and blood and breath. That I have returned and he has not. I would once have given her my blood and breath. But now she tells me that I am too late."

514

"Is that true? Does she not just need time?" Harry blows smoke at the pink sky.

"No. There is not time enough in my lifetime."

"Perhaps returning isn't the right thing," Harry says. "Perhaps we expect too much of it? Perhaps it is better just to keep moving on? Perhaps you're not there yet either?"

"Perhaps, perhaps," says Gabriel, crushing his cigarette. "I don't know that I should have returned. I don't know that I have a place here any longer. I don't know what I am meant to be."

"You need to talk to her. You need to tell her that."

Gabriel nods his head.

He writes to Edie again that night. He sends it all to her in words and images: the significance of a lantern in a window, Gabriel's struggle to settle on the right design for the memorial, and the way that he looks at Madeleine. He sends her sketches of the gold of the hayfield, the shadows of his loft, and the shine of Madeleine's plaits; he draws the folds of the fields, the shape of the walnut trees, and the way the sun glows on the red cliff behind the house; he gives her the streak of the bats against the blue-black sky now, and the glimmer of the ghost-winged moths. He means to let Edie travel with him. He wants her to see it all, to share it all, even though it all means nothing if she's not here with him. He wants her to know that he would still give her his blood and his last breath.

On the third day the hayrick comes, swaggering and creaking, precariously top-heavy. They fork the hay up into the loft from the wagon and the children trample it flat. The gold and green is pressed to the rafters and Harry's aerie is gone. There is something bright and beautiful here, he thinks. Something timeless. Something that will go on. He thinks that, if he were Gabriel, he might stay, that he might make that effort, that he would try to make a future of it.

Gabriel helps him to clear away old straw and implements in a tumbledown cottage behind the barns. He talks of the tools and terminology of his new commission. "I do not expect to get a taste for statuary," he says.

"And Madeleine?"

"I am planning a pilgrimage of my own." He smiles at Harry. "I plan to take Mado to Marcellin, to visit the cemetery together, and through his death to find a future. I will talk to her. I will make her see. Marcellin is lost to both of us. He divides and bonds us. It is not wrong. We have to find a future."

As Harry sweeps the flagstone floor of his new lodgings he thinks about how he would compose a portrait of Gabriel and Madeleine. He has already started putting their gestures, their movements, the way their eyes connect down on paper. He is drawing Gabriel and Madeleine because he has stopped drawing Edie's face. He has made a pact with himself because it has to be this way. Because he has to stop. He has to make himself forget. Sometimes now, when he has the dream about Edie, he can't quite make out the details of her features. Edie is starting to blur. She is slipping out of focus. It is an agony to him, her imprecise face, but how can he have it otherwise?

CHAPTER SIXTY-ONE:
EDIE

Lancashire, October 1921

Those details just aren't there in Rose's letter. Edie reads through it again, although she hardly needs to; she already knows those brief lines by heart, could pick out Rose's handwriting, could recognize his on-paper voice. Among all his pleasantries and kindnesses, there is no mention of any dressing station or a journey back. Surely if Rose had done that, if he had carried Francis back as the ferryman had described, he would have mentioned it? But there is no hint of that journey in this letter. There is only that scant phrase *Missing, believed killed* embroidered around with apologies and well-meaning obituary. It doesn't add up. Why would he not have told her the rest? What motive could he have had for that omission? Could the ferryman's memory be wrong? Might he have mistaken Francis for someone else?

She turns the photograph of Francis between her fingers again. She has spent so long focusing in on that terrible image for the past five months, and had altogether forgotten that this one existed. Francis is carrying a camera in this photograph. A tree is casting shadows across his face, but Edie recognizes the expression. She looks close, at the hands that were once as familiar as her own, at the glint that the image captures in his eye. This is so much more like the man she knows. It is almost like there are two versions of Francis, she thinks. Could this version not have survived?

It was Rose who had sent her this photograph, folded into that momentous letter. He had taken it himself eighteen months earlier, back near Béthune, he had told her. He had recently given Francis his old camera and they had been planning an outing to Ypres together. *To photograph the sights,* he had said in his letter. Edie thinks about the sights of Ypres. She thinks about Francis making plans for photographic excursions. Is it so improbable? Could he really have let go when he yet had plans? Should he not — could he not — still be taking photographs somewhere?

Francis's letters are laid out across the table. Edie had realized, as she retrieved the box, that she had not read his words for a long time. It is nearly two years since she has last pulled the box of letters out from under the bed. How had she accepted it for all that time? How has she never before thought to look through them for more clues? Francis's last letter is dated September 1917 and is brief and purposeful, just full of arrangements for his journey home and complaints about camp food. When she reads it aloud, she can't discern what mood he is in. She can't hear his voice there. She thinks about the man who then made that journey home, who sat silently in her house through the last week of September, and wishes that she had tried harder to get him to talk. Did he already, at that point, suspect that something had gone on between her and his brother? She thinks now that it must have been the case, but where had that suspicion started? Where had it come from? Was he watching her that week and looking for signs? Was he seeing guilt, seeing betrayal, in all her words and gestures? Was he already planning to take Harry's diary when he got back? Did he know what he would do next?

When the telegram had arrived at the end of October, she had somehow known what it would say. There was just something about him when he came back on leave; a recklessness, she supposed she might call it; something precarious; a sense that he had already started letting go. And yet, could she have got that wrong? She can remember so few of his words that week, but as he had readied to leave, he had said, "It will all be over in another year and then I'll start again." She wasn't sure that she believed him then, as he had stood in the doorway, heading back to the station. She had doubted his conviction. But had she just misunderstood? Had she misread him? She had seen weariness on his face and read it as a reluctance to return to the war, but was it rather that his trust in her was dying? Was he giving up on her in that moment? Could he, even then, have been planning a different course? Did he really say "I" and not "we," and if he had, was that significant?

Harry's letters are in the same box. She doesn't mean to reread them, but even the appearance of his writing on the page is so different from Francis's letters. Harry had so many more words. He had spoken to her in his letters, while after Will's death Francis had always seemed to just be repeating a script. At the top of the pile, Harry's *P.S.* thanks her for pencils. *I can see where you have sharpened them with a knife. I can picture you on the kitchen step with the paring knife. It will break my heart when I have to sharpen them again.* And that was just how they were together, Harry and her. It had always been like that, and neither of them would have really let it spill over into anything that they needed to feel guilty about. Neither of them would have hurt Francis. They never even needed to speak about bridges that mustn't be crossed; it was just understood that there was a limit. But, of course, she realizes now that Francis was watching. Of course he was listening to them. Of course he didn't understand that there was a limit. How far did he think it had gone?

She takes the card out of her pocket and looks at it again. She had gone to the regimental headquarters the previous day and the woman on the desk had simply smiled at her inquiry and obligingly copied the address from her records onto the reverse of a business card. Captain Michael Rose is living in Alderley Edge. He didn't die at Cambrai, as Harry had told her. Since the woman smiled at her, and passed the address across the desk, Edie has been asking herself what reason Harry had to lie. What reason did Rose have not to tell her all of the truth? She can't help but think

522

there is something that links the lie and the omission, but what does that add up to?

She pushes Harry's letters away. It is the same voice that writes to her now, only the tone is so different. It is like the orchestra has changed key. *It won't stop,* he says today. *I can't move on. I don't know how to make it stop.*

"I don't know how to make it stop," she speaks out loud.

Does she not have the right to ask Rose? Should she not be allowed to know how Francis got from the dressing station to being missing and lost? She walks back to the table, picks up the pen, and once again considers where to begin a letter. But it is not enough just to put those questions in an envelope. Her fingers turn the card in her pocket. Does she not have the right to hear it directly from him?

CHAPTER SIXTY-TWO:
HARRY

Quercy, October 1921

Gabriel takes him on the horse and trap.

"Do you want me to come with you?"

"No. Don't waste your time. It might be a fool's errand. I don't even really know what I'm looking for."

Saint-Christophe du Quercy already has its war memorial — an obelisk dressed with stone palm leaves and the newly cut names of twenty-eight men. Harry walks around the monument. He reads the names of the twenty-eight men, imagines who these Edouards and Augustes and Jean-Baptistes might have been, what their faces might have looked like. None of these names is familiar. How did an image of his brother's face end up in this remote, ancient village? How is Francis connected to this foreign place and this list of strangers?

They passed through fortified walls on the way in, but it is a long time since war shook the stones of this place. There are arcades around the square and a wooden market hall that might well be medieval. There are no people, though. He shades his eyes from the sun. There is no other soul in the square — only Harry and the names of twenty-eight men who didn't come back. Did anyone come back?

He walks around the arcades and looks out at the bright square beyond and the war memorial at its center. It is like the pivot at the center of this village now. Everything must revolve around it. He wonders if it repulses or draws. Today it does not seem to draw. Noise clatters from the top of the bell tower and vibrates around the square, summoning no one. He walks on until he hears the sound of voices.

Harry stands at the bar to drink a beer. A woman is polishing glasses with a white cloth, holding them up to the light and nodding as she places them back on the shelf. An old man is whistling as he sweeps the floor in the back room. Otherwise the bar is empty.

"Do you know if there is an Englishman living in this village?" he asks, faltering as he sees her incomprehension. *Il y a un anglais qui habite ici?*"

"*Un anglais?*" The woman looks up and

pauses her polishing. *"Il n'y a que l'homme qui prend des photographies."*

"A man who takes photographs?" The glass won't seem to stay still in his hand.

He had felt his heart racing as he had watched the woman drawing the map. All the rhythms of his body seemed to be accelerating as her pencil made a chain of arrows that finally terminated with a cross. As he follows those arrows now, and looks down the long perspective of the narrowing road ahead, he feels something like vertigo and has to put a hand out to the wall to steady himself. What exists where those vanishing points meet?

The woman has taken care to mark all the shops along the street, but her sense of scale is askew, Harry realizes. The drawing diverts him from the road and into washing-strung alleys that twist around and then widen again, past the back door of a baker's, where a youth crosses white arms in the doorway, and a butcher's, where a man in a red-stained apron touches his hat to Harry. He walks quickly, but as he looks at the cross on the map, he is not altogether sure whether he ought to be running to it, or running away; he is caught between urgency, the need to know now, and fear. He steps out beyond the walls that enclose the village, over a bridge, and across a field, and sees the building. It is a symmetrical-faced house, two windows on either side of a canopied door, squarely planted in a garden. Here the order stops, though. The garden, he can see, is overgrown, and paint is peeling from the metal railings that surround the property. The shutters are closed. It looks forgotten.

Harry's hand is on the gate when he sees the man. He is in the field beyond, moving away with what is unmistakably a camera and tripod in his arms. There is something about the man's gait. He walks awkwardly, jerkily, as though he has sustained an injury to a leg at some time, but the way he moves is familiar, and Harry finds himself following.

Though it is a warm autumn day, and Harry is sweating in shirtsleeves, the man is dressed as if it is December. He wears a black overcoat and a homburg hat that looks like it has seen better days. He stops every few paces and looks about. Harry, following, supposes that the man is looking for the right angle for his photograph.

He leans in the shadow of a wall as he watches the figure's halting progress across the field. The valley falls away below, tapering into a funnel of trees. There is a lone ash tree ahead, an antique, noble tree. If Harry was taking the photograph he would center the composition in on that tree. As he watches the man setting up the camera and tripod, he can't help but approach. It is a glass-plate camera, old but quality apparatus, heavy kit.

He is just yards behind the photographer now. He can hear him breathing, smell his breath. Harry realizes that he is holding his own breath. Hands — familiar hands? — adjust the focus. The man steps back to swap over the plates. He half turns as he does so.

"Who is there?" says a voice that Harry recognizes.

He doesn't know quite what it is that makes him run, but suddenly Harry is back pounding through the village streets, past the butcher's and the baker's and the twenty-eight names, his heart banging, pulling away as fast as he is able.

CHAPTER SIXTY-THREE:
EDIE

Cheshire, October 1921

"Captain Rose? I'm sorry, dear, he's long gone." The woman leans in the doorway. Edie's hand had shaken as she had rung the bell, she had felt light-headed as the door opened, and, as the woman pushes her spectacles up her nose now, Edie knows that she can see her foolishness.

"He died?" she asks.

"Heavens, no. Whatever gave you that notion?" The woman laughs and then apologizes. "I just meant that he's moved on. Moved to Altrincham. Not moved to the other side."

"I'm sorry. I really wasn't sure. Do forgive me for disturbing you." She turns to go. She has spent the journey framing questions, rehearsing one side of a conversation, working her way through iterations of possibility, but now it all falls away and she finds herself struggling for the next word. "Only, I don't

529

suppose that he left a forwarding address?"

"Goodness, how pale you look, miss. Yes, they left me an address to pass on the post. He moved in with his sister, you see. I'll find it for you, if you'll give me five minutes, but won't you come in and have a glass of water, dear? You look like you've see a ghost."

There are paintings of gloomy Victorian children all over the walls of this sitting room. Red-faced infants shed great glassy tears and milkmaids sob over spilled milk. Edie had braced herself to walk into a house full of polished leather and brass, compasses, binoculars, and military bearing. She is rather thrown by the inconsolable children, the packs of porcelain pug dogs, and all the cushions embroidered with Bible quotes. She moves THOU SHALT BE SAVED aside, and takes the offered place on the sofa.

As she watches the woman working her way through the writing bureau, Edie considers why Harry had chosen to tell her that lie. Why did he need her to think that Captain Rose was dead? Why had he blocked the possibility of her speaking with him before? She can only assume that Harry doesn't want her to know the parts of the story that were missing from Rose's letter. But what significance does that have? What more can Rose tell her?

"Do forgive my mess. How embarrassing. I do know that it's in here somewhere."

"No, I'm sorry for barging into your house uninvited. It's very kind of you to make the time."

While she sips the glass of water, she pictures a series of scenes in which Francis moves from dressing station, to hospital, to recuperation, to — where? She imagines the chain of decisions that have gone through Francis's head, resulting in his making a choice not to come home. Is he so convinced that she has wronged him? Is he still angry at her? Did he simply decide that there was nothing to salvage? Has he made another life? Found another wife?

"Only my husband rearranges my papers and never thinks to put anything back where he found it. It's like sport to him, like it must always be hide-and-seek. Is that men in general, do you think?"

"I couldn't say."

Edie looks around the sitting room and she imagines a home in which she and Francis are husband and wife again, where possessions are once more shared, and conversations have two halves. Edie finds that it is

531

easy to give their imaginary home a dinner service, and cutlery and upholstery, and to pick out the pattern of the wallpaper, but she doesn't know what face her husband ought to wear. The two versions of Francis seem so far apart. Must she have the man with the sorrowful eyes when she would really much rather have the boy with the rhymes and the smile? The contemplation of it makes her feel foolish. It makes her feel like a failure, and why would he choose to come back to such a shallow woman? She imagines an alternative reality in which Francis is sharing a home with a different woman. Is this what jealousy feels like? Is this how betrayal smarts?

"I knew I had it." The woman turns and puts a looking glass to the piece of paper in her hand. Edie sees rounded copperplate letters and, in the magnification, a female name.

"Captain Rose lives with his sister, you said?"

"Yes, a very nice lady. Lovely manners. We met them both when the house turned over. The captain is a gentleman too, of course, and a decorated officer, only the poor man was suffering terribly with his nerves."

"He told you that?"

The woman shakes her head and plumps

a cushion that is cross-stitched with the words DO UNTO OTHERS. "The neighbors. Noises in the night."

"Oh." Edie thinks about the sound of Harry's fear and tears, and then the cold of his cheek against hers. She is not really sure she wants to hear about noises in the night.

"Don't you think it's a pity? He was a charming man in the daytime, they tell me, meek as a lamb, but there were some shocking things went on, weren't there? Alfred says that no amount of medals on your chest makes up for having that in your head. I suppose that's why his sister wanted to look after him."

"Naturally so."

Is it his nerves that make Harry cry in the night? Is it the shocking things that went on? There was a moment when she had wanted nothing more than to look after Harry, but is he really the man she thought he was?

"Anyway, listen to me rattling on. You are still terribly pale, Mrs. Blythe. Would you like a sherry?"

"No, it's quite all right, I must get on, but thank you. Could I possibly take a copy of the address?"

"Do you mean to get in touch with Captain Rose?" she asks, as she looks up from the writing bureau.

"I'm not sure. I think so. There's something that I perhaps need to ask him."

"Do be careful, dear. Won't you?"

"Of course. But why do you say that?"

"Oh, these men and their memories. It's really not over for so many of them yet, is it?"

CHAPTER SIXTY-FOUR: HARRY

Calvaire du Quercy, October 1921

"It is not from her?"

"No. It's Rachel's writing. It's from a friend." Harry is familiar with the handwriting of several women now, their loops and leans and the way they set down the lines onto an envelope. There are still no envelopes from Edie, though.

"Read it, if you wish," says Gabriel. "I will make the coffee."

He sits at the table and opens Rachel's envelope. It is the second that he has received from her this month. She has gone to David's grave. She had been to that same cemetery before, her letter tells Harry. She doesn't know how she could have missed him, how she could have walked so close by and not known that he was there. She will return to England now, she says. She will pull up the shutters and restart her sewing machine, make a business and a purpose

535

for herself. Harry is not quite sure what emotion he hears between Rachel's lines. She tries to sound determined, but it is tinged with something else. He suspects she is not experiencing the sense of relief that she had told herself she would. What has hit her is not quite the emotion that she was braced for. He thinks about her profile on the boat reciting poems and wonders what lines will come to mind as she reverses her journey. He thinks again about the mystery of the empty photograph.

"Your friend is well?" Gabriel asks and puts the coffeepot down on the table.

"I think so. I hope so."

"This is the tall woman? The Amazonian?"

"No." Harry laughs. "That's Cassie. Her letters are full of wagging fingers. She writes to tell me that I have to write to Edie."

He does not need Cassie's encouragement; though his letters remain unanswered, he carries on writing. It is as if, in describing the details of his days, and committing these acts and images to her eyes, he tests that what he sees is true. He hasn't told her about the photographer, though. He hasn't told Gabriel all of it either. He's not quite sure how to put it into words yet, and suddenly doesn't feel like he can trust his own eyes or his mind.

"Does she realize how many letters you have written to Edie?"

"Possibly not."

Gabriel shrugs and takes the chair opposite. There is paint on his hands. He had shown Harry the canvas the day before and asked for his opinion. It was just darkness at first, and a suggestion of night sky, and Harry had seen nothing more in it. He had looked at Gabriel and then back to the difficult shadows. It was a veiled vista, smoked with soft suggestion, but Harry stepped closer and it slid into focus; the landscape was cross-hatched with white crosses; these fields were dense with dead. Harry stepped back, but the dead, now distinguished, refused to blur. In the foreground was a figure, his shadow-carved face greens and grays, his mouth gasping, as if surfacing from the sea, and his pale eyes communicating torment. It was a lamentation. Gabriel told him that it was a portrait of Marcellin and all the dead of France.

"Madeleine has bought the train tickets for Chaulnes. You don't mind that we go?"

"Of course not."

"We will be back on Saturday."

"Don't feel obliged to hurry back. I can help your mother."

"And then how guilty would she make me

feel?" Gabriel rolls his eyes and laughs.

"I have been developing more photographs," Harry tells him. "I should, shouldn't I?"

"Will you feel better when you have completed it?"

"I'll never complete it."

"You've done enough."

"Have I? I wish I could feel like that." He had left his camera in pieces on the floor of a hotel room in Amiens. He can't recall the name of the hotel, but he can remember the names of all those men who were still on his list. "I'll post the photographs that I've taken back to Mr. Lee. The families have paid for them. I need to complete that much."

He had started the previous week, setting up his trays of chemicals on the table at which they are now sitting, wet images of graves hanging in lines from the beams, thinking all the time of Francis and Lieutenant Rose making a darkroom of a cellar in Arras. Would Edie still want an image of Francis's grave? Is she ready for the alternative?

After an evening in the red light he had dreamed about the red gallery in Denham Hall. He was walking through it at night, the pictures on the walls just mute darkness within the gilt glimmer of their frames. Broken glass stuck in his feet, but on and on he walked, and it was a spiral, a circle. Then she was there, briefly, in the door-frame at the end of the corridor. She was dancing with someone, though the male figure was just an anonymous shape. She looked back over her shoulder toward Harry and smiled. He walked on toward her, but no matter how far he walked, she never seemed to get any closer. The noise of the incoming shell echoed in his head.

"You must finish it, then." Gabriel nods. "Do you have the photograph of Marcellin's grave?"

"Yes."

Harry reaches for the stack of photographs from the dresser. Gabriel stands at his shoulder as he turns through them, and then he is there standing at the side of his brother's grave. Harry hands him the portrait. Gabriel, in the photograph, is making the sort of expression that one ought to make at a graveside, his sepia face solemn but noble. The face at Harry's side, as he looks at his own image, isn't quite so solid. Is he thinking of standing in this same spot with Madeleine? Gabriel rubs his eyes and Harry turns away.

He looks at the next image in the pile,

which is just a wall. He had stared at it as it floated into existence in the bath of chemicals. He had tried to remember why he might have taken a photograph of a wall. It was only a couple of hours later that he had managed to place and recall the significance of that particular expanse of stone. A figure had been sat in front of it. He had talked to that man, told him his name, shaken his hand. Afterward, in the red light, Harry had stood in front of the mirror. He half expected his own reflection to have disappeared then. But, unlike that of Daniel East, Harry's face was there in the glass.

"My mother will never make this journey," says Gabriel. "I am glad that I can show her this image. You must remember that, when you send your photographs back. It is a good and a kind thing that you have done."

Would he have posted the image of Daniel East to Rachel? He thinks of the man's face, as real as his own in the mirror. The only clue in the photograph that he might ever have been there is a wreath leaned against the wall. That is it. He thinks of Rachel and her talk of clairvoyants, of psychics conjuring spirits for those in wishful mourning. Had he wished Daniel East from his imagination? He had almost told Rachel as they stood looking down over Vimy Ridge.

It would have sent her search in a different, and false, direction. He had been on the very edge of telling her.

"Thank you," he says to Gabriel.

"Are you going to go back to Saint-Christophe? I spoke to Lucien Delbos, who owns the bar. He said that there was an Englishman living there."

Harry tries to recall the photographer's face, but all that will come back to him is a blur. He knows there was something familiar there, but in recall it has no detail. His recalled image is not quite sharp enough. As with Daniel East, could he just have been mistaken?

"I don't know," Harry says.

He sits at the table after Gabriel leaves, and stares at the photograph of Daniel East's absence. Was it the camera, or is his mind playing tricks? He almost suspects that if he looks away from the print for a moment, the figure will return. But will it be Daniel East there against the wall this time, or the face of the man with the camera in Saint-Christophe? Harry tries to bring to mind the face of the photographer, to pull it back into focus. He had surely seen it, and known it, but he can't now recall a face at all. Harry watches the lying photograph; he doesn't mean to let it catch him out; he means to reason all of this through, he tells himself; he will go back to Saint-Christophe.

But when he picks up the phantom photograph, he can't make it stay still. Why can he not hold it still? He tries to pin it to the tabletop, but his fingers won't do as he wills them. The photograph falls to the floor and he crosses his arms over his chest. He tries to brace it, to keep it in, to push the shaking back inside his body.

CHAPTER SIXTY-FIVE:
EDIE

Denham Hall, Cheshire, October 1921

"There are only ghosts here now," says the man by the gate. "Did you know it before?"

"Not really. Not well. I came here once. Back in 1917. My brother-in-law was a patient here."

Edie hadn't expected to come back to this place, but it is one bus stop before the street where Captain Rose lives, and somehow, as the familiar walls of the house came into view, she had wanted to rewind and be here, not there. It wasn't that she had expected to step inside the walls, just that she would have liked to lean on the gate and remember it all better, just to see the house from across the water again and to try to put it all back into place, but now the agent is turning the key and it can't hurt to look again. Can it?

"I saw the sign. It's to be sold?"

"It's going to auction at the end of the month. Every stick and stone of it. Every item of it has been catalogued. Every napkin, candlestick, and soupspoon. I'm sorry, I should introduce myself. Alastair Bowen, property agent."

She shakes the man's hand. "How sad for the family."

"They've taken a house in town. These old places are too much of an expense to maintain — all those windows to clean, all those steps to climb — and the roof needs work. The damp is finding its way in. It'll probably become an institution of some kind, or be split up into flats, or just bulldozed to make way for new houses. That's the way it's all going now."

Weeds have grown through the gravel path and the gardens have gone back. Bindweed has choked the rosebeds, and the clipped lawn is now a yellow meadow picked out with bright poppies.

"It was all so tidily mowed and maintained."

"It hasn't been for a long time."

The rhododendrons have grown taller, the elm and ash crowd in more, but beyond them the house is still there, mirrored in the lake. The upper windows have been boarded over and the blinds are drawn on the lower floors, so that it is like a blinkered version of its former self. There are no men singing on the steps. No gramophone music distorts across the garden. It is as still as an Impressionist painting. It is only the light that vibrates.

"The winds last winter weren't kind," says the agent.

A tree has fallen, bringing the far end of the conservatory down into so much buckled metal and fallen glass. Edie remembers the men in wicker chairs looking out in their convalescent blues, all their faces in the glass, looking like they were waiting. Where are all those men now?

"How quickly nature takes it back."

The climbing roses haven't been pruned and they sway away from the walls in the wind. Ivy has crept over the balustrade and is claiming stonework and windowpanes.

"I've already cleared it back from around the door twice," says Bowen. "It blunted my pruning shears. It's like it wants to seal it in, to close the lid on the mausoleum."

Edie watches as he turns the key and pushes the door. Blown leaves shift and skitter across the tiles.

"Don't spook easily, do you?" he says.

"No. I don't think so."

"Good. The last patients left two years ago and the family never really made it a home again. There's nothing here but echoes and mice now. I shan't admit to the number of times that a creaking shutter or a rustling in the walls has made me jump."

Edie steps through the leaves and recalls crossing the same floor tiles four years earlier, struck then by the grandeur of this place. The skylight still casts its yellows and blues down around her feet, but when she looks up she sees how the glass is grimed and the silhouettes of fallen branches break the symmetry of the leading.

Bowen nods at a line of packing cases. "Just waiting to make their exit. A few last personal things. I've got to go up to the library. Do you want to come up with me?"

Edie remembers the sweep of the staircase. She remembers holding on to the stair rail and a flutter in her stomach as she had followed the nurse up. Her knees hadn't felt quite steady. She had felt fear at that moment.

The paint has blistered from the ceiling and flaked down onto the staircase. It is like a sweep of confetti strewn all up the stairs, and there is a smell of damp decay. Can it really be just four years ago? The house has the air of having been abandoned for decades.

Bowen's flashlight leads along the corridor, picking out moldering lampshades and stacks of curling magazines. It lights a birdcage, a box of crockery, and a cob-webbed wheelchair.

"This was the saloon, but it became a ward during the war," he says as he pushes the door. "Though you perhaps already know that?"

"Yes," Edie replies and realizes that she is holding her breath.

How odd to cross this threshold again. How shockingly alike and different it all is. She is conscious, as she stands here, of how many times she has replayed this memory, how she has stored away all its detail. The bedsteads are still here, though stripped back to their metal frames. Without the antiseptic smell and the blue uniforms, they are just boys' beds in a dormitory. The wallpaper is coming away, sheets peeling down from the tops of the walls.

"It's shrugging off its skin," she says. "How sorry it looks."

"I'm not sure that it would be terribly hygienic any longer."

She had looked at all the men in their beds, one by one, hoping for Harry's face, and they all looked back at her, so obviously not him. She had feared how bad the injury would be. Francis had told her that Harry had been caught in an explosion on the barbed wire and that he was pretty nastily cut up. She had looked at the men with bandaged faces and wondered if she would still know him. Edie walks the length of the room again. Just for a second it flashes into cold white daylight, with the scent of larkspur and Harry's eyes lifting to hers.

"Your relative did make it out of here, I take it?" Mr. Bowen's voice brings her back to the dim present.

"Yes. He's a photographer now."

"Grand. We are the lucky ones and must make the most of every day."

His face is lost in the dazzle of the flash-light beam but she hears a melancholy edge in his voice. What secrets they all must now keep stored away. She looks down the corridor from the ward. "May I?"

"Of course. I'll open a shutter for you."

The room is just darkness at the end of the corridor. She pictures Harry in the doorway. Walking through feels oddly like some sort of rite.

"You look like someone has just stepped on your grave," says Bowen's voice, suddenly there at her side again. "It was a picture gallery, I think. Someone in the family was a collector."

There is no light in the room, but she

knows the color of its walls. A pale shape looms. She looks twice before she knows that it is a statue covered over in a dust sheet.

"Open more shutters if you want. I'm just in the library next door. Don't worry, if you see a ghost, I'll hear you scream."

The shutter is stiff, but she manages to pull it back far enough to see it all. The chairs are stacked now, the tables pushed back, and the chaise longue covered with sheets, but it is the walls that most strike her as different. Where the paintings once hung, where there were all those purple mountains and blue cliffs, there are now just darker rectangles of red paint.

"They've all gone," says Edie.

Bowen turns in the doorway. "The paintings? Yes, all sold off last year. So much of it went out of the door, bit by bit, but not enough to settle the bills."

Edie puts her hand to the cool marble of the mantelpiece. For a moment he is by her side, steering her around the walls again.

"It's all downhill from now, isn't it? This might just be the best day of my life," says Harry's recalled voice.

The plasterwork ceiling has come through in places. Older wooden panels show beneath. Could it have been that bad back then? Surely this decay must have already set in. Had she just not seen it?

"If I cling on to you, will you help me not to bounce back down?" she hears Harry say.

Music suddenly swells, and she gasps. Is Bowen right about the ghosts? Jazz music is playing somewhere in the house. She steps into the library as he looks up from the gramophone.

"I didn't scare you, did I?"

"Briefly. Momentarily. Bravo, if that was your intention."

The gramophone crackles through "Crazy Blues." It is the same instrument, she recognizes, that they had out on the steps. She shivers and pulls her coat around her shoulders.

"Mamie Smith and her Jazz Hounds." Bowen shuffles his papers and smiles. "I find it cheers the place up a bit. Drags it into the twentieth century. I'm sorry. I won't be much longer."

"I wouldn't like to be in here on my own."

"Do you wonder why I jumped at the chance of your company?"

There are books all over the floor in the library. Bowen apologizes for the mess. She steps between stacks of Shakespeare and estate accounts and thinks of Francis and Harry in a looted house, his feet picking between sonnets and maps of Abyssinia.

"If you wish to take a souvenir, I'll turn a blind eye." Bowen nods to the stack of gramophone records. "No one will know and I won't tell on you. There's actually some decent stuff here."

"It's quite all right. But thank you."

She sits down in a chair and closes her eyes. For a moment it all spins around her and they are dancing again on the lawn. She sees Harry's up-close, long-ago face. She also sees the photograph that he sent the previous day. It had shocked her when an image of Tyne Cot fell out of the envelope, but he reminded her that he had promised to do it for her. His writing supposes that she hasn't yet stood in that place. He says this is the best that he can give her.

Being there, seeing this, brought it all back to me, he wrote. *I relived those last moments. I saw his flickering eyelids again, heard his stilling breath, felt the weight of him in my arms.* Seeing the scene now through his words, being brought up close to Francis's dying face, she wants to believe that Harry isn't lying. But she has stood in that cemetery, among the eight thousand nameless men, and she knows that Francis isn't one of them. She also knows that this wasn't Francis's last moment. Where in this scene is the journey back in Rose's arms and the dressing station? Why is that not in any of Harry's letters? She wishes that he wasn't lying, but she knows now that he is.

"I shall be sad when it's gone," says Bowen, turning toward her as he locks the door of Denham Hall. "I should be sorry if so much history went under the wrecking ball."

They stand side by side and watch the reflection of the house shiver in the lake. She turns the Saint Christopher in her pocket. If she hadn't given it to Harry that day, if she had given it to Francis instead, would it all now be different? Did it really cause so much trouble?

"It can't do any harm, can it?" She hears her own recalled voice and feels like she has caused so much harm.

There is no drama in its arc, not even a bubble breaks the surface. She has no obvious sense of exorcising a ghost or righting a wrong.

"There's probably a tidy sum in coins at the bottom of that lake. Did you make a wish?" Bowen's grin is no more real than Francis's celluloid smile, but how very far away and long ago that suddenly seems. How fleeting and fragile it all is.

"I'm not sure what to wish for," Edie replies.

CHAPTER SIXTY-SIX:
HARRY

Saint-Christophe du Quercy, October 1921

Gabriel drives him as far as the village walls this time.

"Are you sure you don't want me to come with you?"

"No. As I said, if you'd meet me here again in a couple of hours . . ."

Harry walks back over the bridge and across the field and stands with his hands on the railings. The grass beyond is knee-high and the apple trees untended. Wasps hum among the fallen fruit and he thinks of a long-ago felled orchard, the sweet smell of the newly cut wood, and his brother sleeping in the grass at his side. Should he not still be sleeping? Who do these railings contain?

The gate closes behind him. Weeds have pushed through the gravel path and a trellis of wisteria has taken over one side of the house. There are empty bottles stacked in a crate by the side of the door, he sees as he gets closer, and a cane chair that has blackened with being out in the weather. The drone of a wasp is amplified in the bottles. A shutter hangs aslant.

It is dark inside and he can see very little through the window. There are some items of furniture covered over with dust sheets, so that they look like ghosts in a Victorian melodrama. There is a vase of desiccated hydrangea heads on the other side of the glass, and an open book. He stands on his tiptoes to see and reads the first line of a poem. "I must go down to the seas again, to the lonely sea and the sky. . . ." He hears Rachel's voice speak the line and is momentarily back on the boat with the taste of salt on his lips. "It's not enough: 'Missing'," says Rachel's recalled voice.

With a sudden movement he steps back. A bottle falls and smashes. A rat scurries away.

"Monsieur?"

He turns, expecting to see the man in the homburg hat with a face that is a blur.

"Monsieur? Je peux vous aider?"

It is a woman. White hair. A black dress. A gold cross at her throat. She holds her outstretched hands together as if she is making an offering in a church, as if she is about

555

to dip in front of an altar. There is something humble and tender about the gesture and Harry instinctively wants to stretch his hand out to hers.

"I can help you?" she says.

She unlocks the door and Harry steps in behind her. She introduces herself as Marie-Thérèse and apologizes for the state of the floor tiles.

"I have been looking after the house and *le monsieur. Il était anglais, ce monsieur,*" she adds. *"Comme vous?* The house is available for rent again, but I did not expect anyone to view it today. *J'ai honte de ce bordel!* I am sorry for the mess. *Tout sera bien propre."*

She goes ahead and opens shutters. As light comes into the room Harry sees china dogs that he might recognize and porcelain shepherdesses that he might not. There are several clocks in this room, all stopped at different times, so that their lies vary in scale. He also sees a lot of photographic equipment; there are rolls of film and parts of cameras, stacked glass plates and boxes of chemicals. Photographs are everywhere. Lines of wire have been stretched between the beams, and clothespins remain where drying prints have been suspended. There is only one image now on the wires: the view of the valley, the tapering lines of trees, and the ash tree at the center. With the smell of developing fluid, Harry is back in the cellar in Arras.

"*Voyez!* Looking after this monsieur has not been easy," says Marie-Thérèse. She laughs, throws her hands up, and then frowns. "*Pas facile,*" she repeats with emphasis.

"No," says Harry, looking around. "I see."

The walls are a patchwork of photographic prints, rippling now in the breeze from the window. Many of the images Harry recognizes as being from the immediate vicinity — the arcades of the village square, the wooden timbers of the market hall, the alleys, and the crumbling bastide walls. The valley below the house is a repeated subject. The ash tree is there in mist, in rain, and in snow.

Marie-Thérèse points and pulls back her lips to show a crooked-toothed smile. Her own image is among a collection of portraits. She sits straight-backed, proper, and proud, those hands, linked again, now in her lap. There are faces of farmers and shepherds and circus performers, ancient faces, children's faces, and young women in mourning clothes. There is something quietly dignified about these portraits. Each of the sitters looks like they have some source of pride. He has given a nobility to them all.

"Ma fille," says Marie-Thérèse and indicates a girl with braided hair. "My daughter."

Harry nods. They are accomplished portraits. Sharp. Direct. Their eyes arresting. They speak loudly, these quiet sitters. He would be proud had he taken these photographs himself. He thinks of all the faces that he drew. All those glinting eyes and grins that he had tried to catch on paper left something of themselves behind and come back to him in dreams. He sometimes imagines all of those paper faces flickering behind him like an echo. He sometimes wonders what happened to the sent-home soldiers' smiles. Are they still there on bedroom walls and kitchen dressers, substituted for their owners or looking like something long ago and unlikely? He thinks of all the times that he has drawn Francis's face and how far away but oddly close that memory feels at this moment.

Harry looks at the far wall, and Marie-Thérèse shakes a hand in front of her face and turns her back. "I don't look," she says.

There are faces again here. All male now:

some of them smiling, joshing in a farm courtyard, others unshaven and shadow-eyed. There are faces that Harry does not know, but so many that are familiar. Will is standing on his hands in a Yorkshire field. Pembridge is exchanging cigarettes with a French soldier. Wilkinson scowls at a jar of insecticide powder. Bartley is in the orchard. Harry is by Francis's side on the docks in Boulogne. Francis is everywhere.

He hears footsteps behind and turns. Marie-Thérèse opens the far door, steps into a kitchen, and beckons Harry after.

"*C'est trop, tout ça,*" she says. "Too much. It is necessary to try to forget. *Il faut essayer.* It is necessary to think of tomorrow, not yesterday."

She takes a bottle from a shelf, pours two measures, and squeezes Harry's arm. He watches her as she moves around the kitchen. Her broom shoos cobwebs from corners. There is a stale smell, a rust mark in the bottom of the sink, and husks of dead centipedes on the tiles. She gathers them together with a dustpan and brush and, straightening, says, "*C'est trop triste.* Too sad."

Harry takes it all in — the row of wooden spoons and the rosy-sprigged coffeepot, the pans that hang from the ceiling and the bar of soap by the side of the sink that has shrunk and cracked. Who last turned it in their hands? Whose domesticity is this? There are bird bones and snail shells on the window ledge, a piece of quartz, a clay pipe, and a collection of flints. Harry considers the imagination that has salvaged and arranged these small treasures. He sees his brother, long ago, pull a triangle of flint from the wall of a trench and turn toward him with an outstretched hand. "Look," says Francis's once-upon-a-time voice.

He glances up at a scurry of noise above. *"Que les souris qui dansent."* Marie-Thérèse laughs at Harry's alarm. "Only the mice. While the cat is away, the mice dance."

Harry drains his glass. The spirit is strong and hot at the back of his throat. He coughs, and Marie-Thérèse widens her eyes in amusement. She clinks her own emptied glass against Harry's and crosses her arms over her chest. *"Alors,* you wish to view the house, monsieur?"

Harry suddenly feels like he is trespassing.

"No. I mean, thank you, but I wouldn't. I couldn't. The gentleman is out? He is away today? *Le monsieur, il n'est pas ici?"*

Marie-Thérèse looks at him for a moment before she answers. She counts it out on her fingers and holds up five digits. *"Capit-*

aine Rose, il est décédé. He is dead, monsieur. He is dead for five months."

Perspective shifts as he walks back into Rose's room full of photographs. Harry remembers the grip of Rose's hand on his arm as they had stood at Will's graveside. He remembers Rose's face next to Francis's, laughing in the red glow of their cellar darkroom. He remembers — he is sure of it — reading that Rose had been killed in Cambrai. So many facts are false. So many people aren't where they're meant to be. So much is shaken up.

He looks around this room and Francis's face is everywhere. How could he really have believed that Francis might be in Saint-Christophe du Quercy? And, yet, he so obviously is.

"*Il était un vrai* gentleman, *Capitaine Rose. Sympathique. Très gentil,*" says Marie-Thérèse.

"Yes, he was," Harry agrees.

Rose had joined them while they were still training in Morecambe. He and Francis had met looking into the window of a photographer's studio. A conversation had started as their reflections joined over flashguns and spools of film. Is this where it ended?

"But these journeys! *Cette lourde tristesse!*

561

It was all very difficult. *Cette affreuse guerre.*"

"Journeys?"

Marie-Thérèse's finger makes backward and forward gestures. "Each month. From north to south. *Du sud au nord.* And all of this terrible news," she adds, searching for English adjectives. "Horrible news."

"I'm sorry? I'm not quite sure I follow."

"*Ses gars.* His boys. *Ses soldats.* Are you one of his soldiers?"

Her meaning becomes apparent when she shows him the wall. Marie-Thérèse leads Harry back through the kitchen, back past the flints and the quartz and the rosy coffeepot, which just ten minutes earlier all might have belonged to Francis. Past the spoons and the soap and the snail shells, which Harry had pictured so very clearly turning in his brother's hands. The room beyond looks like it once served as a dining room, a sideboard displays decanters and soup tureens, only now it is something between a library and a command center. The dining table is covered over with large-scale military maps, busily annotated. As Harry looks, he sees familiar villages, and around them clusters of names and numbers. It is some moments before he realizes what the numbers represent.

"His casualties? Our losses?" He turns to Marie-Thérèse. She nods her head.

Something seems to shift under Harry's feet as he looks at the maps. Marie-Thérèse pulls out a chair and encourages him to sit. She goes back through to the kitchen for the bottle of eau-de-vie.

Harry knows the villages, the woods, the terrains, and the names, and it doesn't take him long to figure out Rose's purpose or his code. The names of the missing men are in red ink; the confirmed casualties are in black. Rose had seemingly given himself the task of turning all the reds into blacks.

"He says it is his responsibility." Marie-Thérèse refills Harry's glass. "*Il a dit que c'était son* duty."

He thinks of Ralph Fielding's need to do the right thing by the men he lost. The need to make it up to them in some way. His penance, as Cassie had called it. Was this what Rose felt too? Was this something that he had to make right?

"He was trying to find them all?"

"He had some success. *Il a trouvé beaucoup de ces disparus.*"

"*Disparus?*" Harry repeats. "He found the disappeared?" There is only one name, then, that he needs to locate on the map. "*Il y une carte de la région d'Ypres?"* He searches the table.

"*Je ne sais pas, monsieur.* I do not know. *Mais il y a son mur.* His wall." She points.

It is only then that Harry sees there is a wall of faces in this room too. It is like the crosses that suddenly loom out of Gabriel's canvas. Like those unintelligible shadows that suddenly, with a shift of focus, make sense. The wall behind Harry is covered in photographed faces.

"*Ses gars,*" repeats Marie-Thérèse. "His boys."

Harry's eyes do not know where to look. There is Bartley and Pembridge and Fearnley. Here is Summerfield and Wilkinson and Lieutenant O'Kane. So many of them are familiar. So many more of them he had forgotten. "William," he says as his focus catches the expression of his younger brother. It is a shock to see him here. "*Mon frère,*" he says to Marie-Thérèse.

"*Le pauvre.*"

"And the cemetery," he says as he steps nearer to the wall. There, beside Will's grin, is the cross in Guillemont that Harry had knelt beside two months ago. It is the same for all of them, he sees: next to the photograph of each of these men is an image of his grave.

564

"Et ceux qu'il n'a pas trouvés. Et les soldats he does not find," Marie-Thérèse adds, hesitating through the words.

Her finger indicates the second group. Just faces, these. No accompanying graves. But too many faces. And Harry's eyes cannot search them fast enough.

"He's not there."

"Monsieur?"

"Francis." He searches Marie-Thérèse's face too, but no recognition glimmers. "Francis Blythe? His photograph is everywhere in the other room. Did Monsieur Rose find Francis Blythe?"

It seems a long time before Marie-Thérèse's expression changes. An awful long time until she picks out the place on the wall.

CHAPTER SIXTY-SEVEN: EDIE

Cheshire, October 1921

"You're looking for Captain Rose?" the woman asks.

"Yes. Please forgive me for disturbing you. I'm looking for Michael Rose. I was given this address."

Edie feels embarrassed and confused now, feels a strange urge to run. Does she have any right to cross-examine this man? Is it fair to oblige this stranger to pick over memories that evidently trouble him? Looking at the woman's frowning face, sensing her obvious suspicions and doubt, Edie feels like coming here has been a mistake.

"I'm sorry. He's not here any longer."

"He's not?" It's almost a relief then. Can she now just turn her back and walk away? "Please excuse me. Do forgive me. I must have been given the wrong address."

"You're not wrong," the woman says. She looks at Edie, but then looks away. "You were given the right address. My name is Louisa Davies. I'm Michael Rose's sister. But I'm afraid that my brother is dead."

"It was five months ago," Louisa Davies explains. "I had a phone call from the gendarmerie. It's very difficult to be told in a foreign language that your brother has killed himself. As you stumble through the translation, there's no softening it off with euphemism. He hanged himself."

"How awful for you."

Louisa Davies shakes her head. "Awful for poor Michael, but I can't honestly say it was a shock. My brother wasn't a well man, you see. When I look back, I can see that it was coming for a long time. Sometimes you wonder how you can have missed the signs, don't you?"

Edie insists on helping Louisa with the tea things, and as she looks around this stranger's kitchen, at the coffee spoons enameled with the coat of arms of Arras and the sugar bowl painted with an image of Ypres, she is aware of just how much connects them. But how many other links will never now be clear enough? There have been so many missed signs and missed opportunities. She had wanted to look Captain Rose in the eye, and to hear the story from his mouth, and then to know if Harry had lied and whether there is really a chance that Francis might yet be alive. She is now not sure that she will ever know.

"We thought we'd lost him once before, long ago. My brother was badly wounded at Cambrai," Louisa says as they walk back through with the tea tray.

"At Cambrai? Yes, I think I'd heard that."

"He was in the hospital for months and I wasn't really certain that he'd make it. We sorted all the paperwork out, and my mother and I even talked about what hymns he would have liked at his funeral. It quite spooks me now to remember that! Because one morning we walked into the ward and his eyes were open again. Just like that. He pulled through then, he got stronger every day, but the version of Michael that I got back wasn't the brother that I'd known before the war. He joked once that he'd looked his maker in the eye. I suppose it was coming so close to the edge that did it. Or that's how I reasoned it to myself, anyway. The version of my brother that I got back was a driven man. The war had spat him back out again, but it had taken his mind. He was obsessed, you see."

"Obsessed?"

"By what had gone on. By making it

right." Louisa blows at her tea and makes small waves. There is such difficulty in her eyes, Edie sees, as she looks up over the rim of her cup. "I'm afraid that Michael felt guilty, that he had a sense of unfulfilled responsibility. You see, when he was still in his hospital bed, he made a list of the men in his unit that he'd lost, and he gave himself a mission to account for them all."

"Like a shepherd looking after his sheep?" There is a framed photograph of a young man over the fireplace. He is wearing a tweed jacket and holding a cloth cap in his hand as he leans on a farm gate. His fringe flops over his forehead and there is a sparkle of amusement in his lifted eyes. He looks rather like Louisa Davies, Edie thinks, she can see a family resemblance, but she also recognizes the young man's features, just a little older, from some of Francis's photographs. This is the young man with whom she has needed to talk, only it is now too late.

"Something like that," Louisa replies. "Like a shepherd who has lost his sheep and needs to bring them all back into the fold. He made a list of the men who had died and a list of the missing. He had to be sure that the first group all had a grave marker, and the latter all had to be found. Only, that was such an undertaking. He had set himself an impossible task."

"Absolutely impossible." Edie thinks about Tyne Cot and the words on all those crosses; all the men, so many men, KNOWN UNTO GOD and God alone.

"And, really, I think Michael knew that it was impossible. He probably even knew that right at the start, but he wouldn't give it up. He started going back out there, you see. He'd go out there for weeks on end, going over the ground, picking over it all. Like a scab that he refused to let heal. He went out there with a spade. Can you imagine? Digging over all those terrible places. It was dangerous and it was bad for his health. His health never really recovered after he came out of the hospital, and all of this made it so much worse. I tried to reason with him. Of course I did. I begged him to stop, to give it up, but I don't think that he actually could. It was a torture to him, and it was a torture to see him like that, but at some very fundamental level he needed to do it. Or, at least, he needed to try."

"Did he find any of the men he was looking for?" Edie pictures the young man in the tweed jacket out there in that terrible landscape. She pictures his spade digging and all of the amusement falling out of his eyes. She needs to know what he was looking for and what he found.

"Yes, which gave him all the more reason to carry on, I suppose." She looks at Edie. "Why did you want to speak to Michael?"

"Because my husband is missing. I thought that he might be able to confirm some details for me. Please say no if this is too intrusive, but could I perhaps look through your brother's papers?"

Louisa hesitates. "Could I perhaps ask your husband's name?"

"Francis Blythe."

Louisa nods. "For some odd reason I did think it might be. I know his name. It used to be there so often in Michael's letters."

"You do?"

"Well, they were friends, weren't they? He was the young chap who took photographs with Michael. Isn't that right? And his was the last name that Michael crossed off his list. I think that finding Francis Blythe rather drew a line under things, like Michael felt he had come to a point where he had done enough."

"He found Francis?"

"Oh, how do I say it? I am so sorry, Edie. You shouldn't hear it like this, should you? Michael found Francis Blythe's grave."

■ ■ ■ ■

Edie cries then like she hasn't cried before, not even when the telegram came, or when she got the first letter from Michael Rose. Because now it is final. Because now finally it is real. Louisa puts her arms around Edie as she cries, and Edie feels how Louisa cries too. When it is done, when Edie can cry no more, Louisa pushes the damp hair away from her face, looks her square in the eye, and smiles.

"Forgive me," Edie says.

"Don't apologize. Don't ever apologize. You have every reason to cry, and better out than in, eh? Shall I fetch the bottle of brandy?"

"Your brother wrote to me twice, you know," she tells Louisa as Louisa fills the glasses. "He sent me a letter in November 1917 and told me that Francis was missing and believed killed, and I was grateful to him for that, the fact that he'd taken the time, and that he said such kind things. But then afterward, I heard that your brother had brought Francis back to the dressing station, that he'd carried him back there himself. I haven't been able to make that fit, that Francis could have both been missing and a casualty."

"This is the dressing station at Houthulst Forest, I'm assuming?"

"Yes."

Louisa shakes her head. "Lots of men disappeared from that dressing station. I know that much. It was only a group of pillboxes, you see, just concrete bunkers, and the enemy kept on shelling it. Men got brought back there, brought back to what they hoped might be safety, only to be lost all over again. Michael had nightmares about that place, but he kept going back over that area. He had to keep going back there. A lot of the names on his list were connected with that dressing station."

"But why did he not tell me that he'd made the effort to bring Francis back? Had I known that, had I known that he'd tried, I would have thanked him."

"Because in the end he couldn't save your husband? Because he felt that he'd tried and failed?"

Edie looks at the young man smiling over the fireplace, imagines the weight of Francis's body on that young man's back, and all the effort that must have taken, only for it all to have been for nothing. She is not sure who she feels sorrier for.

"You said that my brother wrote to you twice?"

"Yes, he sent me a package full of Francis's photographs just a few weeks after his first letter. Mostly the photographs that they'd taken together. It was kind of him. I was glad to have them." She thinks about the other photograph, the final one that had come through her door in May. If Francis himself hadn't sent it, could it be that Michael Rose had contacted her a third time?

"I was sent a photograph a few months ago — a photograph of my husband. It came in the post, but there was nothing else in the envelope. No letter. No details as to the sender. I somehow seem to have spent the past few months convincing myself that Francis sent it himself."

"Where was it posted from?" Louisa asks.

"From France."

"What did the envelope look like?"

"It was a manila envelope, a typed address, worn keys. Is it possible your brother could have sent it?"

Louisa presses her lips together. "It sounds like Michael's typewriter."

"Really? Do you think?"

"Yes."

"But why send me that? Why send me that

574

without a note to explain it?"

Louisa turns her glass before she looks up. "Michael seems to have gone through a process of clearing his desk at the end. He tidied and labeled and sorted through all of his papers. He left it all as if he meant to hand it over. I wouldn't go so far as to say that my brother's mind was tidy at that point, but in his own way he was dotting the *i* and crossing the *t*. I guess that he meant to return it to you."

"But why not put in a note? Not even a signature? Why not let me know that it was him sending it?"

"Perhaps he just couldn't bring himself to write again? Perhaps he just didn't know what to say?"

Edie thinks about Francis's black-and-white photograph face, but it is different now, knowing the truth, knowing that he isn't out there any longer. Something has shifted; something that she now realizes was fear and shame and overwhelming worry as to how she might cope if he did come back. She now just feels desperately sad and sorry for the broken man in the photograph.

"May I ask what the photograph looks like?"

Edie takes a mouthful of her drink. It's been six weeks now since she last saw that picture, and she doesn't like to bring it to mind. "He's standing in a square, but it's all broken down. He doesn't look well — tired, exhausted, like he's given up. He seems so much older in the photograph — like he's ten years older than actually he is."

"He looks like he's taking the photograph of himself, doesn't he?" Louisa asks. "Isn't that right? You can see that from the angle of his arms. I think it was taken in Ypres, wasn't it?"

"Yes. But how on earth can you know that?"

"I might have seen that photograph before. I think I might have seen it on Michael's desk. Only it's quite memorable. Once you've looked at that poor man's face, it's difficult to forget it, isn't it?"

"It is."

"I'm sorry. I probably shouldn't say that, should I?"

Edie shakes her head. "But how did your brother come to have it?"

"I suppose because they took photographs together? Because they developed them together? Didn't you say that Michael sent you a package of Francis's photographs after he died? That he'd developed Francis's last film?"

"He did. But why keep that one?"

"A memento?"

"It's a strange choice of memento, though, isn't it? Why would he want to remember Francis looking like that?" Edie wonders where that photograph of Francis is now. She hopes that Harry doesn't mean to remember Francis that way.

"You have to understand my brother's state of mind." Louisa refills the glasses. "He felt guilty. He felt wretched about some of the things that had gone on. He believed that he should have done better — been a better man, a better leader. I'm afraid that he rather punished himself for that."

"He punished himself by looking at a photograph of Francis?"

"Possibly. I can't say with all honesty. I can only tell you that Michael wasn't a well man."

"But why not tell me that he'd found Francis?"

"Perhaps he simply just couldn't bear to. I don't suppose you recall the date on the postmark?"

"Of course. It was sent on the thirtieth of April."

Louisa nods. "I wondered if that might be the case. It was the same day that he took his life."

"I am sorry, Louisa. So terribly sorry. The

577

poor man."

"Yes. Aren't they both?"

In the box of photographs that Edie handed to Harry there had been an image of Francis and Michael Rose together. There's something candid about this shot, something natural and simply sincere that had made Edie pause when she first saw it. Francis and Michael are looking at one another and laughing, and neither of them seems to be particularly aware of the camera. They look like friends in this photograph. They look happy. Edie had quite forgotten the shape of Francis's smile in recent months, but she now means to remember it. As she watches Michael's sister tidying the glasses away, she decides that she will frame that picture when Harry returns the box, and she will also have a copy made for Louisa.

"Your brother lived with you here?"

"For a few months. I wanted to look after him, but then he moved to France just over a year ago. I didn't want to let him go, I didn't trust him to look after himself, and what with his state of mind, I worried. You understand?"

"Yes. Absolutely."

"But he was determined. He rented a

property down in the southwest. He said that it was for his health, for the weather, but I think it was really just that he couldn't stand any more of me fussing around him. I wanted to stop all the business with the graves, you see, I wanted him to think about other things, find new occupations, forget about the war, but he'd made his mind up to finish it."

"In the southwest?"

"I went over and stayed with him a couple of times, but it wasn't any sort of a home, and I'm not sure that he really wanted me to be there. It was a village called Saint-Christophe du Quercy."

"Saint-Christophe du Quercy?" Edie repeats it, and suddenly the letters of a blurred postmark slide into focus, and match a place-name in Harry's letters.

"You almost look like you know it."

"I think I might."

CHAPTER SIXTY-EIGHT: HARRY

Calvaire du Quercy, 11th November, 1921

November 1921 is exceptionally cold. Ships are lost in the Channel in snowstorms, telegraph communication between London and Paris goes down, and fountains freeze solid in Trafalgar Square. The grass beneath Harry's boots is glitteringly brittle. The shapes of oak leaves crunch white. The trees are like negative images of themselves today, and all the contours of the land declare themselves differently. He looks back and sees his own breath hanging in the air. His survival, on this day of remembering death, seems to be making empathetic marks. He is conscious on the frosty lane of his own momentum and bulk and pulse and heat.

Gabriel is waiting for him at the bend, as arranged. The service is scheduled to start at twelve. He stamps his feet and blows on his fingers. Gabriel's breath mists around him, like a soul in a trick photograph. "It's ten degrees below," he says through chapped lips. "This air is like needles in my mouth."

There are strings of red, white, and blue flags across the square. They tug in the icy wind and seem to accentuate the cold. The people of the village, below the bunting, are in black. Harry moves through the crowd, at Gabriel's side, toward the memorial. Gabriel shakes hands. A lot of hands stretch out toward him today. He is nervous, though, he has told Harry on the way up the hill. He fears that they each still secretly hope that the statue will wear the face of *their* son, *their* husband, *their* father, *their* brother.

The figure is still covered over. An apparatus had been constructed that suspends a black cloth over it, worked with ruffles and pleats. Via a system of weights and pulleys it will be unveiled on the stroke of twelve, as the trumpets' blare closes. This apparatus looks like a gallows, Harry thinks.

He steps inside the church, and even in here it is as cold as the grave. It takes a few seconds for his eyes to adjust. Stubs of candles are flickering out, like the sputtering ends of prayers. The walls of the church are Old Testament and last judgment, but it is all pulsing stars and shooting comets above. The blistering plaster on the ceiling

581

suggests the mystery of clouded heavens, and Harry remembers a star-punctured sky over Salisbury Plain long ago, and the faces of his brothers looking up. He also remembers the first night after Francis died, how the sky had seemed to be entirely empty and he had suddenly been certain that no god was looking down. But Gabriel is at his side then, his hand on Harry's arm. "Come away," he says. "We need a *coup de courage,* not a confession."

It is not much warmer inside the bar. Overcoats are kept buttoned. The barman polishes a glass and holds it to the light. There is not much light today. Gabriel clinks his glass against Harry's and says, "Absent friends."

Jacques Delpy, down the bar, is holding forth on the significance of this day, on why it is a start rather than an end. It feels like an end. He says that it will be better now, that they have been shown the way, that henceforth it will be socialist brotherhood and full bellies. The old world is breaking up, he says. It is cracking apart.

Marie Leval cries quietly and takes a brandy for her nerves. She lost her sons, all gone at Verdun but all apart, one by one, and three to mourn. It would have been easier, she says, if they had gone together.

Harry considers: Did his mother feel the same?

It is almost four years to the day since Harry's mother died. He had had to write to her a fortnight previously to tell her about Francis. There had never been a reply. There never would be one. He looks at Marie Leval and thinks about his own mother shedding sons one by one. Only he had come back. He had come through. Did that make him the lucky one? Ought he to appreciate that luck? Was it careless — callous, even — not to?

At a quarter to twelve, the crowd moves from bar to barricade. The village mayor, Marius Ferniot, looks coy in his mayoral chains. It is a big thing to have to preside over, and Harry pities him the struggle for the appropriate words. Gabriel translates here and there, where the sentiments find weight with him. We are *orphaned,* he says. There is *hommage, gloire, patriotisme,* and *sacrifice.* These words sound all the more abstract, all the more alien, in Gabriel's accent. Harry thinks about the service around Will's grave, how Francis had not seemed to be quite there even then. He also thinks about a grave surrounded by crumbled concrete. As Harry had peered closely at that photograph on Michael Rose's wall,

583

he'd seen how the wood was crudely hewn and hammered together, but the lettering was unambiguous enough. As he had finally looked at Francis's grave, he realized how he had clung on to some hope. But both of his brothers are dead today and Harry too feels orphaned.

Marius Ferniot intones the names. Calvaire sent sixty-eight men to the front, to the north to fight for France, out of a population of just over one hundred and seventy. Of these, fifty-seven returned. The statistics and calculations are Gabriel's. Calvaire did well: it beat the odds, fought and won against probability. By the law of averages this village should have lost twelve men. Marcel Mandelli looks up and nods as his son's name is spoken. Guillaume was his eldest, Gabriel has told Harry, gone at Maurepas, where they sang "La Marseillaise" and carried the colors. He is five years dead and never buried. There are eleven names (Harry counts them) recited and now in new chiseled stone, dead in sharp lines, and below them the *disparus* — those who have simply disappeared, the men in limbo between life and death that discretion cannot bear to distinguish.

Harry thinks of a face on a photographic film that ought to be there but isn't — a distinctive pair of eyes that have simply, inexplicably, disappeared. He has written to Rachel again. Would she now rather have David missing or dead? When he looks at the panel of *disparus* he sees the wreath weaver's pale eyes and cannot comprehend that he could just have imagined them. When he reads the list of *disparus* he sees a wall full of once-familiar faces. He cannot comprehend that either.

The notes on Rose's desk told him how he had gone back out again after the failed attack and struggled to get Francis to the dressing station. Rose had carried Francis on his back, across all that awful ground, even though he knew Francis was dying, even though he knew that he couldn't possibly make it. Harry hadn't known that Rose had brought Francis's body back, and he can hardly imagine how he managed it. Rose's notes recorded that he left Francis in the dressing station without much hope, but then, when the shelling started, he knew that all hope was gone. Harry had realized, as he looked at the photograph of Francis's grave, that the eruption of concrete around it is what is left of the dressing station. He remembers the concrete bunkers, the shelling and the screaming and then the meaningful silence. There was so much confusion. There were so many bodies. He is struck by the unfathomable loneliness of the single cross. Where have the rest of them gone? How many unfound men are out there still? Will they all be brought home one day?

As Harry had turned the photograph of Francis's grave in his hands, he had thought of all the images that he has taken and sent back to waiting, needing, doubting families. Is this how those parents and siblings and wives felt when they received Harry's photographs? There is a finality to it now, a final silencing of the nagging questions, but Harry also feels a profound new sense of loss. He has slept, though, for the past week; nights of deep, silent, dreamless sleep — sleep such as he hasn't known for months, maybe years. He thinks of all the names on his list and hopes those men really are resting in peace, truly sleeping silently, and that their families have also stopped dreaming.

Harry sees Rose himself as he looks at the *disparus*. The blur of a face that might for a moment have been Francis's. Was that just imagined too? Captain Michael Alfred Rose committed suicide back in April. Francis was the last missing man that Rose had placed before he took his own life, Marie-Thérèse had told him. Harry wonders what emotions Rose had felt as he stood behind the camera squaring Francis's cross in a viewfinder. What did he feel then as he posted that photograph of Francis to Edie? Harry had spoken to the priest in Saint-Christophe. The priest had walked Harry to the grave where Rose is buried without rank, another anonymous Englishman. He had hung himself from the ash tree. Harry can't help but work (and rework) through an imagined day in which Rose puts Francis's face in an envelope, addresses it to Edie, and then carries a stool and rope down the field.

The close-pressed crowd bristles. Harry can almost see the static between them. He looks at the circle of faces and then feels obliged to look away. He wishes that his eye had found Edie's face in the circle, that she could be here to share in the definition of this. It is a landmark, if not an end. For all of them it is an end of sorts. The trumpets blare and have their silence. Fabric falls, silently seismic. It is done.

They walk to the edge of the square afterward and lean on the balustrade by the church. Harry measures his steps. The wind is the only sound, as if the village cannot bear to speak, cannot bear to break it, to acknowledge it and to pass on. It is a collectively held breath. They stand in black units, in pairs and mute groups, in wordless surmise. There are no words.

Harry looks over the valley. The mist clings to the river, but for a minute the sun breaks through, hedges and barns show their shapes, fields are green, and it is over. They watch the mist roll over the contours of the valley.

Harry feels a strange mixture of sorrow and satisfaction as he sees Gabriel's statue for the first time. The bare feet of the stone woman are planted in a hayfield and her left hand, palm downward, caresses the tops of the grass. Her head is bowed forward and her right hand covers her eyes. She is unmistakable, though.

"It's her. It is Madeleine, isn't it?" Harry compares the statue with the young woman who is standing just feet away from him.

"It is, but she's also France," Gabriel adds. "She is all the mothers, daughters, widows, and sisters, their loss and the weight of war."

"It's just what it should be."

Madeleine is standing at Gabriel's side then. *"T'as froid?"* he asks.

Gabriel rubs the cold from her hands, peels his gloves off, and pushes them onto her fingers. There is a strange sudden intimacy to the action, and Harry is both compelled to watch and feels as if he ought to avert his eyes. Her face is very pale today and unmistakably the twin of Gabriel's statue.

"*Il est malade?*" Her eyes turn to Harry. She wiggles her comically oversized fingers and nods a smile toward him.

"*C'est ces temps.*"

"What does she say?" Harry asks.

"That we all need a drink."

The crowd is finally doubling back and daring to look, to take in the new perspective of the square. They don't get too close to the memorial, though; it is approved, but somehow at this moment it repulses; it is measured from afar, assessed and debated. Only Marie Leval is able to breach and bear that proximity. She leans against the railings and stretches a hand through the bars. It is too distant by design, but her fingers wriggle and reach, and must touch her son's name on the plinth. The village watches aghast.

Gabriel's hand is on Madeleine's back as they walk into the bar. "*En avant,*" he says. Something has changed between them today, Harry sees. He wonders if she recognizes herself in the stone girl on the memorial and what Gabriel meant by it. He wonders if Edie has yet seen his envelope and understood its meaning. Marie-Thérèse nodded when he asked if he could take the photograph of Francis's grave, but he had hesitated as he folded his letter around it. Did Edie really need to see it? But then perhaps for her, as for him, it will draw a line, silence the questions, and let her sleep. And he owed her this truth. Didn't he?

They dance in the bar that night. They sing songs from long before the war, and songs about the future, and the volume and the tears rise. Harry doesn't feel part of it, he doesn't know the words to any of these songs, but Gabriel tells him that he shouldn't be alone tonight, and he knows that Gabriel wants him to be here.

It is hot in the bar, as they spin gavottes and waltzes and ragtime, singing of fidelity and anarchy, of old loves and barricades and cherry blossoms. Harry's head pounds with the beat of the music, and the sounds of their laments and laughter, but he sits by the window and watches as the moonlight pulls the frost on the glass into patterns. Whorls of ice stretch finely, brightly, scrolling into rhythms of divine geometry. As the patterns on the glass multiply, he thinks about the cemetery with the gun emplacement at its center, the crosses of the nameless dead radiating out from it. He thinks about what that vast cemetery must look like in moonlight and what pattern the graves must make from above. Do the graves look like waves of shock radiating out? He pictures Francis's cross and Francis on the cross with his arms splayed out. He feels the waves of shock that radiate from that image.

"Harry, are you all right?"

"Yes, but I might go home."

"Stay. Drink. We shouldn't dream tonight." Gabriel's face glistens in the strange yellow light of the bar. He reaches for the bottle and fills Harry's glass right to the top, but Harry has no thirst for it tonight.

"I am tired."

He shuts his eyes to the polkas and the politics and the drink, and Gabriel and Madeleine's across-the-table embraces, and in his mind he watches Edie dancing in the red room. He tries, as they spin, to see the face of the man she is dancing with. He expects it to be, wants it to be, Francis, but in turns he sees the icy paleness of the eyes of the man called East, the *disparu,* whose image a camera cannot catch. With that, Harry must keep his eyes open. Perhaps Gabriel is right, that this is a night made only for nightmares? He drinks the glass of brandy down, and the words of the songs and the speeches seem to revolve in his head.

He puts his cheek to the cool of the window and watches the ferns of frost curl. His head throbs with the hot and the cold, and the interminably circling beat of the music, and he is Francis in the Blue Angel for a moment, but then, somewhere behind the ice crystals, there is a flash of red.

"You look like you've just seen a ghost." Gabriel's face blurs in the candlelight and fug of drink. His hand stretches across the table. "Are you unwell, Harry?"

"I don't know."

But then Harry knows the color for what it is, and suddenly all the music and the tears and the laughter are silenced, and she is there. Harry stares at her and wonders if he has made her. Has he conjured her up? Is she imagination? He doesn't trust his mind any longer. Like the eyes of the wreath maker, is she madness or a phantom? Is this delirium or drink? He stares at Edie's face. Edie's eyes connecting with his. Edie's mouth making the shape of his name. There is no fantasy in the fierce grip of her hand.

EPILOGUE:
HARRY AND EDIE

Houthulst Forest, north of Ypres, March 1922
Last night Harry dreamed about the reservoir. It is an awfully long time since he last had that dream, since his sleeping imagination last went back to that long-ago place. But yesterday, in their hotel room in Ypres, he had thought about the mirror that he broke here six months ago, the sound of the fracturing glass, and perhaps that was the link that took him back to the noise of the ice.

In his dream he is a boy again, stepping out across the frozen reservoir, in the blue-white, bright crisp cold. Will and Francis are calling from the far side and goading him to step out farther. "Dare you!" their adolescent voices shout. "Coward!" they cry. The breath is icy in Harry's mouth, and coming faster now, but because they shout, he keeps on going.

He hears the cracks before he sees them,

593

and then it is not even a second before they are racing out under his feet. He sees them shoot, suddenly multiplying and accelerating from his boots, and leaps momentarily before he plunges. He makes a grab for the ice, but it just breaks away and there is nothing to hold on to. He flails, his legs wheel, and he screams, but the black water takes away his words and thrusts into his lungs. He is full of it then, numb with it and falling down. He looks up, and sees the light flickering and retreating on the far-above surface of the water, as the cold pulls him down.

No hands break the receding light above. No fingers reach down to save him this time. Harry's legs stop kicking and he lets it take him down. The silence of the water wins — until that moment, at the very edge of it being too late, when Francis's fingers push through the light above and he is hauling Harry out. In that instant, Harry is thirteen years old again and he looks into his brother's face and gasps.

Strangely, it is something similar that he feels now as he stands and looks at Francis's grave. He cannot quite believe that he is standing here. That this really is Francis, and that it has all ended here. The sight of Francis's grave marker takes all of the air out of Harry's chest, and though it is a warm spring day, he shivers like the boy who has just been pulled out of the reservoir by his brother.

"You're trembling," she says. She takes his arm.

"It's real, isn't it?"

"It is."

How odd it is to stand in this place again. To stand here with her. When he looks at the concrete, and the rusting railway tracks, and the bales of barbed wire, it's October 1917 again, he is following a tape line, and Francis is at his side. He remembers it all as it was; the vibration of the hands of Summerfield's wristwatch in the second before it started, and then all the leaping black water and the white of his brother's eyes. Standing here, he can almost feel the convulsion of the bombardment again and, in the heavy silence, hear their screaming. How long will it be before this place forgets all of that, until the signs and the vibrations are all gone, and the silence is really still?

This is not Francis's final resting place and, looking at all the yellow grass and crumbled concrete around, Harry is glad that is the case. Ralph has told him that the grave will be moved now; having been identified, Francis will be disinterred and relocated to Tyne Cot. But it could take months, Ralph says. With all the scattered crosses that they have seen from the car, Harry thinks that it may take years. But they have had to fill in paperwork in preparation for the grave being moved. They have had to give all Francis's details, define their relationship to the deceased, and are invited to choose a personal inscription of up to sixty-six characters to be incised at the base of his new gravestone. It is such a difficult thing to condense it into sixty-six stone-cut letters, to pare all life and loss down to that, but they have talked it over between them, and through those conversations, they have both voiced and shared and agreed what Francis means to them.

They have bought dog violets in Ypres today, the first of the wild spring violets from the market, because she had said she wanted to plant them here for him. The scent of the disturbed petals takes Harry to a looted room, but he shuts that down; he doesn't mean to let his memory go back there any longer; that is not the version of his brother that he chooses to remember. The scent of violets is also her smell and, because of that, this gesture seems right. He recalls Francis's face turning and smiling, his eyes closed, as he curled into Edie's neck. Harry holds her now as she cries, and wants to take her away from here and to make it right, but he knows that she has to have this moment, that he has to let her have this time, to plant violets around his grave, and to say all the words that she needs to say to Francis.

How odd it is to be digging around his brother's grave. He wants to dig the soil out before she does, because he dreads what the trowel may turn over.

"Do you really want to do it? Are you sure?"

He sees Edie's hand shake as he gives her the trowel.

She takes the trowel from him and she can feel his hand tremble in that contact. She looks at Harry. What must it be like for him to be back in this place? What must it be like to stand at his brother's grave? She is so sorry to have brought him back here, and yet she is also so grateful to have him at her side.

Edie pushes the soil back around the violets. As she kneels by Francis's cross, it is so hard to believe that this is him, that it has all come down to this, but she knows that he is here. Finally she believes it. Finally she feels it. She puts her hand to the wood of his cross so that she may know its texture. It is not that she means this to be her remembrance of him, only that she means not to forget. She sits back on her heels and looks at him, all ringed around with violets.

When they had first told her that Francis would be disinterred, she had not liked the idea that he must be dug up and disturbed all over again. But having been to this place, having seen this poisoned, leafless forest, so terribly marked by the passage of war still, and so far off from being made right, she realizes it is better that than this. She wonders if this place will ever be made right.

How very difficult it has been to have to choose an epitaph for Francis, to be asked to summarize all that he was and all that his absence means. In the end, they have decided it together. Somehow, as she and Harry have talked over the past four months, as they have fit together all of the pieces, she feels that she has made her peace with Francis. She has talked to his memory through the long winter nights, has rewound from that man in the photograph, and has decided to remember him as the boy who sat waiting for her on the library steps. It feels as if they have shaken hands at that, she and Francis, because that, not this, is who Francis Blythe really was. She doesn't want a photograph of this grave. This is not what she intends to remember.

"Your hands."

She looks down at her hands, all creased in the earth of his grave. The grit of it is down her fingernails and behind her wedding ring. It is terrible to think what this earth contains, but she also feels strangely close to Francis just now and there is some comfort in that.

"It's all right. Don't worry."

When she looks up at Harry she sees the concern in his eyes. She still sees Francis in Harry's face, and she is glad of that, but there is also something else there now; when she looks at Harry's face, she sees a future. Her legs feel unsteady as she stands up. He puts his arm around her and she leans into his chest.

Harry takes the trowel back from her earth-ingrained hand. When she had sat there, on his grave, he had remembered Francis at Will's graveside, the creases of his palms picked out in brick dust, and how he had ached with pity for them both at that moment. When Edie had looked back up at him, her face was wet with tears, but there was also a smile there as she took his hand.

"Are you all right?"

She nods.

"Shall we go home?"

"Yes. I'm ready now."

PRIVATE FRANCIS BLYTHE
MANCHESTER REGIMENT
22 OCTOBER 1917
AGE 25
LOST AWHILE AND
FOUND AND LOVED

ACKNOWLEDGMENTS

I should firstly, and loudly, thank my fantastic agent, Teresa Chris, for believing in this story and championing it so fiercely. Teresa, your determination is a wonder to behold and I'm so very lucky to have you on my side.

I've been fortunate to have had the chance to work with editors at both Simon & Schuster and William Morrow. This crack team untangled my knots, pointed out my plot holes, breathed life into my characters, and knocked my wonky northern grammar into shape — and always with the greatest patience, thoughtfulness, and care. I'm indebted to Liz Stein, Jo Dickinson, Alice Rodgers, Emma Capron, and Sara-Jade Virtue.

Lastly, and mostly, thank you to Mum and Dad — for putting up with my away-with-the-fairies face and for never once telling me that it was time to get a proper job. X

ABOUT THE AUTHOR

Caroline Scott is a freelance writer and historian. After completing a Ph.D. in history at the University of Durham, she worked as a researcher in Belgium and France. She has a particular interest in the experience of women during the First World War, in the challenges faced by the returning soldier, and in the development of tourism and pilgrimage in the former conflict zones. Caroline lives in southwest France and is currently at work on her second novel. *The Poppy Wife* is partially inspired by her family history.

The employees of Thorndike Press hope you have enjoyed this Large Print book. All our Thorndike, Wheeler, and Kennebec Large Print titles are designed for easy reading, and all our books are made to last. Other Thorndike Press Large Print books are available at your library, through selected bookstores, or directly from us.

For information about titles, please call:
  (800) 223-1244

or visit our website at:
  gale.com/thorndike

To share your comments, please write:
  Publisher
  Thorndike Press
  10 Water St., Suite 310
  Waterville, ME 04901